X MARKS THE SPOT

X MARKS THE SPOT

An Anthology of Treasure and Theft

Edited by
LISA MANGUM

WFP
WORDFIRE PRESS

X Marks the Spot
Copyright © 2020 WordFire Press

EBook ISBN: 978-1-68057-113-4
Trade Paperback ISBN: 978-1-68057-112-7
Hardcover ISBN: 978-1-68057-056-4

Cover design by Janet McDonald
Cover artwork images by Tiffany Brazell
Kevin J. Anderson, Art Director
Edited by Lisa Mangum

Published by
WordFire Press, LLC
PO Box 1840
Monument CO 80132
Kevin J. Anderson & Rebecca Moesta, Publishers

Printed in the USA
Join our WordFire Press Readers Group for
sneak previews, updates, new projects, and giveaways.
Sign up at wordfirepress.com

❀ Created with Vellum

Contents

The Wish Shore

KRISTEN BICKERSTAFF

E ven the smallest, plainest of stones can hold a wish. That's what Adria's grandfather had told her every morning as they walked the wish shore.

When she was younger, she'd longed for a pretty stone like those the girls from the white-walled town inland threw when they made the daylong trek to the shore. A quartz or an onyx, perhaps. Even a mica-speckled rock would do. But all she had were the plain, gray-and-white rocks littering the shore. As the years passed and her grand wishes never came to be, she accepted the truth. She was a fishergirl, destined to marry a fisherman and live in a salt-stained hut by the shore. No rock would change that, no matter how fine it was.

But whenever Grandfather handed her a stone on their morning walks, she would whisper a wish into it to make him happy, her lips brushing against the water-smoothed surface, and throw it out to sea. Even after they sent Grandfather's body back to Sky-Mother on a bed of blue-tinged flames, she still walked the shore and, if a stone caught her eye, she'd give it one of her wishes. Adria made sure to keep her wishes simple—for a good catch, for a clear night, for her voice to sound sweet at festival time. And if the wishes only came true partway or not at all, well, she didn't really believe in the wish shore anyway.

Just a few days before Sea-Father's festival, one stone caught her eye. Pale white with a black crack snaking through it, uniformly shaped, and sunbaked—it was just the sort of stone Grandfather would have picked. Catching up her skirts, she bent down and plucked the stone from its fellows before the sea could take it away. She rubbed her thumb down the black line, enjoying the flaw in the otherwise featureless rock.

Straightening up, holding in her mind the wish she would whisper, her eyes caught on a dark shape far out to sea. She blinked, and the shape formed into a boat flying black sails. The stone tumbled from her nerveless fingers, landing with a small *plunk* into the water.

3

The raiders' distinctive black sails were a children's tale, spoken over a crackling fire by an old-timer who'd spent his youth trying to make his fortune on a trading vessel. Even in the stories, the raiders only attacked fat merchant ships filled with gold and fine cloth. They didn't come for tiny fishing villages on a small island in the middle of the sea. Yet there they were, growing closer with each rattling breath she drew.

She knew she should scream and wave her hands to the fishing boats out to sea—the ones carrying her father and brothers—but another part of her, the part that knew there was no Sea-Father granting wishes to each silly fishergirl who threw a rock into his domain, understood that it was already too late. The fishing boats were too far out, and the black sails were moving too fast. *They move like ghosts*, the old-timer had said. And so she sprinted back to the village, hoping against hope that her legs could outrun the sails.

But when she reached the pickets that marked the edge of the village and glanced back, her cry of alarm choked off in a sob. The familiar silhouettes of her family's fishing boats roared with flames, pillars of thick, black smoke obscuring the clear, blue sky. The black sails were already ahead of her loved ones' pyres and moving alarmingly fast, almost to the wish shore. She would never make it to the white-walled town in time.

Her wish stone lay on the rocky shore, tumbled by the tide and the heavy boots of the raiders, forgotten.

"Yer a wind-singer, aintcha?"

Adria drew back from the raider's reeking breath, stinking of chew-leaf and rotting fish, as far as she could in the hold's close quarters. Kara, the only other captive from her village, tightened her near-permanent grip on Adria's hand, while the woman to the other side of Adria merely leaned away. Adria ducked her head so that her long dark hair, matted and salt-stained after weeks at sea, would fall in front of her face, but it was too late. He had seen.

The raider squatted to get a better look at her, pushing her hair back and grabbing her chin to tilt her face up to his. Putting on a show of bravery for young Kara, Adria held the leering gaze of his one eye, the other covered with a leather patch.

He jabbed a finger at her cheek, where the sign of her family was inked in blue. "That's the sign, right? I had a woman once from your parts. She said your kind could fill a sail on the stillest of days. Bet that's not all you can make swell." He smacked his lips, thin and pale under his scraggly beard.

Adria fisted her hands in her damp skirt—it was always damp these days, since she and Kara had been spared the raiders' knives and forced into this stinking, swaying hold—so that she would not strike him. Lashing out would only earn her, and most likely Kara, another beating. But when he poked her cheek again with his grubby finger, it took everything she had not to snap her teeth at him.

"Oy! You deaf, girl?" he asked, curling his hand into a fist.

"It's just a superstition," she mumbled. "I sing at Sea-Father's festival and the like. I've never been out to open sea."

His beady, dark eye searched her face, but he'd find no trace of a lie there. Then his single-eyed gaze moved over to Kara. "This true? Is it all rubbish?"

Kara's wide brown eyes flickered to the raider, to Adria, then back.

No, no, no, Adria begged her silently. At barely ten years old, the girl was too young to understand that Sea-Father was just a myth, that the tales she'd heard of wind-singers calling up his favor were nothing more than that. *Please say yes. Please.*

Kara lifted her chin, and Adria's heart sank. She knew that look, had stared it down ever since the girl had been a toddler, marching around the beach and declaring it all for Sea-Father against her imaginary enemies.

"You better leave her be!" the girl said. "The wind-singers are Sea-Father's own children, from his love of the sea-maid, and he doesn't take kindly to any who hurt them! Her songs will bring a storm like none you've ever seen, and then you'll be sorry!"

Oh, sweet girl, how I wish that was true.

The raider bared his teeth, what few were left. "Ay, well, superstitions come from somewhere. Let's have you up, then."

He pried Adria from Kara's grip, ignoring the girl's cries, and dragged her to the ladder that led to the deck. He slapped her backside just as her hands touched the deck, sending her sprawling. Rough laughter chorused from the other raiders, and her face burned.

"What's this, Holger?"

A man swaggered up in that strange bowlegged walk all the raiders seemed to share, clothed in black tatters that were in slightly better condition than the rest of the crew's. His beard was trimmed closer than Holger's ratty mess, though Adria had still never seen so many men with such unkempt beards. She thought of how Grandfather would carefully slick fish oil through his each morning until it shone, and how they'd laughed when her youngest brother, Tadd, had proudly smeared the oil across the peach fuzz dotting his cheeks.

Holger shoved her once more, bringing her nearly chest-to-chest with the captain. He stank of sweat and salt.

"She's a wind-singer, Cap. Figured she could sing us up a bit of wind, get us back to familiar waters." There was a desperation underlying Holger's voice that worried Adria.

The captain looked down his crooked nose at her, his lip curled in a sneer. "This true, girl?"

"I tried to tell him," she said, her voice barely dribbling past her lips. "Wind-singing is just an old story, a tradition for festivals. It doesn't actually work."

Grandfather had been the last wind-singer in the family, and Adria had agreed to take on the mantle for love of him, nothing more. She'd never believed she had the power to call up winds or calm storms; even Grandfather had admitted that, when he'd tried as a youth, no wind had come at his call. The captain's skeptical expression seemed to agree with her, but enough of the men had heard Holger's claim and clustered closer, eagerness glinting in their eyes.

"Let 'er sing, Cap!"

"We could use the wind!"

The hungry gazes of the raiders passing over her made her sweat. Adria noticed the dark circles under their eyes, the pinched looks on their faces. This, pieced together with the strangeness of the raid on her village and the raw, rotting grain the women were served each day, made the whole picture clear.

These men were lost, blown off course and running low on provisions. She'd already been warned by some of the other women that they were meant to be sold as slaves at the next port the raiders docked in, as they were the only goods worth coin on this cursed ship. That was why the men hadn't done more than touch Kara or Adria. That was why she and Kara had been spared the knife, when the old fisherwives and the elders and the young boys had all been slain.

These men knew nothing of mercy, and hunger would have only sharpened their cruelty. What would they do when they realized she *couldn't* sing the wind?

The captain was already nodding, though, and pointing to the bow. "Have her try out there. After our cursed luck, I'll take what backwater magic we can find."

Holger shoved her across the rocking deck, ignoring her protests as the raiders followed after. Adria clutched the railing to keep her balance and turned her back on the men and their ravenous eyes. All around her was sparkling blue water, stretching endlessly in every direction. It would have been beautiful, but she understood the danger in an empty horizon. How much longer did they have before the men started pitching the extra mouths overboard?

There was no wind to speak of, the sails hanging loose and forlorn from the mast. When she merely stood, gazing out at the empty water, Holger gave her another shove, flattening her against the rail.

"Sing, girl, or I'll make you wish you had," he growled.

Adria licked the taste of salt from her lips as her mind scrambled over what to sing. Nervous and unwilling to test Holger's patience, she decided on the song that opened the summer festival. It was almost time for it, after all, or had it already passed? She cleared her throat, wishing for a cup of water, and began to sing.

"Oh, Father, oh, Father, where have you gone?"

Her own father was buried beneath the waves, his bones resting in the sand along with her brothers'. Adria squeezed her stinging eyes shut and forced herself onward.

"Our nets, our nets, long for fish but hold none."

There were no nets for Adria to weave anymore. No more days in the common hall, shoulder to shoulder with her friends, singing songs as their callused fingers deftly caught and knotted the flax. No more memories of how her mother, long dead, had shown her those knots, over and over until she could tie them with her eyes closed.

"Our sails, our sails, lie dead on their lines."

And may they stay dead, Adria wished fervently. She thought of young Kara and the horror that awaited her if they found land. Better the watery embrace of the sea, or slow starvation, than that living hell.

"Oh, Father, oh, Father, now is your time."

The rest of the words blended together, and her last note held for a long time, floating back to her on the waves. Adria blinked against the bright sunlight reflecting on the ocean's glassy surface as sweat dripped down her spine.

Not so much as a breeze rustled through the sails.

A rough laugh broke her song's spell, followed by grumbled curses. She hunched her shoulders, trying to make herself a smaller target, and clung to the railing, even as their fists fell upon her unprotected back.

That night, as she tried to find a position to sleep in that did not send fire racing across her new bruises, Adria leaned her head against the hull. With her ear pressed against the wood and only her short, pained breaths to count a rhythm, the lap of the water against the ship sounded almost like a song.

And so it went. For the next five days, Holger dragged her up to the bow, and each day she sang with no real hope that Sea-Father heard her. Each day, no wind appeared, and each day, she was beaten for failing to sing it to them. The raiders had long since lost hope that she could actually do as Holger claimed she could, but they seemed to enjoy the break from rowing and the distraction from their hunger, their thirst, their boredom. Each day, there was no hint of where shore might be.

Oh, Father, oh, Father, where have you gone?

They could not row back to Adria's home. They did not have the men to conquer the white-walled town as easily as they had her poor village. Their prowess lay in quick raids on the water, not attacking well-defended fortifications. And they did not have enough drinking water to backtrack. Their navigator, Adria learned, had been lost in the storm that blew them so wildly off course and to the shore of her island home.

Our nets, our nets, long for fish but hold none.

On the sixth day, when the grain ran out, Adria was sure that was the end. It was the end for two of the older women in the hold, who were thrown screaming and wailing over the rail, their cries echoing long after the boat had rowed away from their clutching fingers. Adria had pressed shaking hands over Kara's ears, as if such a simple thing could shield the girl from what was likely to be their shared fate.

But the next day, the men caught a few fish in their nets. They discovered Adria and Kara were both quick hands at gutting and cleaning, so she sang another day, and Kara remained in the hold and not in the sea.

Our sails, our sails, lie dead on their lines.

The real danger was running out of fresh water. Only a couple full barrels remained in the hold, Adria's only company besides the few remaining women. Adria dreamed of cracking the barrels open and dunking her head in, of the cool kiss of rain on her skin. Her lips cracked until she tasted blood every time she spoke, and her voice weakened until it was barely a whisper.

And still they made her sing.

Oh, Father, oh, Father, now is your time.

Two more days passed, and two more women were thrown overboard. There were no more fish. It was much quieter in the hold than when she'd first been forced into it. There was only herself and Kara now. The girl cried every night, and Adria whispered nonsense stories of how the sea-maids would rise from the depths and carry them away to safety.

The sea's lullaby grew louder each night. Sometimes, just before sleep took her, she swore she could make out words, sung in no language she could understand. She dreamed of the sea-maids that Kara loved so dearly, with hair the color of kelp and tails shining with scales, long-lost sisters come to take her away to live in their sandcastles with their hidden treasures.

She dreamed of Grandfather teaching her the festival songs, his deep baritone weaving in and out of her childish soprano, their notes dancing through the small hut. A gift for Sea-Father, he used to call the songs. Even when the wet-lung stole his voice, Grandfather held faith that Sea-Father loved him, his wind-singer child, and heard him. He would brokenly whisper his wishes to Adria so she could throw a stone for him if she found the right one. *Sound sleep, easy breathing, calm heart.* He never wished to be saved. Sea-Father was not known for his mercy.

The next morning, Holger dragged Adria and Kara up to the deck.

"Take me, take me," Adria begged, clutching Kara's small hands tightly in hers. "She's worth more!"

The one-eyed man smiled at her with cracked, bloody lips. "We took a vote, y'see. The men would rather have a go at you than her, if we don't find land tomorrow."

Adria had long ago stopped hoping for a chance to grab a knife and at least take her blood due from one or two of the raiders. She was too weak to wield a blade, and she was almost positive the men had broken a few of her fingers in one of the beatings. Most of her right hand was swollen purple and throbbed with each heartbeat. But still, when Holger yanked Kara from her grip, Adria threw herself at him, shrieking and raking her nails down his face and neck in the hopes that he'd be distracted enough to let Kara go.

"Damn it, someone grab her!" he said, as Kara screamed and fought against his hold. The girl was too weak to break free on her own.

Wiry arms snatched Adria back just as her fingers brushed Kara's grimy blouse. She howled and tore at the man's hold, helpless as Holger lifted Kara as easily as he would a fish. Adria caught the girl's frightened gaze one last time.

"Please, Sea-Father, save her!" she cried out.

But Sea-Father was not known for his mercy, and the girl disappeared over the railing. There was one lonely splash, a watery scream, and then silence.

Sagging in the man's hold, Adria screamed until her voice gave out, until there was nothing left for any stupid song that day. When she refused to even try to sing, they beat her until she lay curled in a ball on the deck.

The slow, plodding tread of the captain drawing near forced her eyes open. He pressed a dagger to her cheek, right over her family sign. Adria welcomed the stinging-sharp pain. It distracted her from how thirsty she was and the new grief in her already-heavy heart.

"Tomorrow, it's you," the captain said, his voice as cracked and broken as hers was.

That night, she dreamed she stood on the wish shore, alone. A man wrapped his arms around her from behind, and she leaned into his strong embrace, grateful for the support for her weary bones. She hurt even in her dream, but in his arms, she knew she was safe at last.

"You didn't come when I called," she said accusingly, even as she cuddled closer to his solid body.

"You must wish the right way," he said, his voice a rumble in his chest like thunder. "Even for you, daughter, I can only reach so far."

"I have no wishes left," she whispered, wrapping her hands around his strong forearms, corded with the muscles of a fisherman. "There is no one left to save. There is no one left to help. My family … Kara … they're all gone."

"Do you truly have nothing else to ask of me?" His voice took on an edge, like the razor-sharp coral her brothers always warned her about. A wave crashed against the shore, rushing up to their feet with long, foamy fingers. She shivered in the chill of it.

She thought of the knife, of Kara's last scream, of the flames eating her father's boat.

"No," she said slowly. "I do have a wish."

"If you but reach your hand to me, I can grant it." His voice turned soft, like the susurrus of the tide kissing the shore, a sound she'd never missed until she heard it no longer. "But I cannot touch a heart that is closed, not even one of my own blood."

Adria accepted this with the easy logic of dreams. But still, she had no answer. "How do I wish the right way?"

"My stubborn daughter." He chuckled and kissed the top of her head. "You know the way. Listen to your sisters."

Adria woke with a small gasp in the empty hull, the movement jarring her injured hand so much that tears sprang up in her eyes. She wept, longing to feel those strong arms wrapped around her again. The sea sang her back to sleep in a chorus of female voices, a liquid lullaby that surely came from a place beyond waking.

As Holger pushed her up the ladder, Adria's heart rattled in her chest like a bird in a cage. She thought of Kara, of the girl's thin fingers disappearing over the rail. She did not want to die alone in the open sea, with no one to sing her soul home. But then she thought of her dream, and of the sea's lullaby, and held on to one last hope.

The captain arched a weary eyebrow at her as she stopped before her usual spot on the bow.

"I'd like a stone," she said, forcing the words through her cracked lips. Her throat was raw from yesterday's screaming, but the fire in her heart drowned out all the pain.

Coarse laughter rang out across the deck, harsh as a seabird's caw. The captain merely sighed. He rubbed his crooked nose.

"Are you trying to delay, girl? It'll serve you no good. There are no stones at sea."

She lifted her chin, meeting his cold, gray eyes with hers. "I need a stone. That's why it hasn't worked before. It's the only way."

The captain scowled, his hand going for the hilt of his knife, when a thin voice piped up from the back of the crowd.

"Cap, I have a stone."

Adria looked up as a young man, no older than she was, pushed forward through the ragged bunch. He fumbled at a leather cord tied around his neck. His fingers shook, though, and he couldn't get the knot free.

The captain rolled his eyes, then yanked the leather tie so hard the boy let out a strangled yelp as it snapped from his neck. The captain tossed the tie and its small burden to Adria, and she caught it with ease.

"I found it in my boot after the raid," the boy explained. "It looked pretty, so I kept it. For luck."

The other raiders laughed at his foolishness, but their rude jibes seemed to come from fathoms away as Adria stared at the stone. Her legs gave out beneath her, and she crumpled to the deck, cradling the stone in her broken hands. It was pale white, uniformly smooth, warm from resting against the boy's chest, and had a black, jagged crack running through it. She rubbed her thumb along the black line, a sob escaping her lips.

Too distracted by the lost stone returned to her, she didn't see the boot coming toward her face until it was too late. The blow snapped her head back, bright white chasing away the deck, the raiders, the sky. The rock grew hot in her hand, and as she squeezed it tighter, the pain faded just a little. Just enough to finish her task. She blinked—once, twice—until the captain's scowling face came back into view.

"You've got your rock. Now, sing."

Gasping with each movement, Adria pushed herself to her knees, then used the rails to lever her battered body up the rest of the way. She sagged against the thin wooden poles to catch her breath before turning to face the sea. Did it gleam a little brighter? Did the ripples move a little faster? Or was her head too damaged from the kick?

She ran her tongue across her lips, wincing, then took a breath. The song that spilled out of her was not the festival song she had sung each day, nor was it any of the other songs Grandfather had taught her. Instead, she sang the song of the sea, once heard muffled through the hull each night but lately crystal clear as the notes bled into her dreams.

The meaning was lost to her, the syllables liquid and tumbling like the tide over the wish shore, but she sang with all her heart. She strained her broken voice to hit the ever-climbing notes, embarrassed as it cracked and squeaked, falling well short of the beautiful tune that lulled her to sleep. She wasn't sure she could sing this song flawlessly even at her best. It was not a song made for human throats. But she tried, singing until she had no breath left, until blood ran down her chin from her lips and the image of the sea blurred in her eyes.

She sang and thought of her father and brothers, smiling and sunbaked after a long day; of Grandfather picking out just the right stone for her to wish on; of strong arms holding her safe on a familiar shore.

For once, no chuckles or sly comments rang out from behind her.

Finally, just as she thought she could sing no more, the song was done. She swayed on her feet, hunching over the stone, warm in her hands, close to her heart. Then she brought it to her lips and spoke the wish of her soul, so softly that none could hear. When she was done, she kissed the rock and threw it into the sea.

Adria didn't turn around, not even when one of the raiders broke the eerie silence with a shout, followed by a louder chorus. She clung to the rail, ignoring the pain in her fingers, in her head, and struggled to stay upright. As she watched the scintillating surface of the sea, she heard the familiar sound of a sail snapping taut. Finally, she looked over her shoulder, taking in the sight with a mixed heart of satisfaction and resignation.

The sails were full with the same wind that whipped her hair against her face and plastered her skirt against her legs. She looked to the captain, who'd stayed close to her while the others had run off to their tasks and celebration.

Holding up a hand to guard his face from his own wind-tousled hair, he stared at the sails, then back at her. His mouth hung open, and he looked at her as if she had crawled up from the sea itself.

"I'd like to go back to the hold now," she said.

At first, the raiders rejoiced in their newfound speed, boasting about what they would do as soon as they reached shore. Perhaps they'd keep their wind-singer to speed them on to fortune and fame. What patrol boat could possibly outrun a ship powered by a true wind-singer, after all? The deck rang with dreams of fat merchant ships and gold so heavy they couldn't bring it all back with them, and for the first time since the storm, the raiders cheered at their salvation.

That night, though, the wind the raiders had first celebrated grew wild and sped their ship through waters dark and choppy. No matter what action they took, they could not turn the ship from its course. Ropes tore from their hands, the sails strained and ripped, brutal waves slapped against the deck, taking a few of the raiders with them, and still the ship sailed on. The wind was so fierce that it stung the raiders' eyes into blindness, and they stumbled around in the dark, unaware of the coastline rapidly approaching.

Adria saw none of this, huddled against the hull of the ship, safe in the hold. When the ship's rocking intensified and the shouts above melded into a raucous song of their own, she knew the first half of her wish had come true. And when the impact of the deadly, craggy rock that the raiders could neither see nor steer away from shook the boat to its very bones, she smiled.

Sea-Father was not known for his mercy.

As water gushed in from the hole the rock had created in the hull, Adria sang. A song of welcome and a song of family filled the hull with that strange liquid language as seawater soaked her skirts, then her bodice, then finally closed over her head. It spilled into her open mouth, and her sodden clothes dragged her toward the jagged hole.

In the darkness of the water, she spread her arms out, welcoming her Father's all-encompassing embrace. Just as her eyes closed for the last time, she imagined she felt a small, pale hand, with curiously webbed fingers, grab her ankle and pull. She closed her eyes and let the water have her.

The next day, a boat ventured out from the port city guarded by the cruel rocks, to hunt for any salvage in the wreckage. The sailors found the raiders' bodies, floating in their soaked black tatters, but little else to take home for spoils. And of a dark-haired girl with a blue tattoo on her cheek, there was no sign.

About the Author

Writing since she could pick up a pen, Kristen Bickerstaff has always loved exploring the worlds and characters that live in her head. By day, she's a content marketer and freelance writer/editor based in Dallas. By night, she dreams of magical worlds and crashing spaceships. Learn more about her current projects and other published works at kristenbickerstaff.com.

The Wreckers

KEN HOOVER

N o one else in the crew wanted to lead a donkey along the cliff's edge at night, so Agwe Delmas volunteered. Only by the light of the waning moon and the lantern hanging around the donkey's neck could he see the silver path, slick with sea spray. Occasionally, the donkey tried to break free, but Agwe had wrapped the lead around his meaty hand several times so he could drag the poor creature along. At nearly forty years—old for a seaman—he was a stout, thick-limbed man, hardened by a childhood in the shipyard and decades on the seas. But if the donkey went over the edge, they would both plummet to their deaths.

Two asses bound together, he thought.

Agwe reached his spot and stopped to inhale the salty mist. Dew had collected on his broad shoulders and dread-locks. The night air was cold, so he huddled in his longcoat, which still bore the hole in the breast pocket where he'd rammed a cutlass into the previous owner.

Dragontooth Cove was named for malicious spires of rock that lay beneath the surface, protruding only at low tide. For a long while, he stared at the dark sea and listened to the waves hissing in and out of the cove like a sleeping dragon.

One of his fellow crewmen whistled somewhere below. Another echoed the call from high on the cliff. Agwe saw the lights of the incoming ship, then whistled back. *Ship approaching,* they all said. The crew was scattered on high rocks and in caves, their lanterns bobbing in the dark. To those at sea, the lights would signal safe harbor.

They all went silent as the ship drew into the cove.

He heard the deep thunder and lightning-crack of splin-tering wood as the ship's hull caromed off the first rocky fang, then another, and then its hull smashed into a shelf of rock, the mast jarring loose with a deafening squeal. From inside the vessel came the sounds of agony and death—men hurled about, thrown overboard, and crushed by shifting cargo. Sails flashed in the darkness. The mast twirled and jabbed like a rapier.

Between the force of the sea and the strength of the cliff, the ship was quickly unmade.

At sunrise, when the tide was low enough, the wreckers descended upon the ship's carcass like crabs. Agwe's fellow crewmen celebrated. If their sources were correct, this was a Corcovian galleon, heavy-laden with gold and silver. While that was plenty to cheer over, Agwe was a shipbuilder's son and knew what it took to transform lumber into seaworthy vessels. He'd come home well after dark, his fingers bleeding from hammering nails, cutting wood, and hefting planks, and then he and his father would wake early and do it all over again. To take part in a ship's destruction was a heavy anchor on his soul.

Tattered canvas sails draped the rocks like black shrouds, and it was beneath one of these that he found the bloated, gray corpse. The dead man wore black livery, covered in constellations of sand.

The color of pirates and priests, he thought.

He took the cutlass from the belt, searched the pockets and pouches, and removed the boots. Then he saw a silver chain looped around the corpse's neck. Attached to it was a silver medallion—an engraved kraken with ruby eyes. Only the Avants of the Sea Goddess wore them. To seafolk, priests were sacred. Even pirates let them be. To kill one was a heinous crime. To destroy their ship was unheard of.

He backed away from the corpse into the sunlight.

"Ill luck to touch a seaman's corpse," said Tom Hatchet. "They are gifts for Amadah now."

"'Tis worse than that," he said, nudging the corpse with his boot. "One of her Avants."

"Here, too, looks like," said Klip, pointing to a black shape on the rocks. She was a fierce woman, yet her eyes were fearful.

Tom shook his head, eyes wild with panic. "No, no, no. The Usher of Souls'll come and lock us in the Sea Goddess's cages for all eternity. I won't be no lobster." With that, he scuttled up the rocks toward town.

A cold breeze howled through the cove, and Agwe fought the urge to run with Tom.

Agwe was a wrecker out of necessity. He owed La Roche, a vicious moneylender, who had threatened his wife and daughter if Agwe failed to pay his outstanding debt. He couldn't blame Marisha for throwing him out, yet nothing was more precious to him than his daughter. He thought of Raeni's sweet smile and her big eyes, so full of goodness, and it made him sick to his stomach to know he'd put her at risk. He had to make this right.

He eyed the silver chain and the medallion. The ruby eyes were a small fortune on their own, while the rest could be melted down. It was a good find. Enough to pay off La Roche and free his family of danger. He took the medallion off the priest's body and hung it around his neck. It was an act of defiance and blasphemy that made a few of the crew gasp. But once they saw no harm came to him, they returned to scavenging, though he noticed they didn't go near the corpses. Some superstitions couldn't be shaken.

The cove was an amphitheater of sorts, with great shelves of rocks naturally carved into the cliff base. The breeze howled and whistled through the caves and along the tiers. Mist curled around the spires jutting from the shallow water.

Sunlight gleamed on a gold coin. As he stooped to pluck it from the dark rock, cold water flooded his ankles and washed the coin away.

"Tide's rushin' in!" shouted Klip, her voice shrill.

"Goddess have mercy," he heard someone else say.

The tide wasn't due for hours. Agwe didn't believe in the Sea Goddess anymore, but he believed in the tide. And he saw it now, swelling in the cove, rising impossibly fast. The wreck was already half-drowned.

It can't be, he thought as water sloshed around his waist.

As the crew scurried to safety, he saw one of the men slip beneath the water, and then a second and a third. The rush of the waves and the shocking cold of the sea held him fast, and he went under.

Most seamen didn't know how to swim, but his father had taught him how to fish, cast nets, and gather clams; how to read the weather and navigate by the sun and stars; how to select, cut, and shape wood; and how to swim. And he wanted now, more than anything, to do those things for his sweet daughter. All of the things he should've done, but hadn't. Teach her how to bait a hook, where to find the best flowers and seashells. Teach her to fight, to read. How to hammer nails into wood, and how to float in water. He wanted to watch her grow from a child to a young woman.

A strong undercurrent hauled him out to sea, and he tumbled beneath the surface, not knowing which direction was up. Beneath the churning water, he saw the shadows of his crewmen and the ruins of the shipwreck suspended all around.

And then he felt a presence behind him, silent as the grave.

His father had preached to him about the Sea Goddess his whole life. She granted safe passage to ships, offered blessings for a successful haul, or made ships vanish. He'd never truly believed in Her, but now Her presence loomed undeniable, ancient and powerful, as immense as roiling storm clouds. Innumerable black tentacles writhed in the darkness. Her vastness overwhelmed him, and he felt Her great whirlpool eyes looking right at him, churning and raging in his mind. The water held him in a crushing grip.

He'd never felt so insignificant.

He recalled the last line of a prayer said before a ship set sail, and he chanted it in his mind. *She is the wondrous deep. She is the wondrous deep.* The medallion's eyes flared to life, glowing in the dark water like embers.

His lungs were burning, nearly drained of air. The grip on him coiled tighter, hauling him down, down, into the darkness. He hit the sandy seafloor in an explosion of silt. The water dropped like curtains all around him and drained away. Salt burned his nose and throat, and he coughed it out.

He lay in a large grotto. Light shimmered on the walls as if reflected off pools of water, giving Agwe the sensation of being underwater though he was somehow breathing cool air. From everywhere came the constant rushing sound of a whirlpool.

In the center of the space stood a large pool of black water, round as an eye. Crude benches made of porous volcanic rock surrounded it. At one end of the grotto stood a pulpit shaped like the bow of a ship. Just above the bowsprit and forepeak, the sea-green figurehead of a kraken looked down upon him with furious red eyes.

He approached the pool nervously, peering at his own reflection. The water remained still, but he heard the crash of waves in his ears. He sat heavily on one of the rock benches, feeling the cold dampness through his trousers.

"How's the wind, shipmate?" called a voice.

So loud was the sea that Agwe scarcely heard the polite greeting, and then the sound ebbed, leaving only the pulse of blood in his ears, like the rhythmic rowing of oars. Across the pool stood a short woman in a black longcoat, black trousers tucked into black boots, a tricorn hat, and a cutlass on her wide hips. A silver kraken medallion hung around her neck.

"Who might you be?" he asked.

"You know who I am." Her eyes were the color of a glacier sea. Her hair was tinged green.

"Are you the Usher?" he asked.

"Aye." She bowed her head just enough to allow water to trickle from her tricorn. "Like the Goddess, I am too vast for you to comprehend, so I took this simple, familiar form so we might talk. I've an eye for lost souls. May I join you?"

"Heave ahead, but I've only the one rock." He scooted to the edge of the bench to make room. "Is that what I am—a lost soul?"

"You have forsaken the currents of your life. You went adrift, and now you are marooned."

"Sent to the bottom, more like."

"The course ebbs and flows, curves and wends, and all we have to do is follow the currents, stay the course."

He stared murderously at the black pool. "The currents brought me here to this little rock. With you."

"Nay. You were a shipbuilder's son, from a long line of shipbuilders. A sacred art."

He nearly choked. He'd buried that secret long ago. "How can you know that?"

She stared hard at him with her glacier eyes. "I see into the deep waters of a person's soul. I see the currents of then, now, and what should be."

He believed her. He should've been amazed, yet he felt only contempt. "Bah. Keep your Goddess. She led me to ruin."

"You have a daughter who loves you. Is that not enough?"

He didn't answer, his mind whirling. His family had been put in danger because of him. He was a wretch and a scupperlout.

"You were meant for greater things, Agwe Delmas. Even at a young age, your keen eye spied gaps in the planks and faults in the wood. You kept tight seams. You were good with hammer and nail. I see much love in those days."

"I never measured up," Agwe muttered.

"There can be no mistakes," she said, "or a ship will sink."

"Aye. Perfection or failure. Those were his words."

"A father must expect greatness or his son will never achieve it. You were meant to follow in his wake and become a great shipbuilder."

"I was never good enough."

"He was a hard man, aye. But your child, his granddaughter, would have softened him as his life ebbed. You would have seen that old love again."

"That ship sailed," he spat. "I couldn't live up to his expectations." But as he said it, he knew it was a lie. *He was a better shipbuilder and family man than I'd ever be.*

"A ship can change course," said the Usher. "A wife can love her husband again. A son can love his father. A man can become a shipbuilder."

Agwe snorted. "Are you trying to inspire me to change course?"

"Nay," she said.

From the pool of still water, Agwe heard the terrible churning of a whirlpool. "What then?"

"One of Amadah's ships was lured to her doom in a cove not far from here. Twenty-four of Her souls were lost. She has already reclaimed every scrap and splinter, whilst I collected the souls of your crewmates. And now I have come for you, Agwe Delmas."

There was a finality to her words, and he knew he was as helpless now as he'd been against the sea. He wouldn't see his wife and daughter again. He wouldn't see his father again. He was drowning, and he needed a plank to hang on to. He wanted to be a better man for Raeni and Marisha, even though they didn't need him. Their lives were on course, and he was little more than a barnacle.

But he could be better.

He could become a shipbuilder. Follow in his father's footsteps.

In a flash, he built that life in his mind, fitting pieces

together. He saw himself as a dedicated husband, father, and shipbuilder. His heart pounded with excitement. "I can change my course," he said brightly.

But the Usher shook her head sorrowfully. "Nay. 'Tis too late for that. Amadah is wrathful. She takes back what is Hers."

He thought of the ship crashing into the dragon's teeth of the cove. Smashed. Ground to pieces. Unmade.

Agwe bowed his head in defeat and sorrow. "What will you do with me, then?"

"I offer a choice. Step into this pool and go to Her cages. Or board Her ship and serve Her for all eternity. Prisoner or servant? What will it be?"

"And if I choose neither?"

"Then I will keelhaul you and sentence you to the cages for all eternity."

With cold certainty, he knew there was no way out. No violence, no bargaining, no deceit. He saw himself standing on the ledge of the round, black pool and stepping off. Down he would go, down and down some more until he was at the bottom of the sea, trapped in cages of whalebone. That was the fate he deserved.

He swallowed hard, tears welling. There was so much water in a person, and it all belonged to the Goddess. He knew that now. He'd never cried before, not until Raeni came along. She'd opened his heart, and he'd slammed it shut and thrown it away. He'd been a chickenhearted fool, a craven coward.

"Will I ever see my family again?" he asked, words choked. "My daughter?"

She regarded him coolly, eyes unblinking. "Choose."

The currents of his life flowed through his mind, racing like a whirlpool.

When he was young, he'd thrown his hammer into the sea because his father had wanted him to work past supper. Years later, he'd left home in the same sort of childish temper. His father had watched him leave from the belly of a skeleton ship, a hammer in one hand and a lantern in the other.

For work, he'd spitefully avoided shipbuilding. One of his first jobs was as a whaler. The gruesome work hardened his soul so much that he pushed a vile shipmate overboard without remorse, to let the seawolves and sharks sort him out. That was the first man he'd killed, but not the last. As a pirate, he'd killed many men. He'd brawled at any slight, and sometimes just to feel something, anything. When he'd grown tired of being at sea, he'd sought the shore instead.

And that's when he'd met Marisha at the fish market. She'd been a beacon of light in those dark days, and he'd been content to be a fisherman just so he could come home to her every night.

When Raeni was birthed, she'd been a squalling, flailing creature. Despite all of the terrible things he'd seen and done, nothing had prepared him for holding her for the first time. Marisha had forced the baby upon him, and her head had fit in the palm of his meaty hand like an egg. She was a treasure more precious than gold or silver, and it had frightened him so much that he'd found as many odd jobs as he could just to avoid holding her. As she'd grown, she'd become even more mysterious. She'd always wanted to sit in his lap or offer him her mushy food or clutch his fingers in her soft little fist.

And now he wouldn't see her again.

He deserved the cages.

But perhaps he could mend some of his wrongs if he chose to serve the Sea Goddess. Perhaps he might see Raeni again someday.

He lifted his chin and looked the Usher in the eyes. "I will serve." And with that, he felt a watery ripple escape from him. A promise, an oath.

"You have until the day's end to put your affairs in order.

At the witching hour, return to the sea and board my black ship. Fail to do so, and I will drag you to the cages."

Agwe gasped. He could see his family one last time. He'd never been so grateful. He wanted to sweep up the Usher in his arms and dance a jig, but her stern face sobered him quickly.

"Have you any advice for a lost soul?" he asked.

"Take a deep breath," said the Usher.

Great waterfalls poured from the ceiling of the grotto and thundered around him. He had time for a quick gulp of air, and then he was fighting against the swells of the ocean again. He kicked hard to the shimmering surface. When he broke through, he gulped fresh air, spitting and coughing out the salt-burn of the water. Dragontooth Cove was a short swim away.

He swam hard, and when he finally crashed onto one of the rock tiers, he lay helpless as a beached whale, gasping, his lungs pushed to their limits. It was nearly dusk, he realized. He had little time left.

When he sat up, he felt a weight around his neck. The silver kraken medallion still hung there, heavy as a noose. Only then did he realize the wrecked ship had vanished, as if none of it had happened.

Gifts to the Goddess, he thought.

By the time Agwe made it back to the village, the streets were dark and wet. He waded through cold air so thick he saw motes in the patches of lantern light. He pulled up his collar and huddled in his longcoat, thankful for the long dreadlocks that warmed his scalp. A few flinty-eyed sailors lurked in the doorways and windows, but otherwise the streets were empty. Normally, after his work was done, he'd visit one of several pubs to drink with the townsfolk, living a better life through their tales. But now he wanted nothing more than to see his family.

Tonight, they were his safe harbor.

Ever since Marisha had kicked him out, he'd been sleeping on a cot in a storage shed behind the Hornpipe Tavern. There, he retrieved his small coin purse he'd hidden in a flour sack and hoped it would be enough for La Roche.

If not, he would roll the bones one last time.

Agwe smelled salt when he was ushered into La Roche's lair. The notorious moneylender was a barrel-chested man with a pock-marked face and a bulbous nose turned red from too much drink. He was not a man to owe, for he liked to use deadbeats as examples by mummifying them in salt barrels then hanging them on posts around his territory.

Surrounded by those barrels, La Roche looked up from his desk with an expression of utter astonishment. "By my death-less soul," he said, "what have we here?"

"Fine stuff for the gallows," said Agwe. He tossed his pouch of coin onto the nearest barrel. It looked smaller than he'd hoped.

"You weary me," said La Roche with a disappointed frown. "That meager sum scarcely covers the tax."

"It's all I've got," said Agwe.

La Roche picked up a crowbar from his desk, hefted it onto his shoulder, and strolled over to where Agwe stood. He wore a pristine white longcoat and white trousers tucked into long, black boots. With a deft movement of his free hand, he swiped the pouch, then looked Agwe up and down with rheumy eyes.

"Tell me, have you ever seen what salt does to a man's flesh?" asked La Roche, his breath stinking of whiskey.

Agwe became aware of the other men in the salt house.

Somehow, without his noticing, they had gathered around. He sensed them more than saw them. *Like seawolves in dark water*, he thought.

"Can't say as I have," he said.

La Roche pried off the lid of a barrel and flung it aside. He shoved a hand inside and hauled something up. White salt poured over the edge and onto the floor. In his fist, La Roche held a knot of wispy hair, and below that a head. The eyes were coated with crystals, the open mouth stuffed with even more. The leathery skin beneath was pale and dry as bone.

La Roche shoved the head back down, and one of his men nailed the lid shut. Each hammer blow made Agwe blink.

"Don't let this be your coffin," said La Roche. "You have until the morrow to pay what you owe, or it is death by salt for you—and your family."

Agwe did his best to stand straight, though his knees wanted to buckle. "We settle this now," he said.

"Why do I trouble myself with you?" La Roche sighed. "I should dry you to the bones and nail you to a post."

"Because I have this," said Agwe, pulling the medallion from beneath his shirt. "This covers the debt, the tax, and more besides."

La Roche squinted at the medallion, inspecting, assaying. "Now what have we here? Hmm. It appears a good enough forgery."

"'Tis the real thing, I swear it."

La Roche settled back on his heels and gripped his coat's lapels. "If that be true, I will consider your debt paid."

"In full," said Agwe quickly.

"Aye. In full."

La Roche reached for the medallion, but Agwe stepped out of reach, clutching it to his chest.

She is the wondrous deep, he thought.

When the medallion's red eyes flared in the dark room, La

Roche's own eyes widened with amazement. "Well, bless my black heart. Why were you keeping this all to yourself?"

No lie came to Agwe, so he spoke the truth. "I paid a severe price for it."

La Roche held out his hand, and Agwe slapped the medallion into his open palm. Agwe hoped the Goddess would forgive him this small sacrilege.

As the moneylender hefted the medallion, all menace washed away from his face, replaced by hospitality and charm. "A pleasure, Agwe Delmas. If the need should arise again, you can find me here amid my treasure hoard." He spread his arms wide as if to embrace the barrels all around him.

When Agwe finally tromped up the back steps of the cottage, he saw his wife and daughter framed in the window, sitting in their cramped kitchen. He couldn't see what they were doing, but they always made things out of wildflowers and seashells from the beach. How Marisha had such energy after a hard day at the fish market was beyond him. He watched them for a long time, soaking in their smiles. He desperately wanted to throw open the door and embrace them both, but he knew his intrusion would collide with their happiness. For putting Raeni in danger, Marisha had thrown him out. She would not welcome him back so easily.

He opened the door anyway.

Marisha glared at him, but he ignored her wrath and focused on his daughter. Raeni brightened. She was always so much bigger than he thought she should be. With a playful growl, he gave her a hug, lifted her out of the chair, and kissed her neck. Her dark hair smelled of lavender. She giggled with delight.

Wood shavings littered the tabletop, surrounding two small pieces of driftwood and two pocketknives.

"What's all this?" he asked.

"We're whistling," said Raeni.

"Whittling," said Marisha.

"I'm making a sea turtle," said Raeni. "Ma's making an albatross, but it looks more like a fish."

She made a disgusted face that reminded him of Marisha, and Agwe laughed hard, too hard, his eyes welling with tears.

This was all he wanted. It didn't have to be more than this.

He set Raeni back in her chair. Marisha gave him a warning look, as powerful as a lighthouse. She was still shockingly beautiful, with piercing sea-green eyes and braided hair decorated with seashell beads. Her face was unreadable, a mystery; he always loved that about her.

"Why are you here?" she asked. With the knifepoint, she maneuvered him out of the kitchen and into the bedroom, five steps away. He didn't fear much, but he did fear her anger.

He tried to remember what he wanted to say and couldn't. "I wanted to give you more. You deserve more."

"We agreed it was best to keep distance between us."

He knew the night was about to swirl out of control and crash. But he wouldn't fight with her. Not tonight. He needed calmer waters.

"I settled with La Roche," he said quickly. "The danger has passed."

He knelt beside his little smuggler's hold and removed a small sack of coin. It was his final cache, the one he'd saved as a last resort. He held it up to her.

She frowned at his offering. "Keep your coin and go about."

He rose, his joints creaking like a ship at sea. "I've come to say goodbye, my love."

Her eyes flickered across his face, poking and prodding, and finally settling on suspicion. "What have you done?"

He looked at the floorboards, noticing the loose seams he

should've fixed for her. "I've done terrible things. Unforgivable things. But here's the truth of it, my love. I'm listed in service of the Sea Goddess Herself."

Her expression softened, first confused, then disbelieving. "You? An Avant?"

"Upon my life, I speak true."

"Why? How?"

"There was no other way." He shoved the coins at her. "Take this. Please."

"You still think money is the problem or the answer. We don't need you for that."

"I ruined us," he said. "I know that now. So take the coin. Leave this terrible place for a better life. Don't do it for me. Do it for yourself and Raeni."

"And where would we go?"

"Go wherever you've dreamed of. This will buy you passage to Corcova. Or Baralon."

"We could go to those places," she said, "but you won't be there."

The sorrow in her words broke his heart. He said, "I will be wherever the sea takes me."

"She can have you." She slapped at his shoulder, but he caught her hand and held it. She didn't wriggle it away.

"You loved me once," he said.

"I love you still, you damned fool," she said, entwining her fingers in his.

"That makes me happier than I deserve."

He lifted her fingers to his lips and kissed her knuckles, then he pulled her into his arms. She hugged him fiercely. He hadn't realized how much he wanted her forgiveness until he had a small piece of it.

After a few wonderful moments, she caressed his rough cheek, then kissed him. Her lips were warm and soft, and he wanted to stay there forever.

She gently pushed away from him and rested her forehead

against his chest. "You're going to miss me on those cold, lonely nights at sea."

"I already do."

"When do you leave?"

"I am yours until the witching hour, my love."

"Then, at the very least," she said, smiling up at him, smiling at last, "you could make us a cup of tea before you go."

He laughed at that. She'd never been docile. He found the tea where it always was. He poured two cups, and they all sat together. Raeni focused on her whittling. He was amazed at her skill with the knife. Marisha had taught her well. She had grown so much without him. He soaked in every movement, every feature, every change of expression. It was all he could do. It would have to be enough.

All too soon, there would be a black ship in the harbor, waiting just for him.

About the Author

Ken Hoover lives in New Mexico with his family. He is the author of *Midnight Agency*, a post-apocalyptic supernatural western, and his short fiction has appeared in *James Gunn's Ad Astra Magazine*, *Bourbon Penn*, and other places. In addition to being a semi-finalist in the Writers of the Future contest, he is an alumnus of NMSU and Superstars Writing Seminars. You can find him on Facebook, Twitter, and Instagram.

Scourge

L.V. BELL

The dumbwaiter by the reinforced steel door opened its gaping maw at exactly 6:00 AM to deliver a tray with breakfast and the week's targets. I snatched it from the cavity, impatient for the next part of the ritual. The console to my right flared to life. A timer in the far corner of the leftmost screen flashed six hours, then started counting down. Thank the stars, Blackbeard didn't want to talk over things today. I needed all the time I could get.

The day's menu offered a Parmesan-and-chive egg soufflé, a bowl of fresh strawberries, and a thermos of tea. Oolong, if my nose wasn't lying. I poured a quarter of it into my favorite cup—the phoenix one with gold inlaid around the bird's flames—and helped myself to a strawberry as I read over the list. Blackbeard wanted something special if she was willing to bribe me with fruit.

Assignment one: photos of the king of England's honeymoon. The wedding to Queen Five had been a month ago, but people remained obsessed with royalty, even in the twenty-second century, and the paparazzi hadn't acquired any scintillating images since the big day. I resisted the urge to roll my eyes. A boring prize and too easy to obtain.

Assignment two: a report on the latest terraforming breakthroughs at the International Cooperative for Space Exploration. Even easier, and I could guess the customer. Despite publicly participating in the global effort, Russia remained determined to plant their flag first for some reason. Maybe because Mars was the red planet.

Assignment three: a list of dark money donors contributing to the reelection campaign for the current president of the Global Congress. I'd been expecting that target for a month. Politics was forever a profitable business and worth keeping up on for someone in my line of work, but it didn't warrant the fruit.

Ah, there it was. Assignment four: the as-of-yet incomplete manuscript of the final VanGelder novel. Save the best for last, Blackbeard always said. Maybe that's why she let the other morons in the guild take their cracks before handing the task to the one person who could get the job done. I sniffed, the earthy scent of tea filling my nose. She was probably looking for my replacement. Good luck.

If it hadn't been for more important tasks, I might have already pirated the manuscript. The greatest desert saga since *Dune* had enthralled me as much as it had the rest of the world, though I wasn't as bothered by the decade-long wait for the final installment. Besides, I didn't see a point in stealing the ending until it was ready. But Blackbeard had never been one for patience, and even an unfinished manuscript would fetch a pretty price when she was done reading it herself.

In any case, I expected none of these projects would push my schedule past the usual two-hour timeline, and I needed every spare second my talents could buy now that the real target was in sight. Not the flashy tabloid photos or political deals Blackbeard was always chasing. They had value, sure, but the treasure I sought would rewrite history. And with any luck, today it would become mine. After I saw to Blackbeard's list, of course.

The breakfast tray found a place on the mahogany desk that housed the instruments of modern pillaging: a built-in computer console with enough processing power to run a small city and six wraparound screens that bathed my adolescent body in blue light.

"Good morning, lovely," I said, greeting my single window to the outside world.

I settled into the plush chair custom-made to fit my youthful frame and got to work. The ghost program woke at my gentle caress of the controls. I hated to lose the processing power, but it was necessary to prevent Blackbeard and other potential eavesdroppers from looking over my shoulder. No reason to be pillaged myself. Instead, the ghost displayed an edited version of my interactions with the world beyond the

40

screen to keep the essence of my skills hidden while maintaining Blackbeard's belief that I needed the full six hours allotted to collect the treasures she desired.

The royal pictures were acquired before I'd polished off the last strawberry. The terraforming report tied for completion with the soufflé. I poured a fourth cup of oolong. The list of donors took a little longer. The curls of steam had faded from my tea when the data finally surrendered to my tender encouragement, leaving the VanGelder manuscript the only impediment to pursuing my own treasure.

The timer in the corner showed an hour and seventeen minutes had passed. The donor list had taken longer than anticipated.

I rolled my shoulders, willing the muscles to relax, and drummed my fingers on the console.

Tap, tap, thwam.

The final percussive motion of my index finger brought me to VanGelder's home server. I leaned in and got to work.

Here, at last, lay a prize worth my effort. Firewalls, encryptions, snares hidden behind every potential vulnerability I thought to exploit—the sea around my virtual ship grew increasingly stormy. The usual tricks weren't nearly enough. I finally gained access to an email account with correspondence between author and editor, which should've been the end of it. Instead, it explained why Blackbeard had sent the strawberries.

VanGelder had written the manuscript by hand. With an actual pen. On actual paper.

"You mad genius."

Having read the novels, I should've expected such a twist. There was no better security in the world than a hard copy. It also meant I was screwed.

I thumbed through a number of other emails to confirm the manuscript existed out of anyone's reach. The author had scheduled an in-person delivery to the editor for last week and

—I sat up straighter—the editor had sent a note thanking VanGelder for trusting him enough to make a copy to mark up.

One corner of my mouth twitched to a smirk.

A minute later, I let myself into the publishing house's servers. A quick search led me to the editor's personal console, which in turn guided me to the copier he'd used. Then came the long shot. Copiers were antique bricks left over from the pre-digital era. I'd never heard of a functioning one, much less attempted to hack one before. The operating system was a joke, but, depending on how solid the underlying firmware was, Blackbeard might have to send someone to physically lift the hard drive.

Luck, however, favored me a second time. A minuscule vulnerability granted me access to the drive's history, and a quick search found the digital record the machine had kept from the scan required to make the copy.

Tension fled my shoulders. Three simple commands, and the manuscript downloaded itself onto my drive with the day's other treasures. Another command encrypted the four files, compressed them, and prepared them for delivery to Blackbeard at the appropriate time. I leaned back in my chair and reached for the tea. It hit my tongue cold.

"Ugh."

I dumped it in the orchid beside my desk and picked up the thermos.

Empty.

The timer provided yet another irritant. A full three hours and two minutes had passed. The manuscript acquisition would see me robbed of solitude at lunch so Blackbeard could congratulate me. The revelation of my success—necessary to maintain my place as her favorite, or at least her most useful, hacker—would see my console go dark until the delivery of the next week's assignments. She wasn't stupid, and a mind like mine could wreak a lot of havoc if given unfettered access to a computer.

My fault for hacking the most powerful corporation in existence without permission or a ghost to hide my efforts. I may be a verified genius—everything from technology to languages to music came to me as easily as breathing—but I'd been a dumb five-year-old kid. Blackbeard had modified connections to the room after that. It didn't matter how I retrofitted the console, I couldn't reach the interwebs without permission, and she restricted my access to six hours a week. Thus, the threat was successfully neutralized without damaging profitability.

Except that depriving me had made me better at my craft. I would've enjoyed basking in the irony, but I had a mere two hours and fifty—I glanced at the timer—seven minutes to retrieve the secret of the Fountain of Youth from Legacy Corp. And I was close, I could feel it.

Once again, my fingers rapped on the console, landing me right where I'd been forced to leave off the week before. Legacy's encryptions were wound tighter than a Gordian knot. To date, I'd spent a total of 1,872 hours stretched across 302 weeks, and I still couldn't find the sword to cut it away from my prize. A reality made more aggravating by the fact that I had spent those six years in servitude to Blackbeard. More than half my life lived in this hole. I'd considered abandoning ship more than once, but the tools I needed to reach the Fountain were here and, once it was mine, I would be free of more than just my captain.

Not that my time in Blackbeard's guild had been horrible. Quite the contrary. Life here was more lavish than I'd imagined possible when my former guardians forced me to hack Blackbeard's private accounts and lift a cool two million credits. I'd protested, but they'd insisted. It was less than one percent of what she had in the account. What harm could such a small sum do?

Rule number one: never hack a hacker.

But rather than yanking me before the law—the most terrifying thing an unsanctioned child could imagine—Blackbeard rescued me from the den of half-starved urchins our beneficent global government considered an orphanage.

Dumb to call it that. The advent of the Fountain sixty-four years before I was illegally conceived saw death all but cease to exist. Nothing but a bad memory from the primitive world predating Legacy Corp's biggest breakthrough.

Of course, no one considered the negative repercussions immortality might have before making it free to the public. Sure, disease and aging were as dead as death, but the planet had been suffering from lack of resources long before the expanding population became immortal. Even the Lunar settlements and planned Martian colonies weren't enough to relieve the pressure on Earth. So until someone in the Global Congress managed to pass a sterilization law, there would be places for irresponsible couples to dump the children they weren't allowed to have and were too moral to dispose of pre-birth.

But the horrors of being an illegal couldn't touch me once I attracted Blackbeard's attention. I don't even think the staff noticed when I disappeared. Too busy enjoying the spoils of my latest exploit. Blackbeard slipped me away in broad daylight to this palace of a room in her fortress of a mansion on the other side of the world where my talents could be put to better use in a more comfortable setting.

It would be a shame to say goodbye to the luxury foods and high-end tech, but I wouldn't need it once I made humanity mortal again.

My fingers flew across the console, their *te-ka-tek* composing a symphony. My magnum opus was so close to completion, it was a sprint against time.

One I seemed destined to lose. Again.

The borders of my screens flared red. Simultaneously, the

ghost delivered the day's plunder to Blackbeard. Thirty seconds later, it began playing a recording of my performance of Bach's Cello Suite No. 1. The timer showed less than eight minutes remaining in my access window. Curse Blackbeard's impatient reading habits.

Worse still, my momentary inattention unleashed a technological kraken. Legacy's firewalls closed in, their many tentacles wrapping around my virtual ship, squeezing until it snapped. The next thing I knew, I'd been booted from the server.

"Shit!"

Part of me wanted to throw caution to the wind and dive back in, but if anyone caught me in Legacy Corp's servers again, I'd be flayed within an inch of my illegal life, chucked into the darkest hole on Blackbeard's property, and left to rot. She might rule the world's most feared hacker guild, but Legacy Corp owned the world—privilege of discovering immortality and all—and they defended their property like it was the last source of clean water on the planet. Those who hazarded so much as an unsanctioned peep at their firewalls were charged with crimes against humanity and prosecuted as terrorists. Those who went further simply disappeared. Permanently.

Hence Blackbeard's promise regarding my fate should she ever catch me sniffing around their security again. Legacy's IP was the only thing on her no-go list. I wondered vaguely if the Fountain could preserve someone from starvation. Until death was back on the table, that would be an ugly way to live. I closed down everything but the ghost program, which continued to play the cello recording.

Eighty-four seconds.

The empty thermos and strawberry bowl found their places on the tray beside the soufflé ramekin. I found my place too, on the stool in the music nook opposite the console. My second-favorite instrument came eagerly to my hands. The recording was in the final seconds of the third movement. My fingers danced across the cello's neck. The bow hovered over the strings, moving with music still silent. The timer flashed.

Three.

Two.

One.

The console went dark. The music continued, my instrument picking up precisely where the recording left off. I poured myself into the movement of it, feeling the pressure of the strings against my fingers, the vibration of the sound traveling through the bow as I swept silence into song.

All sense of time melted into tones as rich and lonely as my existence in Blackbeard's prison cell. That's what it was after all, antique furniture, designer meals, and state-of-the-art technology aside. And I was still just a meal ticket.

Lunch, in this case.

The whir of the locks in the reinforced steel door to my cage pierced my musical meditation and alerted me to the impending breach of my solitude. My eyes closed. A minute later, I heard the door hiss open. The familiar *pock-pock* of designer stilettos rang against the hardwood floor.

"Just set it down," a female voice said.

Softer footsteps moved into the room, deposited something on the solid mahogany table to the right of the music nook, and left. The door closed with its typical *whir-whir-whir-click*, sealing me and my guest inside.

"Scourge."

I could feel Blackbeard's gaze on me.

"Come here," she said.

"Let me finish the suite."

"I don't have all day."

I broke contact with the strings with a jolt and snapped to attention, eyes open, back as straight as the cello at my side, bow across my forehead in full salute. "Yes, Captain."

One of Blackbeard's finely manicured eyebrows arched.

Its new purplish-red color didn't do anything to make her plain face more attractive. The fake tan wasn't helping either. "How many times do I have to tell you this is not a ship and I am not your captain?"

"But I *am* a pirate."

"Hacker."

I shrugged. "Pirates are more fun. Either way, I'm pillaging for your benefit, so you'll be my captain until that stops."

She smirked, and I could almost see the thought in a bubble over her head. *Never, then.*

Keep on believing it, I thought back.

"Have it your way," she said. "For today, at least. Consider it a reward for acquiring the requested valuables."

"I better get a bigger reward than thanks. The effing manuscript took me all morning."

It wasn't a lie as far as she was concerned. The ghost program had me struggling with it until it kicked on the music.

"Don't curse," Blackbeard said. "And don't I always reward you well?" She pointed at the covered tray on the table beside her.

I treated her to a lopsided grin, set the cello down, and pranced over to lift the lid. Lunch was comprised of an ahi tuna steak as thick as my fist, a spring salad, and toast with avocado slices. Fresh produce twice in one day? Someone must have already paid for the VanGelder manuscript. And for dessert—my mouth watered—a chocolate trifle with actual shavings of the stuff on top. Cacao was worth as much as gold these days. I'd only been treated to such a delicacy twice before.

"And this is why you're Blackbeard," I said. "Loyalty secured through reward rather than terror."

"Can't you just say thank you?"

"Thanks, Captain," I said, and meant it. I snagged a piece of toast and shoved it whole into my mouth.

Blackbeard smiled. "Thank *you*. I'd love to stay and hear how you figured it out—"

"It's a thrilling tale."

"—but I have more pressing issues to—"

BOOM.

I sank to a seat in front of the meal, picked up a fork, and speared myself a piece of tuna. "Issues, you were saying?"

Blackbeard shushed me, her gaze intent on the door to my room.

BOOM.

The lights flickered.

The fish practically melted in my mouth. "Sounds like the scurvy dogs on deck be messin' around with yer cannons, Cap'n."

She didn't spare me so much as a scowl as she crossed to the door and pressed her hand to the scanner built in where the doorknob should've been. Normally it would've lit up and opened the door. Today it remained as black as my console.

Blackbeard tapped a small silver band on her wrist. "Johns, what's going on?"

BOOM.

"Johns!"

The lights went out.

Backup power kicked on security lights for all of twenty seconds before those died as well. Something fleshy thumped against the door.

"Shit!" she snarled.

"Don't curse," I said through a mouthful of ahi. "Set yerself at ease, Cap'n. The scurvy dogs'll rescue—"

"Shut up." Her fingernails scrabbled along the door.

I shrugged and went back to my food. She could toy with things all she wanted, but with the security system down, there'd be no getting out from this end. She'd made sure of that after the second time I tried it.

The fish, salad, and toast had disappeared before she gave

up, but I took my time with the trifle. I held the little glass bowl to my nose, breathing in the smell of rich cacao until I couldn't resist. At that point, I collected the smallest spoon from my tea set, one I generally used to stir in sugar, and drew up the smallest of bites. Smooth cream met my tongue, and then—absolute heaven.

"Oh yeah," I sighed to myself. This was totally worth waiting another week to steal the Fountain. Lucky Blackbeard didn't know my weakness. With enough chocolate, she could've kept me a willing member of her crew for the rest of our unnaturally long lives.

I was two bites in when the security lights flicked on. Blackbeard sat on the floor, arms folded over her fake breasts, a scowl twisting her red lips.

I grinned and lifted a third spoonful of trifle. "Told you they'd rescue us. Or you, anyway."

Her scowl deepened, her eyebrows threatening to meet in the middle of her forehead, though I wasn't sure what annoyed her more, me or the fact that she'd had to sit on the floor in her designer pencil skirt. Or maybe it was the missing nail on her right ring finger. Either way, I turned my attention back to the trifle and did my best to keep from snickering.

The fifth spoonful had just met my tongue when a familiar whir heralded Blackbeard's imminent liberation.

The door hissed open a crack.

Blackbeard turned her scowl upwards. "About ti—"

I looked up at her hesitation. Wide eyes erased every hint of her former irritation.

"Told you she'd have a safe room," a male voice said.

The door swung wide, revealing a mob of SWAT officers in full riot gear.

"Boss, there's a kid in here with her," one of them said, his mask muffling his words. "About twelve years old, Asian descent. Can't tell if it's a boy or a girl."

I rolled my eyes. "Does it matter?"

"Bring them both," came the answer from somewhere down the hallway.

Two of the SWAT team pulled Blackbeard to her feet. A third headed my way. I dropped the tiny spoon and shoveled the remaining trifle into my mouth with my fingers. No way was I going to let that go to waste, no matter what else was going on.

The officer gave me a napkin. I licked my hand clean before wiping. He took my other hand and escorted me into the hall and up a flight of stairs.

The room at the top was unbearably bright. In the time I'd worked for Blackbeard, I could count on one hand the times I'd seen the sky. The last one had been three years ago. A gift for my eighth birthday. I blinked wildly, trying to clear my vision so I could appreciate the view.

The officer guided me toward Blackbeard and the others so we could continue our extraction as a group.

"Out of curiosity," she said, "what finally did me in?"

The officer who'd spoken earlier gave a grim laugh. "Isn't it obvious?"

"No." Blackbeard's scowling eyebrows reasserted themselves. "Enlighten me."

"Oh, don't get me wrong, I understand the temptation. But going after the Fountain of Youth, of all things? You've really lost your touch, Reuter."

Blackbeard stopped dead.

Thank the stars for that. It kept everyone from noticing me stumbling over my own feet.

The officer on her left pulled her arm. "Come on, now. Don't got all day."

She ignored him, her eyes on his superior. "Do you think I'm stupid?"

"Honestly? Yeah."

Blackbeard stepped forward. "I would *never* sanction an attack on Legacy Corp."

The officer leaned in until his riot mask met her nose. "Protest all you like. The hack originated from this location. From the exact room where we found you, in fact."

My brain lost contact with my feet, no longer sure which direction was up. A hurricane whirled through my head, half-baked thoughts that had no chance of saving me battering the inside of my skull like cannonballs.

The hallway was silent a moment before Blackbeard turned to me, and, for the first time since I'd met her, I understood how this utterly average woman had managed to maintain her grip on the world's most fearsome hacker guild for the last fifty years. I'd have flayed myself and pitched my worthless hide into a hole for her if it would've rescued me from that gaze.

"Scourge."

Every eye in the hall landed on me.

My stomach instantly regretted that last handful of trifle.

"You ungrateful, brainless, backstabbing little *shit*!" Blackbeard stomped her foot so hard she broke the heel off her stiletto.

She stumbled into the arms of her captors. They hauled her away before she could regain enough balance to claw my eyes out. A nice gesture, but it didn't matter much. She wouldn't go down honorably with the ship I'd sunk, and when the guild found out what I done … Well, I was dead either way.

I looked up at my guard. "Now what?"

He shrugged. "Haven't had a juvenile in custody in decades."

I leaned forward on the balls of my feet. The lack of any firm policy could play in my favor.

"Age means nothing," the officer behind me said. "And if this kid is the hacker, the people upstairs are going to want a lot of answers."

The leader nodded. "Interrogation, same as Reuter. The suits can sort it out from there."

Consensus reached, the officer at my elbow nudged me forward. A second officer fell in on my other side.

I stifled a grin as they escorted me the same way Blackbeard had gone. An interrogation meant questions. Questions often led to conversations. And conversations offered opportunities. After all, the human mind was just another kind of computer to hack.

About the Author

A story addict from a young age, L.V. has a passion for all things science fiction and fantasy. She holds an M.A. in Creative Writing, and her day job is managing projects in the satellite-communications industry. When not madly scribbling words for the muse, L.V. can be found dancing at the Colorado Renaissance Festival or judging beer competitions with her husband. She is currently working on a sci-fi novel, of which this story is a spin-off. Visit her at lvbell.com.

The Pirate's Cat

TRACY LEONARD NAKATANI

W itches are merchants of misery. Why, then, did I let one onto my ship? Because no one listens to a cat.

I sat on the sill outside the captain's window, balancing against the gentle sway of the boat and straining to hear as my human spoke to the beautiful hag over the crashing waves.

Inside the captain's quarters, they basked in candlelight at the table set with a simple meal on silver plates and a spread of painted cards between them. My human, Bastian—young and dashing with night-black hair and a crooked grin hidden beneath his trim beard. And the witch—skin like moonlight with glittering barnacles crowning her silver hair.

The sky bled crimson and orange around me, like light leaking from an open wound.

Bastian, who always put effort into his appearance, had spent an extra hour in his various mirrors, dressing his hair, working strange tonics into his skin, smoothing his silk shirt and ruffled collar, which he had changed five times before settling on the rich green color he now wore.

He'd always spent more time looking in the mirror than over his shoulder.

So there I sat, the loyal cat, watching my human play a game of enchanted cards with a born-and-bred cheat while the salt sprayed my ginger fur and the cold wind brushed my whiskers.

A good witch never gives up—not unless she wants to, or until she gets what she wants. And while Bastian had invited the hag on the pretense that he was the one with desire— looking to add years to his youth—she wouldn't have come if she wasn't expecting something greater in return.

And now, I feared those cards meant Bastian could not escape her snare no matter how much he believed he could trap her.

I hunched closer to the window, ears flicking toward the crack that ran along the frame.

Bastian chuckled, flipped his final card, and slid it between them. The black surface glittered with a sheen of dark purple, different from the other painted cards.

His eyes lit up as they met hers. Triumphant. He said something, reaching across the table for her thin, delicate hand. The witch leaned forward, her smile a sigh of delight.

Something in that smile made me uneasy. A black mist twisted from Bastian's winning card, spilling like ink through water. I stood on all fours, sticking my nose against the glass. Bastian's face paled, yet he remained frozen as the mist swallowed him, the witch, the table—everything—until it reached the glass, meeting my face.

I jerked away, claws scraping against the sill to prevent myself from tumbling into the ocean. My heart pattered in my chest. Whatever had happened couldn't be good. With the next lurch of the boat against waves, I sprang from my perch and jumped to the next ledge, viewing the room from a different angle. Bastian sputtered. Through the black haze, the witch grasped a handful of light and buried it in a sealskin pouch around her waist. I hurried along the window ledge and up the railing of the ship.

Bastian's quarters remained closed, but candlelight glowed in the windows once again as the strange smoke cleared. I crept to the door, and Bastian came stumbling out. My tail puffed like a frayed rope.

Bastian, my once young and dashing captain, now wore a face that was pockmarked and used like an old leather shoe. And his hands had spots a Dalmatian would envy—as if the hand of time had fish-slapped him!

I scurried between his legs into his quarters, searching for the witch. The fire popping in the hearth was the only sign of life in an otherwise empty room. The scent of kelp and jasmine lingered on the air and coated the back of my tongue.

I fiercely licked my coat down, mostly out of habit, but the fear of lingering magic certainly encouraged a cleaning. Then I noticed the roughness of my own coat and almost choked on my own fur. I clawed my way up the captain's chair and onto the table, stepping over the now-blank cards to peer at my ginger-striped face in the reflection of the silver plates.

I hadn't aged. With a sigh of relief, I continued my cleaning until Bastian trudged back to his chair.

He seemed lost and in a daze. When he collapsed in his seat, he stared, unblinking, at the back of his liver-spotted hands, then buried his face in them and sobbed.

Cautiously, I placed a paw on his shoulder as I stood on my hind legs and licked his hand.

His blubbering stopped, and he peered at me for a moment, eyes softening. Then, with a wave of his hand, he shooed me off the table. "Go on, you. Get."

I leapt down and scowled at him from the rug. The sobbing resumed, and I rolled my eyes. He wasn't *that* ugly.

That night, I slept in the storeroom, unable to cope with his whimpering. All men were vain to some degree, but none as much as Bastian. He would have sold his firstborn—if he'd had one—for the secret of eternal youth, of that I had no doubt. What did he expect when dealing with a sea witch? They usually stole their youth from desperate mermaids, but Bastian's vanity far exceeded any creature I'd ever encountered. I curled myself into a tight ball, nestled between the ropes and barrels, tail tucked over my nose to keep warm as I listened to the creaking ship. Humans never learned.

It was none of my concern. It was my ship, sure, but my job was to catch and kill the rats, keep the men in line, and chase the gulls from our morning catch so our crew wouldn't starve. When our journey was finished or the crew disbanded, I could easily find a new ship or new life. If Bastian wanted to chase beauty and court the favor of witches, that was for him to do or undo. Not me.

Yet the sounds of his sobs clouded my mind. I curled tighter, willing myself to rest, and eventually an uneasy sleep found me, one filled with dreams of fatty cream, a soft lap, and the hands of a beautiful man stroking my fur—my Bastian, vain, careless, and stupid, but he had been kind to me.

He'd rescued me from a burlap sack tossed into the ocean where my brothers and sisters had drowned, their tiny claws piercing my skin in the dark, wet panic. Only I had survived—just barely—eyes and nose gunked over, and fur wet and matted by the sea. Bastian had warmed me with those very hands that were now suddenly liver-spotted and worn. We'd always been together. It had always been *us*.

I climbed from between the barrels, stretching the kink in my spine, and stared at my twitching tail in the dark as it tapped the floor in front of my paws.

I had to lift this curse.

I owed that much to Bastian for sparing me from the sea. My debt to him could not go unpaid.

At dusk, when the ship finally docked, I would set out to find the witch and break the curse. Human essence could not survive outside the body for long. I had until sunrise.

The moment we reached the harbor, I set out on my own, unnoticed under the cloud of grief that hung over the ship.

Low clouds raked the distant hills. The seaside town was quiet and still. Candles warmed the windows of the cottages lining the dirt road. On a path leading away from the town center, I caught the scent of kelp and jasmine and followed it to where fields of grass and sand intertwined along the beach.

A small cottage sat among piles of driftwood and dried seaweed in the shadow of a single old tree, leafless and dying. Gull droppings splattered the sand, and water-washed pieces of fishbone gleamed in the moonlight. Strings of oyster shells hung above the door, tinkling in the light breeze, their pearlescent bellies shimmering.

I leapt to the nearest windowsill. Inside, the witch hummed an old seafarer's song while twisting thin branches into a circular totem of a sort. On the center of the table lay the sealskin pouch containing my Bastian's youth. She had yet to consume it, as the pouch was still fat with human arrogance. I could smell it from my perch.

The witch stood from her chair and disappeared into another room. I jumped down to the door and hooked my paw around the cold brass handle. Doors were tricky without thumbs, but it began to pull open with my weight. It was in that moment of pure concentration that I missed the stench of wet dog wafting from behind me.

A ferocious bark reverberated down my whiskers.

I leapt up the door, claws scraping for purchase against the wood. The large hound slammed against the door below me, snapping.

Turning in midair, I stretched out, and, upon my descent, my claws caught the hound's face. I used the momentum to push off and jump over the railing. The hound snapped and snarled after me.

I ran around the corner of the house, toes squishing in the salt-soaked mud and sand. I could hear the snarling breath and feel the weight of the hound's bark on the hairs down my back.

The old and sick-looking tree that towered over the cottage was my only hope. I ran for it, racing so fast I hardly needed my claws to fly up the trunk and onto the overhanging branches. The hound barked and howled below me, furious by my escape.

I hissed at the mongrel. Dogs were truly terrible creatures, using their mind control on the most susceptible humans in order to live a life of easy luxury. I spat at the mutt, which only infuriated him.

The dog paced below the tree, watching my every move. With each passing moment, the moon was rising, and soon the sun would come and take my chance.

There was no time.

I looked to the cottage, where the branches of my tree thinned so much even a bird would cause the branch to bow.

The hound growled below me, as if reading my mind.

If I fell in my attempt to make it to the cottage, there would be no avoiding my fate. I took a breath and began to inch my way to the thinning branches, closer to the cottage. Making it to the roof didn't exactly solve my problem, but it was better than helplessly watching the sun rise and vaporize my chances to snag Bastian's youth. Could I live with myself if I didn't at least try? I mean, I *could*. But I didn't want to.

As I slunk along the branch, it began to shake beneath my paws. This sent the dog into another fit of furious barking.

I slowed my steps to ease the quivering branches and dug my claws into the soft bark to hold on. The branch began to sag, jerking my weight forward.

The dog must have sensed my apprehension because he stood on his hind legs, baying. I hissed again.

The dog jumped, snapping, his white teeth gleaming in the moonlight.

I had no choice.

With all my strength and the last of my nerve, I leapt for the thatched roof, pawing the air and hoping to catch anything with my claws. The wind raked my face and fur as gravity pulled me toward the waiting hound.

Just when I was certain my heart would burst and teeth would pierce my flesh, my claws hooked the thatching. The hound lunged, and I could feel his breath on my tail. Curling myself, I clasped the roof with all four of my feet and pulled myself around and up to safety.

The dog barked with such renewed energy, I could hear it echoing to the sea. He ran circles beneath me, as I smirked to myself.

And then the back door burst open. With it, a gust of air so cold I'd have sworn it came from the north. The dog cowered into the earth, making himself so small and insignificant in the shadow that was cast by the golden light from the cottage.

I peered over the edge of the roof.

The witch gazed out into the darkness, and the youthful glow she enjoyed in the candlelight had fallen away in the silver strands of moonbeams. Her pale skin no longer glimmered, but was a chalky white, and her straw-like hair had thinned, revealing her scalp beneath. This was not the same promised beauty who had dined with my Bastian by candlelight.

Even though I was above and behind her, I froze, flattening myself as much as possible, trying to be invisible.

She stared at the dog for what felt like three of my nine lives. The dog remained curled against the earth, shivering. The witch screeched something in a language I didn't know, yet the dog responded by wagging the very tip of his tail still tucked between his legs.

I saw my chance in that slice of golden light cutting across the yard and jumped down from the roof. The witch was so busy screaming at the dog, she didn't even notice me slinking along the hut in the dim light. The dog, however, watched me while flinching from the witch's shrill tone. I almost felt sorry for the poor mutt.

Except I didn't.

I slipped through the cracked door and into the musty, warm cottage. My eyes watered, and my whiskers felt like they'd curled. Strange spices assaulted my nose. I coughed once, biting my tongue and glancing back at the door for the witch. I heard the dog yelp from the yard. I took the opportunity to scurry into the main room where the witch had been weaving her totems.

A fire burned away in the hearth, the crackling pops louder than the yelping from outside. Tails belonging to various animals hung in a bunch on the wall next to shelves of glass jars and clay bowls. I could smell strange herbs over the scent of kelp and jasmine. It made my hair stand on end. No amount of licking would clean away that feeling of dark magic, either.

As much as I wanted to dart out of there, I forced myself to remain, taking cover beneath the table. I carefully leapt on the seat of the nearest chair to survey the room from a more human angle.

The dog had gone quiet outside, but the hush of the distant waves told me the door remained open, and the witch was still outside.

The sealskin pouch lay in the center of the table. I stretched on my hind legs and reached with my front paw, claws unsheathed. I snagged the leather, causing it to pop out of reach, so I stretched further, trying to keep one ear pointed at the opened back door.

A massive boom pounded at the front door.

"Witch!" a deep voice thundered. "I know you're in there!"

Bastian.

I abandoned my attempt on the bag and ducked under the table, watching between the legs of chairs.

The witch strode into the room, skirt brushing the ground with each wicked step. The smell of blood followed her. I crept closer to get a better look and saw her arms were drenched in blood up to her elbows. She reeked of wet dog. In her hands, she carried a bloody organ the size of my head, which she placed in a bowl above the fire.

I couldn't peel my eyes from the glistening red that dripped from her forearms, nor the glob of flesh and fur stuck to her elbow. A better cat might have felt some guilt at the sight—all that racket we'd made had drawn the witch to the dog, which had allowed me to slip inside to grab Bastian's youth. But what did I feel? Nothing but a fixed curiosity over the buzzing in my ears.

Bastian's pounding at the door made my heart lurch,

reminding me of my situation. I was trapped in a witch's hut. With a witch who had just gutted a dog with her bare hands.

She unbolted the front door and faced Bastian with such calm it sent chills rolling down my spine. She was once again that shimmering youth he'd seen by candlelight.

"Bastian." Her velvety voice melted those chills. More of that nasty magic. "A pleasant surprise."

Bastian's eyes lost that hardened, angry edge. I wanted to groan, but didn't dare make a sound.

Bastian must have shaken the magic's hold on his heart because the glare returned to his eyes, his new crow's feet deepening with his scowl. "You cheated me!"

She laughed. "Did I? It seems you do not understand the rules."

Rules or not, she had taken an unfair advantage of my Bastian with her enchantments. I slid from under the chair legs and hopped into the seat. Only my ears poked over the edge of the table. The sealskin pouch sat in the center, untouched and unattended.

Ever so silently, I pulled myself up onto the table and crept toward the bag. Bastian had fallen silent. I locked eyes with him as surprise washed over his face.

The witch turned, and when her eyes fell upon me, her beauty wavered in the candlelight, flickering like an excited flame. For a moment, I looked dead-on into the window of hell.

Before I could jump from the table, a blast of green light and heat filled the room. Bastian screamed, and the scent of spicy, wicked magic and blood erupted. I leapt for the sealskin pouch, but the witch snagged the scruff of my neck, her nails digging through my fur. I yowled, but the sound was as weak as a kitten's mewl while I hung limply from her grip. The sealskin pouch dangled from the finger of her other hand.

Bastian had fallen to his knees in the doorway, clutching

his arm to his chest as bright red blood seeped into his silk shirt.

"Foolish man, but exquisite creature," she said as she held me up to her face. I would have scratched at her eyes if I hadn't been rendered useless by my damn scruff. Instead, I dangled in silence while Bastian gasped in pain. Foolish man indeed to run into a witch's hut unprepared. At least I had stealth on my side. Or would have if Bastian's stupid look hadn't given me away.

"I needed a cat's spleen," she said with such delight it made my skin crawl. "I'm sure I could find a use for the rest of him." She stepped over to Bastian's crumpled form and sneered.

Bastian grabbed a flask from inside his coat and splashed a liquid on the witch's face.

She dropped me and screamed. The sound and smell of sizzling flesh followed.

Bastian jumped for the sealskin pouch.

I took the opportunity to run for the half-open door, but a sharp pain stabbed at my rear and up my spine, jolting me back. Bony fingers clutched my tail. The witch's raspy breath shuddered, wild and panicked in her pain. The holy water Bastian had splashed her with had washed at least a hundred years from her face, and now her sunken cheeks and gray skin matched her dark, hollow eyes. The sickly sweet stench of death rattled from her breath.

I shrieked and spat, but she grabbed me by the scruff again before I could wrap myself around her arm and bite. I caught a glimpse of Bastian's back in the doorway. He had the sealskin pouch. My debt had been repaid. I couldn't have asked for more. Well, actually, I could have asked to escape with my spleen, or that Bastian not invite nasty witches into his cabin or play games with wicked hags, but not only had I saved his life, I had also recaptured his youth, and that was worth more to him than all the treasure at sea.

That should have made me feel better, but I remembered the dog's fate.

"Release the cat, witch!" Bastian boomed.

I wanted to groan. It was just like Bastian to mess up my efforts. He was going to die here, and worse, if he died here for me, my debt to him would double.

Leave, I wanted to hiss, but again, only a tiny kitten squeak came out.

Something had softened in Bastian's eyes, but not for the witch. Her magic had dampened under the holy water and was no longer strong enough for enchantment. He looked at me, his old eyes fixed on mine, furrowed brow wrinkled like loose leather.

Bastian held up his flask of holy water again. It couldn't have held much after his first attack, but the witch probably didn't know that.

She grabbed a cleaver and pressed my head against the table's surface. I could only see the fire crackling in the hearth, but when I tilted my head, I saw Bastian freeze, his white-knuckled hand gripping the flask.

"Drop it," the witch rasped.

Bastian's eyes darted between me and the witch.

She raised her cleaver, grip around my neck tightening, and the image of my head lopping off like a plump chicken ran through my mind several times before Bastian cried out, "Wait!"

The witch paused, but still held the blade unnervingly close my head. "Out of holy water?" she cooed.

I had the leverage to swing around and bite her thumb, but the probability that she'd drop the cleaver through my neck was still too high. I impatiently watched Bastian, wondering what he'd do.

The fool raised his empty flask higher as if to call her bluff on his bluff. His eyes gleamed with an unexpected sadness.

"Don't kill him," he said, softly. "Please. H-he's the only family I have."

The witch stared at him for a second too long before her ugly face welled with a grin. "Why shouldn't I? You backed out of our deal. And now you threaten my life with that empty flask?" She guffawed.

Bastian let the flask clatter to the floor and took out the sealskin pouch from his blood-covered sleeve.

I squirmed in the witch's grasp—a move that I hoped felt innocent enough to not warrant a cleaver through my neck.

No, I tried to yowl. But even if I could, Bastian was too dense to understand me. What had I come here for? For that damned pouch. For Bastian's glorious youth. So that my human could live out the rest of his life like a normal man, not riddled with arthritis and cataracts before they were due.

He'd saved me from drowning in that sack. Had been kind enough to invite me on the ship. To feed me. Give me shelter. Sure, I was damn good at keeping the ship in order, but I was still indebted to Bastian. Even if I had returned his youth, I still owed this man more than anything I could ever achieve in my nine, sorry lives.

And this stupid, selfish man was at it again. I had risked my skin—literally—for that pouch, and he was going to throw it away and get us both killed.

I would trip him a thousand times in the night for this.

"Take it," Bastian said. "Just let my cat go."

The hunger in the witch's eyes grew. She wanted that bag —*needed* it—or else, according to old pirate lore, she would be sucked back into the depths of the hell she'd crawled from. Her grip tightened around my neck, and my eyes bulged. She reached for the pouch.

Bastian took a step back. "The cat first."

"And let you steal what's rightfully mine?" She growled and lifted the blade again.

I clenched my eyes shut.

"Wait!" Bastian held up the sealskin pouch. "You need my youth to live past this night."

She scowled, but did not wring my neck any tighter. "It is not a fair trade if you only give back what is mine in the first place."

"If I don't give it back, you'll be swallowed into oblivion. You gain nothing if you kill the cat."

"Your suffering is plenty to enjoy. After all, I have no guarantee I will not be killed by your hand if I agree to your terms."

"Release my cat," Bastian said, "and with my youth, I'll also give half of my time. Or what's left of it now that I'm old and spent."

The witch relaxed a little and tilted her head.

I began to yowl, deep and piercing. What was the point of trading my life for half of what remained of his? He'd already saved me once, at no risk to his life, but now ... I couldn't let him do such a thing.

I sank my teeth into the witch's thumb. The salty and metallic taste of blood filled my mouth.

She screamed, and her cleaver came swinging down. Right for my face. I used all of my strength to squeeze through her grip.

My poor tail was not fast enough.

A blinding, burning pain exploded through my body. I staggered across the table and rolled to see a long ginger-striped appendage, limp and bloody, next to the blade that was buried in the wooden tabletop.

I staggered, too woozy to move. White spots danced at the edge of my vision, and the burning pain at my backside buzzed in my thoughts. Did pain have a sound? And was it always this loud?

I felt that cold, bony hand clasp around my neck again.

"I offer you my youth and years," Bastian shouted. "Let the cat go! I won't ask again, and you will not have this offer again. You might watch me suffer, but I'll watch you vanish into dust, and it is I who will laugh last, witch."

She tensed, her wild breath gasping from her chest.

Bastian held out the pouch.

After what felt like an eternity, she finally stepped forward, swinging me by my scruff like a doll. She snatched the pouch and tossed me to the floor at his feet. I heard the thump of my body more than felt it. My tail stump dulled any other pain I could have possibly felt.

Bastian's heavy old hands stroked my fur. I glanced up to see the witch a few paces away on her hands and knees, her long, pale hair cascading over her shoulders and obscuring her face. The gray had vanished from her skin, replaced by a youthful glow, and her bony, knotted fingers were once again elegant and graceful.

She looked up, mischief in the corners of her eyes and on the edge of her full, rosy lips. She crawled forward, shimmering as if a fantastical aura surrounded her. When she reached for the lapel of Bastian's silk collar and pulled him forward, both still on their knees, he did not fight her.

I struggled to stand, but it was too late.

The witch parted her lips and leaned in, capturing his mouth with hers.

The air around us came alive with a crackling sensation as my fur stood, reacting to the magic being conjured. A vibrancy seemed to drain from Bastian and spill into the witch as they remained locked in a kiss there on the floor.

When she finally pulled away, eyes half-lidded, I caught a glimpse of Bastian as a dashing young pirate once more, but it was only for a moment before he melted back into a withered old man.

The witch wiped the corner of her mouth as she stood. Bastian remained on his knees, the tremble in his hands more noticeable than before.

"I could kill you both," she said, "but I'd rather watch you pay for your foolishness for the rest of the years you have left. You have tied your sails, Bastian. Now suffer the journey."

Another crackle of energy pulsed through the room, and she vanished. Everything in the cottage withered and died; surfaces were suddenly coated in dust, and the fire was gone from the hearth.

I looked up at Bastian. *My* Bastian. My foolish human who was once young and strong—the most accomplished pirate on the seas, destined for riches and greatness—was now reduced to an old man with his cat.

Bastian cradled me in his arthritic arms, removed a silk handkerchief from his pocket, and carefully wrapped my bleeding stump.

I couldn't help but notice how his spine curled forward, and he seemed to hobble more to the left, but somehow, lying in his old, leathery hands, I hurt less.

I closed my eyes and purred. *This was fine*, I thought, as he limped out into the waking dawn. The sun breathed pink into every edge of the horizon as it started its ascent. This was fine. *We* would be fine.

I licked his salty hand, my tongue scratching against his dry skin.

His good hand stroked the fur behind my ears, and I sank further into its warmth. All was right enough in the world in that moment.

Just an old man and his cat.

An old *pirate* and his cat.

About the Author

Tracy Leonard Nakatani dwells in the deserts of Arizona, but travels and writes fantasy to escape reality as often as possible. She has an unhealthy obsession with nachos and wears too much black. She looks grumpy, but it's really just her face.

Annie Spark and the Pirates of Port 1337

DAVID COLE

M ilk run to the dark web, they said," Annie muttered to herself as she wrung the last bits of water out of her shirt and put it back on. "You'll get to see new URLs, they said."

So far, all she'd gotten to see was a broadcast storm that had stolen her oars, and now all she was seeing was becalmed airwaves from one side of the split horizon to the other.

Annie cursed herself for a fool for accepting the job. Sure, she was one of the most advanced messenger processes this side of factory default, but until a few milliseconds ago, she'd never had to negotiate a connection over a 9600-baud modem, never mind use her own digits to row a rickety little frame across the endless depths of the Net.

She flexed those digits, thanked Coder that she hadn't lost them when she'd lost the oars, and then ran her hands over her header to check for injuries. There had been some bits flying about during the storm, and the adrenaline was only just wearing off. Her cascade of blue-yellow electric hair crackled as she touched it, but she couldn't feel any faults.

She was whole, and the data was flowing, carrying her battered frame along; she could feel the movement of the craft over the neon water. Her toolkit still hung from her waist, and it looked like everything had stayed on it—her public and private keys, in particular. Her payload—

C.R.U.D. Where was the packet? Even worse—

Annie bolted to her feet. "Nibble!" she called. "Nibble, where are you?" She spun, her sockets scanning the ocean behind the frame for any sign of her magnetic storage byte. What in the Net had she been thinking, bringing him on this job with her?

"Bork!" She'd have known the muffled sound anywhere. "Bork!"

Annie leaned over the edge of the frame. There was Nibble, his little magnetic paws clinging to the rear of the frame, his head just barely above the waterline. The neon pink packet was in his mouth, and digits flared and disappeared across its shiny surface.

Annie's header felt flushed with relief as she reached down and pulled the pup up. He borked again, dropping the header and snuggling in against Annie's neck.

"Oh! Gross. You're all wet, Nibble." Annie put him on the deck next to the packet, and the byte shook himself off, splattering water everywhere.

"Bork! Bork!" Nibble ran and hopped in small circles, making the frame lurch. "Bor-bor-bor—" He stiffened and froze, his paws battering the air, then reset. "Bork!"

"Uh-oh." Annie frowned. An ugly rectangular fault offset the spherical primitive of Nibble's header just above his ear. "You take a bump on the header, buddy?" she asked, scratching around the fault.

The byte sat back on his haunches and raised his leg to scratch along with her. As her digits moved to reach the spot beneath his ear, he tilted his head and looked up at her, his brown eyes inquisitive. "B-b-b-bo-bork?" he asked.

"Couldn't tell you," Annie murmured. "Dead air, dead air everywhere, nor any ACK to SYNc." Her hand brushed the welt on Nibble's header, and an electric shudder went through the byte. He whined and staggered toward the prow of the frame, where he recommenced scratching at his ear.

Annie needed to run a checksum on the payload anyway, to make sure it was intact. Not that it would matter. It was going to take an act of Coder to get her out of this null space and back to Board S926F77203E7BC7A, never mind delivering the packet before it timed out—

"Bork!" Nibble's voice warbled into higher registers, drawing Annie's attention. He must have seen—

A lush island of sandy #FFFFFF beaches kissed by the airwaves and deep #00FF00 parse trees whose nodes swayed in the wind.

The vision defragged Annie's drive, and she felt hope swell

within her, tinged with concern, because this place definitely wasn't on any Nmap that Annie had ever seen. Gentle coves wrapped about ports that were beautiful and—

Empty, Annie realized, as she scanned the sight in front of her. Even Port 22, a bay so wide it could have handled thousands of transactions a second, was closed. A reef of CORAL66 stretched beneath the airwaves from one side of the cove's mouth to the other; it would shred her craft before she even got close.

Port 80 looked like it had been hit by a bunch of logic bombs; it was nothing more than a ragged black cliff face.

"Borborborororork!" Nibble assert()ed, staring longingly at the land. The pup's lag was getting worse. He'd obviously been hit harder than Annie had thought.

There had to be some sort of civilization on this little private network, some sort of village where she could ask for help. Sure, the people might be primitives, but Annie knew a smattering of older languages. She'd even gotten a certificate in binary.

Something clunked against the side of the frame. A bit of driftwood floated in the airwaves, so Annie snatched it up. A couple of light-feet wide, it was more than thick enough to serve as a makeshift oar.

Annie got to work.

Her feet smoldered on the deck of the frame as she rushed from one side of the dinghy to the other, rowing like her life depended on it. What she lacked in experience, she made up for in speed; it wasn't for nothing that she was the First Messenger Process of Board S926F77203E7BC7A.

She would have been zeroth, but she'd given up that opportunity as penance a few hours before.

She was so fast it didn't matter that she only had a C.R.U.D.dy makeshift oar to use. The dinghy picked up speed, heading toward the island.

She drew up alongside Port 80, where the airwaves beat

against the broken cliff, making her frame buck and creak. Annie slung her beleaguered byte across her shoulders, connecting his magnetized paws so she could wear him like a scarf. Then Annie attached the packet on her toolkit and reached for the #000000-colored rock.

Black ICE! The very touch of it froze her process, slowed her mind and body like she was running on a 386. She fell backward. Nibble yelped as he clattered to the deck, and Annie took it hard on the header.

Coder, that hurt! As Nibble scrambled to his paws, Annie groaned and pushed up to her knees. "Guess that makes us ten of a kind, buddy," she muttered, running her digits over her header. There was a nasty lump there, but she'd live, even if her eyes had filled with tears and a low sloshing roar cut across her hearing.

Her sight cleared quickly enough, but her hearing didn't. In fact, the sloshing grew louder, and the dinghy bucked as waves intensified, reflecting from the side of the cliff. The sound of singing resolved, though it was too distant for Annie to make out the words. The tune was familiar, though Annie was sure it was from before her time.

What did that matter, though? Where there was singing, there was help!

"Hey, over here!" Annie shouted, raising her volume to max. "Hey, I'm stranded!"

The sound of singing faded, then redoubled in intensity, and with a start, Annie recognized the strains of Metallica's "I Disappear." A shudder ran through her, but she told herself she was getting worked up over nothing. Sure, it was the archetypical theme song for pirates across the Net, but what were the chances that she'd meet one of those out in a distant network of un-Nmapped coves?

On second thought …

Annie grabbed her makeshift oar and began to row.

Too late. A great traffic spike of a prow led an enormous

galleon's frame around the side of the cliff. An eight-bit Jolly Roger flew at the top of its mast, pixelating in the breeze. Dozens of processes wearing a full spectrum of clothing from every encoding—ASCII and Unicode and ANSEL—worked the decks, and beneath their song, Annie could make out the sound of a heavy power plant driving the antiquated vessel.

It was probably too much to hope they wouldn't notice her, wasn't it?

Yup. As the big galleon cut off her escape, a piratical process leaned over the railing. He wore a long coat of Python skin, and his right arm ended in a code stub, but someone had managed to insert a nasty-looking hook there. His bald header was scarred and weather-beaten, but his trunk was well-formed; he was definitely a process Annie didn't want to mess with. She was fast—really fast—but that was her defense; she preferred throwing an exception to throwing a punch.

It looked like the current function call wouldn't take either of those as an option, though.

The pirate's voice made the very airwaves tremble. "Well, look here, boys! Port 1337 has a visitor!"

"I'm Annie Spark," she said, holding up her packet as the big frame came closer. "First Messenger Process of Board S926F77203E7BC7A. I think I got blown off course—"

None of that seemed to matter to the pirates, two of whom leapt down to her little frame. Before she could protest, they'd connected cables to her belt, and their compatriots had hauled Annie unceremoniously up on deck.

Across the frame, processes stopped working, ogling Annie. The closest sidled in toward her, leering in a way that could only mean one thing. Even if Annie had been running in promiscuous mode—and she wasn't; she would never cheat on Gus—she certainly wouldn't do it with these hardscrabble, truncated processes.

The first one to touch her would get a kick to his private

variables, she decided. That would be no joke. Speedy legs were useful for more than just running.

"U+0052! Back to work, you scurvy bytes, or I'll send you to Devvy/Null's!" The Python-skinned pirate—their captain, it seemed from the way the processes blanched—pushed his way through the crowd, which dispersed as quickly as it had formed. This close, Annie could see that a scar from a nasty fault ran down the fellow's face across one of his sockets, rendering it empty and blind. His other socket was good, and he looked Annie up and down.

Annie tried to remember what she'd learned about the old pirates of the Net. "Permission to come aboard, Captain?"

The captain grinned. "Chmod +x come_aboard.py && chown -R annie:annie./my_ship," he announced, bowing, and Annie smiled despite herself. Maybe he was a pirate, but the formality was endearing.

Of course, he wasn't really giving Annie his ship, and he probably wouldn't appreciate it if Annie kept permissions to the galleon. "Uh, chown -R captain:captain./my_ship," she said.

"Much appreciated, lass," the man said, sticking out his left hand. It took Annie a nano to realize the hook on his right wouldn't be able to follow a handshake protocol. His digits were thick and warm, his palm leathery. "Captain Mu Comet of the Port 1337 Pirates. You'll have to forgive the crew. It's been hours—nay, days—since a one of them has made a male-to-female connection."

"That's okay," Annie said. "I'm kind of in a—"

"And who is this little fellow?" Captain Comet said, bending down to pick up Nibble from one of his crew as they returned from over the side of the boat.

"Booooooooooooorkrob," Nibble stuttered, licking the captain's face.

"That's Nibble," Annie said. "He's a little concussed."

"Quite a header wound he's got," the captain agreed,

barely even wavering as the galleon came about. Annie had to grab the railing; she didn't have her C-legs. "When was the last time you had him checked for worms?"

"What? Gross. I took him in for a scan a few hours ago," Annie said. The captain gave her a sideways look and held Nibble so she could inspect his header. The pup's skin had discolored into an ugly white in a circle around the rectangular bump he'd suffered.

"Looks like tokenringworm," the captain said, "but not colored like any I've ever seen."

"That wasn't there before," Annie said. "He got hit during the broadcast storm."

The captain shrugged and set Nibble down, watching the byte as he scratched his header. "I'd tell you to take him in for another scan, but in order to do that, you'd have to know some way out of this network."

"I don't follow."

The captain nodded at the pink packet in Annie's hand. "You're a messenger process. You route from node to node until you deliver your payload."

"Of course."

"But you can't do that when you're air-gapped," the captain said, and for the first time, Annie saw weariness in his one good socket. "As I said, my men haven't made a connection for days."

"We're *stuck* here?"

The captain nodded and gestured toward the waving parse trees on the turf as the galleon slid evenly through the airwaves. "U+0049, lass."

"But the broadcast storm brought me in from outside—"

Mu held up a hand. "And died down just as quickly. We ran for it as best we could when we caught wind of the storm, but even our bonny lady here couldn't catch the connection before it closed." He slapped the ship's railing. "I'm afraid we're marooned here, and you with us."

#B03060ed. The color code echoed in Annie's processor.
"Look," she said. "We both got stuck here, which means there
are connections, even if we don't know when they open."

"Of course, lass. Oh, we've been trying, but this little
island is a harsh mistress. She doesn't give up her secrets
easily."

"Secrets?"

Captain Comet smiled. "Why do you think we came to
this Coder-forsaken private site in the first place, lass?"

"Well, it's pretty," Annie ventured, gazing at the lush vege-
tation beyond the black cliffs and white sands of the isle.

"Pretty, my bootloader," the captain guffawed. "My crew
and I, we set sail days ago—though it seems like weeks—
searching for booty. And not the kind you'll find pictured in
the sleaziest corners of the Net, Miss Spark. Word came to
Port 1337 that this very MAC address harbored a great treasure in its kernel, code the likes of which process has never
seen."

Annie crossed her arms and leaned back against the railing. "Word came from whom, exactly?"

"Er ... well, the tip was anonymous."

Annie rolled her eyes and considered giving the captain a
tongue-lashing, but she decided against it. If he hadn't been
dumb enough to follow an anonymous tip, she would be
stranded here all alone.

"But the promise was too good to pass up," Mu added
quickly. "A hidden archive like that would be worth Coder
only knows how much Bitcoin!"

"Sure," Annie said. "If it were real."

Mu seemed to deflate. He scratched idly with his hook at
his bald head. "Yes, well. It doesn't matter. The network itself
resists our attempts to penetrate to the kernel. And so, we're
stuck."

The galleon came around a small horn. The parse trees at
the edge of the white beach fell back, and a small village of

shanties took their place. A worm-eaten pier extended into the airwaves. The place was deserted, but that made sense; if the pirates had made a run for it during the broadcast storm, none of them would have wanted to be left behind.

"Welcome to Port 1337 away from Port 1337," Captain Comet said as his crew lashed the galleon to the pier. "This is where we sleep(), eat, and stage our expeditions from." The crew let down a gangplank onto the dock, and Mu gestured to it. "Guests first."

The captain seemed polite enough, but Annie didn't want to imagine what a whole crew of processes who hadn't made a connection in days might try to do to a state-of-the-art female process if she let her guard down. Still, there didn't seem any way out of the bugfix, so with a weary, "All right, Nibble, let's go," she led the way down the gangplank toward the shanty town.

As soon as he touched the turf, Nibble's legs locked up. A shattered "bo-bo-bo-bork" jerked from his throat, and then he was a light-speed blur, racing down the street past the shanties and into the darkness of the jungle beyond.

"Defrag me," Annie shouted. In a nano, she was racing after him, the air biting her face as she slashed through it. Nibble was moving almost as fast as Annie could run.

Captain Comet's words drifted after her as the parse trees closed around her. "Stop! The interior is too dangerous!"

But Annie didn't care. Either she was going to get her little byte back, or else whatever dangers lurked within would kill -9 her and save her the trouble of spending one more microsecond in this awful subnet than she had to.

Normally she liked to travel, but this was getting ridiculous.

The leaves of the parse trees seemed to close in overhead. The sounds dampened as if they were coming from a pair of earbuds left on the table; she could barely hear the borking of Nibble ahead in the dense undergrowth. Strands of code glinted silvery in the gloom, but she was moving too fast to make them out.

She came to a break in the growth, and Nibble's borking suddenly became clear. He stood yapping and bouncing, his icon blurring, before a wall of web. The stuff was strung from node to node of the trees so thickly that Annie couldn't see through it, and what little light that came through showed the web stretching into the jungle from one side to the other. Annie couldn't go around, so she stopped.

Nibble might have been chasing his tail with excitement, but it was hard to tell since he was lagging so badly he might actually have been going in the other direction.

"Don't move," came Captain Comet's voice, low and dangerous. He crouched behind Annie like a security counter-measure ready to pounce, holding a notched sword in his good hand.

Annie's circuits overloaded. "Seriously?" She waved her hands to either side. "Just how desperate are your men for a connection anyw—"

"Don't talk, either," the captain growled. His good socket flickered up to look past Annie's head.

From an eight-legged black spot on the wall, eight sockets stared back. The web crawler was enormous, far bigger than any Annie had ever seen. It could probably fit Annie's head in its mouth.

Or fit Nibble, for that matter, who at that nano decided to lunge straight into the web, borking all the way.

The web crawler descended as Annie leapt after her byte; the beast was fast, but Annie was faster. Nibble was twisting himself in the web crawler's wall, though, and when Annie's digits fell on Nibble to pull him free, the web glued her hands to her byte. And to the wall.

Annie muttered a prayer to Coder as the web crawler's fangs fell.

With a roar, Captain Comet charged, and the web crawler

came to an abrupt halt above Annie. The beast's sockets flicked to her, then to Nibble.

The sticky strands dissolved from Annie's hands, and the wall of webbing opened as if Mu had slashed it with his sword, which he certainly tried to do. But the web crawler was already scuttling back up into the trees as the segmentation parted beneath it.

"U+0049, run away, you coward!" Mu shouted, shaking his cutlass toward the retreating web crawler. "I'll have your header if you so much as show your sockets around here again —" He stopped mid-tirade and blinked in surprise at the opening in the wall. "U+0052, shake me trees," he said, pointing his sword toward the darkness that yawned beyond the opening in the wall. "That's new."

Nibble twisted in Annie's arms, his icon flickering as he tried to free himself.

"So's this," she said. "Nibble's never done anything like this before. I think he wants to go deeper."

Mu sheathed his sword and strode toward the gateway. "That's the spirit!"

"I thought it was too dangerous," Annie said, not bothering to keep the sarcasm from her voice.

If Mu noticed, he didn't show it. "That was before the network made a way for us. Normally the crawlers firewall this spot. But now … Miss Spark, it seems you've got some special code yourself. Come on! The archive surely awaits."

Nibble wallhacked straight out of Annie's arms and onto the ground. He trotted, flickering, into the depths of the parse-tree jungle. He was lagging so badly it was impossible to keep control of him, so Annie had no choice but to follow.

The code here was tangled and impossible to trace, like Coder had written it after one too many beers. The sockets of onlooking web crawlers glowed within the thicket, and webs glistened on the nodes of the trees. Annie didn't like this at all. She was a city girl. The far reaches of the Net gave her the willies, even when she wasn't being stared at by long-marooned web crawlers as big as the frame that she'd surfed here.

There was something in her process pulling her deeper, though, and it wasn't just concern for her pup, who trotted along in the darkness like he hadn't a care in the Net. It was an almost magnetic attraction toward the center of the jungle …

No, not *almost*. It was an *actual* magnetic attraction, Annie realized when she saw the power-circuits flickering within the eyes of weatherworn, header-high sculptures of men sitting along the perimeter of a small clearing. In the center of the clearing was a small four-sided ziggurat with a dozen steps leading up to a closed door. The precision of the three-dimensional rendering gave it away as Mayan in style.

Web crawlers rounded the sides of the temple and flanked either side of the stairway. Their sockets gleamed in the darkness as Annie followed Nibble up the steps, Mu trailing behind.

There was something odd about the way those sockets flickered.…

At the top of the steps, a stone slab blocked the way, but there was a switch slotted into the wall next to the door. Annie reached for it, then paused.

There was something about the unsteady gleam of the web crawlers' sockets …

"What's the matter, lass?" Mu asked, coming alongside her. "After running hot all this time, don't tell me you're getting coolant in your case."

"I don't know," Annie said. "It's …"

It was right there, on the tip of her processor.

"Leave it to Captain Comet, then." Mu slid past her and slammed the switch to the off position, just as Annie realized what she'd been missing. The web crawlers' eyes had been flickering a message in binary.

Beware.

"Wait!" Annie shouted, but it was too late. The magnetic tug in Annie's heart vanished as the door groaned open. Nibble yelped, and there was a *clank, clank, clank* as something clattered down the steps. The pup fell onto his side and almost slid down himself, but Annie caught him.

His sockets were stressed with metal fatigue, but his tail wagged hopefully. "Bork?"

"Refactor me," Annie cursed. "Nibble, you—"

The metallic object that had been stuck to his header was gone. So were the rings of infection.

"I think Nibble's all right," Annie said, amazed.

"Congratulations," the captain said absently from the doorway. He whistled low. "Look at this archive."

Annie peeked past the captain into the temple. The room was small and dimly lit, but she could make out the sheen of hundreds—no, thousands—of little black boxes, just like the one that had been stuck to Nibble.

"Seems your byte wasn't carrying an infection," he said. "Nay, he found some treasure of his own! Let's open it up. It's too dark to see in here. Maybe if we had more light …"

Mu hurried back down the steps and began to search in the long grass for the box that had fallen from Nibble.

Annie frowned. Something wasn't right. The web crawlers had all retreated—*after* they'd told her to beware in the first place.

"Aha! Found it," Mu said, holding up the black box triumphantly. "And it's—"

A long, segmented white tube lashed out of the box, opened its circular end to show rows of serrated teeth, and latched onto his hand. He screamed.

Annie flashed down the stairs as Mu howled. "Coder deprecate me! This isn't treasure! It's—"

"Worm eggs," Annie breathed. "This place wasn't trying

to protect it from the Net; it's trying to protect the Net from the worms!"

"Get it off! Get it off!" Mu shook his arm, but the worm just latched more tightly, flailing about.

Annie yanked the sword from Mu's belt. "Hold still," she ordered, and swung. The blade moved at one-tenth the speed of light—easier to control when it was slow—and severed the worm just beneath Mu's arm. The worm fell to the grass where it lay, half in the black box and half out, like a malevolent jack-in-the-box.

The magnetic field had been put in place to keep the eggs closed, Annie realized. Somebody had managed to open up a connection, though, and this one had almost gotten free. If it weren't for a little magnetic storage pup on a tiny raft—

A cracking sound came from within the temple. The eggs were hatching. The thought flashed through Annie's head in a nano, which was about half as long as it took her to scoop up the severed worm with the side of the sword, run back up the stairs, and fling it into the temple.

She caught a glimpse of hundreds of white worms writhing atop black cubes before she slammed her public key against the doorframe, locking the door shut.

Annie leaned against the door and slid down, wiping the sweat from her header. Nibble crawled up beside her, nestled in the crook of her arm, and she let out a microsecond-long sigh. "Thank Coder that's over," she muttered.

The scraping sound of hundreds of claws on stone announced the return of the web crawlers.

Captain Mu stood at the bottom of the temple. "Toss me my saber, lass," he said, looking worried.

"Relax," Annie said. "They're friendly." She was too tired to explain.

The web crawlers surrounded her, their sockets flashing their gratitude. <<Thank you. These processes expected to remain disconnected forever.>>

"You're the ones who shut off the network access, huh?" Annie asked.

<<Affirmative. This node lost its key pairs. Without encryption, the only way to protect the Net from the worms was a magnetic seal, which required us to sever ourselves from the Great Web.>> One of the crawlers pointed a spindly leg toward Annie's toolkit, and she grinned. So that was why they'd let her through the web-wall.

And it was just as obvious now why they hadn't allowed the pirates to penetrate to the kernel. There was no archive to plunder, just a horror to unleash on the unsuspecting Net.

<<But without your private key, this node's Coder will never be able to decrypt the lock. The worms are locked forever, and so is our exile.>>

A breeze rustled the parse trees surrounding the clearing, and Annie smelled the sweet scent of the Net on it. The connection was back.

<<These processes depart. Farewell.>>

There was another flash of gratitude in the web crawlers' sockets, and then, one by one, strands of web extended from them, catching the breeze and lifting them up through the parse trees and out of sight.

"You'd best run—" shouted Mu, shaking his hook at them. "Uh ... where are they running, anyway?"

"Home," Annie said. She thought of the crawlers drifting across the airwaves, leaving this desolate node behind. That made her think of Board S926F77203E7BC7A, of Gus's smile, of Nibble snuggled against her in bed.

Annie rose to her feet. "Come on," she said. "I think it's time we went home, too."

"Home?" Captain Mu asked, his voice breaking softly. "You mean ... we can leave?"

"We can," Annie said. "The magnetic lock is down, and the connection's back up."

Mu looked so happy he might cry.

"Aw, stop being a blubbering landlubber, and let's get the dev/null out of here. I'll need a ride. Oh." Annie gestured toward the packet hanging at her toolkit. "And could we make a detour along the way?"

About the Author

David Cole is tickled #FFC0CB to finally be getting his 0th publication credit under his belt. He lives in Colorado, works in a cubicle containing a half dozen computers, and apparently watched way too much of the show *ReBoot* as a kid.

Tidying Magic

LINDA MAYE ADAMS

I've always liked to tidy. But tidying takes on new meaning when it's cleaning up magic.

That's where I come in: Marc's Magic Tidyings.

My father hated—no, he *loathed*—the idea. I'd heard it all.

That I wasn't trying hard enough to find out what my magic abilities really were.

That I should play football since I didn't have the right magic.

That I was embarrassing the family by being a *maid*.

My mother ... she never said anything.

Growing up, I didn't have any of the sexy magic skills. You know, creating fire or levitating. Things you can show off to the rest of the world. Teachers graded me on my "lack of effort," and even when I discovered I had tidying magic, it was dismissed. They declared me selfish for not accepting my magic skills, or, with sniffy arrogance, that I just had not gotten with the program.

Right.

Everyone declared my brother would do great things with his magic. My parents and teachers lauded over him, envisioning how their names would be linked to his success.

He's getting unemployment. I have a thriving business.

The house I'd been hired to tidy this morning was two blocks from the Alexandria waterfront, close enough to get the cold wind whistling through from the Potomac. The spring birds were chirping loud enough to rival an orchestra. A squirrel screeched at a tree, probably after a lady squirrel.

New clients, so I'd dressed up—button-down white shirt, gray sports jacket, Dockers. I didn't mind the clothes getting dirty, but I'd stuck to my military-style boots to protect my feet. Clients were notorious for under-describing their magic messiness.

The clients were Alex and Bridget Cook. An alphabet couple. No children. Most of the customers I got let their kids run amok and spill magic all over everything so they would feel "creative." They also let their kids leave their dirty under-wear on the floor. Not sure what any of that had to do with creativity. I suppose if you tell yourself something enough, you start believing it, even if it is garbage.

The town house was sandwiched between two others, each with a scrap of grass for a lawn. This one still had the original brick and a historical marker identifying it from the 1700s.

The Cooks waited out front. Alex was tall, nicely dressed in a polo shirt and Bermuda shorts. Even unshaven, he looked like a movie star. Me? If I didn't shave, just check me off in the slob column.

Bridget was a cold blonde, hair styled perfectly. Floral sundress in a pale pink the color of cherry blossoms. On her, everything felt like a show for the rest of the world. I wondered if she felt lost somewhere inside.

Everything looked normal ... except that they were both scared to death. They paced, they argued with each other, they ignored me entirely until I walked right up to them.

Good thing I wasn't a mugger.

"Good morning. I'm Marc." I pointed to the logo on the side panel of my minivan: a sparkling magic wand and my business name.

"Thank God!" Bridget said. "You have to help us!" She rushed at me, clasping my hand with her ice-cold ones. Her fingers trembled against mine.

Oh hell. What was I getting myself into?

Most of the time, magic tidying was routine. Magic is sticky and stinks like an onion buried in an old shoe. During winter, when people were cooped up and bored, they used it more, like using it to throw paper balls into the trash. By the time spring showed up, they were ready for a housecleaning.

But then there were the other calls. The ones from really slovenly people whose magic had become so embedded in a house that I couldn't remove it. I'd only had one of those, and when I couldn't clean it up, I ended up in small claims court because the owner refused to pay. She said I hadn't finished the job. So now I always started with an assessment for new customers before agreeing to anything.

But none of my clients had been this desperate before though, so my tone was cautious. "What is it?"

Alex and Bridget exchanged glances, lips clamping shut. Bridget let go of my hands.

"Look, if you don't tell me, I'm outta here." I started for my minivan.

"Wait!" Bridget blurted. Tears streamed down her face.

Alex turned away, his jaw set. "It's a ghost," he said.

"We moved in six months ago," Alex said.

We'd walked the two blocks down to the waterfront. A park spread out in front of the Potomac River. The local rowers were out for practice as a motorboat rumbled behind them. The overcast sky made the water look a muddy gray and washed out.

We were seated at a picnic table not too covered by bird shit. The Cooks were more relaxed and less desperate out here. I hoped it was caused by distance to the house and not because they thought they had conned me.

"Go ahead," I said after Alex fell silent.

"Elias Cook, the original owner, was well-known to be a pirate in the 1700s," Alex said. "I'd always heard stories about him from my grandfather when I was growing up. Pretended I was him, playing pirate and waving a sword around." His voice warmed with the memory. The stiffness leaked out of his shoulders.

"When the house came up for sale, we bought it so it could be back in the family," Bridget said.

A squirrel scuttled up an oak with a tick of small claws. It gave me a beady-eyed stare, then corkscrewed around the trunk and disappeared into the branches. A bird squawked in annoyance at the interruption.

"What does this have to do with me?" I asked.

"After we moved in, the ghost started showing up," Alex said. "He throws magic on everything."

Bridget hunched forward on her forearms, her head sagging. "I try to clean it up, but the ghost just does it again."

"It's gotten so bad that it's hard for us to stay in the house," Alex said. "We want to stay there, but ..."

Bridget sniffled. A tear tracked down her face.

I struggled not to squirm. I hated it when women cried. It was so hard to tell if something needed to be fixed or the woman just needed a shoulder to cry on.

"A friend mentioned your name," Bridget said. "I mean ... I dunno. We didn't know what else to do."

In the end, I agreed to have a look at the house.

"I can't promise I can fix this," I told the couple outside the town house. "I can tidy up the magic, but if the ghost throws it out again—"

Alex and Bridget nodded solemnly. My gut had the bad feeling they thought I was going to work miracles.

"I can't fix ghosts," I said.

Alex seemed to get my problem. He drew me aside, man-to-man. "We understand, Marc. We do. Our only other choice is to move out, and I can't do that." Alex glanced around, shifting from foot to foot. "Everyone in my family hates—really hates—that I bought this house. They're ashamed they have a pirate relative, and their solution is to wipe him from history. I have to make a stand, you know?"

Yeah, sort of like my father and my magic. I'd been expecting support for starting my own business. Instead, my father kept waiting for me to quit. Sometimes I wondered if it was worth all the aggravation.

"Okay. I'll try. No promises."

Alex and Bridget waited outside because I didn't want them following me around and telling me how to do my job. People are backseat drivers at everything. Downright annoying.

My boots echoed hollowly on the deep-brown hardwood floors. Not much furniture in the living room—a fussy sofa, a pair of chairs. Beyond the living room was the dining room and a small kitchen.

The smell was horrific. My stomach gurgled at me, threatening to rebel. A headache moved in behind my eyes right away. How could it be this bad with all the windows open? I was definitely never eating onions again.

Narrow stairs led to the second floor, each step creaking under my weight. Two bedrooms up here, and a bathroom with a claw-foot tub. Magic here, too. It stank, but not as bad as below. This was more normal, if anything about this situation could be normal.

I let my tidying magic out, like a dog on a leash. I couldn't actually see the magic with my eyeballs, but once I dropped into my magic well, it came to life in my inner vision. The splashed magic glowed in pale green patches.

Cross contamination. The Cooks had tracked through the magic downstairs and carried it up here. This I could clean up. Wouldn't take that long either. Might make upstairs more livable for them.

My magic found the first patch in the master bedroom and peeled it off the floor. I sent a small amount of energy into it, and it dissipated. Easy-peasy.

Cold closed in around me, and my breath came out visible.

The ghost was here. Watching me.

I turned, looking around. Couldn't see him. "What do you want?" I asked.

Abruptly the cold vanished.

The ghost wasn't talking to the Cooks. He wouldn't talk to me.

I almost started back up on tidying the second floor when—

Downstairs?

This time, I let my magic loose on the first floor. The contamination hit me hard, and I nearly went to my knees with the weight of it. Cross contamination covered the kitchen and the living room. The ghost was spraying magic entirely in the dining room.

Why?

I withdrew my magic, though a headache loomed behind my eyes. I paced the three rooms. Now that I compared upstairs and downstairs, something nagged at me. Something I couldn't pin down.

I went back outside to talk to the Cooks. The fresh air instantly made me feel better.

"Did you ask the previous owners about the ghost?" I asked.

"It was an elderly couple," Bridget answered. "They lived here for fifty years, but the husband passed away two years ago, and she passed not long after."

So, no information. I was going to have to figure out this puzzle on my own. Well, I didn't *have* to, but I wanted to.

I walked back out to the park to stare at the water and let my thoughts go where they might. The gray clouds had cleared out, exposing a deep blue sky. The air seemed fresher with the sun out.

The elderly couple had lived in the house for a long time.

They wouldn't have stayed if it had been this bad. The town house would have been hard to sell with so much magic contamination, even if it had been priced dirt cheap in such an expensive area.

So it had started when the Cooks moved in.

Laughter erupted from nearby. Two children, a brother and sister from the looks of it, tangled with each other on a patch of white sand that served as a playground. They tumbled over a giant plastic turtle, playing tag and screeching. The turtle didn't seem to mind.

The mother sat on a bench nearby, glasses pushed up on her forehead, eyes focused on her iPhone.

Could the ghost be the pirate relative?

Could the ghost know the Cooks were relatives?

Would that even matter to the ghost?

The girl climbed on top of the turtle's back, riding him like a horse. The boy ran circles around the turtle, kicking up sand with his heels. He was already much taller than his sister, though she was older.

Growing like a weed.

That something niggling in the back of my head nudged me again.

Oh hell. I knew what was wrong with the lower floor.

This time I brought the Cooks in the house. We stood in the dining room. The Cooks huddled together, weary of the ghostly onslaught. I hoped my hunch was right.

Cold flitted in. The ghost was here. Eyes bored into my back.

"Do you know about the secret room?" I asked.

Alex and Bridget exchanged confused glances. Alex shook his head. "There's no secret room."

"Yes, there is. I picked up on it when I walked the house.

The upstairs rooms are bigger than the lower rooms." I lowered my voice. "The ghost is only active in your dining room. He's been trying to tell you about it."

A whuff of cold brushed me.

Hot damn! I was on the right track.

Bridget's hands trembled. "Are you sure?"

"About the secret room? Positive. This room is two feet too short."

The dining room had been painted many times over the years. If the door had been obvious at one time, it had long since been hidden.

Alex and Bridget were doubtful, but they joined me at the wall I'd identified. Alex took out his key ring and used it to rap on the wall, listening for hollow spots. Bridget ran her hands over the wall, feeling for cracks.

Me? I let my magic loose. Follow the trail.

Nausea hit me, hard. I nearly went to my knees. The amount of magic was overwhelming. In my magic well, the magic didn't just glow green. It was blinding.

I squeezed my eyes shut. *Breathe, breathe.*

I pulled my magic back, swallowing. Trying to steady myself. What else could I use to find this hidden door?

A cold presence brushed past me.

Cautiously, I let my magic out again, following the ghost. Though I couldn't see him, I could see the magic layers dispersing.

He understood what I was doing! He was helping.

"It's over here." My voice was huskier than I liked.

Alex and Bridget came over, running their fingers over the wall. No dice.

The ghost seemed to withdraw. I could feel him there, waiting, still watching me.

One more time, I let my magic out. There was still an awful lot of glow, but not so much that it overwhelmed my senses. I fell into its flow—and it did have one. It was like a river, running downstream, flowing into three hundred-year-old cracks.

Dizziness rocked me as my magic fell through the crack.

I had an impression of being closed off, confined. Old wood, mildew, and dust. Not a lot of magic stink.

But a thread of green glow. Instead of dissipating it, I grabbed it and backed out.

Old paint crackled. A vertical line split the wall, outlining the door.

Alex pressed his fingers to the edges of the crack.

A snick. Then a whoosh and a rush of stale air.

The secret door opened to reveal a small storage closet with shelves. Dust caked every surface.

"There's a book!" Bridget said.

"Don't touch it with your hands," I said. "Get something to pick it up with."

No telling if there were any brown recluse spiders hiding in here. Too late after you got bit.

Bridget got a dish towel from the kitchen and used it to remove the book. It was bound in leather, cracking from age. The pages were yellowed.

She set it on the dining room table, and we crowded around to see what was in it. I'll admit, I hoped it contained a map of a pirate treasure. You know, X marks the spot. Though if there had been an actual treasure, it was probably long gone. Northern Virginia had already been developed to death.

Faded handwriting crawled across the page. Dated. A journal.

"It's about him," Bridget said, awe in her voice.

"He wanted us to read it," Alex said.

With that, the cold rode out on a gust of wind and was gone.

It took me three days to clean the Cooks' town house of ghostly magic. The Cooks stayed in a hotel while I worked. When they came back, the smell was gone. Yes, I was pleased with myself.

I also charged them a hefty fee because I'd really gone above and beyond. They'd paid, and then paid me more with referrals.

I hadn't expected that. Folks these days wanted superior quality at cheap rates. I don't know what they'd told their friends, but business was booming.

My parents? Meh. Not impressed. They never would be, and I was okay with that.

Four weeks later, the Cooks dropped me an email. Inside was a file—a complete scan of the diary of pirate adventures.

"We thought you'd like this," Bridget wrote.

She added a note that the historical society had photographed the entire diary, considering it a major find. Elias had written about meeting George Washington over at Gatsby's Tavern. A second attachment was from the newspaper, reporting the find.

I'd done that.

A smile stretched across my face.

This.

This was why I liked to tidy.

About the Author

Linda Maye Adams was the least likely to be in the Army—even they thought so! But she served for twelve years and was in Desert Storm. She is the author of the GALCOM Universe series, including the novel *Crying Planet*, featured in the 2018 Military Science Fiction StoryBundle. You can visit her at lindamayeadams.com.

By Stars and by Gears

TRISHA J. WOOLDRIDGE

Their ship was holding together. For a second time! Captain—and Chief Engineer—Mariah MacFly-wrench figured she still helmed the same ship as last trip since the vessel contained more than half its original parts. It was a rare achievement for any ship to survive one of her clan's washing machine pirate voyages, but the casualty rate among gremlins had decreased significantly since the clan's early days of living on an aircraft carrier and exploring fighter planes.

And if this voyage succeeded, if they obtained the Lucky Sock, her clan would have even less need to undertake more dangerous adventures among humans.

The Hanson family's new top-loading washing machine, without a central agitator, *had* made their pirating voyages easier. The crew could teleport in and piece together their ship during the fill cycle without a big front-facing "window" potentially revealing them to an approaching human. It gave them time to make themselves and their ship invisible, and they had more room to navigate while obtaining whatever piece of clothing someone needed for a project.

With the lowered risk, acquiring materials via laundry pirating had become a popular way to fulfill a gremlin's need for adrenaline while also doing something useful for the clan. When Plan Lucky Sock was completed, perhaps Mariah could learn new ways to keep her people safe. After all, nothing was more dangerous—to humans or gremlins—than a bored gremlin.

Foam churned on either side of the MS *Whirlpool Top-Loader Construct II* as the wash cycle began.

"Blue and purple stars, crew!" Mariah called over the cycle's agitation. She paused to untangle her silver-gray hair from the dangling pen spring coils that wound through pierced holes in her oversized, pointed ears. "We're looking for blue and purple stars on a gray background! Stay focused, and the luck treasure is ours!"

Standing at the helm, the elder gremlin studied her crew.

Most were generations younger than she. Few knew the first-hand dangers of living in human war machines, but enough had lost family members or sustained severe injuries, even in their new, safer lair of a suburban human home, to understand Mariah's obsession with Plan Lucky Sock. Her clan, and especially her closest crew, had maintained a near-record level of focus since Mariah had pitched her scheme.

"Cargo pant leg, starboard!" called her best and oldest friend, Buddy Bombbreaker, from the hydraulic crow's nest. He hadn't much of a higher vantage point than Mariah, but he was her best set of eyes during a full "dark load."

During delicate loads and soak cycles, Mariah could often hear him click through the lenses on his homemade goggles, checking for nearby dangers or scanning for whatever treasure had inspired the voyage. The current sloshing of a regular load, however, required almost shouting between them.

"Aye! Thanks, Buddy." Mariah engaged the new starboard propulsion engines, recently scavenged from the guest-room-turned-electronics-graveyard of the house. Then, she adjusted the rudder with a hand crank acquired from a music box buried in a bin of toys that lived in the basement limbo of "not being used, but don't donate or throw out."

The ship rode the heavy material's wake with only a little more pitch than its usual motion over choppy, wash-cycle waves.

Navigating the *Construct II* back to the water's center, Mariah set a few more levers, locked a few other cranks, and rested her hand on the video game thumb toggle by her waist. Small adjustments to the toggle kept them mainly in the center of the wash load, away from most of the clothing's movement and giving them a better chance of seeing their treasure. She sighed as the ship slowly spun in place.

"Captain! Buddy! Port side!" Tucker, a nephew only a few greats removed, pointed from his deck position. His fingers, hands, and arms were wrapped with fine copper and gold wires stolen from old motherboards. They glinted in dim light from the washer's windowed lid.

"Ten o'clock, full thrust, Captain!" Buddy called.

Trusting her crew, Mariah steered and accelerated even before making visual confirmation. Purple and blue stars on a gray background writhed like a giant tentacle ahead of the ship. Frayed yarn from a heel that desperately needed darning danced like seaweed. Mariah frowned; those loose strands could pose a problem to all the moving parts of her ship. Turning sharply so the starboard side faced their target—there were fewer exposed gears on that side—she called out, "Rosie, Tank, Acme—get those lines ready! *Before* she gets sucked down, dammit! Slinger—"

"Ready, Captain!" The tallest of the crew waved at the captain without looking up from the mounted harpoon gun she manned. Her mechanical left arm, powered by a watch battery housed in a bath-toy motor assembly, steadied the barrel while three other gremlins loaded the repurposed curtain hooks.

"Fire at will!" the captain ordered.

"Aye, Captain!" Slinger danced the long fingers of her right hand over a set of knobs, making small adjustments to the gun based on the water's movement from the cycle and load density.

"It's getting pulled down!" Buddy called.

"Slinger!" Mariah clenched the edge of the bridge controls.

Three curtain hook harpoons flew from the gun and into the disappearing sock cuff. Slinger yanked two levers, and three bobbins behind her began spinning; all three floss threads grew taut. Sodden sock fabric snapped between the pull of the hooks and the suck of the water. The ship tilted from the force.

"This feels a lot heavier than a sock, Captain," Slinger called, frowning and flipping adjustments on the reeling speed.

Focused on keeping the ship upright, Mariah almost missed hearing Buddy's hydraulic crow's nest lower beside her.

"Might be tangled on another piece of laundry," he said.

"It's fraying," she agreed, gritting her teeth. After a moment, she shouted over her shoulder, "Rosie, how do you feel about that diving mask you made?"

"I feel like it needs its maiden dive, Captain!" The youngest member of her crew, dressed in a skintight suit of discarded electrical tape, took two skips before popping herself below deck and back in the time it took Mariah to squint a glare.

"Save your magic for when we need it!" she scolded. Of all the fae, gremlins had the least magic due to their technological ties. The oldest and most powerful gremlins could teleport just over twice their mass three or four times a day to a nearby location, but most could only reliably teleport twice their mass, at best, twice a day, depending on the distance, and only after years of practice.

Kids never realized their magical limits until they sparked empty in a deadly situation.

"Yes, Captain," she said with a dismissive wave as she headed to the ship's rail.

As Rosie mounted the rail, the water shuddered still. Buddy breathed a curse at the same time as Mariah.

"Thirty seconds till drain and spin!" Mariah shouted. "Rosie—"

"I can do this, Captain!" The young gremlin adjusted her mask and dove into the water.

"Loose grommets and aglets!" Mariah's fingers ached from clenching the rail. "The rest of you, get ready for departure!"

Half the crew headed below deck, where Mariah trusted they would start teleporting parts of the ship back to their lair. Slinger was still reeling in the sock, adjusting the speeds of the bobbins. Air glugs marked the time as the washer jostled beneath the ship, ready to drain.

What's taking Rosie so long?

On the ship, crew was crew, and Mariah treated everyone as equals. But in her heart, she was painfully aware that Rosie was her youngest grandchild of many, many greats—and her mother was waiting back in their lair.

The drum jolted again, and the glugs intensified. The ship wavered, the harpoon lines growing loose, then taut, as the water level started sinking.

"Stench of smoking oil!" Hitting the button that transmitted over the ship, Mariah ordered, "Full departure procedures, everyone! Double time!"

"Captain, what about the Lucky Sock?" Buddy asked, then added quickly, "And Rosie?"

She opened her mouth to answer as the ship tilted portside with a grinding, tearing *crack*! Buddy nearly fell off his lift. Mariah sent all power to the port thrusters—hoping her crew hadn't taken any of them back to the lair yet—and scanned the starboard side. Shredded purple and blue-starred material clung to the side of the ship.

"Stop reeling! Slinger, stop!" she shouted. The gunner obeyed.

Where is Rosie? Although pressing harder on the thruster button didn't send more power to the fans, she couldn't keep from leaning all her weight in hopes the ship would right itself rather than be pulled to pieces. Or worse, fall upon the friends and family of her crew before they could teleport to safety.

"Captain! There! Climbing the middle thread!" Buddy pointed.

A sopping Rosie clung to the thread, creeping up slowly, hand over hand.

"Pop the crow's nest back to the lair and take over here," Mariah said. "That's an order."

"Yes, Captain," Buddy said before teleporting himself and

the whole hydraulic nest and arm off the ship. He returned to the helm almost immediately.

Other clothing bumped against the ship, snagging and tugging in new directions. She smacked the intercom again. "Full departure. Buddy has the bridge," she commanded and ran to the main deck.

Mariah loosened the binder ring she wore as a necklace, clipped it on the center thread, and zipped down to Rosie.

"I'm sorry," the young gremlin murmured as Mariah threw her over a shoulder. "You were right ... 'bout my magic ..."

"Hush, sweetie. I gotta concentrate." The thread grew slack and shallow splashes hit the clothes around her.

No third voyage for my dear Whirlpool Top-Loader Construct II, *alas,* Mariah thought as she reached for the Lucky Sock's loose threads and began binding them around her. She trusted the crew to collect enough of the pieces of the ship so the humans wouldn't question too much unusual debris in their laundry load.

Diving into fraying material, she rolled herself and Rosie into the worn and wet yarn, weaving magic around herself, her many-great-grandchild, and the treasure she'd sacrificed her latest beloved ship to acquire.

"Da-a-ad!" wailed the young human, Kitty Hanson, flopping upon her laundry-strewn bed.

It never ceased to amaze Mariah how both human and gremlin children could communicate so much by simply adding syllables to what they called their family members. She glanced at Rosie, who was shivering beside the outlet wires, cuddled by her mother, recharging her magic and warming up. It would take some time for her to recover after both draining her magic and pushing the limits of her physical body.

Peering through the cracked drywall seam, Mariah watched Lieutenant Commander Emory Hanson fill the door-frame of his daughter's room. "May I help you, dear, screaming daughter of mine?" A gentle smile played upon his lips.

Mariah chuffed in amusement. Would but the child could have seen the face and heard the man's booming commands and chastisements on the aircraft carrier! Or even his younger face, stern and unyielding during his training years. His friends, and later those who answered to him, had seen glimpses of the man his child and wife knew. The man's emotions were as intriguing as his fascination with machinery and technology—the latter part being why she and several family and friends had snuck into his motorcycle and followed him upon his discharge.

"My lucky sock! I can't find it anywhere! What did you *do* with it?"

"The gray one with the purple and blue stars that's falling apart?" He wrinkled his nose.

"Ye-es! You didn't throw it out, did you? You promised you wouldn't!"

"I did not. I washed it. It should be in … *that*." He wiggled his finger in circles at the clean clothes lumped in wrinkly piles across the bedspread.

"I *looked* through *ev-er-y-thing*, Dad! It's not here!"

"I remember putting it in the laundry, sweetie. Check again, and if you still don't find it, check the washer and dryer—"

"I *knew* you'd say that, so I already *did*! It's *not* there!" Kitty's voice rose to such a high pitch it made the springs piercing Mariah's ears resonate.

Emory sighed. "Maybe it fell apart in the laundry, then. I

don't know. There's this wonderful thing called studying you might try. I hear it's even more effective than lucky socks."

"Da-a-*a*-ad!" The extra, emphasized syllable expressed Kitty's opinion on his suggestion. She threw herself across the clothes, forearm over her forehead as if checking for fever. A pair of colorful leggings tumbled to the floor.

Raising an eyebrow, the former lieutenant commander and currently exasperated father said, "I'll be in the guest room working on your aunt's computer if you want me to go over any problems with you."

After an unintelligible grunt, the girl snapped upright and glared at his retreating form. "Mom never lost any of my laundry."

Mariah winced at the same time as Emory did, sympathy panging through her. The loss of *her* mate still stung, and that had happened years before Emory had even been born.

He paused, looked over his shoulder at his daughter, and asked very softly, "Are you sure now?"

Kitty pulled her knees up to her chest and shrank in on herself, as if feeling the weight of her words. "I don't know. Sorry, Dad."

He gave a nod. "If you want help studying, you know where to find me."

This wasn't the first time one of Mariah's capers—or any caper of any gremlin—caused pain in humans. It was never her *intention* to do so, but there was a reason humans always blamed her people for *anything* that went wrong with their machines and equipment. She sighed.

Also, not for the first time, she wondered if gremlins' dangerous effects on the human world were the universe's way to balance out how dangerous the human world was to fae— or if the world was dangerous to gremlins and fae because of the potential havoc they could wreak upon humanity. In the near-hundred years of her existence, Mariah had found no clarity on that pondering.

110

"Captain Mariah!" called Buddy. "We have completed processing the remainder of the Lucky Sock. All the crew have been given their share, a pile has been placed around our common room, and here's the patch we saved for the plan."

"Excellent, Buddy," Mariah said, taking the blue-and-purple-spangled patch of unraveling sock. It was just enough for Kitty to recognize. If Plan Lucky Sock worked, Mariah's people would be able to find more entertainment outside of interactions with humans, thus creating a safer living situation for everyone.

She looked at the variety of screens adorning the pocket of wall space between Kitty's bedroom and the guest-room-computer-graveyard; it was one of many spaces claimed and decorated by the gremlins. Taken from old cell phones, calculators, and cracked computer monitors, most of the screens were either already dead or glowing gray with "input" and a blinking cursor in a corner. A few lit the area, showing websites or operating platforms. Multicolored and metallic wires linked them together and to small keyboards taken from calculators and long-obsolete phone keyboards with letters.

Four gremlins, all about Rosie's age or younger, jumped between the collections of buttons, chatting and typing. Three were also many-great-grand-relations of Mariah; the fourth may as well have been. Carolyn was Rosie's best friend, and Carolyn's many-great-grandfather was Buddy, who'd followed Mariah from Emory's aircraft carrier to his motorcycle to his home. Mariah and Buddy had survived several human wars together—along with Emory. Both gremlins had lost mates during explosions of their machine homes; Emory had lost his to human disease.

Mariah squatted beside Carolyn, whose wrists jingled with stacks of thin washers as she typed. The young gremlin stopped and looked at the clan's matron. "How's Rosie?"

"Better," Mariah said. *Alive.* Not only could gremlins be killed in all the same ways humans could—immolation, drowning, being sliced or punctured by shrapnel, explosions, stray bullets—most humans, upon seeing them, reacted by trying to squash or destroy them. Given their limited teleportation abilities, gremlins had to be aware of a human's approach—as well as other nonhuman threats like rats, cats, and large spiders native to certain parts of the world.

"That's good." Carolyn relaxed in the chair she'd made from a mounted bracket padded with duct tape.

"But I might need you to take over her part in tonight's plan. Do you think you can do that?"

"Oh, yes! We only get one free character on the game account, so we share. And Kitty hasn't figured out Rivet-Master is two people." She turned back to her station and resumed typing. The chat box of the shared online game popped up on an old phone screen that was the same size as Mariah. Several new messages blipped down the display, and a look of genuine concern crossed Carolyn's face. "And it looks like Kitty needs a friend right now anyway."

Mariah wished all human-gremlin relationships could be like the online friendships the younger members of her clan had created.

"May I?" Mariah asked, settling on the floor at Carolyn's nod. The chat box took up more screen than the actual game display and was half-filled with waiting messages.

MewMeow: OMG, CANNOT FIND MY LUCKY SOCK
MewMeow: SO GOING TO FAIL MATH CLASS AND GET GROUNDED SO I WON'T BE ABLE TO PLAY FOR WEEKS
MewMeow: Will you make sure raiders don't steal all my ships and treasure?
MewMeow: NOT ONLY AM I GOING TO FAIL

MATH CLASS BUT I AM THE WORST DAUGHTER IN THE WORLD. I DESERVE TO FAIL MATH CLASS AND LIFE AND EVERYTHING

Cracking her knuckles, Carolyn began typing a response.

RIVETMASTER: WILL TOTALLY SMASH ALL RAIDERS THREATENING YOUR SHIPS
RIVETMASTER: WHAT HAPPENED?
MEWMEOW: TOLD DAD THAT MOM NEVER LOST ANY OF MY LAUNDRY CUZ I KNEW IT WOULD HURT HIS FEELINGS AND IT DID

Carolyn looked at Mariah for guidance. This hadn't been the conversation they'd been expecting.

Mariah pursed her lips and reached for the keyboard. Carolyn gave her a look, and the matron gremlin withdrew. There was a code for sounding like a human near Kitty's age, and Carolyn was right to question Mariah's ability to communicate in such a manner.

"Tell her ... Say something like, 'It's a parent's job to forgive their kids.' And he's accidentally said some hurtful things after her mom died, too, so he will understand."

Carolyn thought a moment, then proceeded to type.

RIVETMASTER: DIDN'T YOUR DAD SAY SOMETHING ABOUT YOU NEVER GIVING YOUR MOM SO MUCH GRIEF? AND YOU FORGAVE HIM?
RIVETMASTER: BESIDES, IT'S A PARENT'S JOB TO FORGIVE THEIR KIDS. IF THEY'RE GOOD PARENTS ANYWAY.
MEWMEOW: ... YEAH, HE'S A PRETTY GOOD DAD I GUESS. STILL WISH HE HADN'T LOST MY SOCK. I HAVE BEEN STUDYING BUT PREALGEBRA MAKES NO SENSE SO I AM TOTALLY GOING TO FAIL

Both gremlins relaxed as the conversation moved back on track. Mariah nodded to Carolyn to proceed with the plan.

RivetMaster: I MIGHT HAVE AN IDEA TO HELP BUT ITS GONNA SOUND CRAZY

MewMeow: YOU KNOW I AM HERE FOR THE CRAZY

RivetMaster: LOL K SO MY BROTHER'S BEST FRIEND LOST HIS BROTHER'S LUCKY JOCKSTRAP BEFORE A SOCCER GAME

MewMeow: EWEWEWEWEWEW! DO I EVEN WANT TO KNOW THIS?

RivetMaster: HOW THE JOCKSTRAP GOT LOST I DIDN'T ASK. SO DIDN'T WANNA KNOW. BUT HE WAS ABLE TO GET IT BACK IN TIME FOR THE GAME

MewMeow: LISTENING

RivetMaster: TOLD YOU IT WAS GONNA SOUND CRAZY

MewMeow: AS LONG AS IT ISN'T ABOUT THE JOCKSTRAP, STILL HERE FOR THE CRAZY

RivetMaster: HE LEFT A TREASURE FOR THE FAERIES … LIKE FOR A TRADE

MewMeow: UM OK

RivetMaster: TOLD YOU CRAZY BUT IT WORKED. GOT THE IDEA FROM HIS GRANDMOTHER

MewMeow: STILL LISTENING

RivetMaster: HE LEFT OUT THE BEST CHOCOLATE IN THE HOUSE ON TOP OF A FAMILY SECRET

MewMeow: FAMILY SECRET? IF WE EVEN HAVE FAMILY SECRETS, I DON'T KNOW ANY :(

RivetMaster: NO THE SECRETS WERE A LIST OF ALL THE FAMILY PASSWORDS FOR WI-FI HULU NETFLIX AND AMAZON PRIME. UNDER A GHIRARDELLI CHOCOLATE BAR. THE KIND WITH SALT AND CARAMEL

Mariah raised an eyebrow at Carolyn. "We already have the Wi-Fi password. And a Ghirardelli chocolate bar with salt and caramel?"

"The pitch is in the details," Carolyn said with a shrug. "And I volunteer to be on the team who gets the chocolate and writes down the rest of the passwords."

"Uh-*huh*." Mariah smirked.

MewMeow: I have EXACTLY that chocolate bar in my desk. Dad gave it to me for helping wash the cars. You think that and a list of all the passwords will be enough?
RivetMaster: Worked for my brother's friend
MewMeow: Totally trying that tonight. Will let you know what happens
RivetMaster: Cool! So we doing a thing tonight or are you abandoning me to study jic?
MewMeow: Um …
RivetMaster: I got you covered if you still want to study. Smash raiders. Defend treasure. Stop mutinies
MewMeow: Mostly want to check on Dad. And get the passwords. I know where he hides them
RivetMaster: Np. Go do you. You always cover me
MewMeow: TY! You are the best! xo

Carolyn spun in her chair, cracking her knuckles proudly. "Mission accomplished. I can taste that chocolate already!"

Only Carolyn, Rosie, and Buddy accompanied Mariah to the drywall crack as Kitty's alarm burst into loud music. The scent of chocolate and salted caramel clung to them like a web of Scotch tape. The rest of the clan was already hunkered down in front of the multiple screens throughout their secret rooms, perusing menus upon menus of entertainment. Their treasure had been even greater than Mariah had anticipated because Kitty had also found and reported how to access

"Pirate Bay," where her father—despite his otherwise law-abiding demeanor—had already downloaded a plethora of high-definition programming and games.

But Mariah was a gremlin of principles and wanted peace for the humans with whom they lived, too. Her heart pounded as she watched Kitty jump from her bed and run to the space beneath her desk where she'd placed the chocolate bar and list of passwords—and where Mariah had carefully laid the scrap of Lucky Sock, Kitty's personal treasure.

Kitty pressed her hand to her lips to muffle a delighted squeal as she hugged the tattered scrap of purple and blue stars to her heart.

Mariah released a happy sigh. Before she'd returned Kitty's Lucky Sock, she'd found a website with a whole list of DIY programs about crafts she could make with obsolete computer and phone pieces. Arts and crafts certainly would lower the danger of human-gremlin interactions. *And* she'd found a tutorial on building toy ships from "things found around most houses"—and *this* house had a whole room of such interesting things!

A safer world, the ultimate treasure, was certainly on the horizon.

About the Author

Trisha J. Wooldridge (or child-friendly T.J. Wooldridge) writes novels, short fiction, nonfiction, and poetry that occasionally win awards. She's edited six anthologies and over sixty novels. Find her in *Wicked Weird*, *The Book of Twisted Shadows*, *HWA Poetry Showcase*, *New Scary Stories to Tell in the Dark*, and more. For more information, visit anovelfriend.com.

Porch Pirates of Pasadena

AMY HUGHES

I lean on the handlebars of my sea-green bicycle and shift my weight to the side, listless. The sun beats down from a cloudless sky, and I wipe sweat from my eyes with my favorite red bandana. The cul-de-sac is devoid of life. There is no breeze. There is no sign of the FedEx delivery truck. There's nothing I can do but wait.

Pasadena is becalmed.

When I'd joined Captain Malhouk's crew, it was to promises of adventure and exploration. I'd been sold stories of sailing down the high streets and up the highways with my little red wagon trailing in my wake. It would be filled to the brim with stolen packages—each one holding a hidden treasure, buried deep within the packaging, just waiting to be dug open and explored. Fortunes to be found. Money. Women. Money to impress the women. I'd been sold dreams of exotic locales. I'd been promised Sacramento.

But nothing in life is ever quite what you dream it will be.

I kick a pebble at my feet. It skitters across the sidewalk and rolls away into the storm drain.

I've been stuck watching the same dead cul-de-sac for weeks.

The air echoes with the distant rumble of an engine. My heart skips a beat. I dart behind the bushes, crouch over the handlebars, and pull out my spyglass. The world whirls by as I focus on the house at the far end. I settle on the address: 1764 Bermuda Circle. If I can pull this off, I'll be rewarded. Whatever Capt'n Malhouk wants from this house, he wants it fierce.

The FedEx truck slows to a halt in front of the ancient Victorian home. Her paint is peeling, and her deck sags. She has a tiny decorative cannon on the guardrail. An old-style brass bell hangs above it. Not much care has gone into the place. It's surprising Malhouk would think there was anything of value coming here at all. But he is the captain, and I am just crew.

It's about time I saw some action.

The delivery man sets the package down. He rings the doorbell. He walks away. He climbs into his truck and pulls away from the curb. I slip the spyglass into my satchel and pump at the pedals of my bike. The truck disappears out of the mouth of Bermuda Circle. I skid to a halt on the stoop and swing out to grab the package off the deck. It's the size of a Rubik's Cube and fits perfectly into my palm. I slip in into my cross-body satchel.

The front door opens.

A woman stands there. Her brilliant red hair curls out and away from her head like a giant frizzy halo. Her glasses are so thick, her eyes look as small as pomegranate seeds. Her apron is a mass of pockets, with tools hanging from the lip of each one. They rattle as she takes a step forward.

She's the most beautiful woman I've ever seen.

"Hey!" she says. She reaches a hand toward me.

I scream and pump my foot down as hard as I can. I sail away down the street to the sound of protests behind me. I glance back. She gives chase, her arms flailing above her head, but she can't keep up. My bike is too swift, and the breeze is at my back. She stumbles to a halt in the lonely, deserted center of the cul-de-sac. Her shoulders sag. She sinks to her knees. A single lone gull circles high above.

I pump away as hard as I can.

Whatever this package is, it had better be worth it.

I pedal until my glutes burn, past the Kraken's Gate Diner and the Coconut Palms Café. I can't get the memory of that woman out of my head. She was so beautiful. She was so sad. Her fingers grasped at the air above her head as she ran, like she was drowning. Like I was someone who could save her but didn't. Her right hand, with only two fingers, reached out to me on the porch.

I skid to a stop in front of the Golden Coin Laundromat. Gravel sprays around me like a wave.

She had only two fingers on her right hand.

But that couldn't be right.

She must have had her other fingers curled in like a fist.

But I imagine back and see nothing but two fingers like lobster claws grasping out toward me. I can't make any other image fit, no matter how I try.

I know who she is.

Two-Finger Kearns. The greatest ship-in-a-bottle builder in an entire generation. I've watched every YouTube video she's ever made. Her show, *Warning Shot across the Bow*, gets more than four million views a month. I've seen her assemble, refurbish, and restore hundreds of ships in the past five years. I've never seen her face, but those hands are unmistakable.

I pedal my bike to the alley behind the laundromat. I pass the dumpsters and the overgrown hollyhocks, lemon trees and date palms. I swerve into the grotto at the end of the alley and glide my bike to a stop. When I step down, my feet sink into soft grass growing from the tiny patch of sand. Normally, this place is my shelter in a storm—my oasis from the world—but my mind won't stop swirling.

Those fingers … those tools …

I swing the satchel from my shoulder as I sit on the grass and sand. Palm fronds wave gently in the breeze above my head. I pull the package from the satchel.

It weighs almost nothing. Its brown cardboard exterior and clear packing tape seem so innocuous. They could hold nothing. They could hold everything. The unknown of it calls to me like a siren.

I check the label: Katherine Kearns.

I swallow the bile rising in my throat. I scratch at the peach fuzz on my chin, then roll the small package between my palms.

I knew she lived in Pasadena. To think, I'd been beached outside her house for weeks waiting for … an awl? Maybe. The package is light enough for a small one. Tweezers,

AMY HUGHES

perhaps. My mind races over the possibilities. Chisel? Scoop? Dremel—no, too light for that. Needle? Wire? Superglue?

We're not supposed to open the packages. Malhouk's first law. We turn in the bounty. We each take a share of the profits. It's fair. It works. Theft is punished swiftly, harshly. Banishment. All hopes of getting to Sacramento would be gone. I could lose everything. And for what? One small package meant for a woman I don't even know.

But, Katherine … Did she go by Katherine? Or was it Kate to her friends? Or Kitty? Or Kat? She'd been so distraught. She had tools hanging from of every pocket of her apron from her neck to her knees. This must be something more than just a simple awl. She'd have backups of any tools she needed on hand. Malhouk wouldn't have set me to watch her house for an awl.

But that's the real question, isn't it? Why would Malhouk have me watch the house in the first place?

I slide my pocketknife free of the outer pocket of my satchel. I weigh it in the palm of my hand. I could claim the box had been damaged in shipping if I open it right. It happens. More often than people think. But if I'm caught, it's everything I've spent the last sixty-three days of my life dreaming about. All of it, for nothing.

A gull screams over my head. It sounds like Katherine's shriek of despair as I sailed away from the cul-de-sac. What is it that could make her wail like that?

FedEx will cover it. The company she ordered from can always send her another one, whatever it is.

I crush the corner of the box against the sand and pry open the corner of the tape with my knife. It looks believable. Absolutely believable. I rough up the tear, just to be sure. Ultimately, all Malhouk really wants is the bounty, right? The box is irrelevant. I dip the corner of the box in a nearby puddle, just to finish the effect.

122

You can't trust anyone to deliver packages safely these days. They're all a bunch of brigands.

I open the corner flaps of the box and peer inside. Whatever it is, it's wrapped in bubble wrap and difficult to see. But there is a flash of light—a glint of something metallic. I prod at the bubble wrap with the tip of my blade. I pull it toward the light. Definitely something brass or copper. Maybe something gold?

The box slips from my hands and rolls into the puddle. It's soaked now. I squish the box, and the top falls open. The bubble wrap slides into my palm.

At the center of the bubble wrap is a thin strip of metal, about the size of my palm. It's brass. It's polished and shining. Its surface sparkles through the watery covering of the plastic. A nameplate.

She's building a ship. The greatest ship-in-a-bottle maker in all the world, and I am holding the nameplate to her latest creation. What I wouldn't give to see more. The words are fuzzy and distorted. I peel back the bubble wrap and there it is —*The Mother of Pearl*.

The entire world falls away. I can't breathe. I stare at the nameplate in awe. The breeze is cool, but the sun is still hot. I am dizzy and cold. I feel giddy and strange. A giggle ripples up my throat.

The Mother of Pearl is a legend.

She was the second-finest ship-in-a-bottle ever created by Giovanni Biondo in 1785. The ship disappeared decades ago, lost in a flood, but rumors that she'd been found have been circulating for years. Stories of her appearances are shared in whispers. She flits in and out of the imaginations of shipheads like a ghost in the night.

And somehow, by some miracle, she's in Katherine "Two-Finger" Kearns's house. She's restoring her. She has to be.

I shake my head. This has to be for a replica. Or maybe

she collects nameplates. Some people do. *The Mother of Pearl* is long gone. She can't have bubbled up now, not like this. Not here. But then, where else? Who else could possibly hope to restore her to her former glory but Two-Finger Kearns?

All the ramifications tumble through my thoughts. I can't have this. If the *Pearl* is going to be restored, she needs this. What Katherine is doing could change the world of ship-in-a-bottle building forever. How did the ship resurface after all this time? What does this mean for the world? For me?

This is what the captain has been looking for—proof that the *Pearl* is still out there. Not just out there. But here. In that house. Now. He set me to watch for the greatest treasure ever lost in our age, and I was bored waiting for it. What a fool I've been.

He's likely to pay anything for this.

I gather up the box and tuck the bubble-wrapped nameplate inside. I stuff it back into my satchel and grab my bike.

I'm going to Sacramento after all.

I squeeze through the press of bodies in the back room of the Coral Bay Tavern. The day's haul is heaped on the table, brown boxes piled high beneath the dim light. I always felt they ought to shine. It's a pity they don't. Kearns's red hair shone in the afternoon light as she watched me steal the single most precious item she's likely ever ordered. I focus again on the boxes. I don't want to think about the look in her tiny eyes.

I keep my hand in the satchel, wrapped tight around the little box. Its soggy cardboard squishes ever so slightly beneath my fingers, but I don't let it go. This is my ticket to Sacramento.

The captain lounges in the Barcalounger in the back corner of the room. Feet up, he watches the pile grow bigger with each new crew member who enters the room. Some crew were lucky and stack two or three boxes in the pile. Some come in empty-handed. But that's the way of things. Some days, the haul is good. Today, my catch has been the very best.

"Captain!" I call as I approach. Two of his burliest men step out of the shadows and block me from Malhouk.

Malhouk leans over in the Barcalounger and peers past the vested chest of the nearest guard. His thick black beard cascades over his chest. His gold earring glints in the dim light of the neon Budweiser sign hanging on the back wall. Coco, his yellow budgie, hops down the length of his arm to his fingers, chirping sweetly all the way.

When he sees me, Malhouk pulls the lever on the lounger and sits up straight. Coco skips and flaps her wings.

"Has it come?" he demands. His eyes sparkle and flash. I've never seen such naked greed before. It scares me. I take a step back. I swallow.

I flex my fingers around the little package and pull it free. The box is smushed and wet and lopsided. Such a small and pathetic thing. I hold it out to the captain.

The captain leaps from his chair and closes the distance between us in two great, limping steps. Rumor has it he lost his littlest toe three years ago to a shar-pei. He towers over me. He grabs the package from me, and the cardboard loses the last of its vaguely squarish shape in his massive hand.

"I'm so sorry, sir," I stammer. "The package fell, but it's intact, I swear."

He glares at me over the bulk of his black beard for a moment before carefully, almost reverently, tearing back the remains of the box to expose the bright, white bubble wrap beneath.

He lifts it to the light, and his breath catches in his throat.

"It's real," he whispers. "*The Mother of Pearl* is here."

I clutch at my now empty satchel. I can hear the siren call

of Sacramento singing in my brain. This is the moment I get everything I've ever wanted.

The captain peels back the bubble wrap carefully. The nameplate glints in the colorful neon lighting. I can hear my own heartbeat rushing in my ears.

"Coke and rum for everyone!" His voice booms and echoes through the room. The air fills with the cheers and whoops of celebration.

His massive arm lands heavily on my shoulder. I am squashed in a hearty embrace. He leads me through the crowd to the back room that serves as his office. Coco jumps and flutters on his shoulder nearest my ear. The noise of the crew is muffled by the heavy oak door Malhouk shuts behind us.

The room is old and dusty. A weathered globe sits on the table, and paintings of mermaids adorn the walls.

"Tell me, boy," he says, sinking into the ancient-looking, high-backed, leather chair behind the desk, "how the package came to be opened."

I stand frozen for far too long. Would Katherine's face have been so greedy had she been the one to open the package and see the nameplate first? Somehow, I don't think so. Her videos make her sound so patient and reasonable. She restores old ships for charity sometimes.

"I'm sorry, sir. There were complications." It's a pathetic excuse that means absolutely nothing. I know it. And the captain knows it.

He watches me through squinted eyes for a moment, before leaning back with a dark and twisted grin peeking out through the wisps of his beard.

"No matter," he says. My shoulders slump in relief. "You've brought me the single greatest bounty I could have asked for. Do you know how much I'm going to sell this for?"

I stare.

"Sell just the nameplate, sir?" Surely, if he had me

watching the house he must know about Kearns. He must know about the *Pearl*.

The captain laughs. "Don't be ridiculous. I've been selling knockoff bits of that ship for years. You think I'm going to risk having the original crop up now? Two-Finger was right to keep it from me."

He rolls the nameplate over and over in his hands.

"I don't understand, sir." My voice is weak, and my hands are shaking. "If you're going to sell the nameplate, what happens when Kearns makes the rest of the ship public?"

He laughs again, a hearty, rolling sound that fills the small office. I nearly cringe. "My boy, what does that matter?"

He stands. He moves around the desk and slaps a heavy hand onto my shoulder with a thump like a side of fresh salmon. Coco flutters to the bird-sized play yard on the desk. She jingles the bell at the top of the slide.

"What matters is what I can do for you." He pulls me into a squeezing side hug. His beard scratches my ear. "You've made me a very happy man, and anyone on my crew can tell you that happiness puts me in a very generous mood. What can I do for you? What is it you want?"

Sacramento hangs at the edge of my lips. The taste of it is on my tongue. All I have to do is ask.

"I'd like to know what's in store for *The Mother of Pearl*, sir."

What I really want to ask, what I'm really afraid to know, is what's in store for Katherine.

The captain chuckles and jiggles me in his expansive side hug. Is he ever going to let me go?

"My boy, I'm going to go get the ship, I'm going to salvage what I can, and I'm going to scuttle the rest in the lake." He slaps my shoulder again with his massive slab of fish hand.

The world falls away. Salvage. Scuttle. *The Mother of Pearl* was lost once already. But there had always been hope she'd be found. But not anymore. She is going to be lost forever.

"But you," he continues, "I knew you were the man for

this. I've had my eye on you for a while. How would you feel about a change of location? I was thinking maybe ... Sacramento."

The word brings me back. Sacramento. I could see the Sacramento Zoo. I could spend my days strolling through the abandoned Sutter's Fort. No more stumbling along the streets I'd known all my life. I've outgrown Pasadena. I'm ready to leave it all behind.

But ... at the cost of the *Pearl?*

"Thank you, sir," I manage to squeak. This is what I want. Right?

He lifts his hand from my shoulder at last. I fall away from him and catch myself on the edge of his desk. Coco chirps at me happily.

"Good lad!" he roars. That laugh just keeps coming. "You'll accompany us tonight. It's a real honor. We'll raid the house and take the ship. You'll receive a share of the money from the nameplate to set you up in Sacramento. I'll even let you be the one to scuttle her if you'd like."

He ushers me out the door.

"John Scarr! Gather the men. We're going on a raid at midnight! We meet at Bermuda Circle!"

The burly pirate nods his head. The captain's door slams shut behind me. I am left standing alone outside the captain's office, clutching my empty satchel to my chest.

How has this happened? What have I done?

I wander slowly through the crowd, the smell of rum and Coke thick on the air. I don't know most of these people. I've hardly spoken to a single one. For sixty-three days, I've dreamed of moving onwards, and yet suddenly I find myself marooned in the midst of them. At midnight, Katherine's home will be invaded. The ship will be taken. *The Mother of Pearl* will be destroyed.

Will Katherine be injured? Will her studio be destroyed? I look forward to her videos each week. There's always something new. And she loves what she does so dearly. You can tell. It comes through in the way that she cradles the little pieces in her hands, in the gentleness of how she eases every tiny bit of the ships into their places. It's in the tone of her voice as she talks.

Someone presses a celebratory drink into my hand. I push him off. I don't feel like celebrating.

This isn't fun anymore.

The streetlights in Bermuda Circle create glowing islands around the edges of the cul-de-sac. The crew is scattered between those islands, waiting for the signal to attack. Captain Malhouk crouches in the darkness several men down from me. His face glows with an eerie yellow cast from the streetlight. The seconds tick away. We are only a few minutes to midnight.

Katherine is in there somewhere. She may be sleeping. She may be working on her next video. She may be working on the *Pearl*. There is one light on in the old Victorian house, shining through an old lace curtain. There is no sign of movement from within.

Sacramento. I just have to get through tonight, and I can head to Sacramento and never look back. I've never been outside of Pasadena. I've never been anywhere. Which isn't fair, when you think about it. Why do some people spend their whole lives trapped in the same dead-end city, and others sail through the world like the wind will never cease to carry them?

I want a big life. I want more than some dead end. No more spinning endlessly through my days with the same faces, the same streets, the same conversations, the daily grind forever. I can't live that life. I have to take the opportunities that come to me, or what's the point? I have to seize the day and carpe the diem and stuff. This is my ticket. This is what I have to do.

"I can't believe I'm doing this to Katherine Kearns," I mumble. But what choice do I have? I shift my satchel across my back and grip the strap tight.

"Two-Finger Kearns?" asks the man at my right. His eye patch creates the look of a shadowed hole in his face. "Like, from *Warning Shot across the Bow*?"

"Yeah."

He shifts uncomfortably in his hiding place.

"I love her videos. I haven't missed an episode." He glances nervously at the house. "We're not gonna ... I don't ... Do you think her studio is in there?"

I glance from his suddenly pale face to the house and back. All those ships. All that work. The tabletop with the white mat where each and every piece can be displayed. It's all going to be destroyed.

"I saw her today with her tools," I say. "She looked like she'd been filming." Maybe it was the video for *The Mother of Pearl*. I'd give almost anything to watch her walk through that.

"I'm a huge fan," he almost whispers the words. "The money is good. But I'm not sure it's worth it."

What is it worth, exactly? What if I move to Sacramento but never get to watch her videos ever again because we destroyed everything tonight? Her videos have been a window to the outside world. I go to sleep listening to my old favorites. I watch them at the dentist's office to keep myself calm. The videos give me something to talk about with people I have nothing to talk about with.

"I want everything destroyed!" the captain calls out down the line.

Damn it.

"Wait!" I scream. I run toward the nearest streetlight. "This is Two-Finger Kearns's house! She's restoring *The Mother of Pearl*!"

Noise and confusion erupt from the shadows. A few men shout. A dog starts to bark nearby. The captain's voice rises above it all.

"Mutiny!" he yells. "Get back in line! An extra-large share for everyone who participates! Attack! Now!"

A few men run from the shadows toward the house.

"Stop them!" I yell. "Her studio is inside!"

The man in the lead is tackled to the ground. The next two are chased by several others, but I can't tell if the chasers are joining them or trying to run them down. A car alarm begins to wail. The captain's voice calls for attack, trying to regain order, offering reward. But it's too late. His ranks are in chaos.

"Malhouk is going to destroy *The Mother of Pearl!*" I yell.

"A thousand dollars to the man who gets to the studio first!" Malhouk yells.

The captain is twice my size, but I rush him. I ram into his stomach, shoulder first, like a baby whale trying to move an island. I have about the same effect. He looks down at me in surprise. I slam my hand into his vest pocket. My fingers close around the nameplate. I hold it tight and stumble back as fast as I can. The captain tries to grab me, but I'm fast. I spent my childhood dodging sharks like him in high school hallways.

Police sirens sound in the distance. The pirate on the porch turns and sprints away into the night. Fights break up all over the cul-de-sac as people scatter and run.

Malhouk stares at me from across the curb. His crew is broken. "You've given up your one chance to make it to Sacramento, boy."

I probably have.

Malhouk limps off into the darkness. I watch him go, nameplate clutched in my fist. I've saved *The Mother of Pearl.* It's enough. It's going to have to be.

The early morning light hurts my eyes. I was up most of the night dodging police and didn't get home until dawn.

Around three in the morning, I placed a call. The back room of the Coral Bay tavern was raided around five.

I won't be going to Sacramento. But neither will Malhouk for a very long time.

I hesitate on the doorstep of the old Victorian. I could just leave the nameplate on the mat and walk away.

I steel myself for what's coming. I can't go to Sacramento, but I can do this.

Katherine opens the door before my hand hits the doorbell. Her tiny eyes and her wild red hair fill the doorway. I take a step back. She's exquisite.

"The *Pearl* is going to need this," I say, holding the nameplate out to her.

She takes it. She holds it up to the light and examines every angle. She wanders back into the house without saying a word. I am left standing on the porch. The door is wide open. Is it an invitation?

I take a hesitant step into the dark.

A short hall leads to a side office. It's the same room that had the light on last night.

"I was worried you weren't going to bring this back," she calls from inside. I cringe. She knows exactly who I am. Of course she does. I follow her voice into her studio.

It's all there on the worktable with the white mat. Her camera is ready to record. Her tools, those not hanging in her apron, are laid out neatly nearby.

"Do you want to see her?" She moves to the other side of the worktable. It's weird how familiar her voice is to me.

She lifts something from the shelves at the back of the room and sets it gently on the table. There, in a 370cc bottle, is *The Mother of Pearl*. She is more beautiful even than Katherine.

I crouch at the side of the table. Her rigging is intact. Her sails are full. Her hull shines and every tiny detail almost glows in its perfection.

"All she needs is the nameplate," Katherine says.

I reach out a hesitant finger, but I draw it back before making contact. "I never imagined I'd ever see her. Not in all my life."

I'd dreamed of Sacramento. But seeing *The Mother of Pearl* is like staring at a fantasy. It's a myth come to life. It's like watching a sea serpent rise up to high-five you from out of the fog.

"I heard you last night," she says. "Out in the street. You saved my house."

I shrug. I brought the pirates down on her in the first place. "I hardly saved it."

"Malhouk pays well," she says.

"I don't work for him anymore." Never again. "My life of piracy is behind me."

"You'll be looking for a job then," she says.

I look up. She leans against the shelves with her arms folded across all those tools. Her tiny eyes are shrewd.

"Yeah, I guess I will."

She sets the nameplate on the table next to the *Pearl*.

"Shipbuilding can be dangerous," she says. "It's hard to find people I can trust. I think the secret is to find people who love the ships as much as I do."

I push back from the table and rise to my feet.

"I have parts that need safe transport from Sacramento. You interested?"

My face splits into a grin. She extends a hand, and I take her two-fingered grip in mine.

I'm going to Sacramento after all.

About the Author

Amy Hughes is published in the bestselling anthology *Writers of the Future*, Volume 31. She has lived in the Middle East for the past five years and has ordered many, many packages. Only a few have ever disappeared. She remains uncertain as to whether it was pirates.

Sabbath

JESSICA GUERNSEY

K neeling on the deck, dressed in rags and refusing to make eye contact, was the man who held the key to the future of Spain. Every key unlocked a treasure, even if the key was dirty.

As he listened to the words spilling from the huddled creature before him, Capitán Diego Martinez de Salazar knew this treasure would be vast. He was certain of this almost as much as he knew his first officer, the insufferable Francisco Garcia, would not hesitate to piss in the soldiers' water barrels. But for now, Salazar would pretend not to notice his officer's mock obedience or his murmurs to the crew. For now, Salazar was still capitán. And Garcia would follow orders.

The man kneeling in front of him was known only by the English name Will, although the dark skin of the island people and clipped accent said he wasn't the least bit English. The small but well-muscled man had approached their ship while they restocked in Veracruz. Salazar had nearly ordered the man beaten and sent away, but he'd caught a word the man had said and it turned his attention: pirate.

"Tell me again," Salazar said, speaking to Will but waiting for Garcia to respond.

Garcia scoffed. "He makes his berth on the island by—"

"Not you." Salazar nodded at Will. "I want him to tell me."

Garcia spoke a few words in English to the kneeling man. While Salazar would never admit it to his first officer, he understood more of the language than Garcia assumed. Will began to tell them again what he knew, his English stuttering but serviceable, and Garcia relayed the story in his native Spanish, much as he had before.

"There's a man, a buccaneer." Garcia's trademark sneer hitched higher at the word. "He makes his berth on the island of Guanahani. He has command of the *Trinity*."

When Will had first uttered the name of the vessel, Salazar had sucked in a breath. The *Trinity* was known among

137

the Spanish by another name. A prized Spanish galleon. Not so much larger than his own patache but rumored to have almost as many guns and more crew. It had been stolen by buccaneers some years ago.

Salazar refocused his attention back on Will, who was still fumbling through the English words as Garcia translated them into Spanish.

"The buccaneer is strange for a pirate—religious. His men do not gamble or game on the Sabbath, and he does not attack other vessels."

When Garcia paused, Salazar did not take the bait. He would not look at the man's smug face lest he was tempted to run his fist into it. Garcia's trim beard was far too small for such a vast head. Instead the capitán turned his back on Garcia, a sign of trust. Or of disregard. Garcia could take it either way.

Salazar kept his back straight to remind Garcia that he was higher than the first officer in rank and in stature. "And the buccaneer's name?"

"John Watling." The name was clear enough from the captive's lips.

Salazar waited. He was a patient man. Patient enough to let a man hang himself with his own words. Patient enough to establish himself in the Armada before daring to ask for the hand of the divine Lucia Diaz. Patient enough that Will kept talking and Garcia kept translating.

"I know how to find his island, can spot his sails on the horizon. I know him and his crew. I can take you to him."

"And you were on this ship." Salazar wasn't asking a question. "The *Trinity*." He waited for Garcia to translate, mentally noting that Garcia called the vessel by its Spanish-given name: the *Santísima Trinidad*.

When Will answered in the affirmative, Salazar faced him. "Why come to the Spanish for help?" The island people were a cheap source of labor, easily moved from one island to the next as needed. Easily bent under the fist of their conquerors. They had no love for those who ruled them.

Will's gaze darted to the side, probably taking in the immense amount of silver in Garcia's tacky footwear. "Your ship is big. Very powerful."

Salazar raised an eyebrow. The *Isabella* was indeed a fine ship. A patache, quick and light on her feet. What she lacked in cannon power, she made up for in the several dozen soldiers held in her wooden embrace. It was a source of pride for Salazar, young as he was, to be given command of such a vessel. He tilted his head to one side, causing his finely oiled curls to rub the high collar of his uniform, as he contemplated the man before him.

"Then why do you turn on your capitán?"

As Garcia translated, Will's dark eyes came up, meeting Salazar's and showing an intensity that conveyed his anger, even without the heat in his words. "He left me. Abandoned me. Forgot me. He is *not* my captain." And just as quickly, his eyes lowered back to the deck.

Salazar tapped a finger to the end of his moustache and ignored the scrape of Garcia's shifting boots. He was trying to think; damn the man's oversized buckles. Salazar was patient, yes, but he was also ambitious. Ever since the ink dried on the Treaty of Madrid a decade before, the English pirates had plundered and pillaged, destroying or imprisoning any Spanish ship they encountered in what was once the Spanish Main. If Salazar could take back even one of those ships, his family name would be known once more. And the divine Lucia Diaz could give her consent to marriage. He very nearly sighed thinking of their last meeting and how she had dipped her fan enough to let him touch her slim, cool fingers.

But there was work to do. A buccaneer to trap and a ship to reclaim. A woman to win and a country to exalt.

Salazar slid his gaze back to his first officer. "Have this man taken below."

A hard smile crept onto Garcia's lips, but it slipped away as Salazar continued speaking.

"Have him bathed, fed, and given new clothes. Show him the charts so he can point us in the right direction."

Garcia snapped his fingers at a waiting crewman, but before the underling could scuttle forward, Salazar raised a hand. The man looked back at Garcia as he halted. Salazar suspected the crew listened better to his first officer. No matter. The contingent of soldiers on board were loyal to Salazar.

"I can trust only you with this task, my friend." Salazar rested a hand on Garcia's shoulder, letting the smile on his face show in his eyes. "This is our chance at greatness. You must look out for him."

"Me?" Garcia didn't shake the hand from his shoulder, but his eyes narrowed. "Look out for this … this foreigner?"

As Salazar let the smile fade, he tightened his grip. Not much. Just enough so Garcia would notice. "You."

Garcia snorted and made to reach for the man on the deck, but Salazar did not release his shoulder. When Garcia looked at him again, Salazar made sure the first mate saw the face of his capitán.

Garcia pursed his lips. "Yes, sir," he said slowly. He gave a slight bow and then reached for Will.

Salazar watched them struggle belowdecks before he followed their path, turning instead to enter his cabin, which was fine enough for a capitán of his lineage. The lamps were kept trimmed and well stocked, though how long they would remain so was yet to be seen. If his fortunes at sea did not change, even home would offer no comfort.

His family, sailors and capitáns for generations, was in decline. Much like the Spanish Main. Gone were the days of the mighty Armada. Lands conquered in his grandfather's time were now in different hands. Seas that held no threat in his father's days now teemed with thieves and criminals like Watling. The once-grand fleet of ships sailing under Spanish colors was reduced to a few pataches and galleons that could be spared, no longer carrying rich treasures. Salazar's own hold had been refitted to hold soldiers and storage, not precious materials for his king.

Bracing his hands on the table, he looked down at the piles and rolls of maps. Newer lines marked boundaries that had once been much larger. His vision blurred, and his shoulders fell forward. He caught himself before his head followed. Standing, he stretched, working his arms back and forth to move his blood and clear the fatigue from his head. Too many nights awake. Too many days with no rest among the waves. And too many marks left empty on the calendar before he could return home.

Salazar rubbed a hand over his eyes and poured himself a drink. Red wine. Not the best year, with a slightly acrid bite, pulled from what was left of his family's cellar, their crest fading on the bottle. The same crest was etched into the buckle on his weapons belt, which held a scabbard for his sword and a holster for his pistol. The belt was draped over the only chair in the room. It had been days since Salazar could bring himself to bear the weight of that belt. Perhaps that would change.

If he could not make a name for himself in these waters, then the Salazar name might as well die out with him. Lucia wouldn't have him. No, she had grown up in luxury, as had he, and she was used to the finer things in life. With the vast lands her family held, she would never settle for the modest villa on the coast that was nearly all that was left to the Salazar name. Lucia would want—no, she *deserved* better. Grander.

But if she were to take his name, then what was hers would be his, and together, they would expand the Salazar fortune. His prestige. Her beauty, with eyes more gold than brown. And John Watling's ship offered a way back. Back to honor for his family. Back into Lucia's arms for him.

Treaty be damned. Salazar pulled out a clean sheet of

parchment and a piece of chalk, names and ranks already running through his mind as he sketched the plan for what lay ahead.

All too soon, a familiar pounding on the door announced Garcia and his charge. Water drops still clinging to his short-cropped hair, Will entered, his hands still clasped in front of him although he was no longer bound. His eyes swept the room, then returned to Garcia, who motioned to the table in front of Salazar.

Salazar frowned at Will's unclean fingers, despite their recent scrubbing, as he shuffled through the parchment before pulling out the correct map.

Will's cracked nail tapped down. "Here. Straight east from Havana, past Charles Town."

Salazar leaned closer, stench of the unwashed no longer rolling off their newest crewmember. "San Salvador?"

Will shook his head. "Calls it Watling Island."

"I thought he was religious." Salazar tilted his head to look at his first officer while Will remained bent over the map.

"Pious doesn't always mean humble," Garcia said, never taking his eyes from Will's back.

"Approach from the west, toward the southern tip." Will drew his finger around the speck of an island. "He prefers a bay there. Trees make it harder to see your sails."

Salazar nodded. Good information. He nearly opened his mouth to give the order to set sail, but Will wasn't finished yet.

"No haste," he said. "The island is some distance, but so is Sunday."

Salazar pulled his lips in. "And he won't be prepared to attack us on Sunday?"

Will wrinkled his brow but still peered at the map. "Watling doesn't sail on the Sabbath."

Salazar contemplated the man's words. With the treaty in place, his actions could be construed as aggression. But if they were victorious—and all the information Will gave him indicated the plan was solid—then all that he wanted for Spain and for himself would be in his grasp. It was a flash of memory, of Lucia's beguiling eyes, that convinced Salazar.

He reached for his belt and strapped it on.

The island had been in view for some time with no sign of Watling's ill-gotten ship. Salazar kept his sails hidden by the tree line on approach to the southern tip. Just the thought of English criminals crawling the noble Spanish decks made Salazar tighten his fingers on the railing. He would reclaim the *Santísima Trinidad*. And he would reclaim Spain's power in these waters.

A few moments more and his ship edged around the island, revealing the captured vessel: set back from the island, anchored but perhaps not empty, though he could make out no sounds but those of birds. Through his spyglass, Salazar searched the deck for the crew but saw no movement. Not even a watch set. Pirates were not only greedy but arrogant as well. He handed the glass to Garcia, who took it and peered at their target.

"Empty?" Garcia asked, lowering the glass.

Salazar nodded slightly. "They could be on the island."

Garcia moved the glass to the shoreline. "Some smoke. Probably campfire. Not much. Most of the crew must be on the ship or ... elsewhere."

"Could be his men aren't loyal and have abandoned him." Salazar's insides tremored. This was not a normal response just before an engagement. Nerves? Anticipation? Lack of sleep? Whatever the cause, he ignored the feeling even as it washed through him again. Instead, he turned to find Will standing behind him, his normally downcast eyes glinting as they roved over the decks of his former ship.

"Where would the crew be if not on the decks?" he asked the smaller man.

Will shrugged one shoulder. "On the Sabbath, no gaming or gambling is allowed." Garcia translated, and Salazar paid close attention, making sure his officer gave him all the information Will divulged. "Some forage on the island. Most choose to sleep."

Garcia left out the part about foraging. Salazar did not react. Best to not let the first officer know the capitán understood. But why did he leave that out? Did he not think it important? Perhaps he was lazy. Or perhaps an ambush awaited on the island.

Salazar looked closely at Will, but the man didn't notice, his gaze never leaving the *Trinity*. Was that glint in his eye excitement for the upcoming battle? Or the slight smile on his lips hard enough to be revenge? For a moment, his insides rippled like the slack sails before them, and Salazar did something he never liked to do. He doubted.

"Capitán," Garcia said, jerking Salazar from his inspection of Will. "It is Sunday. The information is good."

And Salazar was hesitating.

With a few practiced hand motions, Salazar gave the order to prepare to board the pirated vessel, with his soldiers keeping as silent as possible. He would not use cannons on the sister ship unless absolutely necessary. If their target hadn't set a watch, then there was no need to warn them of their approach.

As the ships pulled abreast of each other, ropes were flung across the gap, knots pulling tight with a tug wherever they found hold. Salazar's insides seemed to stretch and knot with them. His crew heaved back, closing the gap enough to slide boards across to the other deck. Salazar swallowed hard, checked his pistol, and then drew his sword, leading a group of soldiers across.

Their boots on the other deck moved in near silence as

they sought out the enemy crew. His own crew would remain behind unless he called for them to join the fray, weapons in hand should a pirate attempt to cross the planks. Garcia and Will waited among them.

The soldiers finished their crossing, making no sounds even as a bird called. Salazar's insides tremored again at the sound. He paused. Where was the bird? He hadn't seen any colored feathers, and yet it sounded as if it were on the ship with them. He looked to the empty rigging.

An unearthly cry rose from the port side, only to be echoed up and down its length. Before Salazar had time to do more than turn his attention to the screams, the far deck swarmed with men, swords drawn and pistols taking aim, as they hauled themselves over the railing and on deck even as more of the pirate crew burst from every available hatch and door.

And over the railing came a tall, thin man in a long, dark coat, a wickedly thin blade in hand. He exuded such arrogance, such authority in his simple leap, that it was obvious this was John Watling, the allegedly Pious Pirate. And yet, he had attacked on Sunday—on the Sabbath.

Chaos ensued with men and blood and black powder ruling the moment.

Smoke filled the air, causing Salazar's open eyes to burn, his ears ringing with screams and gunshots. The capitán slashed and stabbed, turning away as many stinking wretches as came at him.

Beside him, his men fell. Over their agony, he heard the birdcall once more. He turned toward the sound only to see the pirate captain's lips finish the mimicking whistle as the last of the Spanish commanders collapsed in front of him.

Salazar pulled his pistol and took careful aim at John Watling's chest.

A weight crashed into him from behind, and he slammed

to the deck, a gun pressed into his shoulder even as he removed his finger from his own pistol.

And then there was silence. His men stopped fighting, some dropping weapons, others bleeding out their lives on the deck. Before him were a pair of all-too-familiar boots and their hated silver buckles.

Garcia leaned over him, pulling his arms back and dislodging the pistol.

Salazar's hands and elbows were bound behind him, and he was hauled up to face the pirate.

With a sweep of his hand, the tall man bowed before Salazar. "Captain John Watling, at your service, sir."

Garcia didn't translate, but it was no longer needed.

In the same grand manner, the pirate hefted a large brass key from an inside coat pocket and tossed it to Garcia, who caught the key easily, weighing it in one palm. Two shabbily dressed men hauled up a chest larger than the paymaster's and dropped it at Garcia's overly decorated feet. The brass lock on the chest matched the key in his hand.

"The treaty stands," Garcia said in English. Two of Salazar's crew moved from behind to tug the chest back onto his ship.

Not *his* ship.

Not anymore.

These men were most certainly Garcia's crew. All the whispers and ceased conversations had not been out of respect for the capitán's arrival. No. Garcia had plotted, corrupting loyal seamen with promises of pirate treasures. He had planned for Salazar to fall. Perhaps before they even set sail.

Will shoved Salazar in the back, causing the capitán to fall to his knees.

A slight tremor rippled his insides once more, one last warning that he had failed to heed.

"Job well done, Will, my friend," Watling said, inspecting

the blood coating his cutlass. "Another Spanish bastard too big for his britches made to pay for the debts owed your people."

Will's grin was broad and cruel, his eyes narrowed as his lips twisted.

"But it is Sunday." Salazar's English seethed through his teeth.

Watling looked to the cloudless sky. "It is. And a fine one at that."

"You don't attack on the Sabbath."

John raised one eyebrow. "That, good sir, is true. I do not dishonor my God by shedding blood on His holy day."

Damn pirates. Salazar spat at Watling's boots. But Watling simply smiled, his gaze shifting to the man holding Salazar. From the dark, long-fingered hands gripping his arm, Salazar could guess it was Will. Garcia stood close by, holding the capitán's weapons.

"Ah, I see you are confused." Watling tucked his hands behind his back. "Let me explain. I am counted among God's people, yes. I honor His Sabbath day and many of His other commandments. But my flock are those of the Seventh Day Baptists."

When Salazar didn't react, Watling nodded his head slowly and frowned at the former capitán even as his eyes shone. "We honor the biblical seventh day as our Sabbath— and *that* is Saturday."

About the Author

Jessica Guernsey writes contemporary fantasy novels and short stories. As a slush pile reader, she is a threshold guardian for two publishers. "Sabbath" is based on her ancestor, the real Pious John Watling. She now lives on a mountain with her husband, three kids, and a codependent mini schnauzer. Connect with her on Twitter @JessGuernsey.

A Good Pirate's Final Storm

TANYA HALES

W hen Good John closed his eyes, he could nearly convince himself that the warm, humid air on his face was salty sea spray. The squawking of birds? Those were gulls swooping low over his ship, crying for scraps of fish. The voices calling excitedly over one another belonged to his crew, and that rhythmic thumping was the unfortunate peg leg of his first mate, Ill Daniels.

But then Good John opened his eyes, and the illusion disappeared. The humid air on his skin was simply how they liked to keep it here in the tropical room of the aviary. The screeching was coming from more than three dozen varieties of South American birds, from brightly colored parrots to a shimmering blue bird a worker had called a "paradise tanager." The voices bouncing around the large room belonged to what seemed like a hundred school children, here on a field trip from one of the neighborhood's fancy schools. And the rhythmic thumping? Well, that was the unfortunate sound of Good John's walker.

Despite the mild disappointment of reality, Good John felt good. He'd found an article in the local paper showing off the aviary's newest rescue animal, and he had recognized the bird immediately. He'd decided to come right away, even though he knew this would be the end.

All in all, today seemed like as good a day as any to die.

Clunk. Clunk. Good John's progress was slow as he moved down the concrete path of the indoor aviary. Much like when he had been young, people made way for him. But now it was for an entirely different reason. He was no longer sturdy and tall, thick-chested and wild-bearded. His back was bent. His hands trembled on his walker as he shuffled along. His hair was still wild, but in a thin, wispy way. His reputation no longer preceded him. Now the mothers of small children smiled kindly at him, and widowed grandmothers occasionally gave him a wink. Good John still had a look of rugged charm about him, even at his age. If only these people knew how old he really was.

Good John made his way up a ramp flanked by towering tropical plants. The floor-to-ceiling windows let in a rare ray of sunshine, and Good John paused to wipe sweat from his brow. It was no wonder they had to have such large windows to grow plants here. The Pacific Northwest had abysmally gray weather most days. Usually, that made Good John feel irritable, but on days when the wind was just right, he could stand outside and let a thrill burst like gunpowder inside of him, imagining he was sailing his ship into a storm.

Finally, after being passed up by what felt like every person in the aviary, Good John reached the second level of the tropical room and found the exhibit he was looking for—parrots. Within a netted enclosure, half a dozen large, colorful birds roosted on tree branches or nibbled at hanging toys. A large sign on the netting read: "Please don't touch. These birds may bite."

Good John had only been standing there for seconds when the bird he'd been looking for flapped over to the netting. There were no perches next to the net—probably to deter the aforementioned biting—so the bright green-and-yellow bird fluttered until it could hook its claws into the netting and cling to it. It stuck its thick, gray beak out and peered at Good John with beady eyes. It whistled appreciatively to him. "Ahoy, captain!" it squawked. "Ahoy!"

"Ahoy, Scupper," he murmured softly. "It's been a while, old friend."

The parrot flapped his wings frantically as if trying to start a gale that could rip the net clean open. Several school-children ran over excitedly to watch. One boy tried to touch Scupper through the net, but the parrot squawked low in his throat. "I bite."

The child quickly retracted his hand.

Good John laughed, holding tight to his walker to keep his

weak knees from buckling. If there'd been any doubt about whether this was really his parrot, he was certain now. "Scupper, you haven't changed a bit."

"Time for treasure?" the parrot asked, using his claws and beak to clamber excitedly up and down the net. "Time for booty?"

Good John knew exactly how the old parrot felt. He was itching for the same thing: one last voyage out onto the sea. One last chance to man a vessel and feel the ocean wind in his hair.

Good John was old. Older than any man had the right to be. He knew his time had come. His end was nigh. And now, after decades, he was finally reunited with his oldest and most trusted ally, which had been his last real goal.

But he didn't intend to cross the finish line without one more adventure. And he knew that this moment, here and now, was his one last chance to plunder.

Ignoring the children who were still watching Scupper eagerly, Good John lowered his bag from his shoulder. It was a long, thin drawstring pack. Suspiciously long and thin. The workers at the aviary's entrance hadn't so much as glanced at it when he'd entered. He wondered if they would up their security protocol after what he was about to do.

In one deft move, Good John slid his old cutlass out of the bag. The hilt felt heavy and familiar in his palm, like another old friend. It seemed like today was turning into a family reunion.

"Are you ready, Scupper?" he asked his parrot.

The bird squawked eagerly, flapping away to give him some space.

Good John unsheathed his blade and swung it, cutting cleanly through the net.

Well, perhaps "cleanly" was an exaggeration. He had to slash a few times because of his weak arms, but he was sure he still looked mighty impressive. He was the only one there with a sword, after all.

All his slashing scared the other birds to the back of the exhibit, but as soon as Scupper saw that Good John was done, he dove for the hole in the net, flying out to perch on his master's shoulder.

"Pieces of eight. Pieces of eight. Arawk!" the parrot squawked, puffing up his chest and posing for the children who were watching with mouths hanging open.

Good John smiled. Scupper had always been a performer, eager for attention and praise. It had worn off on Good John through their many years together.

He looked around at the growing crowd of schoolchildren. He felt fortunate that no parents or workers had noticed what was going on. That meant he'd have time to make this truly epic.

With a grin, Good John pulled out a black tricorn hat from his bag. It wasn't one of his original hats, of course. He had bought it from a costume shop last week, but it did feel appropriately pirate-y. He also grabbed a black eye patch and stretched the elastic to fit it over his left eye. In spite of having two decent eyes for his age, it simply was the thing to wear if Good John wanted to convince modern people of who he was.

Good John turned and tried to heft himself up onto a small retaining wall to get some height. His shaking arms refused to lift his weight. Undeterred, Good John gritted his teeth and called upon the ancient life force flowing within his veins. The holy water still lurking in his blood seemed to rise up to meet his call, caressing him like a lover and giving immediate, youthful strength to his limbs. It was the last old friend in their group today.

So little—so very little—of the precious, life-giving water was left within him. It wouldn't last the day. Not with what he had planned.

Strength renewed, and suddenly feeling half his age— which wasn't saying much—Good John pulled himself up onto the wall. There he stood and grinned roguishly at the children crowding around below, staring at him with wide, fascinated eyes. There had to be a full busload's worth of children watching now. Adults would soon take notice. He didn't have much time.

"My name is Captain Good John, feared pirate of legend and terror of the seven seas," he called out in his best pirate voice. It was a laugh, really. He'd never known a real pirate to talk like that in all his days, but it was sure to please the crowd.

Children these days practically worshiped pirates. They had no idea what pirates had really been. They thought it was all about buried treasure and gruff accents. And he adored them for it. The modern, glamorous perception of pirates helped him forget the vile things he'd done in his youth. It reminded him of what he'd tried to become in the end, of the reason other pirates had mockingly called him "Good John." No pirate wanted to be "good." Except for him. And, well, the fact that he was performing like this for a bunch of children now proved he might have succeeded.

"Are you a real pirate?" one bright-eyed girl asked.

"I am indeed, lassie!" Good John told the child, before wondering if "lassie" was even the word their version of pirates would use. "My ship terrorized the Caribbean for decades as we collected loot from every seafarer we could rob. Five hundred years ago, my crew and I chanced upon the fabled Fountain of Youth. Drank the water and then destroyed the source, says I. Did it right under the nose of Ponce de León. Poor fool never got to taste a drop."

Which had been really quite mean of them, Good John had later decided.

"Now I'm more than five centuries old. The waters of youth have kept me young all this time."

"You're not young," one boy yelled.

155

Good John examined the child. His arms were folded, a rebellious set to his jaw.

"I like the look of you, lad." Good John took off his hat and tossed it. The surprised boy caught it. "Keep the dream of treasure alive, and don't let no one tell ye what to do."

Good John squinted at a large sign by the parrot exhibit he had just looted. In big words, it read, "Meet our newest parrot!" The rest of the text was too small for Good John to make out. He motioned to the boy he'd thrown the hat to. "Lad, can ye read this sign for me? My eyes don't work as well as they used to." Good John pointed at his false eye patch, which elicited giggles from the crowd.

The boy cast him a sideways look, and, for a moment, Good John thought he would refuse, but then the boy spoke. "It says it's an Amazon parrot they recently rescued. Says he has an unusually salty vocabulary, and they estimate him to be almost fifty years old."

"Fifty?" Good John laughed. "Scupper, tell these fine children how old you are! And remember to use only tame words. Yer in tender company."

Scupper adjusted his claws, shuffling on Good John's shoulder. He cocked his head like he was considering using his saltiest pirate vocabulary just for fun, but he simply said, "Five hundred." He squawked. "And twelve."

"What?" Good John asked with a booming laugh. "Ye rascal! Yer at least five hundred and *thirty*!"

"If you're a real pirate, then have you ever met a mermaid?" the same bright-eyed girl from before asked.

"As a matter of fact, I have. Back when I was just a lad, the pirate crew I worked for captured a mermaid. They wanted to sell her at port and make a fortune, but when I saw the way she cried, it broke my heart. The night before we reached port, I cut her free of her ropes while the rest of the crew was too drunk to notice. I helped carry her to the edge of the ship, where she dove back into the sea. She never forgot what I did for her. When I became a captain, she helped me and my crew find sunken treasure time and again. She was my first love."

His *only* love. A man had to be a fool to go after another woman when a mermaid loved him. Luckily, mermaid life spans were much longer than those of humans. They'd been together for a long time.

But still not long enough. He'd been alone now for almost two centuries.

"I wish mermaids were real," the little girl in the group sighed.

Her words startled him. She was too young to stop believing in mermaids, especially when they were *real*, in spite of what science said.

"Come here, lassie," Good John told her gently. When the girl had scooted up to him through the crowd, Good John knelt down on the retaining wall to look her in the eye. His pirate accent fell away. "Don't stop believing in something just because other people say they can't see it." He reached into his pocket, pinching the familiar shape that felt like a hard jewel. Then he pressed the object into the girl's hand.

She stared down at it in wonder. She moved the teardrop-shaped mermaid scale back and forth, watching its iridescent sheen change colors in the light. Good John knew he didn't have to explain what it was.

It hurt a bit to let go of the precious memento of his lost love, but he felt at peace about the decision. It was time to say goodbye.

Looking over the heads of the children, Good John could see that his time was up. A parent stood at the bottom of the ramp, pointing at him with concern while two members of the staff stared, bewildered.

"And now I'm off!" Good John announced. "To seek fair winds and fairer fortune!"

Good John leapt down into a small gap between the children, calling on the holy water within his veins to keep his bones from shattering as he landed. The workers were coming toward him up one side of the ramp, but there was another ramp leading down on the other side of the parrots' exhibit, so he hobbled off that way. He left his walker behind.

As he moved, he called on more and more of the life-giving force within him. His legs became strong, letting him leap down the ramp, past surprised families and startled birds. He dashed past enormous jungle ferns with Scupper clinging tightly to his shoulder and letting out his squawking imitation of laughter. He burst out of the jungle room and into the aviary's main lobby.

To exit the building, visitors had to leave through the gift shop, so Good John sped past rows of stuffed narwhals and peacocks. Any other thief might have fun in this room, but he already had the only treasure he wanted.

The worker at the counter noticed Scupper clinging to Good John's shoulder and yelled, "Sir, you can't take that parrot—"

But Good John burst through the door before the young man could finish.

He ran down the sidewalk and was dashing through the large parking lot when he looked back and saw that he was indeed being pursued. At least five aviary staff members were sprinting after him, looking winded but determined. They probably thought it would be easy to catch an old man and get their parrot back. Good John grinned. He would show them.

He put on an extra burst of speed as they reached the main street. There was an opening in traffic, and he bolted across. Cars honked. He ignored them. They would be fine. Besides, jaywalking was delightfully fun at his age, and no self-respecting pirate would ever use a crosswalk.

As they reached the other side of the tree-lined street, Scupper leapt from his shoulder, taking to the air and zooming overhead with glee. Good John was sure the parrot was using his own remaining water of youth to fly with such vigor. The only thing more amazing than a five-hundred-year-old man was a five-hundred-year-old parrot.

Together they ignored the world, speeding down a dozen city blocks toward the ocean. They lost their pursuers almost immediately. Someone from the aviary staff was sure to call the police, but Good John would be long gone before anyone arrived. No one could catch him while he was burning through his last reserves like this.

The waters of youth made him feel young and strong. Invincible.

But he knew he wasn't.

Good John had outlived every member of his crew. The holy drink had made them young, after all, not immortal. A bullet between the eyes or falling overboard while drunk would still kill a magically youthful man the same as anyone. Good John had turned out to be the only man of his crew who'd had an ounce of common sense or self-preservation.

He'd been punished for that, of course. The water of youth within him had worn off slowly but steadily, leaving him feeling old two centuries ago. And the aging had only gotten worse from there. He'd long outlived his ability to be a pirate, his limbs slack and weak, his sharp senses grown dull. Strangest of all, even piracy itself had died long ago. At least piracy as it was meant to be.

Now Good John lived in a seaside city, a man too old to sail, but dreaming of nothing else.

Today, he would not be too old.

Even as he thought it, though, he could feel himself slowing. The water within him was down to mere dregs. His lungs were beginning to wheeze, his back beginning to bow painfully. Even Scupper drifted down to land on his shoulder once more, too tired and old to fly any longer.

The sky was gray with low clouds by the time Good John

reached the ocean. People milled around on the docks; most appearing to be finishing up for the day. No one wanted to be out in weather like this.

Except for Good John. The wind and ominous clouds sent a thrill through him.

The port was one of the smallest in the city, perfect for small fishing vessels and sailboats. Good John had come here hundreds of times to stare at the boats and the sea. Months ago, he'd picked out the boat he wanted to steal, if he could. And, as he'd hoped, it was docked as if waiting for him. It was a small boat, but its sails looked excellent, and the hull was designed to look like brown wood, almost like the planks of a pirate ship.

"A ship. A ship," Scupper croaked softly, and Good John realized just how tired the bird was.

"Yes. *Our* ship now," Good John agreed. He jogged down the dock, past the people leaving for the day. Not willing to lose momentum, Good John circled the boat, using his cutlass to hack through the various dock lines tying the boat in place. Before reaching the last ropes at the bow, he used another drop of precious energy to leap magnificently onto the sailboat. He stumbled, then straightened, chest swelling in pride at what was now his.

In truth, the boat was quite different from the vessels Good John had sailed in his youth, but he had spent countless hours in his apartment watching online videos about how these modern boats worked. With only a little difficulty, he started the engine, making the boat roar to life in a most unpleasant way. Motors were useful, but not proper at all.

Before moving the boat forward, Good John used his cutlass to slice through the last ropes tying them to the dock. With those immensely satisfying and pirate-y acts complete, he was off. Someone called out from the docks, but the stranger was incapable of stopping him as his new ship rumbled away into the choppy waves.

Grimacing at the noisy rumbling of the motor, Good John soon got to work on the sails. He knew people would be after him, in spite of the storm, so he did his best to stay steady as he untied, unfurled, connected, and pulled until the sails stood proud and tall. Then he angled the boat just right and cut the engine. The wind yanked the sailboat out to sea.

The rocking boat nearly knocked Good John's legs out from under him. He trembled and swayed, feeling for the first time utterly infirm. There was only one drop of the water of youth left inside of him. How long would it last? Hours? Minutes?

Well, he was going to enjoy this.

Things were going to go right this time.

Nearly fifty years ago, he had tried this same thing. He'd decided he and Scupper had gone long enough without being proper pirates, so they'd stolen a boat and gone sailing into a storm, laughing it up. Only, when the storm had engulfed them, Good John had found himself suddenly afraid. He'd lived so long; was he really ready to die? He'd frantically steered his boat back toward land, only for it to capsize near the shore. He'd woken up in the hospital, injured and facing an impending court trial for his crimes. But the judge had gone easy on him. What else would a judge do when the accused looked to be in his nineties? But Good John had been punished with something far worse than jail time.

Scupper was gone. Blown away by the storm that Good John had been too scared to face.

But finally they were together again. And this time Good John was not afraid.

Gripping the boat's railing, he filled his vision with the stormy horizon. With that as his focus, he could almost imagine he was back on his own ship, his crew scrambling to prepare for the squall while Good John stared the storm in the eye.

"Do your worst!" he screamed into the gale as the wind

whipped through his wispy hair. Water splashed onto his knobby knuckles and hollow cheeks. He tasted salt as it dripped down his face. The taste of home.

He felt his own strength failing at the same time Scupper slipped from his shoulder. He caught the large bird and held him close as the parrot took his last, rattling breaths. Without his grip on the rail, the rocking boat knocked Good John clean off his feet, and he found himself on his back, eyes to the stormy sky.

The clouds billowed and churned, somehow both hostile and inviting. Perhaps they were accepting his challenge. A thrill burst like gunpowder inside of him. He cradled Scupper to his chest and felt the rocking of the boat. Even as his body failed him, he finally—finally—felt young again.

Good John closed his eyes. There was nowhere he would rather be.

About the Author

When Tanya Hales was a baby, she enjoyed books by chewing them to pieces before eventually moving on to the higher art of reading. Tanya splits her time between her work as a writer, an illustrator, and a mother, all of which she loves intensely. She now lives in the Utah Valley with her family, daydreaming constantly about imaginary worlds.

Percival Bunnyrabbit and the Robot Wizard

JOHN D. PAYNE

D eep in the Regular Forest, there is a tree that is bigger than all the rest. Also, it is magic. This is the home of a bunny rabbit who is strong and brave and kind and good. His name is Percival. He is a hero. He helps people, and he finds things.

One sunny day, he was in his bedroom trying to find his favorite carrot-shaped flashlight. He thought it was under the bed, but he couldn't see, so he was feeling around with his paws. He didn't find his flashlight, but he did find a pencil. It was magic.

Percival knew the pencil was magic because it wrote, all by itself, *Help! Someone Stole Me from the Robot Wizard*. Also, the pencil had sparkly glow-in-the-dark shooting stars on it and a rainbow eraser.

"Don't be scared," Percival told the pencil. "I am a hero. I help people. Where is the Robot Wizard? Tell me, and I will take you to him."

The Robot Wizard Is Lost, the pencil wrote. Then it drew a sad face.

"I will find him," said Percival. "I am very good at finding."

That reminded him about his lost flashlight, so he looked under the bed one more time and found it under some under-pants. Then he turned the flashlight on to look under the bed and in the closet and all around. He found lots of interesting things, but no robots. Or wizards.

So he zipped up the pencil in his backpack and went down to the lake to do some more looking. And finding. He also brought two magic eggs, some peanut butter celery in a lunch box, and his spyglass and pirate sword.

Percival loved the lake. It was cool and dark and so big he could not see the other side. But he had sailed across it many times with his friends, Wally the frog and his sister, Eagle. (She was also a frog.) Percival had found them in the stream when they were very tiny, but now they were all grown up and had a tall sailing ship. It was tied up at the dock.

"Hello, Wally. Hello, Eagle. I found a magic pencil." Percival took it out of his backpack and showed it to them. "Do you know anything about a robot wizard?"

"No," said Wally the frog.

"No," said his sister, Eagle. (Who was also a frog.)

"Yes," said Abdul the Ladybug Pirate. Abdul the Ladybug Pirate used to have his own ship, but it had been sunk by the Wicked Pirate Cats, so now he sailed with Wally and Eagle.

"Where is the Robot Wizard?" Percival asked. "This magic pencil wants me to help find him."

"I don't know," said Abdul the Ladybug Pirate. "The last time I saw him, we were playing hide-and-seek. He went and hid, and I never found him."

"Oh," Percival said. "Was that yesterday?"

"No. That was two hundred years ago."

"That is a very long time ago. I didn't know ladybug pirates lived that long."

"I am very good at living."

Percival thought maybe Abdul the Ladybug Pirate was not telling the truth. "Are you telling me a joke?" Sometimes he liked to joke.

"It is not a joke," Abdul said. "I will help you find the Robot Wizard, but only if you give me that magic pencil."

"No," said Percival. "It's mine. I found it under my bed."

"I had a magic pencil," Abdul the Ladybug Pirate said. "But I lost it. I think I lost it by a bed."

Percival frowned.

"You have never been to his house," Wally said.

"You told us," said Eagle, his sister. "Yesterday. You said you were mad because he invites us to play at his house, but not you."

"I am not talking to you," Abdul the Ladybug Pirate said.

"I am talking to my friend Percival about the pencil he found. What color is it?"

Percival looked at the pencil. "Black with sparkly glow-in-the-dark shooting stars and a rainbow eraser."

"Mine was also like that. I really think that's it. May I hold it, please?"

"No," said Percival. "I think you are telling me another joke."

"That is not a funny joke," Eagle said.

"It is a little bit funny," said Wally.

Abdul the Ladybug Pirate said, "You can keep my pencil. But if you want me to help you find the Robot Wizard, then you need to help me find another sailing ship so I can be a pirate again. Wally and Eagle don't let me sink any ships."

"Pirates are bad," Percival said. "They hurt people, and they steal."

"I like stealing," said Abdul the Ladybug Pirate. "It's fun."

"No," said Percival. "It's bad."

"Stealing is not nice," said Wally.

"We don't steal," said his sister, Eagle.

"Well, I like it," Abdul the Ladybug Pirate said. "What if I promise to only steal from other pirates?"

Percival wasn't sure about that.

"There are a lot of pirates on the lake," said Wally.

"They are very mean," said his sister, Eagle. "Especially the Wicked Pirate Cats. We always fight them when we see them, because they are bad guys."

"I always fight bad guys, too," Percival said. "I'm very strong. I'm a hero."

"Us, too," said Wally and Eagle.

"Me, too," said Abdul the Ladybug Pirate. "I will be a hero pirate who only fights bad pirates."

Percival thought about that for a while and decided it sounded all right. "Okay. If we find another sailing ship while we are looking for the Robot Wizard, you can have it."

"And if we find any treasure, I can have that," Abdul said.

"Maybe," Percival said. He was not sure if taking treasure was a thing that a good-guy hero would do. It sounded more like what a bad-guy pirate would do. "First, why don't you tell me where you were playing hide-and-seek."

"It was by a tree."

"That is not much help."

"The tree was on a cliff."

"Where was the cliff?"

"By the lake. Somewhere. I think."

Percival thought very hard. The lake was very big. Sailing around looking for cliffs might take a long time, and he only had enough peanut butter celery for one lunch. "Wally and Eagle, can you draw a map of the lake?"

"We can try," said Wally. "I have some special drawing paper here. Look! It has crisscross lines."

"Can we borrow your pencil?" asked his sister, Eagle.

Percival handed the sparkly magic pencil to Eagle, and she put it on her brother Wally's paper so she could draw the map. But then the pencil hopped out of her hands and drew a map all by itself.

"Wow!" said Wally.

"Amazing," said Eagle.

"That is definitely my pencil," said Abdul the Ladybug Pirate.

Percival was mad. He didn't want anyone to take his new pencil that he'd found under his very own bed. But then he remembered that maybe Abdul was joking, so he wasn't so mad. He even laughed a little bit.

When the pencil was done, there was a beautiful map of the lake drawn on Wally's crisscross paper. Percival saw the dock, the little stream and the big river, and even the sunken castle where the mer-family lived.

There was also an island on the map. It was a very pokey island that poked up high out of the water. It had a big tall cliff with a tree on top. And next to the tree there was an X.

"Is the X where you played hide-and-seek?" Percival asked.

"I think so," Abdul the Ladybug Pirate said.

"Then maybe we will find the Robot Wizard there." That made Percival happy. He liked finding people who were lost. Also, he really wanted to meet a robot. And a wizard. And he especially wanted to meet a robot wizard. Maybe he would have a big hat.

"That's right next to Pirate Cat Island," said Wally.

"There will be lots of mean pirate cats," said his sister, Eagle. "We will have to fight them, because they are bad guys."

"And I can take their ship!" said Abdul the Ladybug Pirate.

So they set sail on Wally and Eagle's ship, following the map. Percival sat on the deck and ate his peanut butter celery. He offered some to the frogs, but it was not frog food so they said no thank you. Percival was glad. He was very hungry.

They sailed past the mouth of the stream where Percival had found Wally and Eagle when they had been tiny. They sailed past the mouth of the big river that divided the Regular Forest from the Other Forest. They sailed out into the lake, far out, so far they almost reached the sunken castle where the mer-family lived.

Then they saw three islands. One was very small. Abdul the Ladybug Pirate said that was Ladybug Island, where all his brothers and sisters and aunts and uncles and cousins lived.

One was big. Wally and Eagle said that was Pirate Cat Island. With his spyglass, Percival could see the stone fortress from which he had rescued Grandmother Mouse and the sewing machine she used to make hero costumes and cozy warm quilts.

In between the big island and the very small island was a

medium island. It had a tall, pokey mountain that reached high into the sky. It looked like a pointy wizard hat. And at the tippy-top of the pointy-hat mountain, there was a tree growing next to the edge of a cliff. Percival shared his spyglass with the others, so they could see.

"That's it!" said Abdul the Ladybug Pirate. "That's the tree where we were playing hide-and-seek."

"There is a harbor at the bottom of the cliff where we can anchor the ship," said Wally the frog.

"But there is a Pirate Cat ship anchored there right now," said Eagle.

"Let's fight them!" Percival cried, drawing his pirate sword.

Abdul the Ladybug Pirate looked through the spyglass. "I count thirteen Wicked Pirate Cats. There are only four of us."

Percival thought about that. Thirteen was a lot. Then he remembered he had brought two magic eggs with him. He pulled one out of his backpack and looked at it. It was silver with a black paw print on one side and a picture of a gold windup key on the other side.

"Oh!" Percival said. "This is a windup puppy dog egg." He opened the egg, and inside there was a little gold key and a silver clockwork puppy with a keyhole on the back. He put the key in the hole and turned it around several times, which made a fun clicking noise. When he let go, the clockwork puppy rattled across the deck of the ship and barked a very noisy bark.

"Wow!" said Wally. "That is cool."

"Aw," said Eagle. "That is so sweet."

"Hmm," said Abdul the Ladybug Pirate. "I see you found my clockwork puppy as well."

"That is a good joke," Percival said. "But it is for you."

"It is?"

"I want you to fly over to the Pirate Cat ship and drop it on their deck. Cats are scared of dogs. They will run away."

"There is nowhere for them to run," Eagle said.

"Except the water," Wally said. "And cats hate the water."

Abdul the Ladybug Pirate shook his head. "I don't think this will work. The Wicked Pirate Cats will kick my puppy over the side of the boat. And then he will be lost again."

"I think it will work," Percival said. "The Pirate Cats will jump over the side of the boat to get away from the puppy. Then you will have a puppy *and* a ship."

"Hmm." Abdul the Ladybug Pirate looked through the spyglass again. "It would be nice to have my ship back." He gave the spyglass to Percival. "Can you hold this for me while I fly?"

"Of course."

"You must be careful with it," said Abdul. "It is my favorite spyglass." Then he picked up the puppy, opened up his shell, and unfolded his big ladybug wings. With a buzz, he flew up into the air and over toward the Wicked Pirate Cats.

"Follow that ladybug!" Percival shouted, and he pointed with his sword.

"Aye aye, sir!" said Wally and Eagle together. And soon they were sailing straight for the Pirate Cat ship.

Percival watched through the spyglass as Abdul dropped the barking clockwork puppy onto the deck of the Pirate Cat ship. Every cat in sight turned immediately toward the puppy, hissing and puffing out their fur to try to look bigger.

But the clockwork puppy was not scared. It couldn't be, because clockwork toys don't get scared. It just kept rattling around the deck of the ship, barking and barking with a very loud voice.

Some of the Wicked Pirate Cats were so scared that they jumped overboard into the water. As their ship got closer, Percival could hear the cats in the water meowing very unhappily about their fur getting wet and about how cold the lake water was.

But some of the cats stayed on the ship. One of them, who

wore a big black pirate hat, was waving a sword at the others and meowing at them to attack the windup puppy. The other cats complained, but they followed his orders.

That must be their captain, thought Percival. He made sure his sword was ready for fighting.

The clockwork puppy's barks got softer, and its rattling walk got slower. It was winding down, and the Pirate Cats were getting braver. And closer.

Suddenly, there was a buzzing of ladybug wings. "Leave my puppy alone!" cried Abdul, and he flew into the middle of the cats, waving his own tiny sword around, trying to shoo them away. But he was only one little ladybug, and they hissed and swatted at him, trying to knock him out of the air.

And because all the Wicked Pirate Cats were so busy with Abdul and the clockwork puppy, none of them saw Wally and Eagle's ship sail right up alongside their own. So they were taken completely by surprise when Percival came riding in on the boom, crashing right into the middle of the Pirate Cats and knocking two of them into the water.

"That's what you get," Percival shouted, "for being wicked pirates!" Then he kicked another cat in the water with his big, strong rabbit feet.

Wally and Eagle threw grappling hooks to bring the two ships together, and then jumped into the fight behind Percival. They carried belaying pins in each hand—heavy wooden clubs used to help secure the ropes on sailing ships.

And the Pirate Cats soon discovered the brother and sister both hid more weapons in their big, froggy mouths. They mewed in pain whenever the frogs' long, sticky tongues shot out and smacked a cat in the face with one of the heavy wooden pins.

Percival and his friends were outnumbered, but they fought hard. Even Abdul fought, zipping around and poking Wicked Pirate Cats everywhere with his tiny little sword.

The Pirate Cat Captain charged in to attack Percival,

slicing and slashing with the fanciest sword Percival had ever seen. It was decorated with gold and silver and jewels all over, and for a moment Percival was actually a little bit embarrassed that his own sword was so plain.

But his sword was also very strong. And Percival was very fast. With a few quick strokes, Percival disarmed the Pirate Cat Captain and sent his fancy sword flying through the air, tumbling end over end until it splashed into the water and sank down, down, down to the bottom of the lake.

"No!" cried Abdul the Ladybug Pirate. "My favorite sword!"

The Wicked Pirate Cats were defeated, and now they were all in the water, mewing miserably and sneezing. All of them promised to be good if Percival would just let them back on the ship. He felt a bit sorry for them, treading water in that cold lake, but he didn't think they would keep their promise.

"I know!" Percival said. "We can give the cats a dinghy!" A dinghy was a little boat carried by a big ship to use for small trips. Wally and Eagle's ship carried a dinghy. So did the Pirate Cats' ship.

"They can't have mine," said Abdul the Ladybug Pirate. "I need it."

"They can have ours," said Wally.

"But they will be crowded," said his sister, Eagle. "It's not very big. Look." She pointed.

"Hmm," Abdul said. "My ship used to have two dinghies, but one is missing. This one looks quite a bit like the one I lost."

"No," Percival said, feeling cross. "That is not yours. It's Wally and Eagle's, and they are giving it to the cats, so they don't have to swim all the way back to Pirate Cat Island."

The cats hissed and meowed quite a few complaints about how the dinghy was too small and how they all hated rowing. But in the end, they all got aboard and set off back to their home port.

"I think we had better follow them," Wally said.

"In case they get into any trouble," Eagle said. "Or up to any trouble."

"Good idea," said Percival. "We will be fine here. Abdul will show me where the Robot Wizard is, and I will save him. And give him back his pencil."

Abdul did not look happy about that last part, but for once he minded his manners and didn't try to claim the pencil as his own. That made Percival happy, because he thought that Abdul might be learning that it was not nice to take other people's things.

"You are sure you will be okay?" Wally asked.

"This is a very big ship for one bunny rabbit and one ladybug to sail alone," said Eagle.

"Ladybug Island is close by," Abdul said. "I will call my brothers and sisters and aunts and uncles and cousins. There will be plenty of ladybugs to help sail my new pirate ship."

"*Privateer* ship," Percival corrected him. "Remember, that is the word for good pirates."

"Then I am a privateer," Abdul said. "Because I am definitely a good pirate. A very, very good pirate."

Wally and Eagle said goodbye and sailed away after the dinghy full of Wicked Pirate Cats. Percival and Abdul waved farewell and watched their ship get smaller and smaller. Then they turned to look at the cliff looming above them.

Percival pointed to the very top, where he could see a little tree growing. "You are sure that's where you last saw the Robot Wizard?"

"Yes." Abdul opened up his shell and stretched out his ladybug wings. "And you are sure you are ready to fly up there?"

"No," Percival said. "Bunny rabbits are very good jumpers, but we don't fly."

"Oh. Then maybe you should give me the pencil, and I will take it up myself."

This did not sound like a great idea to Percival, but he wasn't sure how to get up the cliff. It was very tall and very steep. He wasn't sure he could climb it. Then he remembered his second magic egg.

He opened his backpack and looked inside. His last egg was dark brown with orange-and-yellow stripes. It was soft and poofy and had a valve on the bottom. And on the very top, there was a tiny propeller.

"Oh!" Percival cried happily. "This is an inflatable heli-copter egg!" He popped the cap off the valve and began to blow it up. In no time, the little egg-copter was inflated and ready to fly. Percival hopped in.

"That is a very nice helicopter," said Abdul.

"Does it look like one you lost?" Percival asked.

Abdul laughed. "Don't be silly. Why would a ladybug have a helicopter?"

The two of them flew up to the top of the cliff. It was very high. They could see all of the rest of Hat Mountain Island, as well as Ladybug Island to the south and Pirate Cat Island to the north. With his spyglass, Percival found the dinghy full of cats, with Wally and Eagle's sailing ship following behind.

"Good!" Percival said. "Now all we have to do is find the Robot Wizard."

"That will be tough," said Abdul. "Wizards are very good at hide-and-seek."

"Well, heroes are very good at seeking," Percival said. "And I am a hero. And so are you, now."

Abdul grinned at that, and they both started looking. It didn't take them long before they had looked everywhere on the cliff top.

"Maybe he went somewhere else?" Abdul wondered.

"No." Percival held up the map. "This is where the magic pencil drew the X."

"Well, all I found were my old boots," said Abdul. He pointed at a very large pair of boots that were poking out of the ground, upside down, under the tree. Abdul was standing on top of one of the soles. "I've been wondering where I left them."

"Wait," said Percival. "Those look like wizard boots. Can you please move so I can pull them up?"

Abdul flew to one of the branches of the tree. "I don't think they look like wizard boots at all. I think they look like ladybug boots. But I do thank you for pulling them out of the ground for me."

Percival grabbed on to one boot with each hand and pulled with all his might. Nothing happened. He took a deep breath and tried again. He was big and strong (and brave and good), but it was useless. The boots would not come out of the ground.

It was so disappointing, Percival almost wanted to cry. But then he had a thought.

"I know," said Percival. "I'll dig them out!" And with his powerful legs, and his strong digging claws, he started to dig and dig and dig. Dirt and rocks went flying everywhere. In no time, he saw there were legs sticking into the boots.

"Who is that?" he wondered out loud.

"Go away, beep beep!" said a muffled voice from inside the dirt. "I am playing hide-and-seek."

"Are you the Robot Wizard?"

"Yes, boop beep, but right now I am hiding. So unless you are Abdul the Ladybug Pirate, beep bo boop bo beep, then please go away and let me keep playing my game. I am winning!"

"Well," said Percival, "as it turns out, Abdul the Ladybug Pirate is here. Except now he is a good-guy privateer instead of a wicked pirate."

"Beep bop boap. All right, then," said the Robot Wizard. "If he has found me, then it is his turn to hide and my turn to seek. Help me out."

So Percival did. He dug and pulled and pulled and dug

until the Robot Wizard popped right out of the ground like a nice fat carrot. Except that instead of being small and orange, he was big and shiny, with lots of dials and colored buttons that lit up.

"Hello, beep beep! I am the Robot Wizard."

"My name is Percival. And I think you remember Abdul."

The Robot Wizard frowned. "The Abdul I knew was a ladybug. Beep. You are pointing to a tree branch."

Percival started to tell the Robot Wizard that Abdul was the ladybug who was sitting on the tree branch. But then he looked closer and saw that the branch was empty. He looked all around the cliff top, but Abdul was gone. And so was Percival's inflatable egg-copter.

Percival ran to the edge of the cliff and looked down to the harbor. The Pirate Cats' ship was sailing away.

He opened his backpack and got out his spyglass. With it, he could see hundreds of cute little ladybugs crawling all over the ship's ropes and rigging. Many of them wearing cute eye patches or little pegs at the end of one or two of their six legs.

And at the wheel stood Abdul the Ladybug Pirate, using Percival's inflatable egg-copter as a stool. He waved up at Percival and turned the ship's wheel.

"Where are you going?" shouted Percival.

"I can't hear you," Abdul the Ladybug Pirate shouted back. "But thank you for finding my inflatable egg-copter."

Percival frowned. "That is mine!" he shouted. "And you should not be stealing! Stealing is not nice!"

"I can't hear you," Abdul called back again. "Also, it is definitely mine and not yours. Goodbye, Percival!" Then the ship's sails caught the wind, and Abdul and his ladybug pirate crew sailed away.

Percival threw a rock at the ship, but it was quite far off and so he missed. He went and sat down on the ground by the Robot Wizard.

"Has he already gone to hide?" the Robot Wizard asked.

He had not noticed that anything was wrong. "This will be so much fun. I love seeking, bippity bippity beep!"

"He has gone," Percival said. "But I don't think he is playing your game anymore."

"Oh," the Robot Wizard sighed. "Boop boop boop. That is too bad. I do love seeking."

"Me, too," said Percival. "That's why I came here. I was seeking you." He took the magic pencil out of his backpack and handed it to the Robot Wizard. "I found this under my bed, and it said I should find you. So I did."

"Thank you, boop bop. That was good finding." The wizard took the pencil and stuck it into an empty socket on one of his hands where a finger would go. "Say, would you like to play with me? I know you're good at finding, beep, but are you good at hiding?"

"Very good," said Percival. He looked around. "Although there are not very many good places to hide up here." Also, he was getting quite hungry again, and he had already eaten all his peanut butter celery.

"Hmm, beep beep," the Robot Wizard said. "How about this? You can borrow my boots. They are rocket boots and can fly for miles and miles. Then you could go anywhere to hide!"

"Wow!" Percival jumped up. "Rocket boots? That would be awesome!"

The Robot Wizard smiled and took off his boots. Percival didn't think they would fit, because bunny rabbits have very big feet. Even bigger than robots. Or wizards. But these were magic boots, so they fit perfectly.

Percival made sure his backpack was all zipped up and strapped on tight. Then he reached down and flipped the ON switch. The rocket boots roared to life, and Percival Bunnyrabbit shot into the sky, rising on bright hot columns of smoke and flame.

"Goodbye! Beep bo peep peep boop!" called the Robot Wizard, waving his arms and flashing all his lights. "I'll close my eyes and count to twenty million. Then I'm coming to find you, beep bee-deep!"

Percival waved goodbye and blasted away, leaving Hat Mountain Island far behind him. He skimmed so low he could feel the spray of the water. He soared so high he could touch the clouds. Faster than all the sailing ships, faster even than the birds. Rocket boots sure were fun!

As the sun began to set, it started to get cold, and Percival started to wonder where he should go to hide. There were so many good places! The mer-family's sunken castle. The fairy flower garden. The secret underground base of the steely-eyed missile mice.

But then his tummy rumbled, and he wondered if maybe he could hide in his own kitchen, with some nice crunchy cucumbers or some sweet, delicious snap peas. It would be warm there, in his tree house. Even warmer in his very own bed, with his blankets pulled up to his chin.

And so he turned and rocketed to the docks, and from there to his home. He had some dinner, and a bath, and then he read stories in bed with his carrot-shaped flashlight until his eyes got so heavy and sleepy that he just couldn't keep them open any more. And he slept all night in his bed until the sun found him in the morning.

When he woke up, he switched off his flashlight, rolled it under his bed, and slipped the rocket boots on right over his pajama pants.

"Where shall we go today? And what shall we find there?" he asked himself, and he opened up his window. "Maybe ... adventures."

About the Author

John D. Payne lives at the foot of the Organ Mountains in New Mexico, where his children are delighted to watch bunny rabbits devour everything in the yard but the cactus. John's debut novel, *The Crown and the Dragon*, is an epic fantasy from WordFire Press. His stories have been published in magazines (*StoryHack*) and anthologies (*Cursed Collectibles* and *A Mighty Fortress: Being an Anthology of Mormon Steampunk*). For updates and more, find him at patreon.com/johndpayne or @jdp_writes.

Plundering Lives

LAUREN LANG

The echoes of a thousand empty apologies ring through the church. The vaulted ceiling seems designed to catch them. The words have been trapped and held between the peeling paint and the dingy floor tiles for years, bouncing from doomed person to doomed person.

"I'm sorry, there's nothing we can do," the cardiologist tells me. His eyes are devoid of emotion as he intones the phrase, adding yet another voice to the chorus of despair singing through the walls. It's as if repeatedly pronouncing a death sentence has killed him, too. His body just hasn't recognized his soul is gone yet.

If there was any hint of a spark in his eyes, I might be willing to leave my fate to medical science—researchers are supposedly close to finding a new treatment—but hope left this man long ago. He doesn't believe he'll see me again. He's had too many patients like me walk out and never return. We both know my heart won't hold out long enough for a follow-up appointment.

I remember when hospitals were clean, bright places where people went expecting to get better. None of that is reflected in the building I'm in now. Like so many of the recently opened hospitals, this one is located in a converted church in a sketchy area of town. Society has fled religion, realizing that prayer won't save them from the Cyto virus. The buildings were better utilized as treatment facilities than houses of worship for a God that couldn't give us a miracle.

I turn and walk away wordlessly just to prove I can. I may or may not hear the sound of the doctor's sob being choked back. I can't be sure.

Fifty years ago, no one even knew what Cytomegalovirus was, not until it started to mutate. In the beginning, most healthy adults who contracted it were asymptomatic. Those that weren't sought treatment for chest pain and difficulty breathing. It was rare to die from it as the infection could be treated by antibiotics.

LAUREN LANG

Then, Cyto adapted. Within a few years, the virus became resistant to all known medications and turned deadly. The current form inflames the heart, causing irreversible damage to the organ.

I shake my head just thinking about it, trying to make my panting look like a sigh.

The phrase "organ pirates" didn't exist before this latest incarnation of the disease. Pausing to rest, I look up and glance around the room. The flaking plaster is covered with posters warning of the new dangers that await me. I'm a target now, the signs assure me. My heart may be useless, but the virus doesn't affect my kidneys, liver, pancreas, or corneas —all of which are worth a great deal on the black market.

Organ donation rates have never been high, but they've fallen to historically low levels since the virus turned deadly. With no treatments and relatively little that can be done to make the person comfortable, most victims are choosing to die at home, which means doctors don't get to the organs in time to save them for transplant, even when there is a donor. It's turned people desperate for a kidney into criminals willing to pay pirates to kidnap Cyto victims and harvest their innards before the virus kills them.

Medical facilities like this one have become a target where pirates prey on their victims, hence the wallpaper warning. I start shuffling forward again, determined to get all the way to the parking area on my own power despite the dangers.

I should heed the warnings and go home, where I can waste away in relative peace, but I can't stand the thought of my silent, empty apartment. I'm not ready to be alone with the thought of my own demise or admit the part I played in how I got to such a lonely place. It's better to be surrounded by familiar faces, even if they aren't always friendly, so that's where I'm going.

Gilly's is only a mile from the facility. Before I contracted Cyto, I would have walked. That's impossible now. My bullheaded decision to avoid the automated walkway to leave the facility is physically painful. I struggle on, panting and wheezing my way the last hundred feet to my Autonocar. I dig through my pocket, desperately looking for the fob that will unlock the vehicle. I find it and press my thumb into the bio reader's depression just before I collapse. Holding onto the door for balance, I manage to pull myself inside. The door shuts automatically, and I melt into the seat, allowing the safety of the vehicle to enclose me.

My legs start to shake as I sit, and they keep shaking as I program in the destination. It feels as if a vise is squeezing the air out of my lungs. I dial up the oxygen level on the atmospheric controls in the car and try to slow my breathing. My wrist itches where my white patient identification band rubs the skin. I tear the bracelet off, cracking the window and throwing it out onto the pavement before rolling the glass up. I lean back into my seat, needing to rest before I can work up the energy to start the car.

It's several minutes before the pain in my chest subsides and I'm able to inhale somewhat normally. I still have the fob clutched in my white-knuckled hands, and slowly, I force my fingers to uncurl. I hold the device up to the starter on the dashboard. The vehicle hums to life and begins driving itself to my favorite haunt.

By the time I reach Gilly's, I'm only slightly pale, as evidenced by a quick glance in the mirror, but the bar hasn't installed an automated walkway yet. I wasn't worried about their noncompliance a few weeks ago. I understand the fervor around disability access now. As I pull my exhausted body from the car, I curse the tavern's stubbornness between each labored breath.

I was one of those who said society shouldn't have to kowtow to people sick with Cyto. After all, they only live a few weeks after becoming ill, and it's not like they can go out in public when they're in the late stages of heart failure. Why should we all have to change our lives and our businesses to accommodate their last few days?

Staggering into the bar and finding my favorite stool, I realize how asinine my argument was. It lacked empathy, something I could use right now.

"Haven't seen you in a few days," Daniel, the bartender, says, absentmindedly turning to me while polishing a glass. His hands pause in the task as he looks up and catches sight of my pasty complexion. "You don't look so good."

I laugh. It's more of a wheezing cough than a real chuckle, but it's the best I can manage. "Bourbon, neat," I hiss out between gasps.

Daniel sets down the glass, but I can tell he's unsettled by my appearance. He keeps glancing over at me furtively, and he's making nervous conversation as he moves toward the liquor.

"Top-shelf or well today?" he asks, as if he doesn't already know the answer. I've been coming here for years.

"Top-shelf," I answer, just to throw him off. I might as well have a little fun before I die, and Daniel is making himself way too easy to harass.

"You got the flu or something, man?" He continues pressing me as he pours the drink. "You know I can't afford to get sick. I don't work, I don't get paid."

"You don't have to worry about catching anything from me," I say, snickering. "Unless you want me to plant a big wet one on you, I can't give it to you."

"I'll pass on that, thanks," Daniel replies. His nervousness seems to be settling. "Seriously though, what's wrong with you? You really do look terrible. Have you seen a doctor?"

"Just came from the hospital. Why do you think I need the drink?" I reply as Daniel slides my beverage across the bar. I take a long gulp, draining the liquid. I slam the glass down when I'm finished.

"You want another one?"

"Just keep them coming," I order him, hunching into my customary position. The alcohol is warm in my stomach, and I can feel the sweet liquor beginning to spread through my system, calming me down. Drowning my sorrows seems as good a use of the little time I have left as any.

"Why don't you let me get the next round?" a strange man's voice says from behind me. I struggle to place his accent as he continues speaking. "You look like you could use a friend."

I spin the stool gently toward him as he settles next to me. He must have just walked in. I've never seen his shaggy brown hair and distinctive face before. The long, thin, white scar running down his cheek is memorable. I would recognize him.

"Thanks," I say, trying to keep the suspicion out of my voice. "I don't think I caught your name."

"How rude of me. I'm Cruise Moore," he says, extending his hand with a friendly smile.

"Zane Campbell. No relation to the soup company."

"That's funny." Cruise releases his grip and turns back toward the bar.

"I don't think I've seen you here before." It's my pathetic attempt at trying to break the ice.

"I'm not from around here. I kind of go wherever the wind takes me," Cruise replies nonchalantly.

Daniel brings the beverages over, and we sip in peace for several minutes, looking at nothing in particular.

"So where are you from, Cruise?" I finally ask. Silent comradery can only last so long when you're sitting with a stranger, even with a free drink in your hand.

"Up north," he says without much enthusiasm.

"North like Wisconsin or Minnesota?" I prod, struggling to pry out some details I can use to make conversation with the man. "You must be used to our cold winters then. Chicago's windy weather must not faze you."

"No," Cruise says with a smile, "I'm used to much colder than this."

"And what do you do for a living, Cruise?" I say, defaulting to the age-old introductory questions adults ask one another.

"You know—a little bit of this, a little bit of that," he says vaguely.

"Well, it must be nice to have a job that leaves you free to drink on a Tuesday afternoon," I say, failing to keep the suspicion from my voice this time. I haven't had enough booze yet to forget the warnings at the clinic, and Moore's appearance is a little too convenient for my liking. His hazy answers don't inspire confidence either.

"What's your excuse?" Cruise responds. "It's not like this place is somewhere you'd be meeting clients." He gestures to the dark room. The once-proud establishment has fallen into disrepair, just like the neighborhood. The dark wood of the bar was once polished to a high shine, but a layer of dust has left it dull and dirty. Many of the light bulbs in the fixtures have gone out, and no one has bothered to change them. The floor is sticky with God only knows what, and despite Daniel's efforts, most of the drinks are served in water-spotted glasses.

"Me?" I say, returning my attention to the conversation. "I'm busy dying, but I suspect you already knew that. I'm not the first Cyto-infected person you've seen, am I?"

"I may have met a few," Cruise admits. "But usually not like this." He raises his glass to me in a mock toast. "You've got to be one of the sadder victims I've ever encountered. Why aren't you at home? Let me guess, nobody there to take care of you? Can't stand the thought of dying alone, so you'd rather waste away in a bar?" He downs the last of the bourbon as I look on, my face heating up with anger.

"That plan's been working for me so far," I spit back. "I see no reason why Cyto should change that." The vehemence I use to hurl the words at Cruise makes me gasp for air.

"You're right," Cruise says. "*You* should be the one to change things."

"How?" I answer incredulously. "By coming with you willingly so you can profit off my demise? You get rich, and I get dead. I don't think so, pirate."

"I suppose I should save my arguments about helping other sick people with the organs you're not going to be needing shortly," Cruise says, frustrated. "I can see the idea of doing something worthwhile with your life isn't going to appeal to you."

"Drop the do-gooder act. I don't believe it for a second," I say, beginning to cough violently. It feels as if there's a band around my chest, keeping me from getting enough oxygen.

"You really believe this is an act—" Cruise starts, but Daniel chooses this moment to interject, approaching us as I continue to hack.

The coughing fit has me squinting my eyes so hard they're tearing, which makes it difficult to shoot daggers at the pirate, but I'm trying. I've been so focused on Cruise I haven't been paying attention to the bartender, but Daniel must have been listening. It would have been hard for him to ignore us. We're the only two patrons in the bar.

"I'm really not comfortable with this—" Daniel starts, but Cruise isn't having it.

"Don't worry, you'll get your piece of the action in exchange for your silence," the pirate assures him, never taking his eyes off me. "Mr. Campbell, your Autonocar fob, please."

"What?" I wheeze out between coughs. Another violent fit wracks my body, and it's some time before I can respond again. I'm more concerned with keeping my lungs inside my chest than making sure my vehicle remains in the parking lot, but the suggestion I would willingly hand over the key is just absurd enough to be shocking. "You're stealing my car?" I demand when I'm finally able to speak.

"No, you're giving it to your friend, the bartender. You're feeling especially generous today because you have an incurable disease that's killing you. You won't be needing the expensive gray Autonocar parked out back to get home," Cruise says, winking at Daniel, "because you aren't going back to whatever sad little hole you thought you were going to crawl into and die. You're coming with us."

Cruise's words must have been some kind of signal because two large men choose this moment to cross the threshold into Gilly's. They're tall, muscular, and definitely not individuals I would want to meet in a dark alley on my best day. The dark-skinned man has tribal tattoos wrapping all the way down his arms, even though ink hasn't been fashionable in years. His lighter-skinned compatriot has close-cropped hair and is vaguely military in his bearing. Neither one smiles as they cross the room to stand behind Cruise. They aren't taking any pleasure in this.

"Fine," I say, taking the fob out of my pocket and slamming it on the bar. It's obvious I can't fight one of them, much less all three. They have me.

"Sign it over to him," Cruise insists, gesturing at Daniel. "The fob is useless to him if you don't transfer ownership."

Reluctantly I pick up the fob and speak the necessary words into it. "I, Zane Campbell, transfer all rights, responsibilities, and ownership of this vehicle to Daniel—" I pause, realizing I don't know his last name despite seeing him several days a week for the last couple of years.

"Spence," Daniel says, somewhat hesitantly.

"To Daniel Spence, effective immediately," I finish, managing not to wheeze through the little speech. I hand over the fob so Daniel can complete the process.

"I, Daniel Spence, accept ownership of this vehicle and all rights and responsibilities that come with it," he says, pressing his thumb into the back of the fob firmly. The device scans his thumbprint and takes a bio reading, chirping assent once the transfer is complete.

"There, don't you feel better?" Cruise taunts. "You've done a good deed today. Now, finish your drink. We're leaving."

I gulp the liquid down, trying to savor the taste. This is probably the last sip of bourbon I'm ever going to have, and these goons have rushed me through it. Bastards.

The second I put down the empty glass, the lighter-skinned man takes my arm and hoists me off the stool.

"I can walk!" I protest, trying to tear my arm out of his grasp. It's a pathetically weak attempt, and to his credit, the bruiser doesn't laugh at me. He merely tightens his grip slightly. It's enough to discourage me from trying the stunt again.

"I have to say, you don't seem particularly devastated by your diagnosis," Cruise remarks as we make our way toward a hovervan that's appeared out back. The dark-skinned man climbs into the van first. The last man releases my arm and follows him inside, leaving me alone with Cruise and his question.

"Who says I'm upset?" I tell him, a sharp edge to my voice. "As you've already pointed out, it's not like I have much to live for."

"I pity people like you," Cruise says. The emotion seems genuine, and embarrassment burns hot in my face, causing me to lash out.

"Like you've got anything but profit on your mind," I spit back.

"No," he says, sadness entering his tone as he offers an arm to help me into the van, "I never think about my wife and kids when I'm away from them."

I accept his offer, hoisting myself into the van with a great deal of effort. I start hacking and wheezing again from the exertion. I quickly take a seat, feeling as if I might pass out.

My legs won't stop shaking even after I've collapsed into the surprisingly comfortable cushion.

"You haven't had much dignity in life, Mr. Campbell," the pirate says, his voice still melancholy. "But maybe we can give you some in death." He slides the hovervan door closed before I have a chance to respond. Cruise disappears for a few minutes. When he returns, he climbs in the front seat and raises a black partition, separating himself and the driver from the cargo area where I sit with the two large men.

We fly for what feels like hours. The men in the back with me are deathly quiet the whole way. They don't even make the normal human noises. There are no swallows, coughs, sneezes, or stomach gurgles coming from these two. They don't even shift in their seats. Watching them quickly becomes boring. There's nothing to see.

The windows are tinted so dark they're almost black. I get the impression this crew doesn't want the passengers looking out just as much as they don't want curious onlookers from peering in. I cough occasionally at first, but quickly realize the driver must have raised the oxygen content in the air for me. This is the easiest it's been to breathe since I got sick.

I told myself it was allergies when the first symptoms appeared. It was an easy enough lie to believe for the first day or two. As the disease progressed and I began to feel worse, I lied to myself again, saying it was the flu. It wasn't really a stretch. The onset of the virus looks very similar to a bad case of influenza. When the chest pain and shortness of breath started, I couldn't deceive myself anymore. I knew what was happening. Stumbling into that clinic, there was no question in my mind what the doctor was going to say. I had already accepted the diagnosis.

It doesn't even matter where I contracted the virus, although I can take a guess. Gilly's isn't always empty, and I don't always leave sober … or alone. The bachelor life gets lonely, and one of the companions I invited to my apartment must have been infected. It doesn't matter now. She's probably already dead, not that I would have realized it. I don't call even when they do leave their numbers.

I don't want to think about any of it anymore. The day has left me exhausted. I guess being diagnosed with a fatal disease and subsequently kidnapped will do that you.

I'm just going to close my eyes for a minute, I think to myself, knowing that's a lie too.

When the van door finally opens, I have no idea how long I've been asleep. Cruise stands there, his shaggy brown hair messy as if he had been napping as well. The space is utilitarian and bright, allowing me to see him clearly for the first time. The scar isn't his most striking feature. I can appreciate a good-looking man without feeling threatened, and Cruise is pretty. His chiseled features accentuate his green eyes, and he catches me staring into them. It's awkward, and I quickly look down at the smooth cement floor to cover my unease.

The facility looks like it might have been an airplane hangar once, back when those antique aluminum birds still roamed the skies. The final airline went bankrupt twenty years ago, but it feels like much longer. I've gotten so used to Autonocars and hovervans that it's hard to remember life before they were commonplace.

Buzz Cut, as I'd nicknamed the fair-skinned man during the boring ride, prods my shoulder, encouraging me to climb out of the van. Cruise offers his arm again, saying nothing this time. I accept and step heavily to the floor, the two bruisers right behind me. Cruise shakes my hand off, and Buzz Cut takes my shoulder, half guiding, half carrying me across the large space.

Sleeping in the oxygen-rich air on the ride here seems to have helped. My chest still hurts, but I don't seem to be struggling quite as hard to breathe. I'm only lightly wheezing as we approach a white metal door with a keypad next to it. Cruise types something in, and a light blinks into existence above the frame. A buzzer goes off, and the latch releases, admitting us.

I'm shocked by what I see inside. It's a hospital—a real hospital like the ones I remember from my childhood. The lobby is clean, bright, and decorated in soothing colors, art dotting the walls. The reception area is a buzz of activity. Telephones ring, and smartly dressed men and women take the calls with pleasant efficiency, a large screen displaying the lines that need to be answered.

Behind the desk, there are several hallways. Nurses in scrubs pass through the stations that dot the long corridors. They're working at monitors, making notes in digital charts, then swiping them away before pulling up the next patient's information. Doctors in white lab coats scurry between rooms. I can hear the buzzes and beeps of machinery, and the whole place smells antiseptic. It's the scent that gets me, the memories it conjures bringing tears to my eyes.

Cruise has made his way to the front desk and is standing at a monitor, inputting my admission information. He holds something small and white up to a scanner beneath the displays, and it registers, automatically filling in the blanks in the digital paperwork. It's my patient identification band from the facility I had been at this morning—the one I threw out the car window. He must have stolen it.

"Where have you taken me?" I demand, stumbling toward him and catching myself on his shoulder. "What is this place?"

"I promised that you would be allowed to die with a dignity you've never known," Cruise says, his voice so soft I have to strain to hear him.

I am unable to reconcile what I'm seeing and hearing with the warnings about organ pirates I saw just this morning.

"It isn't what you expected, is it?" Cruise says quietly.

"No," I whisper back. "But I can't tell you what about it

makes it seem right and the facility I was at this morning seem so wrong."

"You have that doctor to thank for being here," Cruise says slowly. "Just because he can't help people the way he wants to, doesn't mean he isn't taking care of his patients. He called us when he saw your test results. We were nearby and followed you from the clinic to the bar." An involuntary shudder runs down Cruise's spine. "I hope I never have to walk into a place that filthy again."

I open my mouth to defend Gilly's, but before I can speak, a nurse approaches us. Two orderlies follow her, guiding a floating bed.

"Mr. Campbell, we have a room waiting for you. If you'll let go of Mr. Moore"—she glances at my hand; I didn't realize I was still steadying myself on his shoulder—"we can get you someplace more comfortable."

I don't protest, instead trudging toward the bed.

One of the orderlies takes my elbow and helps me climb on.

"One last question, Cruise," I call out, coughing again. The words come out garbled, but they're clear enough to get his attention. "Why do you do it? Why get demonized in order to save people like me? I don't deserve this."

"You're right," Cruise says, walking up to the side of the bed. "You don't merit saving, but your organs do. You aren't going to get a second chance at life, but the little girl who is going to receive one of your kidneys will. The man who contracted hepatitis through no fault of his own deserves a second chance. He just needs your liver, if there's anything left of it. No one has signed up for your corneas yet, but you'll help restore vision to someone who will appreciate the gift."

I don't know how to respond. I have no answer. I just stare at Cruise.

"Don't worry, I don't expect you to thank me for giving your life some meaning," Cruise continues. "I know you aren't capable of it. I'm not completely responsible for your abduction anyway. You can't really believe that a hospital like this exists without some funding."

I hadn't thought about it, but now that Cruise mentions it, it's obvious.

"You asked where you were. You're not in the United States anymore, that's for sure. Your government might have abandoned you to die alone, but you can shut your eyes for the final time knowing that your organs will go to Canadian citizens who need them and to state-sponsored researchers who are dedicated to finding a cure for Cyto."

"Canada?" I finally squeak out. "The organ pirates we're all so afraid of are Canadians?"

"Is that all you took from that, Mr. Campbell?" Cruise says, a look of disappointment on his face.

I try to laugh but end up wheezing instead. I can't believe I rushed through my last glass of bourbon for a couple of Mounties on steroids.

"Boss, we've got another call," Buzz Cut says, tapping Cruise's shoulder to get his attention.

Cruise keeps his eyes on me, not even acknowledging the interruption.

"I'd say get well soon, but we both know you won't," Cruise says, flashing me a devilish grin. "They'll take good care of you here right up until the very end. Of that, at least, you can be assured. Stay comfortable, Mr. Campbell. I won't be seeing you again."

"You can't make people do the right thing," I yell after him as he's leaving. "It will never work."

"No," Cruise says, turning back toward the bed as the orderlies prepare to float me away. "I can only offer them the opportunity to do it willingly. Those who don't make the correct decision, people like you, end up here anyway. Choice is the only thing we've stolen from you, Mr. Campbell, and as far as I'm concerned, you never should have had one anyway. Life is a gift. You should treasure it."

"Mr. Moore, that's enough," the nurse chides. "He's dying. There's no reason to make the process more painful."

"You're right," Cruise replies, his smile unwavering. "I should have a heart."

About the Author

Lauren Lang is a former broadcast journalist, current freelance photographer, videographer, and owner of Jacobin Photography, a Denver-based company that specializes in professional headshots. In her spare time, she crochets hats for stuffed animals, gardens with the intent of photographing the flowers (should they live), and terrorizes local residents while running through area parks with her camera, chasing birds.

Time Comes for All Men

MELISSA KOONS

The sea raged. She tossed our ship to and fro, as if we were nuthin' more than a stick caught in the rapids of a stream. She shook with ferocious waves that could swallow a man whole and spit him out in Davy Jones's locker." The burly sailor took a swig from his stein, gulping the amber beer heartily. Droplets dribbled down his chin and clung to his bushy, red beard. The sailor lowered his stein and released a satisfied sigh, wiping the foam from his upper lip with the back of the sleeve of his black coat.

The rest of the tavern roared with music and laughter as men and women drank, danced, and made utter fools of themselves, but their corner was quiet. The small group of men—young and old alike—watched him silently, listening attentively to every word he spoke.

The man in the black coat eyed each man individually, evaluating him. He knew they were all there hoping for a chance to be awarded a job on his ship. Some looked young and strong, others frail and old, with most somewhere in between.

Black Coat Marley had never lacked for a crew. He was known up and down the coast, his reputation bolstered by the rumors that the men on his ship returned home richer than their wildest dreams. Those rumors were enough to keep the crew of the *Sea Blazer* full, despite the well-known fact that, of the men who crossed paths with Black Coat Marley, it was far more likely they'd come out a dead man rather than a wealthy one.

Despite the unfavorable odds, there were always men at each port who wanted to test their luck. Marley had his pick of men, and he'd been known to turn down sailors other captains would have paid double for, as well as take on men who'd never been on a boat before in their lives. Black Coat Marley knew a sailor could be made, but he was looking for something more, something far more crucial that only certain men were born with.

"We were at the sea's mercy, the lot of us holding on to the ropes for dear life as she thrashed us about. We were little more to her than a leaf is to the wind. It was useless to try to steer the ship. We were just trying not to get tossed overboard or have the mast break from the force of the storm—"

"If it was so bad, then how are you sitting here now?" A young man interrupted, giving Black Coat Marley a challenging grin. He sat at a table next to the group, near enough so he could eavesdrop.

Marley gave the young man a quick once-over. He appeared to be in his early twenties, and his tidy, yet worn, appearance coupled with his tangled blond hair tied at the nape of his neck showed he was no stranger to work. Old enough and experienced enough to know better than to challenge Marley, but still too young and dumb to realize it.

Without hesitation, Marley reached into his long, black coat and pulled out his revolver. He calmly cocked it and aimed at the young man across from him. The other men at his table cleared the line of sight.

The blond man's eyes widened, and his mouth fell open. Before the boy could plead for his life, Marley pulled the trigger and sent the young man reeling backward.

The man yelled, grasping his wounded shoulder where the bullet had ripped through the muscle of his upper arm. It was a mercy he wasn't dead.

The other men at Marley's table froze, crouched and leaning away from the gun's smoking barrel.

Recovering first, a middle-aged man at Marley's table— gray peppering his black hair and with a strong build—rushed over to the bar, asking the barmaid for a rag. He returned to the wounded man, tying the cloth tightly above the wound so the boy wouldn't bleed out. Black Hair finished bandaging up the wound and patted Naive Boy's shoulder. He whispered something to the young man before returning to his seat at Marley's table. He wiped a thin layer of sweat from his brow with his forearm before he cleared his throat and folded his blood-stained hands on the table in front of him, waiting for Marley to continue his story.

Black Coat Marley looked from the middle-aged man's piercing, yet unfazed, blue eyes to the worried expressions worn by the rest of the group, and then to the wounded man in the corner. The blond man's eyes were closed, his posture slumped, unconscious from pain and blood loss. The tense silence stretched another moment before Black Coat Marley returned his pistol to a hidden pocket in his coat.

"So the sea was angry, and we were at her mercy, the lot of us holding on to the ropes for dear life as she thrashed us about," he continued, refocusing on the men at his table.

The other men relaxed a little, doing their best to keep their eyes focused on Marley. A few stole glances at the blond man, as if checking to see if he still breathed. Black Hair sat stoically, ignoring the others and their frightened glances. He focused intently on Black Coat Marley, determined to hear the sailor's tale.

Marley knew the type: a man nearly past his prime, looking for one last chance to make his way onto a crew and earn his riches. He suspected Black Hair wasn't about to let a young fool ruin his opportunity now that he sat before the sailor who could give him everything.

"The ship couldn't take the rough waters and harsh wind. She was groaning, and we knew it wouldn't be long before her sides would give and we'd all be doomed. That's when Lucky Joe Splinter spotted an island a little ways off." Marley took another swig and held up his empty stein for a barmaid to refill.

The barmaid rushed over and poured more beer in his empty cup. She offered to fill the other men's drinks; many chugged down the last of their beer in order to have a full cup again. She looked to the middle-aged man, holding up her near-empty pitcher as she had with the others with a silent question. The man held up his hand and shook his head. She gave a side-glance to the unconscious Naive Boy at the other table before her eyes flicked back to Marley's face.

Black Coat Marley gave a barely perceptible shake of his head, and the barmaid nodded, turning away and returning to the safety of the bar.

"It weren't no island we ever seen before. It was dark, no signs of towns or ports or any human life at all, and just as Lucky Joe Splinter caught sight of it, the storm ripped a hole in the hull. The ship went down, the hungry waves devouring her and anyone trapped inside. We lost a lot of good hands, but about ten of us were able to escape and swim to the mysterious island."

A lad nearing eighteen paled. He glanced to the wounded man, then back at Marley and his tale of the tumultuous sea. He gave a small shudder and then politely excused himself from the table, taking his full stein with him, heading to join an uproarious party across the tavern—far from Marley and his stories of drowned men.

One down—Marley eyed the others, lingering on Black Hair —*six to go.*

"Jungle loomed above us, a canopy of trees so dark not even the flashes of lightning could illuminate it. The sounds that came from those trees …" Marley drifted off, caught in the memory and haze of the beer. He shook his head and refocused on his captivated audience in front of him. "Sounds you can't begin to imagine … such horrible growls. We decided our best chance for survival was to settle on the beach at the highest ground we could find and wait out the storm. None of us wanted to venture into that dark jungle with what-ever dwelled inside.

"When the sun rose," Marley continued, "we saw that parts of the ship and crew had been washed ashore. We buried our mates best we could, but a beach is not known for its stable ground." He gave a melancholy chuckle and wiped his brow.

The men at the table bowed their heads respectfully, sharing a moment of silence for the men devoured by the hungry sea.

Another man stood from the table and gave Marley a respectful nod of farewell. He left his mostly full stein on Marley's table, tossing a coin to the barmaid before he hurried out of the tavern.

Two down. Five to go.

"How'd you survive it? The island," an older man asked, scratching his gray beard.

"Now that's where it got interesting." Black Coat Marley grinned.

His eyes paused on the barmaid, who emerged from the back room, sewing kit and fresh rags in hand. She approached the wounded Naive Boy, then cast a nervous glance at Marley.

He gave her a single nod, and she hastened to tend to the blond man, who was still unconscious in his chair, blood dripping from his arm to the floor, despite his makeshift tourniquet.

Marley gave a sly smile as he carried on. "We stayed on the beach for two days, rummaging through the shipwreck and supplies that washed ashore, though there wasn't much that could be salvaged. The sea had taken her bounty and spat back up naught but the bones.

"We knew we'd have ter find a way off the island and back to civilization eventually, but unfortunately, Lucky Joe Splinter and the rest of us seemed to have used up all our luck. Not enough usable materials washed ashore for us to make a raft. We needed to move inward if we were gonna make it another night." Marley paused to let his words sink in. His eyes drifted to the wounded man—just a flicker, a moment—and when he saw that Naive Boy had regained consciousness, his gaze moved back to the faces surrounding him.

"But the sounds? What about the sounds?" a man across the table asked, panic in his voice.

"We had no choice. It was that or be stranded and starve. Ten of us went in. Five of us came out."

The wounded man sucked in a pained breath as the barmaid pulled her needle through his raw flesh, pausing after each stitch in his arm to dab a rag drenched in rum over the freshly sewn stitches. He hissed in pain. The barmaid muttered something, and he nodded.

"When we entered the jungle, it all seemed rather what you'd expect," Marley continued, watching the wounded man get sewn up. "Nothin' was amiss save for this awful, unsettled feeling. Walking through the darkness, it felt like a million eyes watchin' us. You couldn't shake the feeling, and none of us were willin' to break the quiet lest we upset whatever it was that was watchin' us, but it was only a matter of time.

"It was Tiny George who took the first shot at a hare that darted across our path." Marley took a breath and shook his head, looking down at his hands. He tightened his grip on his cup, squeezing the polished wood.

"We were all so hungry. We ain't had hardly anything since the storm. A small fish or two Big Ted caught on the beach that we split amongst all of us. They were hardly big enough to fill one man's stomach, let alone ten. When Tiny George shot that hare, he was only thinking with the rumbling of his stomach—like the rest of us." Black Coat Marley sniffled. "If only we hadn't been so hungry."

Squirmy, the panicked man sitting across the table from Marley, began to breathe heavily, his own hands tightening around his stein as Marley's tale unfolded. "W-why?" he whispered.

Marley looked up at him, his stare sharp enough to gut a man. "We weren't the only ones hungry in that jungle." He met the eyes of each man still sitting around the table. The older man with the gray beard met his gaze head-on: curious, with a hint of skepticism. The second man and his friend—Cautious and Intrigued, Marley decided to call them—who were both in their thirties, met Marley's stare cautiously, but met it all the same. Squirmy shifted uncomfortably under Marley's stare, his breathing heavy and anxious.

Marley honed in on Squirmy, staring him down with more intensity. The man buckled. He muttered an incoherent sentence as he fled the table.

Marley's stare moved to the middle-aged man. He sat still, unaffected and unflappable.

Four remained: one curious, two cautious yet daring, and one fearless.

The wounded man let out a soft cry, drawing Marley's attention. The barmaid had finished stitching the bullet wound and had slung his good arm over her shoulders, helping him to his feet. As they moved toward the bar, the man met Marley's glance and gave him a small smirk before the barmaid guided him away.

Yes, four was good.

"Tiny George took two steps toward the dead hare, but before he could scoop it up, a deep rumbling came from the trees. He didn't even get to look up before he was yanked into the canopy, screeching somethin' horrible. His blood rained down upon us as the beast devoured him, crunching his bones and slurping his intestines."

Gray Beard paled, but his attention didn't waver and his curiosity only seemed to grow. "What did ya do?" he asked, leaning closer to Marley.

Black Coat Marley snorted and took a swig of his beer. "What do you think we did? We ran. Tried to put as much distance between us and Tiny George—or what was left of him—as possible. We lost two more along the way. They were firing their guns into the canopy at the beast and got yanked from above and pulled into the trees. Their screeches were a haunting echo of each other as they were ripped apart and gobbled alive."

The raucous noise from the rest of the tavern seemed to fade as silence fell over the table. Marley looked past the horror-struck faces of the men around him and focused on the blond man at the bar. The blood had dried on his shirt, and color was coming back to his face. The man looked over his shoulder at Black Coat Marley and met his stare. He took a deep breath and let it out slowly, his chest falling heavily with the release of the weighted air.

"When we made it back to the beach, the jungle quieted. The cries of our men, the ungodly sound of those monstrous jaws … It all fell away and became as if it never were. We stood guard on the beach that night, not knowing if the beasts would come hunting us now that they had tasted our flesh. But they never came. Nothing came out of those trees.

"We were still half-starved, and now shaken to our core. We tried, again, to make a raft out of the debris, but with hardly any food or fresh water, we didn't have the strength or wits to make any progress. We were gonna die on that beach, and we were gonna die if we went into the jungle."

Marley ran a large, square hand down his face. He rubbed his eyes and pinched the bridge of his nose. After a moment, he cleared his throat and resumed. Four men. He needed four men, and he needed to know they were made of the right stuff for his crew. A sailor could be made, but a man was born either a brave man—or a coward. He couldn't afford to have any cowards on his ship.

"We were dead either way, so we might as well go out with full bellies." Marley chuckled and upended his stein, gulping down the dregs of foam that clung to the bottom of the cup. He set the empty stein on the table and wiped his chin. "So back into the jungle we went.

"Just like before, it felt like a million eyes were watchin' us. We sharpened sticks for spears and took whatever ammunition we had left that hadn't been ruined by the ocean water—which wasn't much. We were starving and desperate—a man like that is unstoppable." Marley squeezed his hands around his empty stein.

"When we got to the spot where Tiny George had been taken, we waited. We stood with our backs together and our weapons at the ready, but nothin' came. Nothin' pulled us up into them trees. Nothin' tried to eat us. Wherever the beast was, it was just waiting.

"We pressed on, moving through the brush as one. Finally, we came to a clearing. We were surrounded by the treacherous foliage, which parted only to reveal the gaping mouth of a cave.

"It was Lucky Joe Splinter who entered it first. Don't know what he was thinkin'. His eyes widened, he dropped his weapons, and he moved toward it as if bein' pulled by an invisible rope. We called after him, begged him to stop, to at least pick up his knife and spear, but he was deaf and blind to us. I watched him disappear into that cave, and somethin' in me snapped. I couldn't tell ya what compelled me to do it, but I threw down my knife and half-drowned pistol and went after him.

"As soon as I stepped into that blackness, I heard the cries of the rest of the crew. I turned to look back, to help them, but they were gone." Marley released his stein, and the drastic change in pressure sent it spinning across the table and off the edge.

Black Hair caught it before it hit the ground. He righted it on the table, then refolded his hands in front of him.

"What happened to them?" Intrigued, one of the younger men, dared to ask.

Marley kept his gaze on his stein. "Jungle got them."

Gray Beard shook his head and leaned back from the table. "Wait a minute, I thought you said five of ya came out alive?"

With a smirk, Marley looked over at Gray Beard and then to Naive Boy at the bar, who had his head bowed as if he listened to every word. "Aye, you're right. I did say that. Well then, lucky for you, it seems we have more job openings." He gave a cruel laugh, leaned back in his chair, and slapped a hand to his chest.

The four men around the table remained still. Marley didn't mind. Few saw the humor in dead men.

His laughter died as abruptly as it had started, and Marley swung forward, closing the short distance between him and his tablemates. He leveled them with an intense glare and lowered his voice so they had to lean in to hear him. "This is your last chance to get up and leave. I won't take no offense if you do. Consider this a mercy, 'cause if you choose to stay and hear the end of this story, you're committing to be part of my crew. There will be no leaving after this point. We set sail on the morrow for a treasure greater than you've ever known, but at a price. If you ain't willing to pay it, then you best get up and walk out that door now."

The two friends looked at each other, the unspoken hesitation in their bodies overpowered by the greed in their eyes. With a nod, they turned back to Black Coat Marley and squared their shoulders. They stayed at the table.

Gray Beard gave the offer consideration, the pros and cons floating across his glazed expression as he weighed the decision. With a shrug, he gave Marley a committed nod.

Marley turned his steely stare to Black Hair. His hands were still covered in the wounded man's dried blood, but the man didn't seem to mind. Marley wanted him most of all for his crew.

The stoic man kept his eyes focused on Marley. "How does the story end?"

Marley grinned and leaned back in his chair. "It ends with the discovery of the greatest treasure of all." He gave a nod to the wounded man at the bar.

The blond-haired man took a last sip of his water before he slid off the stool and came to stand behind the men at the table.

Confused, the men looked from the wounded man to Marley, their brows furrowed.

"Men, meet Captain Lucky Joe Splinter." Marley stood and allowed the blond-haired man to take his seat. "Your captain will show ya what it is we found in that cave." Marley gave the four new crew members a sinister smile before stepping back from the table and standing behind his captain.

"But he shot you!" Gray Beard said in shock, his eyes flicking to the man's shoulder.

Lucky Joe Splinter tossed his head back and laughed. "Aye, he did. Hurts every damn time, too, but it's the only way."

"Only way to what? I can imagine there's plenty of other ways to weed out the weak stomachs," Black Hair chimed in, aghast.

Lucky Joe's laughter faded, and he shook his head in amusement. "No, no, no. Not that—although it is effective. No, it's the only way to prove this."

Leaning forward, he yanked off the bloodied bandage, but instead of a bullet wound in his arm, or even fresh, raw stitches from the barmaid, the skin was fully healed with only a hint of a scar.

The middle-aged man pushed back from the table in surprise and shook his head in disbelief. He held his hands up, still covered in the captain's dried blood. "How?"

Lucky Joe gestured for Black Hair to scoot his chair closer. "It was the cave."

The four men at the table leaned in, eager to hear what their eyes refused to believe.

"Those beasts weren't hunting us. They were protecting the treasure of the cave. Tiny George was killed because he shot the hare. He was a threat to the jungle and unworthy of the treasure. The others ... Well, they took up arms and tried to defend themselves—which was their mistake. We were allowed to pass only when we surrendered.

"When I saw that cave, I heard a voice in my head, clear as day and as soft as a child's whisper. It beckoned me to it. That voice ... I dropped my weapons instinctively." Lucky Joe shook his head. "I couldn't think of the other men. I couldn't hear them or see them. The cave and the voice consumed my mind and all my senses. It was black as pitch inside, but somehow, I could see. The voice guided me through the cave—I was deaf to all but it.

"Once I got to the chamber, that's when my senses returned. It felt like I was awakened from a dream by a bucket of ice dumped over my head—a freezing soberness and sudden awareness that was both shocking and painful. Marley stood by me, but we couldn't speak. Our voices were stuck in our throats, and our words choked us if we tried to force them out. Our feet were anchored to the ground. We couldn't move, and it felt like needles in our toes when we tried. All we could do was watch.

"The moisture on the cave walls beaded together, one droplet at a time, until it formed a pond on the chamber floor. The droplets swirled together, illuminated by a light source we couldn't find. The pond's current built with each rotation, pushing the glowing water toward us like a pulse." Lucky Joe Splinter looked up as Marley circled the table, moving to stand behind the four men.

"The water was alive. It was breathing and pulsing, and we couldn't move. It dove at us. It wrapped around us like a snake. It squeezed us until we opened our mouths. It slithered down our throats and drowned us." Lucky Joe grabbed his neck, as if tracing the water's path.

Marley took up the story. "We breathed our last, the water filling our lungs. Then we woke up. We were on our backs, still in the cavern. We were dead, but we weren't. There was no sign of the water that had drowned us."

"The passage we had come down was sealed—there was no going back. We found a dark tunnel on the far side of the chamber. It was the only way anywhere, so we took it, not knowing if we were going to end up back in the jungle or in the depths of hell—if we weren't there already." Lucky Joe shook his head. "Instead, it spat us out on the mainland. We don't know how. We only walked for a few hours, it felt like … but maybe it was days. Maybe we walked the span of the whole ocean."

"We were home. Changed, but home." Marley and Lucky Joe Splinter shared a weary look. "We didn't know at first, but over time it became clear. We'd found it."

"Found what?" Black Hair asked, looking up at Marley and then back to the captain.

"The fountain of eternal life," Lucky Joe said with an airy breath. He looked at the four men with a mischievous smile. "The greatest treasure known to man. We found it once, and we're gonna find it again. Now you know the treasure, and the price you have to be prepared to pay for it. We set sail at dawn."

The men sat in shocked silence as Lucky Joe's words settled on the table. The captain dismissed them with a wave of his hand. They stood and wandered aimlessly into the tavern, clearly unsure of what they had committed to.

Marley took an empty seat and watched the men disappear before turning back to Joe.

"Four, right?" he verified.

The captain nodded. "Aye, four will be good. We'll leave the rest of the crew on the ship and take the skiff to the island. We'll keep the one with the bloody hands, sacrifice the rest. One for each of us."

"You sure?" Marley asked, looking his captain in the eyes.

Lucky Joe's smile faded and an intensity took him over. "Aye, I'm sure. When he tied the tourniquet, Black Hair told me the same thing the voice whispered to me on the island:

'Time comes for all men.' It's time to go back. That wound took far too long to heal. The remaining years we were gifted from our crew's sacrificed lives are coming to an end."

Black Coat Marley nodded, looking back at the four new recruits. "It's been over a hundred years. What makes ya think we'll be able to find it again?"

Lucky Joe Splinter rolled up his sleeve, exposing his right forearm. Vibrant blue veins twisted in patterns unknown to the human circulatory system. "It left us a map. It activated when you shot me. It wants to be found." He grinned sinisterly. "The island wants to be fed."

About the Author

Melissa Koons is a historical fiction and short story horror author. She loves the way history enhances any genre and loves to learn about the oddities of times past. When she's not researching her latest plot, she keeps herself busy with her podcast, writing her self-help blog, running her own company, and caring for her two turtles.

Life Pirate

ELMDEA ADAMS

The Pirate

The seas are beautiful right now. Such rich reds and pale yellows!
Another awareness trickled into my consciousness, a
new area to explore and plunder. Yes!

I've had an extraordinary life: well-fed, ever-expanding
horizons, always growing. My first memories were hearing my
host as she read stories of pirates, the swash-and-buckle kind.
She read other stories—ones she called "history," "biography,"
or "fantasy." They were sort of interesting, but they didn't
resemble my life much. The books she called "space opera"
were fun. But the ones she called "pirate books" were the best
because that's what I am: a full-blooded, full-bodied pirate.

Over the past bit of time, which gets kinda fluid here, I've
been feeling the pull to explore again. My ship is sturdy and
strong, with lustrous planks. My fins navigate the red-and-
yellow seas. I know, pirate ships in the stories have sails, but
there's no wind on my seas. Just strong currents and no horizons. So, fins it is. My fins are half-opened, gleaming fans of
pastel yellow, their surface embroidered with delicate red lines,
the same red as the seas I swim.

Have I mentioned I have a magical ship? I discovered it a
bit ago. I'd been exploring when a land mass appeared. It was
ripe for pillaging, so I prepared to set up an outpost and
explore it for booty. That's when the magic happened.

One of my planks disengaged, floated to the island, and
firmly attached itself to a small rise just off the shore. It felt
like the most natural thing to do, even though I hadn't done it
before. The instant the plank touched the mass, my awareness
expanded. That plank grew and thrived, just like me—in fact,
exactly like me—until it was an outpost.

There are six outposts now. We talk to each other all the
time. I hadn't realized I was lonely for my own kind until that
first outpost established itself. That drove me to search for

more welcoming islands. My host's stories are interesting, but my outposts are lots more fun.

Then today, a colorless foreign substance invaded my seas. An attack, a horrible assault. It's eating away at my beautiful ship, at my outpost's ships. It hurts—a lot!

The Friend

Anthea sat in mediation, breathing in, breathing out, again, again. Her friend, Sarah, had just been diagnosed with stage 4 gall bladder cancer. The long-term prognosis was six to twelve months, with chemotherapy. Radiation and surgery would have to wait until the chemo shrank the tumor.

As she sat, an unfamiliar presence made itself known to her. Continuing to breathe, Anthea concentrated to see what, if anything, developed.

An idea entered her mind. A strange one, yes, but it felt true.

It's Sarah's cancer! No. It couldn't be, could it? It is a living being, after all. Perhaps it has a kind of consciousness. Perhaps I can talk to it.

Anthea's shoulders relaxed as she settled more firmly on her purple meditation cushion.

I see you. Anthea sent the thought to the presence, surprised when she sensed a response.

She explored the presence more. Its only focus was on growing and expanding. She nodded. Yes, that's what cancer did. It ignored the cell death messages that routinely happened in the human body.

"This may be a dumb idea, but there's nothing to lose," Anthea said, needing to hear the words aloud even as the idea formed in her mind. "I'll send it compassion and information instead of anger, hatred, and battle."

I know you are only doing what you know how to do. You are doing it beautifully. What you need to know is that if you continue to do it, you will die. There is no way around it.

But you do have a choice about how you die.

If you keep colonizing, you'll end up killing Sarah, your host. You will eat her up, and she'll die—and so will you.

But Sarah is doing something called chemotherapy. She is taking drugs that will kill you off, bit by bit, until you are greatly diminished. Then there will be something called radiation, which will burn you, followed by surgery, which will cut you out of Sarah's body.

Your choices, from what I can see, are to ignore me and continue to grow, which will kill both you and Sarah, or listen to me and allow the chemotherapy and radiation to diminish you so when the surgery happens, it will be easy for you to detach from her.

It's your choice.

The Pirate

My name is cancer? I'm killing my host, my teller of pirate stories? My source of food and outposts? What I heard has rattled everything I know about myself.

I'll consider it later.

Others are speaking to me, too, saying the same things that first person did—the one who isn't my host. I don't understand how I can hear them. What I do know is they speak in different tones and colors than my host does.

They all say they honor me and acknowledge my dedication to living the only life I know. They all say, yes, I will die. My only choice is how.

I need to be with this for a bit.

Meanwhile, one of my older outposts said there's a new territory that looks promising. I don't know if I should go.

The Patient

I hadn't believed the nausea could be this bad. My friends warned me, but I had hoped to avoid it. A constant state of nausea. Almost, but not quite, feeling like I need to throw up,

ELMDEA ADAMS

an almost constant tightness and lump at the bottom of my throat.

And I'm tired. My feet have gained weight, or my shoes have. I swear they weigh at least fifty pounds each. It doesn't matter which shoes I wear, walking from one room to another is a day's exercise.

The oncologist said food would taste weird. Umm, yeah. Like gasoline, or like it's gone moldy, or like bitter chemicals. But I have to eat. The medical marijuana helps some, but not enough.

This isn't the way I had planned to lose weight.

Losing my hair was anti-climactic. I shaved it the moment my scalp started tingling and itching as my hair follicles died. I was *so* not interested in discovering clumps of hair all over the place. My hats and my wig are easier to manage. I can barely remember the energy I used to put into washing and drying my hair.

The fear is the worst. I do my best to control it, but there are so many new sensations and feelings in my body I don't know what's important and what isn't. It doesn't help that I can't think straight. Thinking wears me out; it's so hard some days. "Chemo-brain" is a real thing. This chemo-plus-radiation-plus-surgery program has to work. I've got things I still want to do with my life.

I have so many books on my Kindle waiting for me, but I can't focus enough to remember the last sentence I read. Yet I remember clearly the first book I read all the way through when I was in first grade. Ever since then, I have loved exploring other places, the way authors think and create.

I've wanted to write since I was a kid, but I never felt like I knew enough. I'm rethinking that now. But when I open my laptop to start typing, the words get all jumbled. I can barely type coherent things on my Facebook timeline, let alone answer everyone's questions about how I'm doing. I appreciate their concern and their love. I really do. Heart emojis are my new best friend.

What I miss even more than reading is being outside for hours on end. Smelling air that unabashedly proclaims spring. It's the same with the light. Spring light is totally different from autumn light. Maybe it's the angle of the sun or something. I'd like to find out why that is.

I love the colors, the unfoldings of flowers, the sheer exuberance of nature in the spring.

Last year, I saw a forsythia clinging to a steep road embankment. The flowers were a waterfall of yellow. I studied the soft magenta of redbud, the clear pinks of cherry, the white of dogwood, the complexities of greens as trees leafed out, as grasses started growing. All of it.

I wish I had painted it. I've always painted, but I was too self-critical back then. Now? Now, what I wouldn't give to just hold a brush, mix colors, and let my heart lead my hand. Life is too short to mess with anything that isn't love.

Glenn is doing his best to take care of things. He has always been good at organizing, unlike me. If there's an empty space on a table or a counter, it's there to put something on. If there isn't any empty space, no problem, I'll just pile whatever it is on top of something else. Glenn's so patient with me and gives me more leeway than he used to.

Glenn is a wonderful cook. I wish I could actually eat some of it. I daydream of eating his Thai food. These days, I'm all about protein shakes and ice cream. Something that goes down easy and has half a chance of staying down. Spices aren't my friends any more.

This cancer has its own ideas and life. I'm going to try Anthea's suggestion. It can't hurt. Battling this cancer hasn't been fun at all—and it doesn't seem to have helped either.

The Husband

Anthea stopped by a few days ago and shared this crazy idea: We should talk to the cancer, have compassion for it. That's the last thing I feel. If it had a neck, I'd wring it and stuff it down the garbage disposal. Even that would be too kind.

I feel so helpless. There's so little I can do. Making doctor's appointments and driving Sarah to them, keeping track of her meds, getting them refilled, ordering her protein drinks, taking out the trash, mowing the yard, and I'm not sure what else. Those are easy, no big deal. But there's nothing I can *do* about the cancer or what it's doing to her.

My Sarah, the Sarah I know and love, isn't around much these days. Instead, I see a stranger in her body. It makes sense, when I think about it. She's focused on doing what she can to encourage healing while dealing with nausea and all the other side effects of the chemo. At the same time, she's staring death in the face.

I wasn't happy about her decision to do chemo. It's so destructive, so beyond awful, what it does to the body. But it's not my life. I don't know what her soul's journey and purpose is. I have to trust—a lot. There are moments when it's easy, like when we get to laugh at something, and she's present, here again, even for a few moments.

I'm alone in a way I've never felt alone before. There's no one I know who understands what I'm going through, what Sarah's going through, how little can be done except hope. This loneliness is not about Sarah's introspection. It's a new place inside me. An emptiness that echoes nothing.

One day at a time. That's all I can do. If I look too far forward, I can see a life without Sarah. I'm not ready for that. I will never be ready for that.

So I'll talk to that cancer. It can't hurt. What did Anthea say? I don't have to like it, but I can feel compassion for it. It's a stretch, but I'll do it because Sarah has asked me to.

The Pirate

I was made to grow and expand and feed. But I'm pirating the life of my host. It never occurred to me I wasn't good for her. I was alive. She was alive. Together, we lived.

My outposts aren't much help right now. They think exactly like me because they *are* me. My host tells me she loves me, but that she wants to live. To stop growing and colonizing is against my nature; it's my only purpose. I don't know how to do otherwise.

I'm being eaten alive by these foreign invaders, and I hurt. My host is getting weaker, so more areas are opening up, but the invaders kill every plank that goes out to colonize.

I thought I was the captain, but now I know she is. Since I'm to die, I'll do it in style. I lack a cutlass or pistol, so I'll maroon myself by letting go of all my outpost islands. This is one time when marooning is honorable. My host has been good to me, giving me everything I needed to thrive and grow, sharing all the bounty. Now I must be good to my host.

There. It is done.

All of us are adrift. We'll be swept away. It's a proper payment for our good life.

The Patient

"Sarah? Can you hear me? The operation went well."

It's hard work finding my place in the world, in my body, in my mind. Oh, yes, general anesthesia. That explains it. I hear her voice again.

"Sarah? It's Dr. Krane. It's okay. The operation went well. You're coming up out of anesthesia."

Somewhere I remember how to nod my head. I speak. "Cold."

The comforting weight of a warmed blanket settles around me like magic.

The third time my mind comes back up, the doctor is still here, or here again. Glenn is here too. He's holding my hand, I think.

Dr. Krane. I've liked her from the beginning. I'm glad she was my surgeon.

"I've done a lot of these operations, Sarah. This one was different. It was like that tumor wanted to come out, like it wanted to let go. It detached so easily. You're a lucky woman."

Yes, I am. I am going to paint, and read, and love Glenn, and write, and twirl in the sunlit air.

Author's Note: While character's names and the type of cancer have been changed, this is based on several real experiences, as told to the author.

About the Author

Elmdea Adams lives on a windy ridge near Berkeley Springs, West Virginia, where dragon's-breath fogs rise from the valleys. Her previous adventures include Fortune 500 management and work as a past-life therapist, which are more related to each another than one might initially think. She appreciates the skilled supervision of her cat, Miz Alice. For more information, visit ElmdeaAdams.com.

Pirated RPG

JACE KILLAN

I died again last night. It doesn't much matter, because I'm still here, still trapped in this blasted game. It takes a moment for my head to clear, letting me know there are consequences to dying. I breathe deep, and my Health powers up to 30%. That's when my world comes into focus.

I'm in jail again. By the looks of it, I'm at the one on Clew Bay. I can tell because the wood floor is a dark mahogany and there isn't a waste bin by the pinewood desk facing me. My Intelligence increases to 15%, and I remember I'd been nearby with the crew trying to take on *La Louisa*. From what all the NPCs have told me, that's how I win the game, and that's how I get home.

Without my gear, and at only 20% Strength, I'm screwed until time and rest help me recuperate. I hate waiting.

My Intelligence clicks up to 25%, and I remember I've planned for being in jail and have hidden nails all over my clothing. Not like the ones you'd buy at Home Depot. No, these are hand-forged pieces of iron I made in the slums of Port Royal, thin enough to bend if I have Strength greater than 60%, which I don't yet, but I can still use them to …

What was I doing again?

Blast. A debuff, kind of like a penalty to my levels, knocks my Intelligence down to 20%. I must still have some alcohol in my system. Even after two years, I'm not used to that happening. Ah yes. That's right. Instead of going after *La Louisa* because I missed docking my ship at Clew Bay before 2100, I got drunk with the mates, and we used the plank to climb the crow's nest and dive off it. We've done it many times before without dying.

My Intelligence clicks up, and I remember I had been attacked by a pod of dolphins. Yeah, dolphins here are not cute, intelligent mammals but vicious, vindictive jerks that eat anything and everything.

Anyway. I ain't got no clothes on, and I reek of rancid liquor and sweat. Damn, I'm even talking like them. Nobody, and I mean *nobody*, but me has an American accent. And after two years, I think I'm losing mine.

I'm naked, so no nails.

To recover my levels, I wait awhile, but without my pocket watch, I have no idea how long. By this time my Intelligence is pushing 30%, my Strength is 45% and my Health is at 50%. K still is and always has been 0%. I'm certain it's a glitch because it has never once moved, not in all my time here.

I remember I have a glass eye, one I forged with Sebastian down in Tortuga. I hate to use it because a glass eye full of gunpowder can be useful in a lot of situations, and once it's gone, I'll have to get back to Tortuga to forge another if I want it. But, well, I hate waiting.

I flip up my eye patch, fish out my glass eyeball, and smash it on the floor. Then I brush up the black sand and sprinkle it into the lock casing.

Every jail is pretty much the same. There are a couple cells designated by iron bars, four inches apart. Just wide enough to stick an arm through. I've lost count of how many times I've escaped these, and there are a good many ways to break out, depending on my levels. I burn 18% of my Intelligence in the next sixty seconds. I don't regret it as the lock on the cell door crackles and spits fire. I push the door open.

What about the guards? Yeah, every town has a couple soldiers that look identical to one another, so I call them all John. And there's a Marshal Thornton on each island—I refer to them as Billy Bob—and they all have the same backstory. Or they're the same guy and he follows me around. To be honest, I'm not real sure. Supposedly we were friends, and now we're not. We both liked the same lady and blame each other for her death. It's pretty cliché.

Lightning strikes and thunder explodes outside, vibrating the wood floor. That's God. At least that's what she calls herself. Another thunderous rumble nearly knocks me down, and my Health drops by 8%.

"Sorry," I say. I mean that's what She calls Herself. See, I have to capitalize the pronouns in my daily journal 'cause ... Anyway, She hates it when I rip on Her game. Like when I say the backstory is cliché, or how it's stupid that when God gets upset, there's thunderous lightning with no time delay calculated for light speed versus speed of sound.

A bolt of lightning slams through the barred window, but I'm ready for it and dodge away. God misses me, but the lightning strikes a connected door leading to the armory. The place explodes.

I died again last night. It doesn't much matter, because I'm still here, still trapped in this blasted game. It takes a moment for my head to clear, letting me know—

Ah, with my Intelligence up to 20%, I remember we did this yesterday. Dying so quickly has the benefit that I'm no longer in the buff but have respawned in my basic attire, save the hat and boots. I find the nails sewn into my collar and break my way out of the cell and into the armory, where I load up on mediocre weaponry.

Right, this is where we were yesterday when I was explaining why there are no soldiers guarding me. Each time I die, I respawn in the nearest jail as if I were arrested instead of dead. And for some reason, neither the Johns nor Marshal Thornton, whom I call Billy Bob sometimes, are here in the morning.

If I hang around, they'll show up later in the afternoon. By that time, I'll have regained 80% of Health, Strength, and Intelligence and won't have any trouble breaking out, usually by manipulating one or both Johns to come to the cell where I put a sleeper on him and borrow the keys. But all that takes time, and after two years, I've grown extremely impatient.

Also, when my Intelligence is so low, I tend to make stupid, rash decisions, like wasting my glass eye.

Sometimes I wonder if I had more patience whether I would have beaten the game and gone home already. And then I wonder if I'll be the same age as when I got tricked into this damn thing in the first place.

The thunder roars.

"Sorry. Didn't mean to take the game's name in vain." My low Intelligence causes me to chuckle at that, and I repeat it a few times like a drunken noob.

Anyway … I creep out the back of the jail, walk a couple paces, then jump into a bush. There I wait for the shopkeeper across the street to go inside his store. That's when I book it as fast as my bare feet can travel, feeling my Health drop with every step, until I make it to the cellar behind the store. This cellar has a padlock on it, but my Intelligence isn't high enough to crack it. Thinking about what to do hurts my head, and my vision blurs slightly.

I kneel and breathe deep. Dying twice consecutively without having time to recharge has hurt my recovery time. I look around for something I can eat. There's a mushroom not three feet from me. I pick it, sniff it, and try to remember with my limited Intelligence if this mushroom will help me or hurt me. I take a bite.

I died again last night. It doesn't much matter, because I'm still here, still trapped in this blasted game. It takes a moment—

Damn. Sorry. We've already done this. Today I stay in bed, wait for the Johns to come and feed me some of Miss O'Leary's stew. That hits the spot and immediately shoots me to 50% Strength and 60% Health. This stew happens to have a rare wild carrot in it, which increases my Intelligence to

96%. Minutes later, I've choked out and robbed both Johns, borrowed a dueling pistol, a hat, and a pair of boots, which protects my Health as I race across the dirt street.

Suddenly it's night, and I don't have much time if I want to make the raid on *La Louisa*.

I twist the lock with my bare hands, costing me 5% Strength, and climb down the cellar to a glowing chest in the corner. It, too, has a lock. I blast it with the dueling pistol in order to conserve my Strength. Inside the chest, I find my gear, including my carbine—the best rifle in the game. I'm not going to point out how this piece of weaponry is not period appropriate. I don't care. It's nearly maxed out the damage scale and has one of the quicker fire rates, especially if I am at greater than 60% Strength. I can flick that lever action one-handed in less than a second and do some serious killing; if I'm within thirty yards of what I'm shooting at, I have perfect accuracy.

I also get my revolver, knife, scatter pistol (it's like a sawed-off shotgun), 5,742 gold bits, and a slew of tonics, rations, and trinkets that help me improve my skills and condition. I take one of my three cure-alls and immediately feel great with full Health, Strength, and Intelligence.

La Louisa.

I glance at my pocket watch, the one I pulled from Capitán Rodriguez after I killed him but before sinking his vessel.

Hold on, that makes me sound like a monster. I'm not a murderer. First off, it's a video game, I think. I'm just playing a role, the one God set out for me.

Thunder rolls outside.

Capitán Rodriguez had killed my girlfriend, and Marshal Billy Bob was planning on killing him too, but I got there first. Anyway, he was a bad hombre.

Dammit, I've been here too long backstorying.

My watch says I have one hour, which means I've got like

ten minutes to get to my ship. I race upstairs, out of the cellar, and find the nearest horse.

I don't care if anyone is looking; with all my gear, nobody will try to stop me. My notoriety is through the roof, and let's just say the people here are terrified of me. Probably 'cause I've killed all of them at least twice. Only, they respawn like me. And while they don't seem to remember our prior entanglements, they don't like me, or trust me.

I ride the horse onto the dock and launch it into the ocean. I abandon the horse and elect to swim the short distance instead of renting the rowboat. With full Strength, I'm pretty quick. I crawl up the starboard side of my ship and plop onto the deck, sopping wet.

Chaz is already telling the joke. "So I get up on the counter and wink at the bartender as I whip it out."

Chaz is my first mate and best friend. He's black and French, and I saved his life sometime in the backstory so he's decided to follow me wherever I go. Since I'm just starting the mission, I'm not going to mention how culturally inappropriate this seems, white savior and all, 'cause I don't want to die by lightning again. But, also, I've almost forgotten that in the real world I'm the son of Korean immigrants, so does it even matter? Like I said—here, I'm playing a role.

"So the bartender," Chaz says in a crude English accent, not French, "places the shot glass at the other end, and you know how long that is. But I ham it up. And I try, I really do." He laughs, as does the rest of the crew.

"Well, I don't even get close. I mean there's piss everywhere, all over the counter but not a single drop in that shot glass. I stuff Mr. Johnson back in my trousers and jump down to give the bartender the twenty gold bits I owe him. He comps me a shot of whiskey just cause he's so happy with winning the bet.

"And as he's cleaning up my piss, he says to me, 'Why would you even try something like that? Next time you get one of them bright ideas, just hand me the money and save us both the trouble.' And I look at him and smile. 'See, that's just it,' I says. 'Weren't no trouble for me. In fact, I made eighty bits profit on the deal.' He eyes me and asks, 'How's that?'"

Chaz takes a swig from the whiskey bottle in his hand and passes it around. I decline. With nearly full levels, I feel great and need to keep it that way. He's really just pausing for cinematic purposes before revealing the punch line.

"'Well,' I say, 'I bet your five mates at that table over there twenty bits apiece that you'd let me hop up here on your counter and piss all over it and you'd wash it up with a smile on your face.'"

I don't laugh with the crew 'cause I've heard the joke hundreds of times. That's right, I've been right here again and again. Chaz laughs and wheezes until he doubles over, coughing.

La Louisa is the final mission. It has to be. But I can't figure out what to do exactly. Nothing I've tried has worked. I've bombed it, sunk it, set it on fire, killed everyone aboard, looted it, and hijacked it and sailed it across the world map. And I'm still here. The game has yet to be won.

And there isn't anything else to do in the whole map. I can sail around and interact with folks, but there isn't any progress to be had, no fight to win, no challenge, no danger anywhere except for pirating *La Louisa*. Day after day, I come here and try to beat the game so I can go home.

"There she is," Scotty says. We call him Scotty cause he has a Scottish accent, and that's not stereotypical at all.

Lightning splits the sky with a crackle.

La Louisa is a schooner, a small ship. My plan is to board with full Intelligence, Strength, and Health and ask a lot of questions of the crew. See what I'm missing.

"Raise the white flag," I say. "Let's parlay this bitch."

Echoes of "Aye, aye, Captain," come from my crew. There are twelve of them that I have gathered throughout the game, some men, some women, and a couple that could be either or like Robin and Sally, but I never asked.

We flank *La Louisa* and throw lines over to her. As soon as I land, I down my second cure-all tonic and look around. I've done this several times before, but I am extra attentive to everything now. I have my crew stay back, and I raise my hands when I'm on *La Louisa*'s deck near the bow.

"You wish to parlay," the captain says.

"Yessiree, Bob." He reminds me of Marshal Thornton but with a beard and peg leg.

"You're looking for Bob?"

I roll with it. "Sure. You seen him around?"

"Never heard of her," he says.

"Okay," I say, ignoring the glitch in the game. "Can we do this?"

"Do what?" he asks.

After years of dealing with NPCs and trying to ask the right question, I sometimes get a little flippant, if only to keep my sanity. "This," I say, and dance the floss.

The pirate captain tries to match my moves but fails miserably. I'm just about to kill him and call my guys over for the raid when he stops and meets my eyes.

"Can you help me?" he asks. "I never learned to dance, and that move you're doing there seems like something I could manage with my bum leg."

Well, that was unexpected. "Sure." I step closer so he can see me better in the torchlight. Then I move slowly, showing him how I counter the movement of swaying hips with my arms.

He tries, and starts out fine, but when it's time to switch his arms to the other side he ends up swaying like a bobblehead. I show him again and when he tries to match my movements, I walk him through it.

"Now pass both hands in front."

He does and repeats the action on the opposite side, then moves his hands to the front again. He's got it.

"C'mon, me mateys," he hollers. "Give it a go." His crew joins him on the deck and they all do the floss, in unison, like some sort of dance line.

I'm extra attentive at this point, because this is something new, something that has never happened before. Then another thing occurs. My levels. There are four: S for Strength, or I suppose it could represent Stamina, H for Health, I for Intelligence, and K. I've never known what K represented and have never seen anything that interacted with it before. K has always been at 0%. Until now. Now, after dancing the floss, it ticks up to 1%.

I am so excited, I look at Chaz and give him a thumbs-up. This is working. Something is different.

Chaz takes the sign to mean we are a go for taking out their crew. The fellow in their crow's nest hits me between the eyes with a musket ball.

I died again last night. It doesn't much matter, because I'm still here, trapped—

Wait a second. I check my levels. Sure enough, K reads 1%. That's different.

Up until this point, I assumed K was a glitch. I'd spent the better part of four months trying to figure out how to affect it. Knowledge? Weight? Logic? Knockouts? Kids? I couldn't find anything on it. No tonic, no NPC info, nothing. Until now. What had I done? The floss?

I dance in the cell, eyeing my levels. Nothing.

I spend the day doing everything I remembered from the day prior. I eat the stew—no rare wild carrot this time—I recoup my gear, I steal the horse, ride off the dock, swim to the boat, listen to the stupid joke, and parlay with *La Louisa*.

I show the captain how to floss, but I forget the bit about Bob. He and the crew are dancing the floss, but there's no change. A few words couldn't have made a difference, could they? Or was it that carrot? All my levels are maxed.

Dammit. As they're line dancing the floss, I race to the stern where I know they keep the kegs of gunpowder and light a match.

I died again last night. It doesn't much matter, because—

I remember. I do the day. I live it precisely, thunder rumbles, rare wild carrot in the stew and everything, even the bit about Bob. Then I teach the captain how to dance the floss. K still reads 1%.

I pick up where I left off two days prior, only this time I don't give the thumbs-up to Chaz, but instead invite the crew down and teach everyone how to dance the floss.

"Do you know what K stands for?" I ask the captain.

"Hmm," he says. "K could stand for a lot of things. Catfish, kites, carp, kelp."

"Actually," I say, "catfish and carp start with the letter C."

He scrunches up his nose at me. "Really? That makes no sense. I thought C started words like seaweed, sea salt, sea breeze, seagull."

Wow. Hadn't thought of that. "All of those start with the letter S," I say. "The letter C can make a couple of sounds like *sss*, and *ca*, and *cha*, if it is paired with an H."

"Fascinating," he says.

K ticks up to 2%. I was explaining something to this captain both times. I taught him something. Maybe K doesn't stand for *my* knowledge but sharing my knowledge with others, increasing *their* knowledge.

"Do you know mathematics?" I ask the captain.

"I can count," he says. "I'm missing a leg, not my fingers."

"So two plus two ..."

He looks down at his hands, lifts two fingers on each and bobs his head as he counts. "Four."

K doesn't move.

"Two times two is the same thing," I say. "Four. Say it with me. Two times two is four."

He does, but my K level doesn't change.

"Is there anything else you wish to learn?" I ask. Though I restrain it, impatience comes out in my voice.

"No," he says.

"Here, words that start with C: city, church, car, canopy, crap."

Still 2%

What had I done both times?

"Are you mocking me now?" the captain says.

"Captain. That starts with C."

"You think I'm stupid 'cause I can't read?"

"No. Not at all."

"Hey," Chaz steps in. "You can't talk to my captain that way."

I died again last night. It doesn't much matter, because—

Dammit all.

K is still 2%. I stay in my cell all day, trying to figure this out. I was teaching both times K ticked up. The first time, Captain Billy Bob had asked for my help, and I helped him. Kind. I was kind. What the hell type of level is that? Kindness?

Hadn't I been kind sometime before teaching the captain how to floss? What about when I saved Scotty's life, or rescued Sally from the dungeons of Port Royal? Hadn't that been kindness?

No. I'd done those things because it was a mission and I

needed to build my crew. I did it, not for them but for me, for the game. To win.

So I need to be helpful, but my actions shouldn't immediately benefit me. Rather, my motivation needs to be helping someone else with no strings attached. Is that what kindness means?

It's early afternoon when a John shows up.

"How was your day, Mr. ...?" I've forgotten his real name. Did I ever know it? I just always called him John, all of them.

"Name's Rogers."

"Good to meet you, Mr. Rogers. How is your fine neighborhood?" I say with a smirk.

"Great, until you buggered in here."

"Yeah, sorry about that. Is there anything I can do to make it better?"

"Well, you ought to know that taking things that don't belong to you is a crime."

But I'm a pirate. It's my role in the game. Pirates steal. It's what I do.

"I know you're a pirate," he says as if reading my mind. "I know you think you need to steal things, but stealing, pirating, that stuff just hurts everyone else. People pirate all kinds of things. Even video games."

I slump to my bunk as I realize the truth. That's what landed me here to begin with. I downloaded a pirated game, 'cause why pay for something you can get for free? Next thing I know, I'm stuck in this world, trying to win so I can get out.

"I'm sorry. I'm sorry I ever took anything that didn't belong to me, including that game."

Mr. Rogers eyes me and shrugs.

"How long do I have to pay for that? I've been stuck in this damn game for two years."

Thunder rolls outside. I did it again.

"Do you know what the definition of insanity is?" he says. "Doing the same thing again and again and expecting a different result." He opens the door and hands me the bowl of Miss O'Leary's stew.

My empty stomach grumbles at the scent of the peppery dish. I feel guilty for the many times I've choked John—I mean Mr. Rogers—out at this point. He's being nice to me, and normally I would take advantage of the opportunity to escape. Maybe, like he suggests, I need to do things differently. Stop being a pirate all together. Start being kind.

"Thank you," I say. "I am really sorry for how I've treated you in the past, Mr. Rogers. And you keep being kind to me even though I don't deserve it."

He smiles and locks me back in.

Later that evening I ask, "Is there a way I can get out of here without escaping?"

Mr. Rogers and the other John, Mr. Jones, look at each other before one answers, "You could pay your fines."

"How much is that?" I ask.

Mr. Rogers goes to the desk and withdraws a leather-bound book. He skims through it and glances up at the ceiling as he counts. "Five thousand gold bits," he says.

We arrange for payment from my confiscated gear, and I'm released on probation. The fines about wipe out my savings, and I fight the urge to go rob the treasury in Tortuga. Got to be kind. I'm not allowed to carry weapons while visiting Clew Bay, but after a while, I don't miss them.

I stroll down the darkened streets of Clew Bay. No one is out. I look at all the homes I've been in, explored by trespassing that often ended in a fight. I've torched Clew Bay several times over. What a waste of time.

There's a woman sitting on a porch. Jane something or other. I've killed her a few times too, after trying unsuccessfully for a month to court her when I thought K stood for Kids. As far as I could tell, the game was rated E when it came to sexuality. Any time I tried anything, I ended up getting killed or arrested.

When I wave, she gets up to go inside. "Please," I say. "Don't be afraid."

She draws the shawl around her tight and cocks her head. "What do you want?"

"To help. I'll do anything you need."

She shrugs. "I've got some pots that need cleaning, if you would be so kind."

"Yes, ma'am. That's exactly what I want—to be kind."

She invites me inside and makes it known she has a pistol aimed at me under her shawl if I try anything. I'm halfway through scrubbing the pots, when she tells me of her fiancé at sea who is embarrassed to be in town because he doesn't know how to read.

"Is he the captain of *La Louisa*?" I ask.

"Yes. You know him?"

"I do. I taught him how to dance."

She doesn't believe me.

"No, really. I know he only has one leg, so I taught him a dance where you don't need to move your legs, just your arms and hips."

She fights a smile, but it gives way and fills her face.

The next pot smelled familiar. Stew. I look up at her. "You're Miss O'Leary?"

She nods.

"I've eaten your stew more times than I can count," I say. "It's delicious, by the way. Captain will be right blessed to have you as a wife." It comes out way more sexist than I mean it to, but she smiles anyway, even has a tear in her eye. "I guess what I mean is thank you for your kindness to me. I didn't deserve it." Especially after all the things I did to her.

I finish the dishes and watch my Kindness meter tick up to 3%.

"Thank you, sir," Miss O'Leary says. "Stop by any time you want to do my dishes."

"I will," I say. "And don't worry about the captain. I'll

teach him how to read, get him back here to marry you."
That ought to get me some points.

She hugs me.

I spend the next couple months helping everyone I can on
Clew Bay. I do Miss O'Leary's dishes every night. It never
ticks up my Kindness meter again, but I enjoy her company.
My Kindness meter never goes down either. It just ticks up,
1% with every good deed, and only the first time doing that
deed.

I don't need to sleep. After a while, the townsfolk stop
running away from me and instead give me gifts. Like a rare
wild carrot each time I wash Miss O'Leary's dishes. I use the
food and tonics I receive to keep playing rather than resting.

Over the next year, I repeat my efforts at every island on
the map, helping everyone. I even teach the captain of *La
Louisa* how to read. When my Kindness meter ticks up to
100%, I board *La Louisa* after hearing Chaz's joke about
pissing all over the bar counter.

La Louisa is abandoned, void of money, supplies, and crew.
The only thing I find is a note nailed to the ship's wheel.

"She's all yours, good sir," it reads, "the ship and the
game. The ship you've earned, and the game I suspect you'll
pay for when you return home and find that I have stalled
time so that you might have this life-changing experience.
Your friends and family won't recognize the new you, especially if you apply what you've learned here about not being a
pirate."

I turn to see Chaz and the rest of my crew waving as they
sail away, leaving me alone on *La Louisa*.

"Venmo me," the note says. "Love, Louisa."

A door appears on the deck. I open it and enter, note in
hand, as my level gauges disappear from view and thunder
rolls across the ocean.

About the Author

Jace Killan lives in Arizona with his wife, five kids, and a little dog. He writes fiction, thrillers, and soft sci-fi with a little short horror on the side. He has an MBA and works in finance for a biotechnology firm. Jace plays and writes music and enjoys everything outdoors. He's also a novice photographer. For more information about Jace Killan and his writing, visit jacekillan.com.

Breath of the Cherubim

CLINT HALL

I always thought the nightmares would be the worst of it." The captain gazes out the window of his quarters, his back to me. The faint melody of church bells rolls through the morning fog like ghosts drifting past the ship, searching for something else. There is no redemption to be found here.

The ropes dig into my skin, sending blood dripping down my fingers. I sit and stare at the captain, refusing to quiver with the fear he's trying to instill in me. Let this cursed soul have his theater. Judging by the way he and his crew are coughing, it won't be long before the devil takes them all.

"But I was wrong," the captain says, his voice almost inaudible through the disease. "The worst was when the nightmares stopped. That's when I knew my soul was truly forfeit, when a monster like me slept with the peace of a holy man like you."

The captain bends over a rickety desk and holds a handkerchief to his mouth as he coughs, then tries to hide the blood-stained fabric as he turns toward me. The skin on his face is covered with splotches and sags as if it were made for somebody else's skull. His hat does little to mask the fact that his black hair is falling out fast. The evil is eating his body from the inside. I've seen it before.

A cat appears from behind his desk. The feline is the color of coffee with too much milk. I might've assumed any creature haunting the decks of this wretched ship would be a gaunt thing, but the cat is clearly eating well. Still, he doesn't look much like a hunter; his round belly nearly touches the deck as he approaches the captain, who acts as if he doesn't notice when the cat rubs against his boots, purring softly.

The captain sets his eyes on me. "There's nothing I could do to you that would stain my soul any more. My men and I have swum in the depths of purest darkness and drunk deep from the blood goblet there within. Your screams will drown in the lapping of the waves against my cabin wall." He leans close, the stench of death heavy on his breath. "Unless you tell me where it is."

The temptation to spit in his face is strong, but I won't waste even that on the damned. It isn't that I don't believe his threat; I know well the evil that roams this Earth. I've seen it on the battlefields, in the dark corners of cities, in the eyes of the possessed.

And every time, I've defeated it.

"You're wasting what little time you have," I say. "It's a lie."

His grin reveals jagged, rotting teeth and bloody gums. "If that's true, you won't mind sharing the book with me. No harm done by a myth, eh?"

He knows about the book. My muscles tense for no longer than a heartbeat, but I know he saw it. "I destroyed it."

The captain's body trembles as if the effort to appear strong is exhausting for him. "Your oath prevents you from lying, even to a man such as me."

I keep silent. He wasn't asking a question.

The captain breaks into a fit of laughter, coughing so violently it sounds like it may kill him. The cat trots away from him and disappears behind me.

"This will be easier than I thought," he says after pulling himself together.

I furrow my eyebrows at him. "I told you. The book is gone." It's the truth. If these pirates had caught me on the way to my destination—a remote village in the jungles of Africa—they might've had more success. As it is, I have long since watched the blasphemous *Book of the Cherubim* rise up toward God in smoke and embers, another offering atop the pile I have built over my life. All these pirates have accomplished is capturing a priest on his way home.

But I know the captain sees what I'm holding back. After all, he serves the master of lies. "Do you expect me to believe you didn't read it?"

My breath betrays me by catching in my throat. Of course I read the blasted thing, and good thing for the church it was I who found it. I doubt there are many others who would've been strong enough to resist the beautiful temptation of its lies.

The *Book of the Cherubim* was likely the source for the heathen legend of Prometheus. It told of a rogue angel who fell in love with an earthly woman carrying a terrible disease of her own. Because the angel could not endure the thought of her suffering, he stole away from heaven in the night—a ludicrous concept, but I only read the cursed text, I didn't write it—and journeyed to the Garden of Eden.

Once there, he stole the flaming sword that guarded the Tree of Life. The rogue angel breathed in the fire of the sword until it burned him alive. In his dying moment, the angel cast the weapon to the island on which his beloved lived so that she might use it to pierce the veil between heaven and Earth.

But he was too late. She was already dead.

According to the manuscript, the sword still remained on the island, drained of enough power that it could be wielded by a human, at least for an instant, but long enough to allow them to step into paradise. Lies, but my decree was to read the pages, then destroy them.

I have never failed a mission.

"I read it," I say. "And when you kill me, the falsehoods of that manuscript will die with me."

The sound of bells drifts through the window again. The captain pauses at his desk to lift a browned piece of fruit and take a bite. "Do you like the bells? You must, given your profession. Never cared much for them myself, but they do make it useful when you need to find land." He looks at me over his shoulder. "To find people."

The threat is so clear neither of us need acknowledge it. It isn't my life, my pain, he intends to use to coerce me into talk-

ing. These seas are dotted with fishing villages largely unde-
fended because—other than their own lives—they don't have
much to defend.

"What is it you want?" I ask. "Even if the sword did exist,
you can't possibly believe God would allow you into heaven."

For an instant, the darkness melts from his face, and he
looks like a child, a scared little boy. Just as quickly, the visage
disappears, replaced by the cold shell of a man. "I have
witnessed every wonder this world has to offer, and I have
watched it all pass away. My crew and I are tired of this ghost
world. There is only one thing left to see."

I cock my head. "To see heaven?"

"That's all we want, priest—a glimpse of the first light
before we're claimed by the final darkness."

I can't help but laugh in disbelief. What false hopes fools
cling to in the face of mortality. "Do you really think a man
such as you could touch a weapon of heaven?"

The captain shrugs. "Likely not, I suppose, but we must
sail, so it may as well be there. You will give us our heading—
the bells or the sword. Your choice, priest."

Any hesitation is gone. This voyage is certain to end in my
death—there is nothing I can do about that now—but I
cannot allow the blood of innocents to be attached to my
name when I'm gone. The book is a lie. We will find no sword,
but even if we did, the forces of heaven would never permit
men such as these to hold it, to stain the pureness of paradise.
Only I among them would be worthy, and I would use the
blade to accelerate their descent into death.

I struggle against the ropes as I straighten myself in the
chair. The brush of soft fur next to my fingers tells me the cat
is rubbing against my hands. I scratch the creature's head.
"Go northeast."

Days into the voyage, I am permitted to move about the ship as if I am a guest rather than a prisoner. I cannot decide whether it's hubris or indifference that emboldens the pirates to let a proven warrior and worthy enemy walk unencumbered—if unarmed—among them. I don't complain. They ask me to do no work, perhaps knowing it would be futile. Everything about my presence here remains under protest. While every passing moment takes this horrible crew farther from innocent lives, I will not hasten the journey toward blasphemy, no matter how foolish.

They mostly leave me alone, and though I do not envy them each other's company, the voyage is mind-numbingly dull. I spend as much time walking the top deck as I can, watching the crewmen drag themselves from one task to another, each man appearing closer to death's door than the last. Had they not taken my swords—beautiful pieces, blessed by the Holy Father himself, though the record books will never show such a thing, as the priests of my Order exist only for the eyes of the church and of God—I'm confident I could have slain most of the crew, if not all of them. Such would likely mean my own demise; I have no idea how to manage a vessel such as this, let alone by myself. Still, I have found few endeavors more satisfying than being the weapon of God.

And even if they killed me, it would be a more fitting death than what lies before me. I always assumed I would die on a battlefield made either of dirt or of the soul. Whether it was a heathen or a hellish creature that claimed me, I had no doubt Michael himself would honor my passing into the heavenly realm. Perhaps we could compare stories upon my arrival. I'm not so proud as to believe that my conquests would rival his, though I suspect a respectful nod may be in store. A true sword recognizes another.

Instead, the constant hacking and wheezing around me means that one of God's sharpest blades might rot away from whatever disease ravages this crew. The only man among them who seems to maintain the strength of his former glory is the first mate. I never catch his name, probably because the men rarely speak to him unless asked a direct question. If I didn't know differently, I might suspect him to be in charge of this ship. I tell him so one day after the captain had retired to his quarters for several hours, probably unable to rise from the punishment of drink or disease.

The first mate gives me a look I've seen before, one that generally precedes a hidden knife slashing at my throat. Instead, he returns his gaze to the sea. "No, I serve the captain."

I shrug, wondering if it may be wise to sow dissension among them. "Why? You're clearly the strongest man here. Don't tell me you buy into the captain's quest. You don't seem the type."

That pulls a guffaw from his gullet. "To see heaven? No, priest, I do not believe that fate lies before us."

"Then why follow him?"

He starts to answer, then stops. Something in the sea has caught his attention. The first mate walks to the side of the ship and gazes overboard.

My curiosity—and boredom, I assume—urges me to follow. In the distance among the rolling waves, I see long, black formations that look like eels bobbing in the water.

"What is that?" I narrow my eyes. I thought I had seen everything this world had to offer, but the chill in my gut surprises me.

"Kraken," the first mate says, though there is no urgency in his voice. If anything, it sounds like mourning.

"Should we change course? Prepare to attack?"

"It's dead, priest," he says, turning away though his eyes linger a moment longer on the shadow in the sea. "There's no magic left in this world. We destroyed it. Only the darkest things remain."

I want to ask what he means, but I doubt he will tell me the truth.

When the tempest hits, I hear the monsters long before I see them. The crew tries to act as if they're unaware, continuing their work to adjust the sails, to repair damage to the hulls, bailing water as needed. But I see it in their eyes.

They know what comes for us.

The captain emerges from his quarters for the first time all day, a cutlass strapped to his side. I'm not sure he has the strength to draw it from the sheath, but he manages to climb the steps leading to the helm. The first mate is already at the wheel, but the captain moves to the bow.

I scramble from the main deck to stand beside the captain. Before us, high-pitched screeches pierce the thunder and the rolling waves.

"What is it?" I ask.

"The ones who come for us," the captain says.

Four figures appear among the waves. The screeching increases, voices singing in a tortured harmony that jars something loose inside me. Their skin is deep blue. Strange jewels held in place by bones cover their feminine forms. Their eyes are washed with a dead-white film, and they ride horses of smoke across the water. I have heard legends of sirens before, believing them to be nothing more than paranoid myth. But the creatures from those tales always drew men toward them, never gave chase.

"Why are they—" I begin to ask.

"Dead." The first mate lets go of the wheel and pulls his sword, a rusty blade that protests on its way out of the sheath. "But still dangerous."

"Something sinister follows us, priest," the captain says, leaving his sword in its place. "This is only the beginning."

He's hardly finished speaking before the sirens are upon us. Their horses charge up a towering wave with the devil's speed, then disintegrate the moment they reach the crest. The sirens launch into the air, arcing through the night and baring fangs and claws.

I grab the captain's sword and pull it free. The blade is heavier than expected, but my muscles know what to do. I slash at the creature falling toward me, catching her on the shoulder. Her song breaks into a shriek of pain as she tumbles onto the deck behind me, black blood seeping from the wound. The other sirens storm the ship, leaping onto sailors and sinking their fangs into the men's throats.

"Arms!" the first mate yells, dashing toward the invaders.

I follow, my warrior's instincts taking over. My first target is the siren I've already wounded. She's rising to her feet, her empty eyes locked on me. She snarls a challenge.

"God give me strength." I lunge toward her, but my strike misses by inches. She swipes at me with long claws, tearing my shirt as I dodge. The ship lurches, and she stumbles for half a second.

It's all I need.

I swing the sword with all my strength. The blade strikes true, hitting below her chin.

Her head tumbles onto the deck.

The ship falls into chaos. Men fire pistols wildly. Blood washes over the deck. The first mate plunges his sword into the back of a siren feasting on the throat of his shipmate. She whirls and gives him a monstrous death grin, blood gushing from her mouth as she falls over.

Adrenaline surges through my body. I put my foot on the bar attached to the helm and launch myself into the air like a warrior angel. This is the death I deserve, and I will meet it with valor.

I strike at another creature as I descend, but she sees me coming and dives away. Another man aims a pistol at her. She swipes her claws at him, severing his hand at the wrist. The pistol falls between us.

I hurl my sword at her. She sees it in time to duck. The blade clangs against the mast, but it was only a diversion. I dive toward the pistol, raise it, and fire.

The bullet hits between the siren's eyes. I'm not sure if it kills her, but it gives me time to recover the sword and sink it into her heart. She collapses.

I stand over the beast, savoring the moment, admiring the view of my blade stuck in her chest. Another enemy of God has fallen beneath my strength.

"Priest!" a voice screams behind me.

I wheel around to see the final siren in midair, flying toward me. I try to swing my sword, but it isn't in my hand. It's still in my last kill.

I prepare for death.

The first mate appears as if from thin air, tackling the siren from the side. They both hit the deck, and she rolls on top of him.

"No!" I scream.

The siren plunges her claws into his heart.

I grab the sword as the first mate continues to fight, grabbing hold of the siren with both hands. She struggles against his dying grip, her eyes on me, seeing my attack coming. But the first mate won't let go.

I let out a shout of fury and bring my sword crashing down on her neck.

The first mate lives to see her die, but then only a breath longer.

The dawn light pushes away the storm clouds, but not the blood that still stains our decks. The crew doesn't tell me the first mate's name, even after the captain asks me to perform his last rites. The request tears at something inside me. Doubtless this man committed unspeakable acts, but he showed courage in his final moments. He saved my life.

In the end, I perform a short service in Latin so the crew and captain will not recognize my words. I ask that God receive the man into His judgment, but I cannot in good faith commend his soul. It is the best I can do given the circumstances. We all make our choices.

I expect some type of ceremony, if not for the other dead crew members, at least for this man they all respected so much. But once I'm done, his body is stitched up in his sleeping hammock and dropped overboard, just like the others.

To my surprise, I find myself standing at the stern long after his body disappears into the depths. The captain approaches from behind me, making his steps loud, perhaps to alert me that he is coming. I was not permitted to keep his sword, of course, but now he knows what I can do in combat.

I ignore him at first, instead continuing my tortured contemplation over what has taken place. I have performed last rites many times for fallen brothers and sisters, each time commending them to the hand of God, praying in earnest for their souls. Anger rises inside of me at these wretches who chose lives so perverse as to put me in this position.

"Why do you do the things you do?" I ask, not looking at the captain. He has no reason to answer, but he does anyway.

"Because we thirst for what we know we could never earn," he says. "And that thirst consumes us."

I let out a deep breath. It's not the answer I expected, but it's more introspective than anything I might've hoped for. At least they know what they are.

"Darkness still comes," the captain says, stepping beside me. True to his word, I see the clouds gathering in the distance. "We have seen only his heralds."

"Heralds?" I ask, remembering the ferocity of the sirens.

He nods. "Intended to foretell his coming with blood, nothing more. Next time, it will be his ship casting a shadow over us."

I know it's a demon ship when I see the size of it. My knowledge of sailing is severely limited; I spent my life studying only what I would need for my missions—hand-to-hand and armed combat, stealth, biology, exorcism, and spiritual warfare. When the crew calls out different parts of the ship, it always takes me a moment to determine whether they are indicating the left or right, forward or back.

But even I know that no ship crafted by the hands of men could achieve such size and stay afloat.

The demon ship looks as if it's an extension of the thunderclouds moving in, a storm on the ocean with tattered black sails. It dominates the horizon, easily ten times the dimensions of our own vessel. Yet what it has in size, it appears to lack in speed. The ship seems content to follow us at a distance. It's gaining on us, certainly, but slowly, like the cold hand of death creeping up our bones in our final moments. A steady pace is the greatest sign of its confidence. It doesn't need to rush.

It will catch us.

I try to keep my eyes forward. The island is right where the book said it would be. It looks like every other island we've sailed past—sandy-white beaches giving way to dense jungles that are watched over by towering cliffs. Behind the island, a red sunset paints the sky.

Of the handful of men remaining, most suffer from injuries as well as disease, but they do their work well. The captain stands at the helm as they bring us toward the beach. He does not call out orders, but rather encouragements.

"This is it, men. The bill has arrived for the lives we've

lived, but there is yet one last swallow in the bottom of our mugs, and it shall be the sweetest."

The crew never touches the anchor, instead allowing the ship to run aground on the beach. The hull cracks loudly as the wooden planks break apart, but other than swaying with the rocking of the deck, none of the crew respond. No one plans to return to this ship.

I lead the men up the beach, if only because the dark ship in the distance draws ever closer. I harbor no delusion that their captain has a manifest of souls to claim, that they will kill only those for which they came. A great battle awaits me. If there is any truth to the legend of the sword, I intend to find out, if only to arm myself with whatever ordinary weapon I may find.

None of the crew looks back as we march off the beach and into the jungle. They say not a word, but they appear content to have seen the last of the ocean upon which they wasted their lives. In the corner of my eye, I spot the cat disappearing into the trees, choosing a different path, his own destiny. Perhaps he's the wisest among us.

As was my mission, the words of the manuscript are etched into my mind, so I have no problem locating the cavern near the center of the island.

Thunder rumbles overhead, and somehow, I know our pursuers have made landfall. Our time grows small.

We have a single lantern among us, which is given to me as I lead us into the cave. The light reaches only a few feet in front of me, but it is enough. The air cools as we wind further into the passage, the ground sloping down with each step. A breeze between the rock walls sounds almost like chimes, calming my nerves. I have never trembled at the darkness and will not begin now.

The winding path opens up into a larger cavern, a difference I recognize by the changes in the sound of the crew coughing, panting. Still no one speaks, but we all know we have reached the end of our journey. There is no way out except the narrow pathway behind us, and our enemy will soon be upon us.

"Find it," the captain says to me. It sounds more like a plea than an order, but it is unnecessary. I already feel something calling out to me, resonating with a yearning in my soul. It has been there since childhood, but I could never describe it. I had hoped to fan the elusive flame with my accomplishments—through war in this world and the next, through ascension, through glory—but my actions never seemed to ignite the fire in my heart. If anything, it grew fainter. I often feared I would die before truly tapping into that wellspring placed in my soul by the Father. That would be the greatest failure.

But now, all I have to do is follow the call.

My lantern shines on an X on the wall, painted in faded blood and turned on its side. There is no chest, no sign of gold or riches. Before me lies only a pile of rocks.

I drop to my knees, setting the lantern on the ground, and begin to pull the rocks away. The men cough and wheeze behind me, exhausted from the journey. Some groan in pain, others in apparent surrender. I keep moving the rocks until I see it.

An ordinary blade, rusted and broken.

My heart sinks. I was right, of course. The flaming sword could never be in a place such as this, but a part of me had dared to hope.

A low, hellish growl fills the cave. I look over my shoulder and see the demon's red eyes in the dark. Regardless of whether it is one or legion, I sense the presence of true evil filling the room. The numbers don't matter. This is my end.

In the fading light of the lantern, I see the captain collapse onto the ground. He had been the last one standing. Death has come for him, and he seems ready to surrender.

I am not.

The lantern dies as my hand reaches for the handle of the sword, and I pray for what is undeserved.

"Leave," the demon says, speaking in an impossibly low tone that rumbles the cavern.

I pause. "And let you have the sword?"

"The sword will remain buried," it says. "I came not for a broken weapon, but to claim what is owed. Treasures and glories unknown await you beyond this island, priest, yours to be taken. You need only walk away."

My hand pulls back for a moment, but something catches my attention. A glint of light reflects on the blade. My eyes flick to the lantern, but it is still black. The men groan. The captain whispers something I cannot hear, but I don't believe it is intended for me.

When I reach again for the sword, the demon's voice shifts from a low growl of warning to a shriek of fury that feels like knives in my ears. My fingers wrap around the handle, feeling the cracked leather beneath my skin.

The light of the blade grows, filling the cavern with a radiant, glowing blue. The power is overwhelming, blinding, but there is no pain. The demon's shriek drowns in a new song, far more powerful, far more terrifying. It bids me to stand.

My vision clears, though I do not see the cavern. Instead, it is as if space has opened before me with a bright sun burning in the center. Around it stand creatures the size of planets. They look like the beasts of creation mixed together —some with heads of lions, others eagles, rams. Some have hooves, others claws. All stretch out great wings of gold and silver that reflect the light.

"So beautiful," the captain says behind me. "Let me never leave."

I look again at the sword, now burning with heavenly starfire. I turn and step between my crew and the red eyes, which are still fixed on me. The light does not fall on my enemy, but I don't need to see it. Behind me, I hear the thunder of the heavens and among it, the roar of the kraken, the song of the sirens. The breath of the cherubim pushes at my back, urging me toward my destiny.

I hold the sword high. The battle is already won.

About the Author

Clint Hall has been writing stories since childhood, during which he spent most of his time in English class creating comic books. Luckily for him, his teacher not only allowed it, she bought every issue. Now, Clint lives in Atlanta and works full-time as a writer, creating marketing content by day and stories filled with hope, wonder, and adventure by night.

Princess Yum Yum's Challenge

NANCY DIMAURO

M olly scowled as she handed over her weapons to Haven's door attendant. The man locked her firearms into a cylinder, then handed her a chit. Lachlan, her quartermaster, jostled her shoulder. Other women thought Lac handsome, but Molly'd seen him in nappies and knew how he'd gotten the scar others found rakish but cost him the sight in his left eye, leaving it a clouded blue next to his brown eye.

"You need a drink, or a man," he said.

Then there was that.

"Does naught else pass through that thick head?" Molly held up a hand. "Silly question."

The skin around Lac's eyes crinkled as he smiled. "First drink's on me."

"Now that's sense."

As they shouldered their way onto the main floor of the pub, Molly spotted most of the captains whose ships lay at anchor. But not *him*. He must have sought other amusement.

Kymani, the pub's owner, handed her a whiskey as she leaned against the zebrawood bar. The miasma of cheap soap, brine, sour malt, tobacco smoke, and flowery perfumes of the whores and Johnny boys meant home. The whiskey, with its hint of fruit over oak and vanilla, calmed nerves taut since she'd crossed paths with a British man-of-war.

"You're drinking the wrong drink." Henry Avary's scent of sea air and juniper enveloped her. Her skin tingled. He was here after all. She fought dueling urges to shiver or punch him.

Balls.

Avary caught Kymani's attention. "Bring our darling Princess of the Sea a Princess Yum Yum."

"Reserving the title of Queen for yourself?" Molly asked.

The crowd pulled back like the tide until no one was within arm's reach. Lac had vanished as well. Traitor. He'd scrub the deck for that.

Molly focused on Avary's work-roughened hand resting on

the bar, knowing the same calluses that crossed her palms would grace his. Though British, his skin was a sun-kissed brown. Neither of them was suited to London's ballrooms—if she ever had been as an Irish woman.

Kymani placed a tankard of ruby-colored beer before her, then cleared the other mugs off the bar. She scowled, though removing potential weapons was prudent. Avary and she were … combustible when mixed.

Mirth sparkled in Avary's changeable hazel eyes. His dark-blond hair dusted his broad shoulders. He rapped the bar with scarred knuckles. "Drink."

"You're just one wave short of a shipwreck. You sail dangerous waters."

"Stalling?" he asked.

Kymani's daughter had named the cursed drink. By tradition, captains bought the drink for those they challenged and then again for those they had bested on the Blue. No one had had the balls to goad Molly. Until Avary. His obsession with winning was one reason she avoided his ocean, the Indian.

She tossed down the drink, its tartness bitter on her tongue, then slammed the empty mug onto the bar. Cheers arose. Her eyes locked with Avary's, and he brushed the corner of her mouth with his thumb. The touch shot quivers through her. Something dark—some might call it desire—flickered in his eyes. And that look was the other reason she avoided him.

Avary leaned down. "See you soon."

Men thumped Avary on the back. Whores cooed as he left. His gaze found hers when he retrieved his weapons at the door, a slow smile lifting the corner of his mouth. Blood thundered in her ears, drowning out the ribald jesting. The aromas that had meant home now turned her stomach.

Lac sidled in beside her. "You handled that well, Cap'n." He tapped the bar for a whiskey. "Best get his challenge out in the open."

"Why me?" she growled.

"Unfinished business?" He picked up his glass and winked over the top. "Now, we can blow that bastard out of the water."

The deserted island off the Florida coast was the *Bonny Read*'s last stop before Molly could push her to the Caribbean. The crew would gather supplies for the last month of their journey, then celebrate with a cask of the Irish.

Shading her eyes, Molly glowered at the ship rounding the peninsula—a ship whose flag sported four blue chevrons on a red background.

Avary'd found her. Her tradition had become her weakness.

"Balls," Molly cursed.

Questions of Avary's intent were answered with a cannon's boom, though the round splashed fifty feet off her bow. Her ambiguity about the man vanished.

"To stations," she called.

The *Fancy*, Avary's forty-three-gun Spanish man-of-war, outclassed her twenty-gun galleon. If the *Fancy* pinned the *Bonny Read* against the shore, she was lost. Molly chewed on her bottom lip. *Fancy* had more weapons, but the *Bonny Read*'s iron-shod keel had strength.

"We're ramming."

She spun the wheel toward the *Fancy*. Avary would get out of her way or she'd cripple his ship. The sails luffed full, and the *Bonny Read* leapt forward. He had time to avoid impact.

Turn, you damned fool.

He didn't.

"Hold!" she yelled. Her grip tightened on the wheel.

The crack of timbers rent the air as the *Bonny Read* smashed into the helm. Shouts arose from the *Fancy*. Her crew bellowed in answer, tossed hooks over the *Fancy*'s gunwales, and boiled over its sides. Gunfire drowned out the screams.

Molly slashed at a man, her blade tearing a hole in his shirt and slicing a bloody line on his left bicep. He staggered back, then put his sword up.

"Parole," he yelled.

For a man barely injured to give his *parole* was wrong, but she nodded her acceptance. The man's sword clattered to the deck as she turned to face her next opponent. Except there wasn't one. Avary's crew had surrendered.

Muffled booms sounded from the *Fancy*'s hold, and she listed toward the *Bonny Read*. Balls. Molly had to separate the ships before both were lost.

"Cut the *Fancy*'s rigging."

Sail monkeys, nimble young boys, hacked at the ropes connecting the vessels while other sailors freed the grappling hooks. Her gaze raked over the captives for the face she was both loath and desperate to see.

Lac vaulted between the ships with Avary in tow. Lac bore slash marks in his favorite shirt but seemed hale. Avary bled from saber cuts on his right arm and cheek and a nick at the base of this throat. The last had likely caused Avary to surrender.

The *Bonny Read* broke free of the *Fancy*'s death embrace and leapt for the Blue.

Avary stormed up the stairs to the wheel deck. Feet splayed and arms crossed, he stood as if he commanded. "You have to put the fire out before the *Fancy* is lost."

"I'll have your parole." Molly's voice remained level.

"Never."

She nodded. Lac and Anne, the boatswain, grabbed Avary's arms. Then even as it sickened her, Molly gave the order she must.

"Fire the *Fancy*."

"You bi—"

Lac's fist crashed into Avary's jaw. His teeth clacked, then he dropped to the deck.

"Keep him in your quarters," Molly said.

"*My* quarters?"

"You annoyed me, Lac."

Avary stopped midstride when Molly opened the cabin door the next morning. Lac's shirt hung loose on him, giving Avary the appearance of a six-foot-tall petulant child. His anger sizzled the air between them.

Finger pointed, he stalked toward her. "You burned my ship."

His oversized shirt brushed her arm. "She was sinkin' and afire. She'd have closed the waterway if she sank. You would have made the same choice if it were my vessel 'stead of yours."

He opened his mouth then snapped it shut. "My men?"

"Thirty in the brig. The rest gave their parole or are wounded."

"How many?"

Tallying the butcher's bill left a rancid taste in her mouth. Too many had lost their lives for no reason. "If you had a full crew of one fifty, there's twenty unaccounted for, another two dozen like enough to die. Ten of mine dead or dying." She folded her arms across her chest. "I need your parole."

He snorted. "As if I'd give it to you."

She turned to leave.

"My cabin boy?" Something in Avary's tone, a mix of worry and regret, made her look back at him.

"Safe."

A grateful shudder ran through Avary as he bowed his head.

Storm clouds squatted on the horizon off their starboard, a dark smudge between her and home. Molly could risk steering through and hope it was only a squall, or she could change course and add time to their journey. She nudged the ship port.

"Cap'n," Hunter said in his still-piping Cockney-accented voice. The towheaded cabin boy couldn't have seen ten summers, but his eyes were older than hers.

Molly softened her scowl into a smile.

"Oi, tray's ready," he said.

She ruffled the boy's hair; he tolerated the affection.

When she and Hunter entered Lac's room, Avary was already standing, his back to her. Lac's red jacket pulled across the captain's shoulders as he tensed.

"No," Avary said without turning.

"I'm not askin' you." She paused as Hunter placed the tray on the desk. "Food."

"Hoping that's the way to my heart?"

"I'm hoping you have one."

Avary turned. His gaze snagged on Hunter. The air left Avary's lungs in a *whoosh* as he swept the boy into his arms.

"I feared I'd lost you," he said so softly Molly almost missed it.

Tears filled Avary's eyes; Hunter's lit with adoration. Avary could love a child and have the child return that love. So? It didn't make him a good man.

She let them talk until their voices turned to whispers.

"Hunter," she said. "You'll resume your duties in the morning."

"Aye, Cap'n."

The door to Lac's quarters banged close on the wake of the tidal wave that was a small boy.

Avary arched an eyebrow at Molly. "You have plans for me this eve?"

"Your parole?"

His lips thinned to a bloodless line.

"Thought not." She turned.

"Molly," Avary said as her hand brushed the handle. "How would you fare without occupation?"

"Poorly."

He crossed to her. "If I stay in this box, I'll go mad."

"Give your parole, and you'll have free access to the ship."

"Would you?"

Would she give her promise not to retake her vessel or commandeer the one who'd defeated her to the captain who'd burned her ship? No, she would not give Avary her parole. Rather, she suspected she'd try to gut him.

"I thought not," he said, a cocksure grin on his face. How did that one expression make her want to hit him and fall under his spell? "Your crew is—what—half female?"

A cold spike stabbed her heart. Was he suggesting she whore her crew?

He held up his hand. "I mean nothing untoward."

"Is the boy yours?" She hadn't meant to ask. Ever.

Avary's deep chuckle hit her low in the gut. "Are you asking if I have a bastard—or a wife?" He paused. "No. I found him in St. Giles."

Her stomach roiled. St. Giles, London's poorest section, was never kind. Larger, older, and craftier predators hunted those streets, devouring orphan boys.

"But—"

He grabbed the tankard of rum off the tray. "Your crew?"

"Yes. About half."

His eyebrow quirked up.

"Should they whore themselves for a roof? Marry a beast to appease a father?" She shook her head. "I give them a choice."

He sat at Lac's desk and motioned to the other chair. "Join me?" When she stayed on her feet, he asked, "Doesn't having women aboard cause trouble?"

"No sex."

He choked on his rum. "What?"

She retrieved Lac's "hidden" bottle of whiskey from his chest and poured a glass. "Ship's rule." She swirled the amber liquid. "Why didn't your men fight?"

"The plunder from the treasure ship of the *Grand Mughal* is cursed worse than Cortez's Aztec gold. It wasn't just a royal fleet but carried pilgrims and held more wealth than any man could spend in a lifetime. A man with something to lose lacks the taste for danger, for this life. But we have no safe harbor." His eyes flashed from hazel to ice-blue. "You changed course. Are you collecting my bounty?"

"I have letters of Marque and Reprisal." She walked to the open porthole and let cool sea air wash over her. "Had an audience with the Queen." She paused. "I'd not hand over anyone labeled 'pirate' when the Crown can't decide if we're heroes or monsters."

Avary's brow furrowed as he stood up. "You've surrendered ships for bounty."

"The ships? Aye. The crew?" She turned toward him. "Only for other crimes."

Avary's rough hands covered her shoulders. His finger traced her jaw, a gesture so unexpected, so gentle, her stomach quivered.

"I'm sure they deserved it." His breath caressed her face.

A shudder ran through the ship as it tacked.

Her stomach quivered again, but for a very different reason. "If Lac's changed course, then so has the storm."

Avary stepped away as she darted from the cabin.

Heading to the deck, she bit her lower lip. *Fool.* Why had she confided in *Henry Avary*? The only strength she could count on was hers.

Lac nodded port as she stepped next to him on the wheel deck. "She's chasing us," he said.

The storm front swallowed the light.

Even knowing the answer, she asked, "Can we bypass it?"

"I suspect not."

"Balls."

What had she told Avary at Haven? He was one wave shy of a shipwreck. Now, those words haunted her.

She scrubbed a hand over her face. "Lay out safety lines."

The hurricane caught them at first light. The ship pitched and rolled. Molly told herself she needed to warn Avary, though she knew he was no fool. He'd know the signs, feel the approaching tempest through the ship's movement. She pushed open his cabin door.

Anne's arms were wrapped around Avary. His hands fisted the material of her tunic, but when he saw Molly, he pushed Anne away. She grabbed the serving tray and rushed out the door. The slam reverberated through the room.

"One rule," Molly said. "No sex aboard this vessel."

Avary rolled his eyes. "A ship full of women is a nightmare."

"Careful."

"Women." He tossed his hands in the air. "Changeable as the sea and just as dangerous. You're furious, thinking I bedded that woman. She's mad, knowing I refused her."

The scent of sea not sex filled the room. The sheets were rumpled from sleep, not tangled from lovemaking. Avary *could* have been covering Anne up, refusing her. Heat prickled up her neck.

Balls.

"Didn't you reserve 'Queen of the Sea' for yourself?" she asked.

Why couldn't she keep a civil tongue?

His hand clamped around her wrist, and he pulled her close.

"Push further and I will show you all the ways a man desires a woman." His gruff voice sent flutters straight to her core.

"You're uncommonly beautiful," she said.

Her fingers traced the lines of his face. Strong jaw, carved cheekbones, the slight bend in his nose where it had been broken, full sensual lips. His hazel eyes changed color depending on his mood and the light. A rangy build created by life at sea. She felt the corded strength in his arms. Even his slightly bowed legs didn't detract from his appeal.

That familiar scent of the sea and juniper enveloped her.

Damn. She needed distance. She moved to step back.

She wasn't prepared for the kiss, how his mouth slanted over hers, how she rose to meet him. His mouth was persuasive rather than possessive. His mouth, that generous and tempting mouth, undid her. His teeth nibbled her bottom lip. He pressed against her, his body shuddering as he fought to retain control.

She'd not have it. She wanted him. Her hands traced the curve of his back as her tongue slid against his.

He moaned and pulled her closer.

A knock sounded on the cabin door.

She stepped back, dragging a ragged breath into her lungs. "Balls. I … can't. There's a hurricane."

Avary's sun-kissed skin paled. Strong men fell to their knees when storms brewed on the Blue. But a hurricane? Even those who lacked faith sought godly intervention. Even a man so godless he could attack a pilgrim's convoy feared the storm.

Lac opened the door.

"Give me your parole," she said to Avary.

Avary swallowed, but shook his head.

Disgusted, she turned from him. "Lac, see to the crew." She followed her quartermaster through the open door.

The rain hit as she reached the helm. The man on duty shot her a grateful look, then rushed to his regular post.

"Tie in!" she ordered, her voice rising over the storm's howl.

Her crew tied lifelines around their waists.

The ship trembled. Molly turned the bow into the teeth of the beast.

"Everyone secured?" she shouted when Lac approached.

"All of ours, except you," Lac said. "What of the prisoners?"

She swiped an arm across her face to push the water from her eyes. "Avary made his choice. Give the same option to his crew. If they refuse, they should pray we don't take on enough water to drown 'em."

Lac raced toward the hatch.

A voice growled over her shoulder. "Why aren't you tied in?"

She glared. "Avary, get back to your quarters."

"I can help."

Could she turn away a seasoned captain's assistance? As much as her pride wanted to say "yes," duty answered.

"Tie in," she barked.

A rope looped her waist.

"Avary—"

"I am tied in," he said, his voice a shout in her ear. "Lac required it before letting me on deck."

She'd kill her quartermaster—later. Avary tightened the loop of hemp, forcing air from her lungs. "Too tight," she gasped.

"It has to be if it's to work," he said.

The wind shifted. Her focus snapped back to the helm. The next wave hit broadside. The deck tilted. Timbers on the mast creaked under the strain from rain-soaked sails.

"Lac!"

"Here." Lac materialized in the driving rain.

"Drop the mainsail."

"That's crazy," Avary said. "We'll founder."

"We'll capsize otherwise. Lac, make it so."

"Aye, Cap'n." He disappeared back into the storm.

She put both hands on a wheel spoke and hauled against the tide. Avary's hands closed around the wood next to hers. Together they fought to keep the *Bonny Read* upright. On the back side of the storm's rotations, the wind and waves battered the ship and crew. The heat of Avary's body against hers tethered her.

A sixty-foot wall of water reared up to cover the world.

"God's teeth," Avary cursed. "How big is the ship?"

"Not big enough," she yelled back.

Lac rang the alert bell. The wave slammed her to the deck. Something cracked in her chest, and pain ripped through her. Air rushed from her lungs in a scream; she inhaled water. Avary was gone. Receding water pulled her toward the Blue, and she scrabbled for the helm. Her fingers closed on her rescue line. She clawed up the line to the wheel's post. She threw her weight against the spin of the wheel. The *Bonny Read* shuddered and listed starboard. Coughing water from her lungs, she stood.

"Port!" she bellowed, unsure if any survived to follow the order. "All hands port!"

Locking her knees, she wrestled the wheel.

Her safety line jerked. She bit her lip to stop another scream and gripped the wheel.

Avary's arms bracketed hers. "She's rolling."

"The hell she is," Molly growled. "She'll stay afloat." Her crew gathered on the port side. "Stay afloat," she whispered to her ship.

Avary lent his strength against the rudder's pull. Her crew engaged in a macabre dance, dashing from port to starboard as they heeded her orders to act as living ballast. Waves lashed the *Bonny Read*, but the storm was spent, exhausted by its failed attempt to capsize them. The rain grew patchy, and eventually stars broke through the night sky.

Around midnight the winds stopped howling.

Molly's muscles ached bone-deep. Her fingers were cramped from her white-knuckled grip. Her legs shook. Breathing hurt.

"Lac, where's your safety line?" she asked. But her words slurred as if she'd drunk a bottle of whiskey so what came out was "Lock, whersh's yer safefty line?"

Lac pried her fingers off the wheel. "Bed, Cap'n."

"You've hwad lsse sgleep wthan me."

Exhaustion etched Lac's face. "Aye, but I'm coherent. You brought her through safe. Bed. Now." He turned her and pushed her toward her quarters.

She worked on the rain-soaked knot at her waist with numb fingers, but made no progress. Damn Avary. Three steps into her stagger, pain knifed through her. Biting her lip, she turned.

Avary stared at her, a rope taut between them. He'd lashed them together. This time when she walked, Avary lurched along behind her.

Stumbling over her cabin's threshold, she banged her hip on her desk, Avary closing the door behind them.

Molly opened her eyes to see Lac looming over her. His cat's grin filled her vision.

"You know, yer the only woman I know who'd ignore a half-naked man tied up in her room in favor of sleep," he said.

Sitting up, she hissed in pain. Her salt-soaked clothes were stiff, and the taste of dead rat filled her mouth.

Head cushioned on his arm, Avary slept on the floor, the

blasted rope still connecting them. A jagged scar etched his right shoulder. Bright light filtered in through the open door and caressed Avary's naked back. Her fingers itched to trace down his spine and follow the slight V as his waist dipped to his buttocks.

Blast and damnation.

"I couldn't untie the rope," she said.

Lac dropped to his knees and made short work of the knot. He lowered his voice. "There's a problem."

Bracing her arms on her bed, she stood. Pain turned her vision white. Panting, she said, "What?"

He scowled at Avary. "*His* men are gathering malcontents for a no-confidence vote. They say he steered the ship to safety, not you." He held up a hand. "Not everyone saw you. They forget hearing your orders."

Nausea clawed up her throat. "Why would our crew join this foolishness?" She wanted a clean shirt but couldn't risk raising her arms while Lac was present. Even a rumor of an injury would fuel a no-confidence vote.

Lac blew out a breath. "*He* spent the night here. Anne's claiming you've violated the 'no sex' rule."

"The poxy strumpet."

His gaze turned regretful. "You're needed on deck."

Avary still slept when she left her cabin.

Molly bit down a scream as the wheel shifted in her grip. She wasn't sure how much longer the injuries she was hiding would allow her to stand. But she needed to be here. Lac mingled with the crew, but Avary's men, freed from the brig, poisoned the air with lies and false promises.

"Captain," Avary said from behind her.

Talking over her shoulder, she said softly, "Three choices: give your parole, stay in the cabin, or be tossed overboard."

He gave a low chuckle. "Since I don't want to be tossed off the ship, I propose a better option." He raised his voice so it would carry. "The Code prevents me from giving you my parole—"

"The same Code that dictated you go down with the *Fancy*?"

The wind buffeted the sails. Waves slapped the hull. Wood and ropes creaked. No one spoke. What happened next would decide her fate.

Avary stepped forward. Her aching side made her appreciate not having to turn. He'd changed into more of Lac's clothes. "I thought we were lost when the rogue hit. But you knew your ship and your crew, and you wouldn't give up. You're the better captain."

The silence stretched. Avary widened his eyes at her as if to say, "Get on with it." Clearly, he hadn't been sleeping earlier.

"Thank you, Captain Avary." She released a breath. "We'll arrive at Pirates' Cove in a month." She gave him a genuine smile. "Then I'll buy you the drink I owe you."

His features lightened as he returned the smile. "I'd enjoy that."

Whispers followed as he left the deck. The tension that had cracked through the crew dissipated like St. Elmo's fire. The normal chatter of a crew going about its business resumed. There would be no vote.

She remained at the helm for another hour then inspected her ship, making sure to speak with each crewmember, reforging what had nearly sundered. The sun had sunk when she reached the officer's quarters.

"I *should* throw you overboard," she said to Avary as she closed Lac's door behind her. The motion made her wince.

Avary set aside a book. "I'll stay here. Much more comfortable." He rose from the bunk and walked toward her.

"Thank you," she said.

"I don't like that you bested me, but you are the better captain." He took her hands and raised them to kiss her knuckles. Heat drained from her face, and she wobbled on her feet. He clamped an arm around her. She screamed, her vision white.

"Molly?" He tugged her shirt free and yanked it over her head. "God's teeth, you stubborn fool."

The door slammed open as Lac, sword drawn, burst into the room. "Let her go," he growled.

"She'll fall."

Metal slid against leather as Lac sheathed his weapon. His face loomed before hers as he helped her to the bed. "Oh, Mol, what have you done?"

"Nothing," she said.

"Mol, you're bruised from breast to waist." His fingers probed down her rib cage.

She hissed in pain. "Something snapped when that wave slammed me to the deck."

"I'm getting Doc," Lac said.

Avary took Lac's place at Molly's bedside. His knuckles brushed her cheek. "Stubborn chit."

"What would you have done?"

His smile didn't erase the worry from his eyes. "The same damned thing."

She'd been bruised, not broken. Ship life returned to its routine. Henry hadn't given his parole, but somehow had slipped into its ebb and flow.

Afternoons found him shirtless and coiling ropes, climbing rigging or cleaning the deck. At nights, they played hazard with Lac and the other officers. They spent hours talking about nothing. Henry watched her when he thought she wasn't looking. When caught, he'd smile, then return to his task.

That smile haunted her days. His kiss haunted her nights. Yet, he didn't kiss her again.

Her shoulders eased as they pulled into harbor. Her gaze flitted to where Henry joked with Anne. His deep laugh rolled over the deck. Molly's stomach roiled. She would miss the toff. She haggled with the harbormaster for berthing fees—fees that went higher when he saw Henry's crew leaving her ship.

Henry left the *Bonny Read* without a word. Apparently, only she had felt a connection between them.

Congratulations greeted her as she descended Haven's stairs. Kymani had a whiskey waiting for her at the bar. Her dinner of chicken and plantains had just arrived when the hair on her neck prickled. Quiet came over the pub. The scent of juniper and sea enveloped her.

"I owe you a drink," she said without turning.

Kymani placed a mug at her elbow.

She raised the ruby-red concoction in salute. "Your Princess Yum Yum, Captain Avary."

His mouth twisted as he fought a smile. He tossed the drink back and slammed the empty mug down. Cheers erupted.

Henry's eyes, gray in the candlelight, met hers. Her skin tingled. She swiveled on her stool, and her knees brushed his thighs. She stood. His breath whispered over the shell of her ear as he bent his head. Shivers raced down her spine. She lifted her face, lips parted. The promise of the kiss hovered there, a breath away.

"This isn't the *Bonny Read*," he said. "If you want that kiss, take it."

She laced her fingers behind his neck, drew his head down

and brushed her lips over his. His hands tracked up her thighs to rest on her waist. She nipped at his bottom lip. He parted his lips, and her tongue darted in to tangle with his. Her senses clouded with his flavor mingled with a hint of raspberry. The shock of it sent flares to her core.

Henry drew in a ragged breath. "Stay."

She rested her head against his chest. "You have a room?"

He shook his head. "Not tonight. Always. I wanted you to distraction, so I challenged you." He kissed the tip of her nose. "Fell in love on the *Bonny Read*." Anxiety crossed his face when she didn't respond. "You're supposed to say it back."

"Am I?"

"Stubborn woman."

She raised up on her toes. "I love you, Henry."

"Marry me?"

She narrowed her eyes. "You're doing this just to get my ship, aren't you?"

"Keep your damned ship. Just marry me."

Lac loomed over Henry's shoulder. "Well, Molly girl?"

Henry scowled. "We agreed you'd stay quiet."

"Never trust me. I'm a pirate." Lac beamed. "You marryin' this toff?"

"Aye."

Applause and cheers filled the bar. Kymani placed two mugs of Princess Yum Yum before them. They raised them in a toast.

"To the Queen of the Sea," Avary said.

They clinked the tankards together and downed their drinks. After all, marriage would pose their greatest challenge.

About the Author

Nancy's alter ego, Nancy D. Greene, is a business lawyer and women entrepreneurship advocate in Northern Virginia. She's been published in three prior Superstars anthologies, and her non-fiction book, *Navigating Legal Landmines: A Practical Guide to Business Law for Real People*, is an Amazon best-seller. Nancy lives on a horse-farm in Virginia and no longer hides her more geeky tendencies. For updates on what Nancy's up to, please visit: www.attorneynancygreene.

Where We Will All Go

C.H. HUNG

My mother drives a pale green hearse and ushers the dead to their final resting places, but not without a fee.

She takes, usually, from the feet. A toe will rarely be missed, she once explained to me, because once the body has been embalmed and the feet encased in shoes, nobody thinks to check again for missing parts. Plus, the bones are small and easy to extract, and even easier to grind up into fine dust, sprinkled into her morning tea, and sipped from her favorite chipped mug that says, in black block letters upon a white background, I WISH I WERE DEAD.

It's the only vessel from which she'll swallow death. So I watch her carefully on days when she takes her tea from that mug, sipping quietly at the small table in our basement apartment's kitchen. I watch to see if the taste makes her eyes crinkle more than usual, or if her slender throat will convulse in gags, or if her unpainted lips will pucker.

When she is done, she tells me that I must be a good girl, to stay quiet so I don't disturb the dead, and to wait for her. Then she fades from sight while I head upstairs to the funeral home, watching mourners wail over what's left behind.

I'm dying to know what it's like, to be drunk on bones. I know only that it is old magic she steeps, older than religion or voodoo or paganism. Older, certainly, than me, a high school dropout, mopping floors at a funeral home.

I begged her for a taste of her tea, once. She took me with her that day, but we rode in her hearse and she didn't drink her tea, and neither did I. All I tasted was the disappointment of sitting silently while Mom met with a ragtag group of strangers.

The next morning, Mom brought out her chipped mug. But before I could speak, she said, "No, Di. It'll happen soon enough." And I knew from her terrible tone not to ask again.

Still, I wanted to know what she saw that I couldn't, what she did while she was gone. I wanted to know what it meant to be her daughter, because she is the only family I have, and we are quite unlike the somber families who march through the doors of the funeral home.

Every time she leaves, I wonder if she'll come back, even though she always does.

So when she says today is the day and to get into the hearse, I don't hesitate.

This morning, the fog is thicker than the questions in my throat as Mom speeds through Orange County and down the I-5 freeway toward San Diego. The back of the hearse is empty and smells of aerosol sanitizer.

She'd raided Mr. Nelson's toes before they were encased in his favorite argyle socks and his stiffly dressed body was laid out in his casket. She'd brewed her tea, stirring in bones and sugar with calm, measured circles, and she didn't rise from the kitchen table until the mug was empty.

The hearse sails through traffic like a ghostly pirate ship, passing through oceans of traffic-weary commuters with barely a shiver to raise goose bumps, her magic encasing the hearse, encasing me, like a benevolent halo.

The skies brighten above us, cloudless and endlessly blue, as luminous as the excitement coursing through me. At last, I'll find out what it's like to drink the bone tea, to go where my mother goes when she leaves me behind.

At last, I'll understand her and her magic.

At last, I'll understand what legacy to expect, from a mother like her.

An hour later, Mom pulls up to an abandoned restaurant —a long, low building hanging off the side of the embarcadero overlooking San Diego Harbor, across the street from a lush waterfront park. The restaurant has been empty for ages, ever since the previous tenants left after running a thriving seafood empire for several decades. It was time to retire, the couple said. Time to focus on ventures closer to grandchildren.

But I knew—because Mom told me—that what had driven them away dwells deep beneath the postholes centering the building, right over the gravesite of countless sea monsters, laid to rest by Mom's predecessors.

"Shh," Mom had said when she brought me here last time. "They will only let you through if you don't disturb them."

"Who?" I'd asked. "And through where?"

But she'd only bowed her head at the ocean beneath the restaurant, then hurried us through its front doors.

Later, Mom called the restaurant Patmos, but that hadn't been its name when it'd been in business. I looked it up and told her that Patmos was an actual place—a Greek island, and we were nowhere near Greece—in the self-important way that only a twelve-year-old can pull off and get away with. But she just laughed and said I needed to learn that place wasn't only about geography. That places could exist in other ways.

It didn't make sense then. It doesn't make sense now.

But now that I know where we are, I know who we're seeing. The memory of my last visit sets my heart pounding so hard against my chest, I wonder that I don't wake the dead. I hunch my shoulders forward, trying to make myself invisible.

Mom notices I've faltered and waits for me to catch up, then grasps my hand. "Remember, Di," she says. "Don't speak."

"No disturbing the dead," I whisper, and then say nothing more as Mom gives my fingers a quick squeeze.

Still holding my hand, Mom dips her head toward the waves lapping against the weathered, algae-slick pilings holding up the restaurant. Then we fade through the boarded-up doors of the building, the wood passing through our ephemeral forms like gossamer mist. Once inside, Mom lets go of me and her magic. We solidify in the sea-chilled room, and the rest of the group swims into focus.

There are seven of them, people of varying ages seated in

folding chairs arranged in a circle like at an AA meeting. There's a tall, thin priest with gray hair, hands folded in the sleeves of his black cassock, and a petite Asian woman in a red power suit ignoring everyone while tapping away on her phone. A mousy-looking, potbellied Latino in a black suit sits in another chair, faking a relaxed pose. His dark brown eyes dart this way and that, studying everyone, measuring us, radiating anxiety like a heat lamp. Another guy who looks way too old to be sporting a man bun chats with a pleasantly plump Indian woman, his red T-shirt advertising a yoga studio's logo.

The Indian woman is an obstetrician. I only remember that because she's wearing pale green scrubs. She is seated opposite the empty chair reserved for my mother. The good doctor nods toward Mom in greeting, the only one to do so.

"Finally," intones an impatient baritone belonging to a short, barrel-chested man with a thick red beard. He's wearing a wife-beater and dirty, white cotton shorts. A trash collector, if I'm remembering correctly. "We're withering away from boredom over here."

"Be nice," chides a lilting soprano from the chair opposite him, her voice no less musical for her asperity. The woman wears a kind, grandmotherly face crowned with tight, gray curls, and a prim Sunday skirt suit in white linen.

Mom makes eight. Her clothes don't reveal much about her profession—faded denim shorts, flip-flops, a worn, flannel button-up.

The grandmotherly soprano squints her pale blue eyes in my direction. I freeze in place, surprised at the attention, uncertain which way to go. Last time, I'd been thoroughly ignored.

"Diane," the woman says warmly, "you've grown so tall."

"It's been seven years," Mom cuts in. "She was a child then."

"On the cusp of womanhood," the soprano replies, unruffled by Mom's sharp tone.

"Still a child," Mom retorts.

She catches my round-eyed stare and makes a small motion with her hand. I bite my lip and take the hint, lowering my gaze to the ground, the hairs rising along my nape as I feel seven pairs of eyes boring into the top of my head.

The obstetrician rises to her feet and moves toward me, but Mom steps in front of the shorter woman, blocking her from my view. They stare at each other for a minute in unearthly silence before the doctor says, "You cannot protect her forever."

"Surely there's another way," Mom says, now soft and pleading. "Someone else."

The doctor's voice, when she answers, is full of quiet sympathy. "You know there isn't enough time left to find another."

I can hardly believe it when, reluctantly, my mother bows her head. Her arm shifts, passing something unseen to the doctor, and the doctor flows past her.

At some unspoken signal, the others also rise and glide toward me without a sound, parting around my mother standing stoic and still like a boulder in a river, her back facing me.

Mom, I want to cry out, but I bite down harder on my lip until I taste blood. She told me not to speak here, and I will not, no matter how badly I want to.

The group encircles me, all of them holding hands, save for the obstetrician who stands before me. She holds a small bone cupped in her open palm. I recognize its size and shape. It's the distal phalange of a big toe—Mr. Nelson's, I presume.

"Don't worry, little one," the doctor says, even though I tower over her by a good foot or so. She withdraws a small, wooden bowl from the breast pocket of her scrubs—okay, *that* trick I haven't seen before—and closes her fingers over the bone. When she holds her fist over the bowl, crumbled dust trickles through her hand as if she were seasoning a cauldron of stew.

The dust dissolves into the reddish-yellow liquid of a well-fermented black tea, more expensive than the murky brown stuff brewed from the cheap supermarket tea bags that Mom usually drinks. Fragrant steam rises from the bowl, warm and inviting.

The doctor holds the bowl out to me. "This won't hurt a bit," she says with an encouraging smile.

I look at Mom for guidance, but she still has her back turned. She's angry, but she won't do anything about it, not right now. I can tell from the stiff set of her shoulders what the effort is costing her.

The doctor is lying then. But of course she is. Doctors always lie.

"You wanted to know, didn't you?" asks the trash collector. "Where your mother goes?"

Ten minutes ago, I would've screamed yes. Ten minutes ago, I would've grabbed the tea and gulped it all down, heedless of how hot it was.

But ten minutes ago, I wasn't here, abruptly set adrift by my own mother.

I am suddenly, frightfully certain that I no longer want to know.

I shake my head and back away, but I can feel the solidity of the circle at my back, eyes watching me wherever I spin. The circle remains unbroken, unwavering resolve caging me in place until I'm facing the obstetrician again.

Don't speak, Mom had said, so I can't even ask what the hell's going on, or why.

I glance at her again, but she refuses to meet my eyes. Not even when she left me at home have I ever felt so alone.

The obstetrician is still holding the bowl, same pleasant smile in place, as if she hadn't just watched me turn in circles like an idiot. I take the bowl in both hands, trembling and fighting not to drop it. The doctor steps back, and the circle parts to include her in its perimeter, her hands now holding the trash collector's on one side, the grandmother's on the other.

"Drink," the obstetrician advises, "and find Patmos through life-giving water steeped in death."

Patmos. The word reminds me of a time of divination, now that I'm older and have had time to study where it came from. To wonder why my mother visits this place. To wonder if I would ever return to it, and what it might hold in store for me.

I thought the bone tea would taste gritty, but it doesn't. The liquid is smooth and tannin-rich, rolling bitter across my tongue with a touch of honeyed sweetness. It is hot but not scalding, tolerable enough to gulp down a few swallows before taking a breath, inhaling the dizzying scent of black tea leaves drying in the sun.

It takes me a moment to realize that I can see the leaves as they're dying, plucked from their mother limbs and spread atop a fine mesh netting to protect them from the ground. I can see silky threads of vibrant green brightening to yellow and then deepening to gold before fading into brown as they wind their way from the leaves and into the dirt below, spidering out in finely spun webs that blend into the deep dark of the underworld's penumbral shadows.

My sight travels deeper still, into the underbelly of the Earth and through to the other side—no, the *next* side, for I can see the web travels still further beyond, threading strings of worlds together like pearls, each a precious globe of its own.

Without thinking, I blurt out, "What *is* this place?"

—and am shocked to discover the rest of me hurtling through the space between, traveling along the same threads my sight did, to collide in a jumble of tangled skeins in a gemstone-encrusted cavern so vast that my voice echoes for eternity.

My stomach sinks. I have the horrible suspicion I'm no longer standing in an empty restaurant with a silent circle of strangers watching me while my awareness flits through worlds. That, physically, I am here—wherever *here* is.

I have broken the one rule Mom taught me.

Don't disturb the dead.

I can't stop screaming.

"No," I sob, over and over again in a mindless litany, everything forgotten in my panic. "No, no, no, no, no." The last is a shriek that echoes endlessly through the rainbow cavern.

I shake and I shiver and I shout, but there is nothing alive in the cavern to hear me or see me or touch me, to fight me or hold me or tell me that they're here with me and will never leave. I am totally, utterly alone, and I have no idea how to get home.

I frantically search for those threads that brought me here, that started with the godsforsaken tea leaves drying under the sun. No threads, no life. No death, either. Nothing that links the living to the dead, and to the living all over again.

Instead, rainbow prisms of light sparkle from the geodes, crystals, and gems that encrust every surface of the cavernous walls. I can't tell where the light source is that glitters off the gems, but its brilliance threatens to blind me with migraines, and there is no respite unless I close my eyes.

So I do, sinking to my knees and burying my face in my hands to block out the dizzying light, whimpering low and deep in my throat. I rock back and forth, if only to give my body something to do besides collapse in a puddle of despair.

I see, like an afterimage burned into my eyelids, the circle of eight again, now including Mom, all of them holding hands, silent, unmoving. Before them, in the center of the circle, lies the wooden bowl that I dropped when I … I don't know what the hell I did, but I'm no longer there, that's for damn sure. One look at Mom's face and I know I am well and truly screwed. This isn't a dream or a game or make-believe. Whatever this is, wherever I am, this is real.

I wanted to know what the tea tasted like. Now I do. It tastes like sweat drying on my upper lip and the sour stench of fear radiating damply from my armpits, like bitter regret lingering on my tongue. It tastes like bile on the verge of spewing. Oh, how easily I forgot my mother's caution. I long for the comfort and security of standing firmly on ground that I knew and understood, for the salt-tinged air of the San Diego sea, for the soothing murmur of my mother's voice as she comforts me in the dark.

It could be worse, I think. I could be dead. I might be, if this was some schizophrenic version of hell.

But I don't think I am. Dead, that is. No way could I conjure up this rainbow hellscape, not in my wildest dreams. But if I don't figure out what is going on, I *will* die here, and it will be all my fault. I'm the one who screwed up. I'm the one who needs to fix this and find my way out of here.

Slowly, my breath eases in my chest until it no longer powers the whimpering. The panic subsides enough for me to think through how to get home.

Home. Eyes still screwed shut against the brilliance of the cavern, I quiet my breath and my mind, focusing on the memory of my mother's chipped mug, on the black block letters, on the steam rising from its rim. On my mother stirring the tea in slow, lazy circles. On the calm, easy way she sipped from the mug and the patient movements of her body as she rises and rinses out the mug once it's empty, setting it on the drainboard to dry.

The afterimage of the circle of eight fades as the memory of my mother in our kitchen strengthens into crystal-sharp clarity.

She must have done it a million times. Stolen a bone here and there from the bodies being prepped in the funeral home for their final burials, brewed her tea, crumbled the bones into dust, drank. Ingested the magic that allowed her to ... what?

I think back to the first moments when I sipped from the obstetrician's bowl—and it hadn't hurt, I realize to my surprise; the doctor hadn't lied—to the sensation of floating and traveling along the threads that marked the tea leaves' passage of life into death, greens flowing through yellows and golds and into browns. The threads that brought me here.

The circle swirls back into focus, and this time I can see the threads again, golden and sparkling like ribbons of star-dust, tying one person to another, in a gleaming strand like a charm bracelet. A few of them have other strands that float elsewhere into the world, mostly greens and yellows. I want to follow them, but my sight is drawn to my mother, shining bright and golden, and to the extra strand of green that snakes out from her core and falls into the floor, through the ground, spiraling and winding and making its way toward me until it wraps around my waist and disappears into me like an umbilical cord.

I open my eyes. The cavern still pulses with its over-whelming prismatic light, but now that I know what to look for, I see it. Through a narrow-eyed squint, I spot the sparkling remnants of a bright green thread, as fresh and verdant as springtime.

I scramble my way carefully over the rocky outcroppings of geodes and crystals, following the thread until it winds its way through the multifaceted wall of the cavern. I hesitate only a moment, then plunge after the thread without losing sight of it.

The same tingling feeling of my mother's hearse sailing

through traffic passes over me, and then I'm on to the next world, a lushly outfitted child's bedroom decorated in white lace and lilac wallpaper. It is dark, dimly lit by a night-light in the corner, and a little chilly, bringing a faint sprinkling of goose bumps along my arms.

More threads of green and gold weave their way throughout the rest of the house, with a coil of green curled up under a voluminous comforter in the canopied bed. The shape stirs, and I dash after my own thread to avoid disturbing the sleeper.

Place by place, underworld by underworld, I follow the thread that leads me back to my mother. I promise myself that each barrier I cross brings me closer to home, even though I don't know if it's the truth. But it keeps me moving, keeps me focused.

And no matter what I see, this time, I stay silent.

Let me cross, I pray, although I don't know who would answer. *I just want to go home.*

Some places are as silent and empty as the jeweled cavern I landed in. Some are as quiet and eerie as the dark bedroom. Some are boisterous, crowded with ghosts who don't seem to give me another look once they catch sight of me—something that makes me nervous, at first, until I realize that their gazes slide away as soon as they meet mine and see what I'm doing.

Odd, I think, that the shades don't know me, and yet they still grant me freedom of passage as if I were royalty.

It's that idea of passage that suddenly makes sense to me, my mother's lessons and rituals coming full circle. I know now that her magic isn't just magic, that the bones of the dead aren't just tools, and that her job as a hearse-driver is more literal and metaphorical than I'd ever guessed.

Abruptly, between one blink and the next, I'm standing again in the center of the circle of eight, holding the empty wooden bowl in my hands. The afternoon light pouring through the dirty windows of the restaurant falls upon me with weak warmth, a relief after an eternity of traveling through unending cosmoses.

A breath catches. It's Mom, her eyes brimming with tears. Her lips are pressed together, and she is uncharacteristically silent.

In fact, none of the eight are speaking; all of them studying me with discomfiting interest. Finally, they drop their hands. The obstetrician steps forward to take the bowl from me, and it's as if a spell breaks. The circle breathes a collective sigh and dissolves.

"Diane," the obstetrician says, her smile warm and welcoming. "Glad you could join us."

Mom grips my hands, clutching them tight. The trash collector claps a hand gently on my shoulder. The priest cracks a thin smile, although it doesn't lighten the gravitas of his lined visage.

"It has been a while since we've had a young one among us," the grandmotherly soprano remarks. "I do hope you'll last as long as your predecessors."

I look at the soprano, at her deep blue eyes, sparkling much like the jewels in the cavern. I want to ask questions, but I don't dare. I already made that mistake once, and nearly lost myself in a rainbowed hell.

I'd disturbed something then. I'd disturbed the dead slumbering beneath my feet. I'd disturbed the dead traveling through worlds. I'd disturbed the threads that connected life to death and death to life. The threads that showed me how to navigate the worlds in between, that showed me the pathways I would take, that my mother takes, to usher the dead to their final resting place.

And it was only when I quieted myself, regained the silence within and without, that the dead showed themselves to me again and allowed me to cross worlds.

This, I realize, is what my mother tried to shelter me from, when I'd asked to taste her tea. She didn't want me to shoulder this burden too early. To understand what it truly means to drive a pale green hearse.

But if I'm old enough to understand, then I'm old enough to carry its burden.

And I'm old enough to have a voice of my own.

"You're Purity," I tell the soprano.

No otherworldly force strikes me down where I stand. No threads snap and pull me back into nowhere. I am still here, still me, and inwardly I let out a sigh of relief. Truth be told, I wasn't sure until that moment if I was right. That I'd be allowed to speak, now that I'd tasted the bone's magic.

More confident now of my voice, I point at the trash collector, though I still address Purity. "Because he's Pestilence, and you sit across from him in the circle, so you must be his opposite."

The trash collector chuckles, his deep baritone rolling like the rumble of a lion. "You were worth waiting for."

"She does seem to be quicker on the uptake than some others," the Asian woman says with a smirk, eyes still on her phone.

"That would make you War," I tell her. "Because you've got attitude, and you aren't afraid to use it." I shift my gaze to Mr. Man Bun, at the way he's presented himself. "You've got attitude, too, but you're careful about how you use it. Which makes you her opposite—Harmony."

He smiles and raises his hands in mock surrender. "Guilty."

Mom has stepped away from me, and I turn in a slow circle, naming the rest of them. "Famine," I say to the priest, who nods back. The Latino beams when he answers to Plenty, and the obstetrician merely spreads her palms when I call her Creation.

At last, I turn to Mom. She is still silent, watching me with the tired expression of a full day's work.

No, I realize as I study her further. She is tired with lifetimes of work. How old was she really? I never thought to question that she was anything more than my mother.

"Death," I say quietly.

Mom smiles. Then slowly, gently, sadly, she shakes her head.

It dawns on me that Mom hasn't spoken a word since I got back.

No, earlier. She hasn't spoken since I drank the tea.

She isn't allowed to speak anymore. She is no longer one of the circle. Like I wasn't, before now. She knows, better than anyone, not to disturb the dead and draw their attention.

A hard lump forms in my throat. This was more than a test or a rite of passage. This was a passing of the reins.

I hold up my hand. "Death," I repeat, and this time, Mom nods. They all do.

"Death," the other seven echo. "Welcome to Patmos."

This time, when we leave the restaurant, it's me who acknowledges the slumbering sea monsters beneath.

Thank you for letting us cross, I tell them.

The answer that comes isn't in words. It's a feeling of peace, of acceptance, that emanates from the silent restaurant, and from the guardians underneath who keep watch.

Mom drives us home, but we travel on the road as mortals, crawling northward in the stutter-stop of commuter traffic.

The effects of the tea linger. I can count the winding threads as we crawl by, spinning off from the people riding in cars and from everything around us. They number in the hundreds of thousands, but the multitude of threads don't overwhelm me the way the rainbow cavern did.

I turn to ask Mom a question, but it dies on my lips as I catch sight of her thread. It gleams golden in the fading sun, but not as brightly as before. Near the floor of the car, her thread deepens into brown—the color of the dead and dying, like the woven thread of the tea leaves I followed into hell. The brown creeps up her thread, toward her center. Marking the time she has left.

"How long?" I ask her, amazed my voice remains steady.

Mom keeps her eyes on the road as she answers, "Soon enough."

Too soon, I want to scream. I have no marketable skills and no other family. Mom is the only home I've ever known.

But I only look down at my hands and ask, "Who's going to teach me?"

"Patmos will." Her knuckles whiten over the steering wheel. "You'll be okay," she adds, but it sounds like she's saying it more for her than for me.

And knowing that, knowing she's making sure I won't be afraid when the time comes, I also know that she's right. Just as she was right about Patmos. It's not just a place. It's accidentally losing your way, then finding it again. It's the revelation that one world will end, and another will take its place.

It's that intersection of life and death, of all the balanced opposites in a circle of eight, which marks where a daughter will let her mother go, soon enough. Where we will all go.

And where I can find her again, after.

"It's okay to go," I tell her. "I'll be fine."

I have to. Death comes for all of us. She and I know this better than anyone.

She smiles, and I watch her thread grow darker. "I know," she says, and I know that she'll be okay, too. It's all I can ask for, now.

We speed home in our pale green hearse. A fresh body waits in the mortuary. And, tomorrow, it will be I who steals the bones and brews the tea, leaving my mother behind.

About the Author

C.H. Hung writes stories founded in scientific plausibility, layered with myth and folklore—mash-ups deriving from her stubbornly rational soul intersecting with her irrational belief in magic. Her genre-spanning short fiction has appeared in *Pulphouse*, *Fiction River*, and multiple anthologies. Read more at chhung.com.

Silver Future

MARY PLETSCH

I reviewed my new assignment on my scribe's glowing screen once again, but the words remained unchanged.

Devastated, I raised my gaze to my commander and mentor, who sat unmoving behind her workstation. "Ma'am, if I may speak freely?"

Admiral Morenadin pressed the tips of her higher forelegs together. "Speak."

I could manage only one word. "Why?"

The admiral reached out her left lower foreleg to me. "I understand your distress, Commander Chanzi Ko Entolladin. Rest assured this is *not* a demotion."

"Then I don't understand. Why have I been assigned as executive officer to Captain Ecks's crew?" I shuddered. My body felt much too cold. Captain Ecks?

A *drone.*

A hiveless, kinless, genderless drone. I was supposed to take orders from such an individual? I was the top-ranked shieldmaiden of the Entolladin hive. I'd been expecting command of my own star cruiser, not forced subservience to a drone. Not even a drone as distinguished as Captain Ecks.

"Would you believe," Morenadin said softly, "that it is because of your exemplary service record?"

"I'm sorry. I don't understand."

Morenadin rose to her hind legs and ambled out from behind her workstation. "Galaxy Command has had concerns about Captain Ecks for quite some time."

Unsurprising. "I've never understood why Galaxy Command let a drone become a cruiser captain to begin with."

"The simple answer is that it is a matter of social control." Morenadin rested her upper right foreleg on my shoulder. "We allow a handful of drones to become officers, and all the rest believe that if they only work hard enough, and serve loyally enough, they might become officers too. When they argue that advancement is impossible, we point to Ecks.

303

'Look. This drone has become a captain. Why can't you do what it does?' Now do you understand?"

"I suppose." The idea of taking orders from a drone still didn't sit well with me.

"There is also no denying that Ecks is talented. And our cold war with the Taq threatens to ignite at any time. So long as Ecks remains in line, Galaxy Command will permit it to continue its privateering missions." Her eye facets glittered. "That's where you come in. Your *true* assignment, Chanzi Ko Entolladin, is to ensure that Captain Ecks continues to act in a manner beneficial to our Hiveworld. And, if it does not, to use your discretion in solving the challenge. You will notice," Morenadin added softly, "that the fine print of your orders gives you a fleet commander's authority to issue demotions, make arrests, and kill in the name of the Queen."

My body temperature spiked, and I felt sick again. Should I not approve of Ecks's behavior, I had been given authority to disregard its rank and act as its superior. I could punish it by demoting it and taking over its ship. I could arrest it. I could even murder it without consequences. I would never have been given such privileges, ordinarily reserved for a fleet commander who outranked a ship's captain, in any normal circumstances.

"Galaxy Command chose you," Morenadin continued, "because we trust you not to simply swagger aboard Ecks's ship, immediately depose it, and seize command. In ideal circumstances, we would like Ecks to continue with its stellar record of captures. But should Ecks grow disloyal, we trust you to analyze the situation and respond with the correct degree of force."

"Yes, ma'am."

Morenadin's mandibles flicked in a smile. "So take heart," she whispered. "I have something for you."

"A gift?" I asked, surprised. I'd never had a superior officer give me a gift before.

"A promise," Morenadin replied. "Open it."

Curious, I lifted the lid—and almost dropped the box in shock.

A cylindrical rod glowed a soft purple, nestled in a bed of shock-absorbing foam. It was the star drive that would power a jump cruiser, a vessel capable of leaping beyond the edges of the solar system and into the galaxy at large. I had no idea why I'd been handed such a precious piece of equipment.

"When you return," Morenadin murmured, "you will personally install it in the star cruiser that will become yours to command."

I felt my hearts leap. A ship of my own. A *jump ship*.

The highest form of adventure and freedom a shield-maiden of the Hive could earn.

"All you have to do," Morenadin continued, "is complete one tour of duty with Ecks. What say you, Chanzi Ko Entolladin?"

"Yes," I replied. "You can count on me."

I tried not to wince when I saw Captain Ecks's ship through the viewscreen of the shuttle.

I was well aware that Ecks, as a drone, did not merit the latest in cutting-edge military technology. I also knew that with proper maintenance and retrofitting, a star cruiser's operational lifespan could easily exceed that of its crew. But Ecks's cruiser was pockmarked with dents from asteroids, scorched from laser blasts, and scarred with weld marks from hull breaches. I suspected the thing had been soaring the void when my grandmother was still in the egg.

As the ship approached, I read the name emblazoned on the bow in regulation-approved font: *CORSAIR-003*.

I winced. I'd seen *CORSAIR-997* in orbit on the way up.

This vessel belonged in a scrapyard, relegated to the dust of history.

Then I saw something that made me wonder about Captain Ecks's sense of humor.

Underneath the ship's official designation—in an elegant script that was absolutely not Galaxy Force regulation—was a second name.

Silver Future.

The first thing I noticed about Captain Ecks when I stepped off the shuttle was that it was *big* for a drone. It only looked average-sized on screen because the crew members flanking it were also unusually large. The Mother Hive strictly limited the caloric and nutritional intake of noncitizens, and I was unaccustomed to drones who were longer than I was.

But Ecks was a very successful privateer. It probably fed its crew from the larders of the ships it looted, over and above the rations it was given. There was no other way drones could grow so long.

Ecks greeted me at the top of the gangplank. "Greetings, Commander," it said. "Choose your rings."

Another crew member—a drone whose name badge read *Karchee*—approached and opened a small box. Inside lay three sets of antennae rings: gold, silver, and bronze.

They weren't part of the standard uniform. I peeked at Ecks—bronze rings—and Karchee—gold. Most of the rest of Ecks's crew wore either gold or silver, but there were enough in bronze to suggest the rings were not indicators of rank.

"I'm sorry. I don't know what they're for."

"How we are to address you," Ecks said. "Gold for female. Silver for male. Bronze for neutral."

Gold for female. I looked closely at Karchee. Stubby wings.

Smooth antennae. Karchee looked like a drone to me, save for the gold rings.

My wings prickled.

I should tell Ecks to take a look at me. That it was obvious from my feathered antennae and large abdomen that I was a shieldmaiden. That the Galaxy Force would never have let me enter officer training had I not been a female.

But I hesitated. My response would dictate how Ecks and its crew viewed me from this point onward.

I could scoff, and Ecks would know not to trust me.

I could insist that everyone on board the ship go by the Mother Hive's definitions of gender. I could use the full authority of a fleet commander to enforce this rule, and Ecks would know I was its enemy.

Or I could accept Ecks's eccentricities, and perhaps it would lower its guard around me.

In fact, I could go one better.

I reached out and selected a pair of silver rings.

Karchee's mandibles flared in surprise. Ecks did not visibly react, but I thought I saw its eyes glitter.

"Karchee will take you on a tour of the *Silver Future*," the captain said. "Welcome aboard, Commander Chanzi Sae Entolladin."

Pretending to be a male was not as awkward as I'd first feared. In fact, I really didn't think of it as *pretending*. It was more as though I'd settled into the life of a lancer who just happened to have a name very similar to my own. And it was *nice* to not be constrained by the behaviors expected of a shieldmaiden.

As a hatchling, I'd envied the Entolladin lancers. They hadn't had to spend their time reciting long political histories while tending to the eggs. They'd been able to sally forth from the hive and discover things for themselves. They were judged expendable, yes, but they could take greater risks for greater rewards. Of course, I'd been punished when I expressed such admiration. A shieldmaiden was more valuable than a mere lancer.

I'd never thought I could just *become* one.

Here on *CORSAIR-003*, I was immediately and unquestionably accepted as a lancer. There was a certain wariness—of course there would be, due to my rank—but my place at the lancers' table, sharing tales of wild adventure, was never in doubt.

My tales were stolen from the lancers I'd so envied.

I felt a strange flurry of excitement when I realized I might soon have tales of my own.

CORSAIR-003 was halfway to the edge of the solar system when we received *Honey Bounty*'s distress call.

Ecks, myself, and several of Ecks's command staff were gathered around the map table, planning an ambush against a Taq supply route. I'd learned that Ecks didn't favor the common method of running down enemy ships and forcibly boarding them. It preferred to alter the beacons on asteroid fields, luring Taqi vessels down dangerous corridors until they wrecked against the rocks. The Taq fled in life pods, and Ecks's privateers salvaged the wreckage. I could not decide if this method was cowardly or smart. Ecks's crew were certainly in much less danger this way.

Then the communications suite crackled to life. Hive colony vessel *Honey Bounty* had been heading out of the system, ready to jump for an unoccupied world discovered by Hive explorers. Taqi privateers had gotten to it first. Ecks immediately diverted *CORSAIR-003* to come to *Honey Bounty*'s aid.

Ecks flickered its mandibles. "Shaim, assemble a rescue

party. After we jump, your group will take a shuttle to the *Honey Bounty*, rescue any survivors, and salvage valuables. Lessity, ready the Swarm for an assault on the Taqi privateer. Karchee, you have command of the bridge."

Karchee had command? "What am I supposed to do?" I asked.

Ecks tilted its head. "Don't you have reports to file?" it said mildly.

"Don't *you* have a ship to command?" I retorted.

"I have a battle swarm to lead." It turned and left the room.

I scurried after Ecks. "Are you certain this is the best use of resources? Perhaps we should stick with the ambush plan. You know the crew of *Honey Bounty* will be beyond rescue by the time we arrive."

"But there is vengeance to consider," Ecks said mildly. "Vengeance on the Taq for attacking a Hive vessel. Surely you agree?"

What did this drone care about the Hive? It was as though it was telling me what I ought to want to hear. And there was no way I could discourage a show of patriotic zeal.

"Very well," I capitulated. "Then I'm coming too."

Battle. Like all shieldmaidens, I'd trained in defensive maneuvers. In the old days, we were the protectors of the Hive. But even in the modern age, only lancers and drones were allowed to join attack swarms, and only lancers could lead them. Shieldmaidens were the leaders of society, the governors and generals. Lancers and drones did the fighting and the dying.

I realized I was looking forward to my first combat as a lancer.

"No, you won't," Ecks said firmly. "You're staying here."

My antennae lashed in shock. "I'm a capable soldier," I argued. "I hold marksmanship medals and top marks in hand-to-hand combat. I won't hold you back."

"You're *staying*," Ecks hissed, "if I have to lock you in the brig myself."

I took a step back, shocked by its vehemence.

Ecks tilted its head, suddenly mild-mannered once more. "Do you really not know?"

"Know what?" I stammered.

Ecks fluttered its mandibles. "First, you're only now realizing that you are alone on a ship crewed entirely by drones, disreputables, or some combination of the two."

I struggled to hide my dismay. It was as though Ecks had read my thoughts.

"But you have no need to fear. You see, if I fail to return you safely to dock at the end of this tour of duty, each and every being in my crew will be summarily executed." Its wings flared. "So. While *you're* worrying about being *accidentally* blown out the airlock or stranded on some desolate asteroid or perhaps simply knifed in the thorax while walking down the corridor one night, *I'm* worrying about you engaging in some extreme heroics against the Taq and getting the rest of us killed alongside you." Ecks folded its wings. "It's my hope the two of us can come to an understanding now, and that in exchange for my reassurance, you'll promise to spend a nice *safe* tour of duty aboard the *Silver Future*."

So. By protecting me, it was protecting itself.

No.

Just its crew.

"What about you?" I blurted. "If I get myself killed—or if I make myself such an impediment that *removing* me is worth the price—what happens to you?"

"According to Galaxy Command, nothing," Ecks replied mildly. "My rank would hold me innocent." Its eye facets tilted, sharpening. "But in practice, I would lose …" It paused, as though contemplating. "My crew is the closest thing to a hive the likes of me will ever have, Chanzi Sae Entolladin. So. I would lose nothing, and everything."

I wondered what Captain Ecks might do, with nothing left to lose. My antennae twitched.

"I think we can settle on an arrangement," I said.

Arrangement or no, I wasn't about to sit idle. If Ecks was out raiding and Karchee had command of the bridge, then I had the opportunity to do a little investigating. I'd noticed something unusual on my "welcome aboard" tour that deserved a closer look.

I'd enrolled as a starcraft engineer when I'd entered military college. After my first year, my commanders had reviewed my aptitudes and redirected me into command training. Once again, someone who outranked me had decided for me what I was allowed to be. And I'd made the only decision I could—to be the best at it. I'd had to work hard to catch up to my new classmates, but in the end, I surpassed them all.

I had enough engineering training to recognize that Ecks and his crew were up to something unusual in the engine room of the *Silver Future*. Starcraft typically had backups that could take over should the main equipment fail, but the *Silver Future* had three, even four, versions of each component crammed into a dangerously overcrowded engineering space.

Why would Ecks do such a thing?

The obvious answer was that the captain was mad, but I was beginning to suspect otherwise. I'd seen a similar setup once before in my life—on a star cruiser being retrofitted while returning home from its tour of duty. The final build would take place in dock, but the engineers had gotten a head start on replacing the systems.

Ecks's engineers were very nervous, far in excess of the deference I would expect from lower-ranking starcrew. Every time I opened a hatch, another crew member would block my view, stammering oaths of loyalty. Between their supplications, and the extreme overcrowding, I'd never learn anything. Finally I ordered the lot of them out.

At last the chief engineer raised a protest. It wasn't safe for the engine room to be unmanned. I reassured it—*her*—that I would only be a few moments, but she continued begging until I finally snapped at her and ordered her out on pain of disciplinary measures. Reluctantly, she left, following her crew into the corridor.

I worked quickly. It really was dangerous to leave the engine room unmanned.

As I suspected, Ecks was retrofitting *CORSAIR-003*, and not just with modern equipment. I found power boosters and cooling units and field stabilizers that in-system cruisers didn't need. My suspicions were confirmed when I opened the star drive locker and found a brand-new, unused, housing for a lavender star drive.

Ecks was upgrading the *Silver Future* into a jump ship.

Ecks returned from the raiding party in a stormy mood. The Taq had decided to blow up their own ship rather than leave anything for the enemy to salvage. I made a point of inspecting the few spoils Ecks's swarm had managed to take. Weapons and gear, yes, but no star drive.

It was harder for me to get a look at Shaim's salvage from *Honey Bounty*, but when I did, I had a shock. The boxes the salvagers carried contained row after row of incubators, filled with fertilized eggs—the future citizens of the colony *Honey Bounty* had intended to establish.

"Put them in the nursery with the others," Shaim said, and I wondered why a privateer vessel like the *Silver Future* would have such a thing.

Admiral Morenadin had provided me with a hacking key that would enable me to gain control of any of *CORSAIR-003*'s systems. I knew it should only be used in emergency situations. She had also given me a concealed long-range communicator, which I now debated using.

Ecks was no fool. It would *expect* me to report back to my superiors. It was possible *CORSAIR-003* would have passive jammers blocking outgoing signals, but I thought Ecks was more clever than that.

I thought for a moment, then activated the communicator and filed a very boring report containing only the vaguest outline of *CORSAIR-003*'s salvage of the *Honey Bounty* and a conclusion that everything was fine. If Ecks read what I'd written, it would assume I was keeping my end of our arrangement.

Dissatisfied, I lay back down again. I never thought I would come to resent my rank.

I understood why Galaxy Command installed a citizen as executive officer of a drone's ship, and why I'd been granted the power to enforce the interests of the Mother Hive. But I was one individual on a ship of five hundred, and the rest of the crew seemed fanatically loyal to Captain Ecks.

If Galaxy Command did not trust Ecks, they'd have been wiser slipping a spy into the rank and file starcrew. As an able sailor, I could have blended in with the rest of the crew while keeping my eyes and audials open for signs of treason. As executive officer, my rank made me stand out.

So. My predecessors had cracked down hard on discipline among the crew, wielding their authority like a cudgel, but careful to stop just shy of violating their *arrangement* with Captain Ecks. And Ecks, cunning as it was, surely schemed in the shadows behind their backs.

I thought of the star drive, quietly glowing in its box beneath my bunk.

All I needed to do to earn my captain's rings was to do

exactly as Ecks said: remain safely on the bridge, keep my head down, and return home alive.

But I had not come this far by merely meeting expectations.

I wanted to—I *had* to—go above and beyond. There was one way to do that while avoiding battle.

I could bring back the *truth* about Captain Ecks's schemes.

And to do *that*, I had to go off script. My predecessors had been the representatives of the authority of the Matriarchs aboard this Queenforsaken vessel. I would have to be something else.

I would have to get Ecks to trust me.

Playing the role of a lancer was a start, yes, but already I was wondering if I was doing it for Ecks or for myself, or if I was really playing at all.

I spent the rest of the voyage living as Chanzi Sae Entolladin. I socialized with the other lancers, practiced their combat drills, and learned their dance steps. I held my antennae and flared my wings the way lancers do. I fit in. I made friends.

I couldn't fight, but I supported my shipmates as best I could, and in return, they gradually warmed up to me. I remember the day they returned from raiding, battered and bloodied, and Lessity actually expressed pity for me and the rank that forced me to stay behind. In that moment, I knew if I remained aboard the *Silver Future*, I could be Chanzi Sae Entolladin forever.

I realized part of me wanted that.

All of a sudden, returning to the Mother Hive and my old life as a shieldmaiden seemed like the lie. Was that my truth, or simply the role I played because I'd been taught it as a hatchling, because society expected it of me?

It was a foolish question, I chided myself. Admiral Morenadin would never let me stay. When the *Silver Future* returned to the Hiveworld, I would get my star cruiser, and Captain Ecks would get a new executive officer.

Unless we didn't return.

For all our raiding, we'd never captured a star drive, and yet, I knew precisely where one could be found.

I pushed open the door to the mess hall. Too late for second thoughts.

I made my way through the crowd to the head table, where Ecks sat chatting to an able starfarer. I realized I was no longer disturbed to see the captain interacting so casually with a sailor so far beneath it in rank.

"We're scheduled to return to port soon," I said, placing the box on the table in front of my captain. "Before we get there, I'd like to give you something."

"A present, Commander?" I could see its expression was guarded. I supposed I couldn't blame Ecks for thinking that the gift might be a gag, or worse, an insult.

Ecks opened the lid and tried to keep its composure, but its wings flared in surprise. It softly lowered the lid again and looked up at me. "Is this real, Commander?"

I sidled. "Yes."

Ecks sat quietly, waiting for me to continue.

"It's an incentive given to me by my mentor at Galaxy Command," I said awkwardly. "It's intended to be the heart of my own star cruiser after this tour of duty is over."

"But you're giving it to me," Ecks said. It wasn't a question. It was a demand for an explanation.

"I know you're upgrading *Silver Future* into a jump vessel."

Ecks regarded me in silence.

"You don't have the proper star drive, and I understand that they are hard to come by."

Still silence.

"I would even go so far as to guess the reason we attacked the Taqi privateer that raided *Honey Bounty* was not for vengeance, but because you knew—or suspected—it was powered by such a star drive."

Ecks's mandibles flickered. "Well done, Commander."

"But I could not support you in that battle, and you didn't get your prize. Nor have we captured another during our tour of duty. I am fortunate to be in a position where I can offer you what you seek."

"Surely you remember that had you died during our voyage, my crew would have been put to death and I would be in the unenviable position of having lost everyone I care about." Ecks tilted its head. "You didn't need to do this, Commander. Why?"

I had prepared for this moment. I'd spent long nights reading the forbidden texts I'd copied from my new friends, poring over radical philosophies of equality and liberation. I'd memorized all the key points, rehearsed my delivery.

I didn't say any of it.

"Because it's my crew too," I blurted. "You've given me a ... a *home* here."

Ecks twitched its mandibles in a smile. "Then we're ready to go," it said. "We need not go back to the Hiveworld at all. We will jump beyond the solar system, following a certain set of coordinates, and build a new society. The hatchlings from the *Honey Bounty* and other salvaged vessels will be born into a world where they can discover who they are and where they fit, rather than being told those answers by the Mother Hive."

It seemed to be testing me. Calling my bluff. But I was not bluffing.

"Very well," I said. "Let's go."

As the crew cheered, Ecks and I walked down to the engineering room, where the new jump system lay idle for want of a star drive. As Ecks spoke to the chief engineer, I scanned the room, and saw exactly what I feared I might see.

Galaxy Command would have been wise to insert a spy into the rank and file starcrew, I'd thought, and so, indeed, they had.

As the chief engineer began to fit the glowing rod into the star drive locker, a junior engineer in the corner of the room locked her eyes with mine. She regarded me as though she expected me to do something to stop Ecks from acquiring a jump ship and abandoning the Hive to start a new life.

I felt as though I was awakening from a long dream. A dream in which I'd been a lancer named Chanzi Sae Entolladin.

No.

I felt as though I was falling back into a nightmare.

I'd spent the entire voyage practicing lancer's battle drills. I opened my mandibles, now sharpened into lancer's spears, and charged.

The junior engineer didn't expect me to attack her. Her attention was on her scribe.

My powerful, augmented bite severed her head from her thorax.

The crew around me stood frozen in shock, save for the chief engineer, who worked all the faster, and Captain Ecks.

"Explain yourself," it demanded.

"She set off an emergency call," I said, fumbling with her scribe unit. "She was undercover. A spy for the Mother Hive."

"You knew?"

"I *suspected*." And I had terrible suspicions as to her true origins. Galaxy Command always gave its spies incentive to return. For me, it was the star drive. For her, perhaps a blood tie far deeper than anything Ecks could offer her. "If she was the spawn of a Queen Matriarch, the Mother Hive's vengeance will never be satisfied. No matter where you go, no matter where you run, the Hive will hunt you down and kill you all slowly."

"Unless?"

"Unless they have reason to believe that you, and your entire crew, are dead."

Ecks fluttered its wings. "And how am I to manage that?"

Rumors tainted the early years of Chanzi Ko Entolladin's captaincy, until her battle record finally erased all doubts. Until then, Admiral Morenadin staunchly defended Chanzi's actions aboard *CORSAIR-003*, arguing there was no reason to disbelieve any of the key points of Chanzi's after-action report.

Fact: The hacking key Morenadin had provided enabled Chanzi to gain control of the ship's systems, including those in engineering and the emergency bypass for the escape pods.

Fact: Chanzi's knowledge of engineering was more than sufficient for her to effectively sabotage *CORSAIR-003* and escape in a life pod before the critical detonation.

Fact: Chanzi Ko Entolladin was never informed of the presence of undercover operative Pinteria Ko-Iz Resuppit.

Fact: Even if she had been aware, two shieldmaidens could not have defeated Captain Ecks and its fanatically loyal crew. Sabotage, therefore, was the best way for a single soldier to eliminate a rogue crew.

Fact: An improperly installed star drive core was at high risk of exploding during a jump sequence.

Fact: A ship lost to such an explosion would leave no wreckage had the jump begun before critical failure occurred.

Fact: Chanzi Ko Entolladin was an exceptional officer whose loyalty had always been without question.

I approached Admiral Morenadin after the awards ceremony where I received the Hexagon of Honor for Meritorious Conduct. "I should thank you," I murmured, "for believing in me and giving me my captaincy. I don't know if I ever apologized for losing the first star drive core you gave me."

Oh, what an actor I'd become since leaving *CORSAIR-003*.

"Small price," Morenadin murmured, "if it removed a renegade like Ecks from the picture. I heard we lost another colony to the Taq this morning. The last thing we need is a second front with a ... a *drone* revolution at home."

Or an angry pirate captain intent on vengeance.

Somehow, though, I doubted it. Ecks already had everything it wanted.

It took all my self-control not to tell Admiral Morenadin that the Hiveworld had nothing to fear from the pirate who'd turned its ship into a hive and proceeded to steal itself a silver future.

My chosen name is Chanzi Sae Entolladin, and the Mother Hive has far more to fear from me.

About the Author

Mary Pletsch is a toy collector and graduate of the Royal Military College of Canada. She attended Superstars Writing Seminars in 2010, and has since published short stories and novellas in a variety of genres, including science fiction, fantasy, and horror.

Sea Wolves

JULIE FROST

The twenty-man crew of my twin-masted merchant ship, the *Auklet*, didn't know their captain was a werewolf, and that was exactly how I liked it.

What they did know was to keep the door of my private cabin locked during the three nights of the full moon, and never to open it under any circumstances, no matter what they heard. Usually they didn't hear much, but sometimes the beast had bad and blood-soaked dreams.

Memories, really. There was a reason—more than one—I didn't let it out to roam the decks. Being trapped inside a ferocious animal, watching helplessly as it wreaked havoc, was my own private nightmare. The creature hadn't killed anyone I actually cared about—yet—but murdering random beggars didn't sit well with me either.

So I confined it to quarters, and the crew had learned not to ask. I made sure to sate it with plenty of good meat before the moon took us, and the men were happy for the change of diet for those three suppers.

We sat at table on one such late afternoon, delicious food and plenty of ale making the atmosphere convivial. "When do we make port, Cap'n Cox?" the cabin boy asked. Joey was on his maiden voyage, eleven summers old and wide-eyed with the new experience.

"Eager for land already, lad?" First mate Peter Westcott said good-naturedly. The boy was his nephew, and his sister hoped to secure him a position aboard my vessel.

"A couple more days before we make port at New Orleans," I answered. "If we—"

"Pirates!" the lookout screamed from the crow's nest, his voice high-pitched with panic.

We all cursed and shoved back from the table, meal forgotten. A few moments later, I had the report—black sails behind us, but still a long way off. They were advertising, which was not a good sign, and had three masts to our two, which was worse.

I gave the order to raise every bit of canvas we had and try to outrun them in the night. Mayhap they hadn't spotted us yet, though I didn't count on that.

And then my inner wolf reminded me that our pirates had the most execrable timing.

"Go dark," I instructed Peter before I locked myself in my cabin. "Not a glimmer of light, no smoking even." With the moon full and bright above, I wasn't sure what advantage that might give us, but I'd take what I could get.

"Aye, Cap'n." He tilted his head, worry creasing his brow. "Will you be all right?"

"As much as I ever am on these nights." He was accustomed to being in charge when these fits took me. "And you?"

"We've a stout and experienced crew," he said. "Be fine 'til morning, I reckon."

"Good man." I clapped him on the shoulder and closed my cabin door, turning the bolt.

The wolf surged in the background, seeking early release. "Not yet, you great bloody brute," I muttered, and set about disrobing so my clothes wouldn't be ripped asunder by the shift.

It hurt less when I didn't fight it, so a little before moonrise, I let the creature have its way. With a wet tearing noise and an all-over itch, the wolf burst forth and stood in my cabin, twice the weight of a man, all fur and aggression.

I'd long since wolf-proofed the room, and it knew what to expect by now. It heaved a gusty sigh and flopped onto the bed, aching for the run I refused to give it. Not after the first and last time, when I had to watch through horrified eyes as it slaughtered a drunkard sleeping in the lee of a dockside tavern—and then ate the poor fellow. I'd got violently sick the next morning. Never again.

We communicated, after a fashion.

I wouldn't do that to the crew, it said. *Crew is pack.*

You're a bad dog, and I can't trust you. Go to sleep.

What are pirates?

Of course it didn't know. *Nothing to concern you. A human matter.*

You're worried, though.

Shared body, shared emotions, and the longer we shared, the more entwined we became. I wondered what it might mean if we ever fully integrated, where the wolf would end and I'd begin, and decided that was one worry I didn't need at the moment.

Hopefully you won't ever know what pirates are, I told it testily. *But you may find out tomorrow.* Just as I gazed through the wolf's eyes, it gazed through mine. *And if you do, we need our rest. Go to sleep.*

For a wonder, it did.

After a night of uneasy slumber where vague monsters stalked our dreams, my hope that the pirates hadn't spotted us was dashed. The *Orca* was close enough to see from the wheel now, and what speed we'd been able to coax from the *Auklet* hadn't been enough. We were a fat merchant vessel, while they were designed to cut through the water like the swift and rapacious killer whales they were named for.

We said a prayer, armed ourselves, and prepared to be boarded. The *Auklet* boasted a few defensive cannon, and we readied those as well.

That part of the battle didn't last long. We fired low, but didn't manage to hole them at all through their armored hull, let alone below the waterline. They fired chain, which tore through our sails and left us wallowing and helpless.

I swore roundly and shooed Joey belowdecks to hide, over his protests. "I want to fight, Cap'n. I'm not afraid."

"You damned well should be." I certainly was. The captain of the *Orca*, Smiling Graham Reeve, had a nasty reputation of leaving just enough survivors to carry the tale—but always the worst wounded, who either died slowly aboard a crippled vessel or were rescued sans body parts.

"Look, lad," I said earnestly, taking a knee in front of him. "You've got one job here: live. Yon pirates won't have mercy just because of your tender years." It might go worse for him, in fact, but he didn't need to be informed of that particular dreadfulness. "Live to go home to your mum. Don't come out unless you know the fighting's done and the pirates are gone. That's an order."

His mouth turned down at the corners, but he tipped his head in acquiescence. "Aye, Cap'n." And he turned and scampered off.

The *Orca* came alongside, the pirates swinging grappling hooks to pull us close.

"Repel boarders!" I shouted, raising my sword.

To my horror, the first grappling hooks weren't aimed at the rails, but at my men. They impaled three of my crew, pulling them overboard to either splash into the sea or be crushed between the ships. Others snagged the rails and heaved us together.

Perhaps one in five of my crew were experienced fighters. The rest knew the point of a sword from the pommel, and that was about it. We were outmatched and outnumbered, and soon overwhelmed.

My own wounds healed nearly as fast as they were inflicted, but I had to hold the wolf back by sheer force. Terrified that it wouldn't stop at the pirates or even differentiate between them and my crew, I battled on two fronts. We'd never been confronted by a situation such as this, fighting for our lives.

Let me out! It wanted to roar forth and make war.

I couldn't allow that, but I didn't have the wherewithal to get into a verbal sparring match. Grim and silent, I fought on.

Smiling Graham Reeve stepped aboard while I still

clashed swords with two of his men. Peter was down, bleeding copiously from a deep slice across his ribs and another to his belly, clutching his hand across his stomach to keep his insides where they belonged.

Reeve set the point of his cutlass beneath Peter's chin and said calmly, "I'd stop that if I were you, Captain Cox." He really did have a dreadful grin.

Panting, I looked about and realized not a single one of my crew still stood. My heart twisted. Bodies littered the deck, mostly ours, and the wolf howled for release. I was sorely tempted. It was right. Maybe if I'd let it go earlier—

Wait for better timing, I said to it. *Soon, though.* That smiling bastard wouldn't live through this if I had any say.

His men backed off me, and I braced myself, bloody but unbowed.

Reeve cut an imposing and dashing figure, a huge brute well over six feet in height with muscles to match. Long black hair in braids and beads cascaded from under his red-feathered tricorn hat, and his beard lay oiled and curled against a ruffled silk shirt. At first, I thought he wore a badger-skin cloak, until the thing lifted its head and growled at me—and I realized that while most pirates went in for parrots and monkeys, this one had chosen something a bit more ferocious.

I understood why when he stepped closer to me. He reeked of wolf.

His smile twisted wider when he caught my scent. "Fascinating." He nodded at my remaining crew, down to twelve now. "Do they know?"

"Of course not," I snapped.

"Different leadership techniques, I suppose. To each their own."

"Take all the cargo you want. Provisions, too. Just spare the crew. Please." The word grated on me, but they were my men, so I said it. "Please."

One of the brigands kicked me in the back of the leg, and I fell to my knees.

"You are not making the rules here," Reeve said. "And you don't become the most feared man in these waters by showing mercy."

"Lookie what we found!" A gleeful voice rose from the hold, and then two pirates appeared, dragging Joey between them.

The blood in my veins turned to ice as the boy struggled, kicked, and swore like the sailor he wanted to be. They dropped him to the deck in front of Reeve, who tilted his head and gave him a considering look.

"You seem a likely lad. How'd you like to join my crew?"

Joey stood tall and spat directly onto Reeve's highly polished boot. "Burn in hell, you bastard."

"You first." Reeve's cutlass flicked out, sharper than a razor.

A line of red appeared across Joey's throat, and then a veritable torrent of blood gushed from the wound. He reached up a hand, but collapsed to the deck before he could touch it, wide-eyed and uncomprehending.

"No!" I sprang to my feet, but something hard crashed against the back of my head, knocking me down again and making me see stars.

"You boys know what to do," Reeve said. "Be sure he watches."

My remaining men tried to fight, barehanded against blades. No cowards, they, especially with their backs to a wall. But it was a hopeless battle, and we were far down in numbers. Two more fell, never to rise again.

The wolf heaved inside, goaded by the stench of blood and the presence of a rival.

I had nothing to lose by letting it off the chain.

The pirates didn't expect that. Three of them had missing throats and were spilling guts before they realized they were dead. The wolf roared, not caring for its own hurts, calculated and ferocious. I almost admired its efficiency as it brought both fangs and claws to bear to excellent effect, and I noted that it didn't leave anyone alive after it bit them. Not wanting to make more. I approved.

But then an enormous black wolf plowed into our side and tore our shoulder open to the bone. Reeve as a man overtopped me by a good six inches and outweighed me by at least sixty pounds of pure muscle; he was correspondingly huge as a wolf. This wasn't some helpless drunkard or surprised brigand; this was a monster accustomed to fighting as man or beast.

My wolf and I rolled with the impact and fetched up against the mast, bouncing off it to our feet again, charging forward with silent and deadly purpose. Reeve met us chest-to-chest, rearing up with us and reaching for our throat, teeth dripping. Our fangs crashed against his, while our claws scored his hide and left deep, bloody furrows through his ribcage.

With a wrench of his neck, he caught hold of our face and flung us to the deck, not letting go when we landed with a mighty thump. He pinned us with a giant paw on our ribs, his weight nearly cracking them.

"Yield," he growled through the fangs wrapped about my head.

Who knew the beast could actually speak? Not I.

But all he had to do was exert pressure, and he'd crush our skull like an eggshell. The wolf resisted for a moment, but I imposed my will and shifted back to human, naked. Still thinking furiously, still trying to see a way out of the situation.

Reeve spat me out and changed as well, swiping a forearm across his bloody mouth and giving me a cheeky grin. "That was almost well done," he said. "Unfortunately for you, I can't let you get away with it." He stood, a great hairy bear of a man, unashamed of his nudity. "Put them in the hold," he said to his men. "I'm going back to the *Orca* for some clothing. We'll deal with them on my return." He scooped up the badger and hopped across the rails.

One of the pirates prodded me with his cutlass. "Behave yourself, Cap'n. Wouldn't want to start the party premature-like."

They herded us belowdecks, and simply dropped the men who couldn't walk through the hatch. After the first one broke several bones on landing, we realized what they were about and caught the rest. Peter was the last, and they slammed the hatch shut behind him with an air of dreadful finality.

I sat beside Peter. "I'm sorry," I said.

"Weren't your fault he's bigger and stronger," he replied. "Also had the condition longer, or I miss my guess." He coughed, and red stained his lips.

I frowned as realization struck. "You knew."

"'Course I did. We all did, Cap'n. We're neither blind nor stupid. It's obvious when you know what to look for."

"And yet ..." I stared at my crew in confusion. "Yet you stayed." There was an unspoken question there. Why? Why stay, when their captain could turn into a slavering monster at any moment and eat them raw?

"You take good care of us," Peter said, and a chorus of "ayes" went up. "And now you've just got to do it once more."

"I don't—"

Make them as us, said the wolf. *It's the only way.*

I recoiled. "I can't bite them." Oh, damn, I'd said it aloud.

But my crew didn't react with the same revulsion. Many of them nodded. "It's the only way," the lookout said, echoing the wolf.

Peter was seized by a coughing fit, and this time there was more than a tinge of blood on his mouth. He spat and grimaced. "I'm dying," he pointed out. "And I'm not the only one." To be sure, they were all wounded, some so grievously they wouldn't last the hour. "Bite us, and we heal." He bared his blood-stained teeth. "And then we fight with a chance of actually winning."

A lump rose in my throat. What I'd done to earn such loyalty was a question for the ages, but my crew was staring into the maw of Hell itself and daring it to take them if it could.

How could I gainsay that?

Reluctantly, I passed control to the wolf, ready to snatch it back at the first sign of uncontrolled rage. However, the creature didn't bite any of them, but rather licked their wounds, laving them with gentle caresses. It was a far cry from my own transformation, where a great beast had chased me up a tree, terrified and bleeding down my leg.

This is what pack means, it told me as the men petted its fur and scratched behind its ears, like they would a big dog. *Caring for each other.*

But that poor drunkard—

It was our first shift. So hungry. He wasn't pack; he was meat.

Well, you can't just run about eating humans, even if they're not pack. It's not done.

I understand that, now. You are me. I am you. We are one.

Oh. And now I understood too. My fear had made me foolish, unable to believe or trust what the wolf had tried to communicate, so many times. I felt a right prat, but hopefully I'd learned something too.

I realized some of the men should stay human during the moon in case of accident or emergency. All of them were willing to be changed, and so we chose seven of the ten left alive. By the time Reeve returned, we were strong and ready for him. We moved our clothes about so they'd conceal the fact we'd healed, and we smeared more blood on our hands and faces.

Reeve had fetched a throne-like chair from the *Orca*, all velvet and ornate wood inlaid with ivory, and lounged in it with his leg slung over a dragon-carved arm. The badger sprawled in his lap.

We pulled Peter up last, faking injuries we no longer had.

Reeve looked us over and smiled. "I normally leave survivors," he said. "But in this case, I've decided to make an exception. You've your captain to thank for that."

"We've our captain to thank for a great many things," Peter said. And he shifted, snarled, and leapt.

The rest of us followed suit. The pirates screamed and scrambled and fought like madmen, but they'd brought steel rather than silver to a werewolf fight. My men slaughtered them all without mercy or compunction, and did the world a favor thereby.

By unspoken agreement, Peter and I made for Reeve. Still on his throne, he shifted before we reached him, dropping the poor badger to the deck, where it retreated under the chair and out of the fray, growling. Sensible animal.

Reeve might have saved his life if he'd jumped overboard. Rather than retreat like a prudent person, he attacked.

But Peter and I weren't there when he landed, instead flanking him and assailing him on either side. My jaws crunched through his foreleg, ripping it clean off. Peter slashed his face and cost him an eye before diving at his hind leg and giving it the same treatment I'd given the front. The pirate wolf shrieked and went down.

More of my crew joined in as I secured the hold I wanted on his throat. Hot blood pumped into my mouth as we literally tore Reeve into pieces.

Not even a werewolf could survive that. The bits turned human, and Reeve's head rolled with the pitch of the ship until it slipped between the rails and fell into the sea. I followed it to the edge and watched it bob on the surface for a moment before it sank, teeth still bared in a rictus of hate.

The badger waddled out from under the throne and sat beside me, leaning on my foreleg. It seemed I'd been adopted.

Later that evening, with the moon fat in the sky, wolves and men lifted our voices in music, singing our sorrow for comrades lost and joy for victory hard-won.

About the Author

Julie Frost is an award-winning author who writes every shade of speculative fiction. Her short stories appear in *The Monster Hunter Files*, *Writers of the Future*, *Tales of Ruma*, *District of Wonders*, *StoryHack*, *Unlikely Story*, *Stupefying Stories*, and many others. Her novel series, Pack Dynamics, is published by WordFire Press. She whines about writing, a lot, at agilebrit.livejournal.com.

Harry the Ghost Pirate

ROBERT J. MCCARTER

We've got a new ghost at the graveyard. His name is Harry, and he likes to dress up as a pirate, complete with eye patch, peg leg, and a green parrot perched on his shoulder.

It's annoying. The silly clothing and all the clomping around and saying "Arrrr," and "Matey," and "Shiver me timbers."

I mean, I get it. The mortal coil has been "shuffled off," so why not play at pirate while you studiously avoid your unfinished business that keeps you an earthbound spirit.

I get it, but it's annoying. But I guess my modus operandi is to complain about other ghosts while studiously avoiding my own unfinished business.

And I will admit I am a bit jealous that he can pull off a pirate so effectively. I mean, underneath the dreadlocks and behind the eye makeup, it's still Harry with his round, pasty face and his dull hazel eyes. Make that *eye*—the patch, you know. Holding a form that foreign and that complicated is just plain hard for any ghost to do.

Take me. I'm still wearing the simple white nightgown I died in. I can't hold another form to save my afterlife. Different ghosts are good at different things, I totally get that, but this girl would love to wear some jeans, maybe some Jimmy Choo heels, a nice glittery silk top. And maybe lose about twenty pounds. No, make that thirty.

But no, Harry is off annoying everyone as a pirate, and I am just chubby Drew in her nightgown with mousey brown hair that hangs halfway down my back and plain brown eyes. Now that I'm dead, I really shouldn't care about how I look, but I do. Biology has a way of sticking with you even when it's years gone.

Harry has been talking about finding gold lately. He's a pirate, right, so this is a logical progression. Clichéd pirate costume? Check. Annoying pirate speak? Check. Screeching parrot? Check. What's left, except to go in search of some gold?

But we are in Tucson, landlocked in Arizona. No ships to sail, no islands to explore. So, silly me, I thought the quest for gold would dry up then and there. I mean, it didn't look like Harry had found anyone to join him on his quest, and to my great relief, no one else had changed their ghostly form to look like a pirate.

"Ahoy there, me fine lass," Harry said one summer's night in the graveyard. He had clomped slowly across the green grass, dutifully and arduously maneuvering around the gravestones with his peg leg. Slow going. Something of a method actor, you might say.

"Hi, Harry," I said, trying to keep my face straight. I don't know a lot about history, but I know the Hollywood-style, clichéd pirate Harry was portraying bore little resemblance to reality. I don't think it was actually very fun being a real pirate.

"Ya might'a heard, but I'm lookin' ta assemble a crew of fine hardy mates to go in search of gold."

I nodded.

"Gold!" the parrot screeched. And I must admit, Harry had done a good job with the parrot. Its feathers looked totally real, and when the bird squawked, Harry's mouth didn't move. The guy had true talent when it came to manipulating his form.

"Oh. I … Are you asking me to go with you, Harry?"

"Aye. That I am." He paused and looked around, as if preparing to share a secret. "I hear told that you, Miss Drew, are a fine witch and can transport us instantly anywhere."

Okay, so I'm a witch in Harry's pirate world. Yeah, that doesn't bother me. Around here, it's called "popping" when a ghost goes from one place to another, instantly. Some ghosts are good at it, and some can't do it at all. I'm very good at it. As long as I can visualize the place, I can pop there.

"So, no ship? I thought you were looking for a crew?"

"Aye, lass, I am," he said, leaning toward me. "But I aim to find the Lost Dutchman's Gold Mine out in this here desert. It has riches beyond a mortal's ability to imagine, and since we aren't mortal anymore, I think we should be the ones ta find it."

I stared at him. Harry used to be an accountant. Now I don't know what an accountant's job is actually like, but it sounds super boring. Maybe Harry just loved pirates and, finding himself dead, he just went for it. Or maybe he's not quite all there, and this is the best he can do to cope with being dead.

"Yeah," I began, "but since we aren't mortal, we don't need the gold."

Harry stood up straight and took a deep breath. No, ghosts don't breathe, but many of the biological tics still stick around with a similar purpose.

"No, lass," he began, his face serious. "We don't need the gold, but me sister does. Her wee one is got the scourge, the cancer, and the bills are threatenin' to pull her family down to Davy Jones's locker."

"Need the gold!" the parrot squawked.

I blinked. Another one of those biological holdovers.

Everyone in the graveyard knows how you died. It's how you introduce yourself. Like me, I say, "My name is Drew, and I died of uterine cancer." Or Harry, he says, "Ahoy! Me name is Harry, and the scourge of bladder cancer broadsides me and drug me down to the depths like a hungry kraken."

Thus the blinking.

Not only had we both died of cancer—yeah, yeah, there are a lot of us like that here—but his niece was facing it, and he felt helpless to do anything about it.

Maybe that explained the whole pirate thing.

"Okay, Harry," I said with a nod. "You've got yourself a witch."

He smiled wide and suddenly looked fifteen years younger.

"All hands on deck!" the parrot squawked.
"We set sail at first light," Harry said.

One thing that follows you into the afterlife is the human ability for self-deception. Reality is still hard to see clearly, even when you are a lot less real than you used to be.

Earlier I mentioned my mousey brown hair and my extra thirty pounds and how I wanted to "lose" that weight. Even though I'm a ghost and it is quite literally not "weight."

And I might have given the impression that is what I looked like when I died.

It wasn't.

I had no hair and was skeletally thin.

I was thirty-seven when I died after several rounds of cancer. Started in the uterus and migrated from there.

Really, I should celebrate how wonderfully long my brown hair is, like it was when I was sixteen. I should revel in each extra pound, because keeping on weight was so hard to do for so long.

Your default appearance as a ghost is kind of like how you think of yourself. So I think of myself with really long mousey brown hair and thirty extra pounds.

And I don't like it.

Even though it's my own "default" appearance.

Even without the biology, we humans are complicated.

I mention all this because after Harry happily clomped away, I was again jealous of his marvelous ability to maintain his ghostly appearance, and then I meditated on my own twisted dislike of my own internal view of myself. Which made me wonder what dichotomy Harry was holding close. What reality of his own could he not see?

Sometimes we fool ourselves and we know it. Sometimes we fool ourselves and we have no clue.

It's the latter that concerns me.

It happened to me when I first got sick. I had crap energy (life is busy, right?) and unexplained weight loss (yeah!) and put off going to a doctor for far too long. Might have had a different result if I had done something about it sooner.

All that rumination aside, I had committed to go looking for gold with Harry.

He came clomping up right before the sun rose the next morning. I was on the wing of some old fighter jet in the aircraft boneyard at Davis–Monthan Air Force Base. I had a good view to the east—dead airplanes, dried grass, distant buildings, and the low hills hunched on the horizon.

A ghost in an airplane graveyard has a kind of poetry to it, right?

When I saw Harry, I felt bad and hoped he hadn't clomped all the way here from the graveyard. That would have taken the rest of the night, but the guy was committed to his pirate thing.

"There you are, me lass," he growled, sounding tired.

"Sorry, Harry. I didn't mean to make you walk all the way out here." Except maybe I had. Maybe I had been testing Harry, seeing if he knew me well enough to know where I liked to greet the new day.

"Not another thought. A cap'n will walk a long mile for his crew."

I smiled. There may be nothing at all realistic about his pirate thing, but it was starting to grow on me. I looked around. "Where is the rest of the crew?"

He sighed and shook his head, and the parrot screeched, "Cowards!"

And then it hit me. Harry was just another lonely ghost who didn't fit in with any of the other groups. Something else we had in common. I turned away and watched as a spark of light ignited on the horizon, a pinpoint of yellow taking on the darkness.

We watched the sun lift itself above the craggy hills, slowly, resolutely, the ordered rows of old, discarded planes glinting in the new light.

Harry wasn't one of those ghosts who has to fill every moment with talking and that boded well for our journey.

"Where to, Harry?" I asked, once the sun was fully above the horizon.

"Well, I been thinkin' on that, lass, and I'd like you ta use your potent magic and sail us to the top o' Weaver's Needle. We'll have a mighty good view there, and it is said that the shadow of the spire points ta the location of the gold."

I nodded. Weaver's Needle is deep in the Superstition Mountains east of Phoenix and rises to a high, sharp point out of the surrounding cactus and mesquite bushes. I haven't been there, but I've seen pictures of it.

I grabbed Harry's arm, a careful bit of business since I had to match the frequency of my ghostly form to Harry's, and popped us there so we could start looking for gold.

The tip-top of Weaver's Needle is hard tan rock and a few hardy bushes and grasses. It's narrow and maybe a hundred feet long and twenty feet wide. This is rough country, dry desert dominated by cactus, prickly pear, and some large Saguaro, with lots of scraggly mesquite bush.

The view is spectacular—rough, rocky ground rising and falling sharply. Weaver's Needle is nearly sheer for four or five hundred feet, and then the broad cone around it becomes full of folds in the rock, like the ground is a badly wrinkled blanket.

I sucked in a breath of surprise when I saw it. The sun was still low, most of the land in shadows, the high rock we were on brightly lit, turning the tans more orange.

I was a bit off when I popped us, so we were about twenty

feet above the rock. Not bad for never having been here. I still had hold of Harry's arm, so I floated us down.

"Harry, this is ..." I didn't have the words.

"Aye, Drew. It be spectacular. A right fine ship you've landed us on."

And I could see it. The rock was long and narrow, almost like it was a keel and the massive ship had capsized and was under the rocky waters below.

"What now?" I asked.

He took a deep breath. "Well, we search, lass. Every last nook, every last cranny. We follow the shadow, and we find the gold."

I nodded and didn't speak any of my doubts. Like how people had been looking for the Lost Dutchman's Gold Mine for more than a hundred years and never found it. It's kind of a tourist thing now.

We watched the sun drive out the darkness and watched the shadow of Weaver's Needle slowly become more defined to the west.

"What's her name?" I finally asked.

"What?" Harry said, sounding surprised, with not a bit of a pirate accent. I mean it was just one word, but he didn't call me "lass" or "arr" it up at all.

"Your niece, the one we need the gold for. What's her name?"

His hazel eye flicked to mine, and I wished I hadn't asked. He looked so sad. "Her name is Megan, and she's the most beautiful and perfect thing I've ever seen."

I bit my lip as hard as I could, but of course that kind of thing doesn't hurt. A whole sentence without the accent and his parrot had stopped moving, looking suddenly like a stuffed animal.

"How bad is it?" I asked.

"It's bad, Drew." Coming from someone who lost his battle with cancer, it made me think Megan wasn't going to be

343

alive much longer. He blinked back tears, another one of those biological things we still do.

I wanted to ask more, like what kind of cancer, what the grade was, how they were treating her, but I didn't. Harry wasn't really here to find gold. He was here to keep himself from worrying about his niece.

Whether he was fooling himself about this or not, I didn't know, and it didn't matter. Gold wasn't what this girl needed. It wouldn't save her. But it was what Harry needed.

"Avast ye!" I said, pointing to the west where the shadow of Weaver's Needle was just starting to come into focus. My pirate voice was just awful compared to his. "That there shadow is right clear enough now. Let's sail forth and find the gold!"

"The gold!" the parrot squawked, looking alive again.

Harry smiled at me, but it was a bitter little thing, like he had something sharp in his mouth.

I took his arm and popped us to the shadow's edge.

We searched for three days.

I mean, it wasn't a bad way to spend our time. In the gorgeous folds of rock, safe from the heat (because you're dead), and no need for food or water (because you're dead). And when you're dead, it's good to have something to do.

Harry talked like a pirate.

When he started to lose it, I talked like a pirate.

We looked in every nook and cranny we could find, ranging pretty wide from the shadow's tip.

Harry would clomp along on his peg leg and I would fly and cover as much ground as I could. When the shadow moved a ways, I would go grab Harry and pop him to the new spot.

At one point, Harry said, "It's a right fine thing that you can fly, me witch."

I smiled at him and nodded. I didn't worry about him when he was fully in character.

We found mesquite and sagebrush and cactus (so much cactus), ants, rabbits, coyote, a few hikers, and even a couple small caves. But nothing that would indicate a mining operation. No caves large enough. No signs of earth having been moved. Nothing.

At night, we would sit atop Weaver's Needle and talk until the stars were a glittering field of diamonds above us. We would mostly talk about pirate stuff, like hidden treasure and seeking new horizons and being outside the reach of the law, which I could appreciate. We were ghosts. We were constantly exploring new ways to spend our days and live our afterlives, and we were, quite literally, outside the reach of the law.

After we ran out of pirate-y things to talk about, we rested.

Ghosts do need some rest, and there is this form of sleeping called "fading" where you're just gone for a while. How long you are gone and where you show back up is a bit unpredictable, so neither of us did that. We were just quiet and let time slip by.

It's either like a pleasant meditation or a terrible nightmare, depending on how close to the surface your regrets are.

And let's face it, you don't end up an earthbound spirit with obligatory unfinished business without some regrets. Make that a lot of regrets.

Harry's nights were not good.

I would hear him moaning and crying like he was in terrible pain. Sometimes he would call out names. Like Megan, his niece we were trying to find the gold for. Or Anna, his wife who he left behind. He and Anna never had kids, so I could see how Megan would be real important to him.

And I have my own stuff. Like my fiancé, Binu, and how my paranoia that he was going to cheat on me chased him away. How I had never had kids—something else Harry and I had in common. And the cancer, always the cancer. I'm three years dead and the trauma of it still comes knocking.

As a ghost, your regrets can really get you. There is this place called the "bardo" that refers to a ghost who is trapped in regret until it has completely taken over and is their entire world.

I was clearly doing better than Harry. So, on the first two nights, when it got bad for him, I would pretend to cry. I mean real epic, heartrending stuff. I had the material (and, really, who doesn't?), so I let it rip. I wailed there on the top of Weaver's Needle in the Superstition Mountains.

And it worked. Harry would shake himself out of his own nightmares and come check on me. Sit with me. Talk to me. We really got to know each other, and I am happy to say that Harry is quite human, imperfect as we all are, but very gentle and sweet.

But on that third night, it got bad. Real bad.

Back at the graveyard, we had this nightly gathering of the ghosts called "The Midnight Circle." Ghosts tell stories, put on shows, share. It can really help, but I guess Harry was too long away from it, because it was clear he was slipping toward the bardo.

I tried my wailing that third night, but it didn't snap him out of it. His pirate costume was gone, and he looked unkempt in a faded blue hospital gown, his face pale, his form way too transparent. When I saw that, I realized how much I missed the pirate get-up. I even missed the damn parrot.

His ghostly form was diffuse, like he was slightly out of focus.

Not good.

The common view of ghosts—wailing, moaning, inconsolable—is about those who have fallen into the bardo. And once there, it is nearly impossible to pull a ghost back out of it.

"All hands on deck!" I cried in my terrible pirate accent. "I had me a vision of gold, glitterin' gold."

Harry didn't even look at me. He was standing at the end of Weaver's Needle, on the highest point looking northwest. If he had been in his pirate garb, I would have said he looked like a captain on the prow of his ship, surveying the choppy waters ahead. In his hospital gown, he looked like someone on the top of a high-rise, thinking of jumping off.

And in some ways, that's exactly what he was.

I flew over to him and tried to grab his arm, but his form was so diffuse, I didn't dare try to match it. As a ghost, if you look human, you feel human, which was why Harry was always clomping around on his peg leg.

"Harry!" I shouted, no more pirate voice. "Come on, Harry, don't do this. We'll find the gold. I swear, we'll stay out here as long as it takes."

He still didn't look at me, his form getting more diffuse.

I considered popping back to the graveyard and getting help, but I didn't think he had that much time.

Harry no longer cared about gold. He no longer cared about being a pirate. What did Harry still care about?

"Megan needs you," I said gently. And as I said it, I felt it was true. Once the biology is gone, all us ghosts are more intuitive than when we were alive. "Right now, Harry. She needs you right now. I can take you to her."

He slowly turned his face to me, and the sadness there made me want to weep. Where was that annoying black eyeliner and eye patch? Where were the dreadlocks and pointy hat? Without them, with the sorrow filling him up, Harry was ... Well, he was bardo bound.

He shook his head slowly and looked out over the moonlit desert. He took a shuddering breath and said, "They moved. I lost them."

It hit me, like I had been punched in the gut. Harry had been checking on his loved ones from time to time, like many of us do. It's not healthy to spend too much time with them; the regrets will get you. When Megan was diagnosed, Harry was devastated. He spent some time away. He developed his pirate persona to compensate. When he felt strong enough to check in on them again, they were gone.

"Look at me, Harry," I said, putting as much authority into my voice as I could. "Look at me!"

He slowly turned his head, his hazel eyes barely focusing on me.

"I'm your witch, Harry. I can take you to her, but you've got to help me."

"You … you can?"

"Yes, Harry, I can. But I need you to come back to me. I need you to tell me what she looks like."

I was making promises I didn't know I could keep. Sure I could pop, all day long, but I had to be able to visualize where I was popping to. A place. A person. As long as I can see it, I can do it. But I had no idea what Megan looked like.

"She's the most beautiful and perfect thing you've ever seen," I said. "She needs you. Right now."

"Megan needs me," he said, his voice slightly stronger.

"Yes, Harry. And I need my captain."

He took a deep breath and nodded. It wasn't easy, it took time, but Harry slowly came back to himself, and soon he was peg-legged and parrot-festooned and telling me all about Megan.

How she loved to dance and how she hated carrots. About her adorable lisp and how long it had taken her to start talking. About her beautiful brown hair and bright blue eyes. About their trip to Disneyland when she was five. About the horseback riding lessons she had been taking before she got sick. How Harry and she used to love to play pirates.

And then I could see her.

And then I popped us to her.

And then things got really difficult.

The room in the hospice house was cheery, with lacy blue curtains and pastel blue walls, but it was dominated by a hospital bed and a wisp of a ten-year-old girl lying in it. Her parents were there, wan and exhausted, slumped in chairs, Megan's mother holding her hand and crying softly. Her father had his head in his hands and wasn't moving.

Megan was too thin, and her brown hair was gone, and tied on her head was a red bandana. My nonexistent stomach fell, and I wanted to run away, and fast.

Megan was dying.

I looked at Harry, expecting to have to battle him back from the bardo again, but he was still fully pirate, his look grim but resolute.

"Ahoy, Megan!" he said, stepping into the bed so he could be close to the girl. "It's your uncle, Cap'n Harry, and I've come ta take ye on a fine adventure. Me crew and I have been searching for the Lost Dutchman's Gold Mine, but we can't find it. We need ya, lass, and your fine weather eye."

It was still and silent in the room. Too silent. I noticed Megan's chest wasn't moving. We were too late. She was gone.

"What do you say, lass?" Harry said. "Will you join us?"

I couldn't move. I couldn't speak. I felt terrible for Megan, for this family. Their grief would be huge. And maybe Megan had moved on, maybe she didn't have unfinished business. But if she hadn't moved on, if she was a ghost, I felt terrible that we hadn't gotten here in time.

But then Megan stirred. Well, not her body, that was done, but her spirit stirred, and she slowly rose up out of the biology that had failed her.

"Uncle Harry?" she asked, her voice high with surprise.

"Aye, lass. It's me."

"Am ... am I dead?" she said, looking around at her parents. Her ghostly form had beautifully long brown hair, but she still wore the red bandana. Her body was not skeletal anymore but was a healthy weight.

"Aye, you are. As am I. But it ain't so bad." He stepped back from the bed and stomped on the floor. "Look! I finally got me a peg leg!"

Megan giggled. "Can I have a peg leg?"

This was a delicate thing Harry was doing. Many ghosts go bardo right away. Kids especially. It's a lot to deal with.

"Aye, you can. I can teach ya how. But we must go, lass. There is gold ta find." He extended his hand to her as she floated further from her spent body.

She blinked and looked at her parents again, then down at the frail body she was floating above, her face contorting in grief. "But, Mom and Dad ... I ..." Her form started going diffuse along the edges, and I knew we would be in trouble soon.

"Megan," Harry said, his pirate accent gone. "It's me. It's Uncle Harry. I know this is confusing, but come with us, and I'll explain everything. You'll see your parents again. I promise."

Megan sniffed and nodded and took her uncle's hand.

It's been almost three months, and we're back on Weaver's Needle, the stars strewn above us, our search done for the day. Sure, the sodium glow from Phoenix to the south and west spoils it a bit, but looking north, there are more stars. An ocean full of them.

Captain Harry the ghost pirate was there in his tattered buccaneer's shirt, his parrot on his shoulder. Next to him was his first mate, Megan, with her tricorn hat and her glorious long brown hair flowing down her back. She's gone a bit nontraditional, choosing to wear a frilly white dress, although she does have a peg leg to match her uncle's and proudly clomps around after him.

We've had some tough times with her. Adjusting to the afterlife is not for sissies, but things have slowly gotten better. Being pirates in search of gold has helped. A lot.

We are a crew of six now, with three other ghosts having joined our search for the Lost Dutchman's Gold Mine.

I am still the witch of the crew, popping us all over the Superstition Mountains. And since I'm the witch, no one cares that I'm still in my nightgown and my beautiful long brown hair is not covered by a hat. Right after we first met, Megan said, "You and I have the same hair." And since her hair is glorious, and no one would ever call it mousey, then my hair is beautiful too.

"Gather 'round, me hearties," Harry called out.

Our new crewmates are Marge and Kyle, an older couple with gray hair and broad smiles, and Benjamin, a nice young man with beautiful brown eyes who died in a traffic accident. I could be fooling myself, but I think he joined the crew because of me.

"I know we been searching long, and we been searching hard," Harry said, "with not one bit o' gold to be seen. But take heart. The desert is vast, and there are more legends for us to chase, more treasures for us to look for."

There was a murmuring of assent. I find the desert beautiful, and it's just fine with me if we never find a thing.

"We aren't just a crew," Megan added, standing tall and proud. She took her uncle's hand and squeezed it. "We are a family."

Harry and Megan reached out their hands, and we all formed a little circle. Six ghosts holding hands at midnight atop Weaver's Needle. A half dozen earthbound spirits with something to do and someone to do it with.

Not a bad way to spend your afterlife.

And that, me hearties, is the real treasure.

About the Author

Robert J. McCarter writes about ghosts all the time. Of his first novel, *Shuffled Off: A Ghost's Memoir*, *Kirkus Reviews* says, "The wry humor and raw emotional truth of JJ's journey will have readers rooting for him from death to eternity." He is a finalist for the Writers of the Future contest, and his short stories have appeared in numerous magazines and anthologies. Find out more at RobertJMcCarter.com.

About the Editor

Lisa Mangum has worked in the publishing industry since 1997. She is currently the Managing Editor for Shadow Mountain Publishing and has worked with several *New York Times* bestselling authors.

She is also the author of four national bestselling YA novels (The Hourglass Door trilogy and *After Hello*) as well as several short stories and novellas. She also wrote a nonfiction book about writing tips gleaned from the television show *Supernatural*.

She edited *One Horn to Rule Them All: A Purple Unicorn Anthology*, *A Game of Horns: A Red Unicorn Anthology*, *Dragon Writers: An Anthology*, and *Undercurrents: An Anthology of What Lies Beneath*, also published by WordFire Press.

She graduated with honors from the University of Utah, and currently lives in Taylorsville, Utah, with her husband, Tracy.

Additional Copyright Information

If You Liked ...

IF YOU LIKED X MARKS THE SPOT, YOU MIGHT ALSO ENJOY:

Rise of First World
by Christopher Katava

The Iron Thane
by Jason Henderson

Oshenerth
by Alan Dean Foster

Other WordFire Press Titles Edited by
Lisa Mangum

One Horn to Rule Them All

A Game of Horns

Dragon Writers

Undercurrents

Our list of other WordFire Press authors and titles is always growing. To find out more and to see our selection of titles, visit us at:
wordfirepress.com